Dark Horizons
Science Fiction and the Dystopian Imagination

Edited by
Raffaella Baccolini
and Tom Moylan

ROUTLEDGE
NEW YORK AND LONDON

Published in 2003 by
Routledge
29 West 35th Street
New York, NY 10001
www.routledge-ny.com

Published in Great Britain by
Routledge
11 New Fetter Lane
London EC4P 4EE
www.routledge.co.uk

Routledge is an imprint of the Taylor & Francis Group.

10 9 8 7 6 5 4 3 2 1

Library of Congress Cataloging-in-Publication Data

Dark horizons : science fiction and the utopian imagination / edited by Tom Moylan and Raffaella Baccolini.
        p. cm.
Includes bibliographical references and index.
ISBN 0-415-96613-2 (alk. paper) — ISBN 0-415-96614-0 (pbk. : alk. paper)
1. Science fiction, American—History and criticism.   2. Science fiction, English—History and criticism.   3. Science fiction films—History and criticism.   4. Utopias in literature.   5. Utopias.
I. Moylan, Tom, 1943– II. Baccolini, Raffaella, 1960–.

PS648.S3D367 2003
    813'.0876209372—dc21

2003001024

In the dark times
Will there also be singing?
Yes, there will also be singing
About the dark times.
—Bertolt Brecht

poetry
isn't revolution but a way of knowing
why it must come
—Adrienne Rich

Contents

Acknowledgments

Our first acknowledgment is to our contributors not only for their essays but also for the discussions leading up to them and, not least, for their promptness, cooperation, and overall enthusiasm for the project. More broadly we want to thank the community of utopian scholars, in particular members of the Society for Utopian Studies (North America), the Utopian Studies Society (Europe), and the Centro Interdipartimentale di Ricerca sull'Utopia (Italy) for the conversations and the collective body of work that provides the most immediate context for this collection. We are especially grateful to Barbara Goodwin, Colin Davis, and Lyman Tower Sargent for organizing the Millennium of Utopias Conference at the University of East Anglia, in June 1999, which directly inspired this project. We would also like to thank our undergraduate and postgraduate students who, at several universities in several countries, shared in and challenged our engagements with utopian and dystopian science fiction.

More particularly, we want to thank Lyman Tower Sargent, Jack Zipes, and Giuseppe Lusignani for encouraging and facilitating our work; and Roberta Baccolini for finding the cover image. We thank the people who worked with us at Routledge—especially our editor, Matt Byrnie; our cover designer, Pearl Chang; our production editors, Julie Ho and Danielle Savin; our copy editor, Norma McLemore; and our indexer Lydia Lennihan. We are particularly grateful to our computer adviser and technician, Piero Conficoni.

Raffaella would like to thank the SITLeC Department (Translation, Language, and Cultural Studies) and the SSLMIT (Advanced School for Interpreters and Translators) of the University of Bologna, at Forlì, and in particular her colleagues and friends Sam Whitsitt, Patrick Leech, and Rita

Monticelli for their encouragement and inspiring discussions. Most of all she would like to thank all those who variously created "spaces of writing" to make her work possible: Adua Nesi and Roberto Baccolini for all their support and assistance; Roberta Baccolini, who was often there when nobody else could; Anna Vitiello for her collaboration; Bruna Conconi for relief and friendship. She is particularly grateful to Giuseppe Lusignani for his intellectual and political discussions, but most for his love and support. Finally, she wants to thank Giacomo Lusignani who, more or less patiently, daily reclaims her from those spaces of writing, thus continuing to help her to redefine perspectives and priorities on life and loving.

Tom would like to thank Nickianne Moody, Tim Ashplant, Roger Webster, and Ross Dawson at Liverpool John Moores University for their encouragement, and the Department of Media and Cultural Studies and the Research Committee of the School of Media, Critical, and Creative Arts for research release and travel funds in the early stages of the book. He thanks Sean Ryder and Louis de Paor at the National University of Ireland at Galway for their interest and support, as well as the Faculty of Arts for the visiting fellowship that allowed him to complete his own essay. He especially thanks his new colleagues at the University of Limerick—in particular, Martin Chappell, Pat O'Connor, and Tony Bretherton—and is grateful to Louis and Loretta Glucksman, the University Research Office, and the College of Humanities for support that enabled the completion of the book. He also wants to thank Adua and Roberto Baccolini for their hospitality in Premilcuore and Tadhg Foley and Molly Fogarty for their hospitality and friendship in Galway. Finally, he thanks Katie Moylan and Sarah Moylan for enthusiastically being there through yet another book.

Permissions

Every effort was made to reach the copyright holders of the documents included herein. Any additional arrangements or oversights will be corrected in subsequent editions.

Excerpts from the following copyrighted material appear by permission.

Cover image, photograph from "The Iceland Project" (1992); Magdalena Jetelova, architect; Werner Hannappel, photographer. Used by permission of the artist.

"Dreamwood," the lines from "Dreamwood," from *Time's Power: Poems 1985–1988* by Adrienne Rich. Used by permission of the author and W.W. Norton & Company.

Dystopia and Histories

RAFFAELLA BACCOLINI AND TOM MOYLAN

I

In the twentieth century, the dark side of Utopia—dystopian accounts of places worse than the ones we live in—took its place in the narrative catalogue of the West and developed in several forms throughout the rest of the century.[1] No doubt prompted by H. G. Wells's science fictional visions of modernity, a number of other works—E. M. Forster's story "The Machine Stops" and, more famously, works such as Yevgeny Zamyatin's *We*, Aldous Huxley's *Brave New World*, and George Orwell's *Nineteen Eighty-Four*—came to represent the *classical*, or canonical, form of dystopia. In a more diffused manner, works that shared the cultural ambience of the dystopian imagination (though often with ambiguity or irony) appeared on the margins of mainstream literature. These include titles as diverse and contradictory as Franz Kafka's *The Metamorphosis* (1915), Ayn Rand's *Anthem* (1938), C. S. Lewis's *That Hideous Strength* (1945), Vladimir Nabokov's *Bend Sinister* (1947), Evelyn Waugh's *Love among the Ruins* (1953), and Don De Lillo's *Underworld* (1997). In the direction of popular culture, a more overt dystopian tendency developed within science fiction (sf), and this resulted in the "new maps of hell," as Kingsley Amis put it, that appeared after World War II and continues in the dystopian sf of recent years (by authors such as Ray Bradbury, Frederik Pohl and C. M. Kornbluth, Judith Merrill, A. E. Van Vogt, John Brunner, J. G. Ballard, Philip K. Dick, Thomas M. Disch, and James Tiptree Jr./Alice Sheldon). In all these instances, to a greater or lesser extent, the dystopian imagination has served as a prophetic vehicle, the canary in a cage, for writers with an ethical and political concern for warning us of terrible sociopolitical tendencies that could, if continued, turn our contemporary world into the iron cages portrayed in the realm of utopia's underside.

Against this dystopian tide, the oppositional political culture of the late 1960s and 1970s occasioned a revival of distinctly eutopian writing, the first major revival since the end of the nineteenth century. The imaginative exploration of better, rather than worse, places found a new form in the "critical utopia." "Critical," in this sense, incorporates an Enlightenment sense of *critique*, a postmodern attitude of self-reflexivity, and the political implication of a "*critical mass* required to make the necessary explosive reaction" (Moylan, *Demand* 10). Shaped by ecological, feminist, and New Left thought, the *critical utopia* of the 1970s—represented by writers such as Ursula K. Le Guin, Joanna Russ, Marge Piercy, Samuel R. Delany, Ernst Callenbach, Sally Miller Gearhart, and Suzy McKee Charnas—combines vision and practice:

> A central concern in the critical utopia is the awareness of the limitations of the utopian tradition, so that these texts reject utopia as blueprint while preserving it as dream. Furthermore, the novels dwell on the conflict between the originary world and the utopian society opposed to it so that the process of social change is more directly articulated. Finally, the novels focus on the continuing presence of difference and imperfection within the utopian society itself and thus render more recognizable and dynamic alternatives. (Moylan, *Demand* 10–11)

This revival was actually a transformation which had to pass through the destruction of utopian writing as it had been known in order to preserve it. Aware of the historical tendency of the utopian genre to limit the imagination to one particular ideal, authors of critical utopias reclaimed the emancipatory utopian imagination while they simultaneously challenged the political and formal limits of the traditional utopia. By forging visions of better but open futures, these utopian writings developed a critique of dominant ideology and traced new vectors of opposition.

In the 1980s, this utopian tendency came to an abrupt end. In the face of economic restructuring, right-wing politics, and a cultural milieu informed by an intensifying fundamentalism and commodification, sf writers revived and reformulated the dystopian genre. As the utopian moment faded, only a few writers—such as Pamela Sargent, Joan Slonczewski, Sheri Tepper, and Kim Stanley Robinson—kept the narratives of social dreaming alive. Moving back in the dystopian direction, in the mid-1980s, the new creative movement of cyberpunk (initially seen in films such as Ridley Scott's *Blade Runner* or novels such as William Gibson's *Neuromancer*) generated a usefully negative if nihilistic imaginary as the impact of the conservative turn of the decade began to be recognized in both the social structure and everyday life.

By 1984, a more clearly dystopian turn began to emerge within the popular imagination of Anglo-American societies. The "anniversary" of Orwell's *Nineteen Eighty-Four* (with new editions, a new film version, commemorations, and conferences on his work) helped to spark a general interest in the creative possibilities of dystopian narrative. In 1985, Margaret Atwood's *The Handmaid's Tale* directly drew on the classical dystopian narrative even as it interrogated its limits and suggested new directions. The republication of Katharine Burdekin's 1937 classic, *Swastika Night*, the same year added to this dystopian resurgence. Finally, the "second wave" of cyberpunk—written mainly by women such as Pat Cadigan, and moving beyond nihilistic anxiety into a new oppositional consciousness—opened the door to a dystopian narrative that was, like its eutopian predecessors, *critical* in its poetic and political substance.

By the end of the 1980s—moving beyond the engaged utopianism of the 1970s and the fashionable temptation to despair in the early 1980s— several sf writers confronted the decade's simultaneous silencing and cooptation of Utopia by turning to dystopian strategies as a way to come to terms with the changing social reality. Works by Octavia E. Butler, Cadigan, Charnas, Robinson, Piercy, and Le Guin refunctioned dystopia as a critical narrative form that worked against the grain of the grim economic, political, and cultural climate.

II

Gradually, critics began to track this dystopian turn, noting its innovations in formal flexibility and political maneuvering. In particular, at the round-table session devoted to a draft of Lyman Tower Sargent's essay "The Three Faces of Utopianism Revisited" at the eighteenth annual Conference of the Society for Utopian Studies in November 1993, a discussion on dystopia ensued in which Sargent urged a general reconsideration of the concept and a specific discussion of the new dystopias of the 1980s and 1990s. In the published version of the essay, Sargent observed that politically engaged texts such as Piercy's *He, She and It* (1991) "are clearly both eutopias and dystopias" and thus "undermine all neat classification schemes" ("Three Faces" 7), and he suggested that these new works might usefully be understood as "critical dystopias." Parallel to Sargent's contribution, others began to investigate this new body of work. Constance Penley, in "Time Travel, Primal Scene and the Critical Dystopia" (1990), identified as "critical dystopias" those films such as *Terminator* that tend "to suggest causes rather than merely reveal symptoms" (117). Jenny Wolmark in *Aliens and*

Others (1994) recognized a complex mixture of "utopian and dystopian elements" in works by Atwood and Tepper as they "critically voice the fears and anxieties of a range of new and fragmented social and sexual constituencies and identities in post-industrial societies" (91). Drawing on the work of Søren Baggesen, Jim Miller (1998) argued that Butler's *Xenogenesis* trilogy and *Parable of the Sower* were "critical dystopias motivated out of a utopian pessimism in that they force us to confront the dystopian elements of postmodern culture so that we can work through them and begin again" ("Post-Apocalyptic Hoping" 337). And working in broader strokes, in a commentary on Fredric Jameson's extensive work on Utopia, Bryan Alexander observed that "[i]n the face of enforced global more-or-less complacency as postmodern nigh-utopia the dystopian trope provides what Jameson describes as a 'bile [which provides] a joyous counter-poison and corrosive solvent, to apply to the slick surface of reality" (Jameson, qtd. in Alexander 55–56). In this range of work, the contemporary historical moment is interrogated by critical positions that necessarily work within a dystopian structure of feeling (and perhaps that "moment" has recurred, as has the dystopian genre, in one form or another since the onset of twentieth-century capitalism—beginning in its monopoly and imperialist phase, taking another form in the 1940s and 1950s, and yet another in the 1980s and 1990s).

During this time, we had each begun independent projects on the dystopian turn. After sharing drafts on several of our own essays that we wrote in the 1990s, we arrived at a shared understanding of the critical dystopia that ultimately came into focus at the Millennium of Utopias conference organized by J. C. Davis, Barbara Goodwin, and Sargent at the University of East Anglia (23–26 June 1999).[2] The discussions at that conference about the new dystopias between ourselves and others (including Ildney Cavalcanti, Maria Varsam, Peter Fitting, Naomi Jacobs, Lucy Sargisson, Ruth Levitas, and Sargent), led to our own work ("Gender and Genre in the Feminist Critical Dystopia of Katharine Burdekin, Margaret Atwood, and Octavia Butler" and *Scraps of the Untainted Sky: Science Fiction, Utopia, Dystopia*) and the beginning of an extended conversation with our colleagues. From this beginning, we eventually solicited essays from those above and others. The result is the present collaboration and collection, which represents the work of an international group of critics working from and across several disciplines.

III

Dystopia is distinct from its nemesis, the anti-utopia, and its generic sibling, the literary eutopia. Whereas some critics conflate dystopia and anti-utopia, in our work we have agreed with Sargent's differentiation between the "complex of ideas we call utopianism" and that "constant but generally unsystematic stream of thought that can be called anti-utopianism" ("Three Faces" 21).[3] Indeed he argued, as early as 1975, that the term *anti-utopia* as distinct from dystopia "should be reserved for that large class of works, both fictional and expository, which are directed against Utopia and utopian thought" ("Definition" 138). On the other hand, *dystopia* shares with *eutopia* the general vocation of utopianism that Sargent characterizes as "social dreaming," a designation that includes "the dreams and night-mares that concern the ways in which groups of people arrange their lives and which usually envision a radically different society than the one in which the dreamers live" ("Three Faces" 3). Dystopia, however, achieves this vocation through specific formal strategies that are distinctly different from the literary utopia.

Unlike the "typical" eutopian narrative with a visitor's guided journey through a utopian society which leads to a comparative response that in-dicts the visitor's own society, the dystopian text usually begins directly in the terrible new world; and yet, even without a dislocating move to an else-where, the element of textual estrangement remains in effect since the focus is frequently on a character who questions the dystopian society. While this observation resonates with Fredric Jameson's recognition of dystopia's narrative concern for what "happens to a specific subject or character," we identify a deeper and more totalizing agenda in the dystopian form insofar as the text is built around the construction of a nar-rative of the hegemonic order and a counter-narrative of resistance (*Seeds* 56). Since the text opens *in media res* within the nightmarish society, cog-nitive estrangement is at first forestalled by the immediacy and normality of the location. No dream or trip is taken to get to this place of everyday life. As in a great deal of sf, the protagonist (and the reader) is always al-ready *in* the world in question, unreflectively immersed in the society. However, a counter-narrative develops as the dystopian citizen moves from apparent contentment into an experience of alienation and resis-tance. This structural strategy of narrative and counter-narrative most often plays out by way of the social, and anti-social, use of language. Throughout the history of dystopian fiction, the conflict of the text turns on the control of language. To be sure, the official, hegemonic order of most dystopias (from Forster's machine society to Piercy's corporate order) rests, as Antonio Gramsci put it, on both coercion and consent. The material force of the economy and the state apparatus controls the social order and keeps it running; but discursive power, exercised in the repro-duction of meaning and the interpellation of subjects, is a complementary and necessary force. Language is a key weapon for the reigning dystopian power structure. Therefore, the dystopian protagonist's resistance often begins with a verbal confrontation and the reappropriation of language, since s/he is generally prohibited from using language, and, when s/he does, it means nothing but empty propaganda. From Kuno's conversations in "The Machine Stops" to Sutty's in *The Telling*, from D-503's diary in *We* to Lauren's journal in *Parable of the Sower*, from the book people in *Fahrenheit 451* to Jim's history in *Gold Coast*, the process of taking control over the means of language, representation, memory, and interpellation is a crucial weapon and strategy in moving dystopian resistance from an initial consciousness to an action that leads to a climactic event that attempts to change the society. As opposed to the eutopian plot of dislocation, education, and return of an informed visitor, the dystopia therefore generates its own didactic account in the critical encounter that ensues when the citizen confronts, or is confronted by, the contradictions of the society that is present on the very first page.

With these narrative structures and strategies, dystopia negotiates the historical antinomies of Utopia and Anti-Utopia in a less stable and more contentious manner than many of its utopian and anti-utopian counterparts. As a narrative mode that of necessity works *between* these historical antinomies, the typical dystopian text is an exercise in a politically charged form of hybrid textuality. Although most dystopian texts offer a detailed and pessimistic presentation of the very worst of social alternatives, a few affiliate with a eutopian tendency as they maintain a horizon of hope (or at least invite readings that do); while many are false "dystopian" allies of Utopia as they retain an anti-utopian disposition that forecloses all utopian possibility; and yet others negotiate a more strategically ambiguous position somewhere along the antinomic continuum. To be sure, the typical narrative structure of the dystopia (with its presentation of an alienated character's refusal) facilitates this politically and formally flexible stance. Indeed (and contrary to Jameson's hesitations about the nature and virtues of dystopian narratives in *Seeds of Time*), it is precisely the capacity for *narrative* that creates the possibility for social critique and utopian anticipation in the dystopian text. Paradoxically, dystopias reach toward what Jameson recognizes as the non-narrative quality of Utopia precisely by facilitating pleasurable and provocative reading experiences derived from conflicts that develop in the discrete elements of plot and character.

While dystopia faded in the 1960s and 1970s, the power of its counternarrative proved useful again in the 1980s. In the face of a powerful anti-utopian campaign, dystopia's potential for exploring utopian possibilities in bad times was tapped by a number of writers by the end of the decade. These writers confronted the devaluation of Utopia by an official, neoliberal discourse that proclaimed the end of history and celebrated simultaneously the end of radical social dreaming and the achievement of an instantaneous "utopia" of the market. While drawing on the classical dystopia, writers such as Cadigan, Robinson, Butler, Piercy, and Le Guin transformed the genre into what has come to be known as the *critical dystopia*.[4] These works carry out an intertextual intervention that negates the 1980s negation of the critical utopian moment and thus makes room for a new expression of the utopian imagination. These historically specific texts negotiate the necessary pessimism of the generic dystopia with a militant or utopian stance that not only breaks through the hegemonic enclosure of the text's alternative world but also self-reflexively refuses the anti-utopian temptation that lingers in every dystopian account. Thus, Sargent has added "critical dystopia" to his list of definitions: "a non-existent society described in considerable detail and normally located in time and space that the author intended a contemporaneous reader to view as worse than contemporary society but that normally includes at least one eutopian enclave or holds out hope that the dystopia can be overcome and replaced with a eutopia" ("US Eutopias" 222).

In our own work, we read critical dystopias as texts that maintain a utopian impulse. Traditionally a bleak, depressing genre with little space for hope within the story, dystopias maintain utopian hope *outside* their pages, if at all; for it is only if we consider dystopia as a warning that we as readers can hope to escape its pessimistic future. This option is not granted to the protagonists of *Nineteen Eighty-Four* or *Brave New World*. Winston Smith, Julia, John the Savage, and Lenina are all crushed by the authoritarian society; there is no learning, no escape for them. Conversely, the new critical dystopias allow both readers and protagonists to hope by resisting closure: the ambiguous, open endings of these novels maintain the utopian impulse *within* the work. In fact, by rejecting the traditional subjugation of the individual at the end of the novel, the critical dystopia opens a space of contestation and opposition for those collective "ex-centric" subjects whose class, gender, race, sexuality, and other positions are not empowered by hegemonic rule.

Another device that opens up these texts is an intensification of the practice of genre blurring. By self-reflexively borrowing specific conventions from other genres, critical dystopias more often blur the received boundaries of the dystopian form and thereby expand its creative potential for critical expression. Drawing on the feminist criticism of universalist assumptions—fixity and singularity, and neutral and objective knowledge—and recognizing the importance of difference, multiplicity, and complexity, of partial and situated knowledges, as well as of hybridity and fluidity, the critical dystopias resist genre purity in favor of an impure or hybrid text that renovates dystopian sf by making it formally and politically oppositional. In *Kindred*, for example, Butler revises the conventions of the time travel story and creates a novel that is both sf and slave narrative, while her *Parable of the Sower* combines survivalist sf with the diary and the slave narrative. Similarly, Atwood employs the conventions of the diary and the epistolary novel to narrate the life of her protagonist. By fragmenting her account of the future society with a tale (itself the record of oral storytelling) of sixteenth-century Prague, Piercy creates a historical sf novel. Thus, it is the very notion of an *impure* genre, with permeable borders which allow contamination from other genres, that represents resistance to a hegemonic ideology that reduces everything to a global monoculture.

Whereas the dystopian genre has always worked along a contested continuum between utopian and anti-utopian positions (that is, between texts which are emancipatory, militant, open, indeed critical; and those which are compensatory, resigned, and anti-critical), the recent dystopian texts are more self-reflexively critical as they retrieve the progressive possibilities inherent in dystopian narrative. In short, the radical openness of the critical dystopias results from steps they take beyond not only the 1970s moment of the counter-hegemonic Left and the critical utopias but also the 1980s moment characterized by the politics of identity, reform liberalism, and the separatist eutopias and pessimistic cyberpunk novels of the 1980s. Necessary as those moments were, the wheel has turned again. In the emerging historical conjuncture of the 1990s, the open dystopias resist both hegemonic and oppositional orthodoxies even as they inscribe a space for a new form of political opposition. With an exploration of agency that is based in difference and multiplicity yet cannily reunited in an alliance politics that speaks back in a larger though diverse collective voice, the new dystopias not only critique the present triumphal system but also explore ways to transform it that go beyond compromised left-centrist solutions. These texts, therefore, refresh the links between imagination and utopia and utopia and awareness in decidedly pessimistic times.

IV

Focusing on Anglo-American sf literature and film and on the question of the political future of utopianism in this historical period, the essays in *Dark Horizons* address a range of topics and issues. Working in the transdisciplinary approach that has become characteristic of utopian studies, they engage in historical and theoretical issues as well as close textual analyses. While they explore the general topic of dystopia and critical dystopia, in doing so, they also challenge assumptions and formulations, old and new. In the spirit of the critical utopia and critical dystopia, these investigations speak to and engage with one another in ways that take our collective thinking further, bringing us, in this new century, to the edge of new possibilities in politics and form and preventing even the work in this volume from hardening into a fixed paradigm.

As arranged in this book, the essays express one way of seeing how the form of dystopia and the politics of Utopia were explored in the 1980s and 1990s. The volume opens with an overview, "Utopia in Dark Times: Optimism/Pessimism and Utopia/Dystopia," in which Ruth Levitas and Lucy Sargisson engage in a dialogue on the political value of utopian thought and action in this decidedly anti-utopian moment in the history of the world. The focus then shifts to a series of textual readings, beginning with Jane Donawerth's investigation, in "Genre Blending and the Critical Dystopia," on how merging genres opens opportunities for radical vision in satire, epic, and sex role-reversal sf. Moving from Donawerth's reading of A. M. Lightner's sf in the late '60s, Samuel R. Delany's in the 1970s, and Connie Willis's in the 1980s, Ildney Cavalcanti, in "The Writing of Utopia and the Feminist Critical Dystopia: Suzy McKee Charnas's Holdfast Series," takes up the concept of the critical dystopia in order to read Charnas's tetralogy as it has developed from the 1970s to the 1990s. Next, David Seed, in "Cyberpunk and Dystopia: Pat Cadigan's Networks," traces the link between cyberpunk and dystopia by reviewing the work of Cadigan as she negotiates the move from what we call first to second wave cyberpunk. Shifting from cyberpunk to the politics of the feminist cyborg, Naomi Jacobs, in "Posthuman Bodies and Agency in Octavia Butler's *Xenogenesis*," proffers a reading of Butler's 1980s trilogy as a critical dystopia that preceded Butler's *Parable* series. In "'A useful knowledge of the present is rooted in the past': Memory and Historical Reconciliation in Ursula K. Le Guin's *The Telling*," Raffaella Baccolini moves to the end of the century and reads Le Guin's 2000 critical dystopia in the context of the relationship between utopia, history, and memory and recent debates on reconciliation. Also working with Le Guin as well as Robinson's novel from 1997, in "'The moment is here . . . and it's important': State, Agency, and Dystopia in Kim Stanley Robinson's *Antarctica* and Ursula K. Le Guin's *The Telling*," Tom Moylan examines the political imaginary of these texts in light of debates on agency in the recent anti-capitalist movement. Continuing this concern but shifting focus to film, Peter Fitting, in "Unmasking the Real? Critique and Utopia in Recent SF Films," distinguishes between militant or optimistic and resigned or pessimistic tendencies in *The Matrix, Pleasantville, The Truman Show,* and *Dark City.* Also working with film, Phillip E. Wegner, in "Where the Prospective Horizon Is Omitted: Naturalism and Dystopia in *Fight Club* and *Ghost Dog*," connects an analysis of dystopia's roots in naturalist narrative with a consideration of the move away from critical dystopian agency in the two films. With a focus on definitions and distinctions, Darko Suvin, in "Theses on Dystopia 2001," moves from readings of specific texts to an exploration of the relationship among utopia, history, form, and politics. Continuing in this vein, in "Concrete Dystopia: Slavery and Its Others," Maria Varsam looks at the relationship between dystopia as a literary form and the manifestation of dystopia in history in her reading of slavery and its narratives. In an essay that returns to the spirit of the opening dialogue, Lyman Tower Sargent ends the volume by moving from its focus on dystopia to a final consideration of the necessity and use of Utopia itself. In "The Problem of the 'Flawed Utopia': A Note on the Costs of Eutopia," he reminds us that Utopia is not a question of perfection and indeed is potentially flawed and dangerous. And yet, if we are not to live in dystopia, we must again and again "commit eutopia."

In addition to the order that we have selected, there are obviously other ways of reading each essay and the relationships between and among them. For ourselves, we see three sets of concerns that are of interest to us in our ongoing collaboration. One, taking up the recognition of dystopia's hybridity, is the investigation of its roots and intertexual relations with other literary forms. In this regard, Wegner and Donawerth give us an understanding of how the pre-twentieth-century forms of epic, satire, and naturalism have shaped dystopian narrative, for good or ill. On the other hand, Seed and Jacobs look at more recent intertextual connections between the critical dystopia and cyberpunk and the feminist cyborg imaginary. Catching the creative flexibility available to a single author, Cavalcanti tracks the oscillation between eutopia and dystopia, critical utopia and critical dystopia in Charnas—thereby giving us a way to read a similar fluidity of form in writers such as Le Guin, Piercy, and Robinson. Finally, Fitting and Wegner open new ground in addressing the specificities of sf/utopian film.

A second concern has to do with the relationship among utopia, history, and memory. While Varsam develops the intriguing notion of a "concrete dystopia" as a way of looking at the question of history and representation in the context of slavery, Baccolini explores the contribution that a utopian theory of memory and history can make to current debates on forgiveness and reconciliation. A third line of interest can be located in the considerations of the relationship between the dystopian/eutopian imagination and current debates on oppositional political agency that runs through all of the essays. Perhaps more pointedly, Levitas and Sargisson explore the overall possibilities for a utopian stance in these "dark times," while Moylan focuses on the potential for specific forms of utopian/oppositional alliances. Finally, Suvin and Sargent bring the discussion back to the question of the responsibility of intellectuals not only in utopian scholarship but also in utopian politics.

Whatever points of interest or lines of thought may occur to people when they read this volume, we will end our own reflections by recalling the properly didactic quality of sf and utopian writing. Whether we are talking about eutopia's potential for providing an education of desire or dystopia's for an education of perception, our hope as scholars, teachers, and citizens is that the thought experiments we read and write about, including those in *Dark Horizons*, will support or catalyze a social transformation that will bring an end to the conditions that produced the twentieth-century dystopias.

Notes

1. We use uppercase to refer to the historical antinomies of Utopia and Anti-Utopia; we use lowercase for instances of utopian expression (texts or practices).
2. See Baccolini, "Breaking the Boundaries"; "Memory, Desire and the Construction of Gender"; "Journeying through the Dystopian Genre"; and Moylan, "On Dystopia and the Novum"; "On Science Fiction, Totality, and Agency in the Nineties"; "US Dystopia, Nation, and State."
3. For approaches that conflate dystopia and anti-utopia, see, for example, Hillegas, Kumar, and Fortunati and Trousson. The descriptive definitions that we find useful are those by Sargent: "Utopia—a non-existent society described in considerable detail and normally located in time and space; Eutopia or positive utopia—a non-existent society described in considerable detail and normally located in time and space that the author intended a contemporaneous reader to view as considerably better than the society in which that reader lived; Dystopia or negative utopia—a non-existent society described in considerable detail and normally located in time and space that the author intended a contemporaneous reader to view as considerably worse than the society in which that reader lived," as distinct from "Anti-utopia—a non-existent society described in considerable detail and normally located in time and space that the author intended a contemporaneous reader to view as a criticism of utopianism or some particular eutopia" ("Three Faces" 9).
4. To these literary texts, one can add what can be called critical dystopian films, examples of which include *Men with Guns* (Sayles 1997), *The Matrix* (Wachowski and Wachowski 1999), and *Pleasantville* (Ross 1998). Specific discussions of filmic texts can be found in this collection in the essays by Fitting and Wegner.

Works Cited

Alexander, Bryan N. "Jameson's Adorno and the Problem of Utopia." *Utopian Studies* 9.2 (1998): 51–58.

Amis, Kingsley. *New Maps of Hell: A Survey of Science Fiction.* New York: Harcourt, 1960.

Atwood, Margaret. *The Handmaid's Tale.* 1985. Boston: Houghton, 1986.

Baccolini, Raffaella. "Breaking the Boundaries: Gender, Genre, and Dystopia." *Per una definizione dell'utopia. Metodologie e discipline a confronto.* Ed. Nadia Minerva. Ravenna: Longo, 1992. 137–46.

———. "Gender and Genre in the Feminist Critical Dystopias of Katharine Burdekin, Margaret Atwood, and Octavia Butler." *Future Females, The Next Generation: New Voices and Velocities in Feminist Science Fiction Criticism.* Ed. Marleen Barr. Lanham: Rowman, 2000. 13–34.

———. "'It's not in the womb the damage is done': Memory, Desire, and the Construction of Gender in Katharine Burdekin's *Swastika Night*." *Le trasformazioni del narrare.* Ed. E. Siciliani, A. Cecere, V. Intonti, A. Sportelli. Fasano: Schena, 1995. 293–309.

———. "Journeying through the Dystopian Genre: Memory and Imagination in Burdekin, Orwell, Atwood, and Piercy." *Viaggi in utopia.* Ed. Raffaella Baccolini, Vita Fortunati, and Nadia Minerva. Ravenna: Longo, 1996. 343–57.

Baggesen, Søren. "Utopian and Dystopian Pessimism: Le Guin's *The Word for World Is Forest* and Tiptree's 'We Who Stole the Dream.'" *Science-Fiction Studies* 14.1 (1987): 34–43.

Blade Runner. Dir. Ridley Scott. 1982.

Bradbury, Ray. *Fahrenheit 451.* New York: Ballantine, 1953.

Burdekin, Katharine. *Swastika Night.* 1937. Old Westbury, NY: Feminist, 1985.

Butler, Octavia E. *Kindred.* New York: Doubleday, 1979.

———. *Lilith's Brood.* (*Xenogenesis* trilogy). Compilation of *Dawn,* 1987; *Adulthood Rites,* 1988; *Imago,* 1989. New York: Warner, 1989.

———. *Parable of the Sower.* New York: Warner, 1993.

De Lillo, Don. *Underworld.* New York: Simon, 1997.

Forster, E. M. "The Machine Stops." *Oxford and Cambridge Review* 8 (1909): 83–122.

Fortunati, Vita, and Raymond Trousson, ed. *Dictionary of Literary Utopia.* Paris: Honoré Champion, 2000.

Gibson, William. *Neuromancer.* New York: Ace, 1984.

Hillegas, Mark. *The Future as Nightmare: H. G. Wells and the Anti-Utopians.* London: Oxford, 1967.

Huxley, Aldous. *Brave New World.* Garden City, NY: Doubleday, 1932.

Jameson, Fredric. *The Seeds of Time.* New York: Columbia UP, 1994.

Kafka, Franz. *The Metamorphosis and Other Stories.* 1915. Trans. Stanley Appelbaum. Mineola, NY: Dover, 1996.

Kumar, Krishan. *Utopia and Anti-Utopia in Modern Times.* Oxford: Blackwell, 1987.

Le Guin, Ursula K. *The Telling.* New York: Harcourt, 2000.

Lewis, C. S. *That Hideous Strength.* London: John Lane, 1945.

Miller, Jim. "Post-Apocalyptic Hoping: Octavia Butler's Dystopian/Utopian Fiction." *Science-Fiction Studies* 25.2 (1998): 336–61.

Moylan, Tom. "'Dare to Struggle, Dare to Win': On Science Fiction, Totality, and Agency in the 1990s." *Science Fiction, Critical Frontiers.* Ed. Karen Sayers and John Moore. London: Macmillan, 2000. 48–61.

———. *Demand the Impossible: Science Fiction and the Utopian Imagination.* New York: Methuen, 1986.

———. "'Look into the Dark': On Dystopia and the Novum." *Learning from Other Worlds: Estrangement, Cognition and the Politics of Science Fiction and Utopia. Essays in Honour of Darko Suvin.* Ed. Patrick Parrinder. Liverpool: Liverpool UP, 2000. 51–71.

———. "New Ground: US Dystopias, Nation, and State." *Utopianism/Literary Utopias and National Cultural Identities: A Comparative Perspective.* Ed. Paola Spinozzi. Bologna: COTEPRA/University of Bologna, 2001. 233–44.

———. *Scraps of the Untainted Sky: Science Fiction, Utopia, Dystopia.* Boulder: Westview, 2000.

Nabokov, Vladimir. *Bend Sinister.* New York: Holt, 1947.

Orwell, George. *Nineteen Eighty-Four.* New York: Harcourt, 1949.

Penley, Constance. "Time Travel, Primal Scene and the Critical Dystopia." *Alien Zone: Cultural Theory and Contemporary Science Fiction Cinema.* Ed. Annette Kuhn. London: Verso, 1990. 116–27.

Piercy, Marge. *He, She and It.* New York: Knopf, 1991.

Rand, Ayn. *Anthem.* London: Cassell, 1938.

Robinson, Kim Stanley. *Gold Coast.* New York: Tor, 1988.

Sargent, Lyman Tower. "The Three Faces of Utopianism Revisited." *Utopian Studies* 5.1 (1994): 1–37.

———. "US Eutopias in the 1980s and 1990s: Self-Fashioning in a World of Multiple Identities." *Utopianism/Literary Utopias and National Cultural Identities: A Comparative Perspective.* Ed. Paola Spinozzi. Bologna: COTEPRA/University of Bologna, 2001. 221–32.

———. "Utopia—the Problem of Definition." *Extrapolation* 16.2 (1975): 137–48.

Waugh, Evelyn. *Love Among the Ruins.* London: Chapman, 1953.

Wolmark, Jenny. *Aliens and Others: Science Fiction, Feminism and Postmodernism.* Iowa City: U of Iowa P, 1994.

Zamyatin, Yevgeny. *We.* 1924. Trans. Clarence Brown. New York: Penguin, 1993.

CHAPTER 1

Utopia in Dark Times: Optimism/Pessimism and Utopia/Dystopia

RUTH LEVITAS AND LUCY SARGISSON

But I like those who come with the passion of a vision,
Like a child with a gift, like a friend with a question.
—Leon Rosselson, "Bringing the News from the Nowhere"

Dear Lucy,   17 July 2001
You asked me to explain why I am so pessimistic about the possible role of Utopia in the contemporary world. The answer stems from the reason why I became interested in utopianism in the first place. I wanted, and still want, the world to be changed. Our current social arrangements condemn most of the world's population to poverty and premature death, and subject even those of us who are very affluent to forms of alienation, repression, competition and separation from each other, which are incompatible with a fully human existence. I don't believe this is necessary. So the strongest and best function of Utopia must be the exploration of alternatives in a way that supports or catalyzes social transformation.

Of course, this isn't the only reason to be interested in utopianism. If Utopia is understood as the expression of the desire for a better way of living, then in one form or another it is present in most, if not all, cultures. Tracing its patterns is a proper part of cultural anthropology, the sociology of culture, literary criticism, the history of ideas and of social movements.

If Utopia is understood as a partial or holistic model of an alternative society, it has a role as a heuristic device in normative political thought. Most of utopian studies is, at least overtly, concerned with these utterly intellectually respectable pursuits. Some of us have even built successful academic careers on these. But in my experience, most utopists are also more or less overtly utopians, who are interested in the different manifestations of Utopia in part because this constitutes a resource for thinking about real alternatives to the present.

Catalyzing change is only one possible function of Utopia. It may even be the rarest one, depending as it does on some version of the idea of progress. The transformative potential of Utopia depends on locating it in the future, on thinking through the process of transformation from the present, and identifying the potential agents of that transformation. Many expressions of the desire for a better life are not of this kind. Myths and literary depictions may be located elsewhere in space rather than in time, or in the past, or a world beyond both space and time. Intentional communities may be concerned with living otherwise in present time, not—as was undoubtedly the case with, say, the Owenite communities—with prefiguring and effecting a wider social transformation. Utopian imaginings may be located in the future, but without any convincing account of transforming agents and processes that could turn wishful thinking into political action. The alternative functions of Utopia, then, are compensation (or retreat or escapism) and critique. Both of these have their merits. In the face of a hostile world, retreat, escape, or simply a compensatory fantasy to cheer yourself up may be reasonable and humanly valuable responses. Holding up a critical mirror to the present to expose its negative characteristics and effects is also important, and indeed a necessary precursor to developing and pursuing positive alternatives. But it is not enough.

My pessimism, then, derives from an observation that, at least for the time being, Utopia has retreated from being a potential catalyst of change to being merely a bearer of consolation or a vehicle of criticism. This is one of the reasons for the dominance of the dystopian mode in contemporary culture—for example, in films like *The Matrix*. As Raffaella Baccolini and Tom Moylan have argued, this dystopianism is not anti-utopian, and its critical potential depends on the presence or absence of a route out. Ursula K. Le Guin's story "The Ones Who Walk Away From Omelas" concludes an ambiguous utopia/dystopia with the words "they seem to know where they are going, the ones who walk away from Omelas" (5). They do not stay to address collectively the problem at the heart of Omelas, but leave individually, presumably to find or make some other, better, place. But we are never, in the critical dystopian mode, shown the alternative or the collective agents of its creation.

This is not a failure of imagination so much as a consequence of the intellectual and political conditions of late capitalism. The term *utopia* itself has been tarnished by association with totalitarianism. This is partly the result of deliberate attempts to invalidate any proposed alternative to capitalism; anti-utopianism is a standard weapon in the armory of the status quo. But this doesn't altogether explain the difficulties of imagining the pursuit of visions of an alternative social order (which have, in any case, generally not advertised themselves under the banner of utopianism). Rather, pluralism and postmodernity have made it difficult to articulate committed alternatives. Pluralism means that it is impossible to ignore the fact that all knowledge and all aspirations emanate from specific standpoints, that others will see things differently, that negotiation is necessary. Values and desires are relativized, solutions partial and provisional. Postmodernity is radically anti-foundationalist, so that at least those forms of utopianism which entail claims about truth and morality are called into question. François Lyotard's challenge to "grand narratives" makes it difficult to assert a historical route from here to Utopia. I am not suggesting that this has led to a collapse in utopian thinking. As Moylan (see *Demand*, *Scraps*) has demonstrated, both the "critical utopia" and the "critical dystopia" are responses to those challenges, in which Utopia itself becomes more fragmentary, provisional, contested, ambiguous. The emphasis shifts from content or structure to process—with Jürgen Habermas suggesting that it is now only possible to consider the communicative processes whereby Utopia may be negotiated, rather than the nature of Utopia itself. Although Moylan, in *Demand*, sees such utopianism as having a positive role in social change, I am more pessimistic. The critical utopia is, simply, critical. Utopia is not dead, but the kind of utopianism that is holistic, social, future-located, committed, and linked to the present by some identifiable narrative of change—a kind of collective optimism of the intellect as well as the will—is culturally problematic. This shift from structure to process has taken place both in the way that utopias are written, and the way in which they are written about in utopian studies (see Levitas, "For Utopia"). It has strengths, but also weaknesses. As Raymond Williams said: "The heuristic utopia offers a strength of vision against the prevailing grain: the systematic utopia a strength of conviction that the world can really be different. The heuristic utopia, at the same time, has the weakness that it can settle into isolated and in the end sentimental 'desire,' a mode of living with alienation, while the systematic utopia has the weakness that, in its insistent organization, it seems to offer little room for any recognizable life" (203). He also said that it is not a question of asking which is better or stronger, but I think there is a weakening involved in the almost total shift to heuristic or critical utopia, as what is lost is the drive to change and the assertion of its possibility. Utopia may still express desire, but it does not articulate hope.

Critical utopias are commended because they disrupt the ideological closure of the present. But for Utopia to be transformative, it must also disrupt the structural closure of the present. The material political difficulties may be more important than the cultural ones. The collapse of the idea of progress and an accompanying social pessimism have material roots—in widening inequalities, persistent armed conflicts, ecological destruction, and the tightening grip of "globalization," or, more properly, global capitalism. It is very difficult to identify either mechanisms or agents capable of effecting a real transformation of the global social and economic system. Without this, the conditions for the serious envisioning of committed alternatives simply don't exist—and Utopia will continue to be confined to the function of critique rather than transformation.

Dear Ruth,   23 July 2001

Thanks for your letter, and I see what you mean: desire is not enough. Holding up a mirror to expose the flaws in the present is not enough. Criticism is not sufficient to change the world. I'd have to agree with all of these points, but for me Utopia does far more than this, and I'm more optimistic (hopeful?) about its potential than you are. In many ways my position is close to those that you deplore, although, like yours, my reasons for studying Utopia are personal and political. Like you, I want the world to be different.

You say that the best and strongest function of Utopia is to *catalyze* change, and I agree. However, we seem to view the route and mechanisms for this rather differently. For you, Utopia should explore alternatives in such a way as to "support or catalyze social transformation." For me, the exploration of alternatives is a transformative process in itself. I suppose I'm interested in the process of change—utopianism as process or moment of change.

I am at once more cautious and more ambitious for Utopia than you are. Utopia has always been a soft target for accusations of totalitarianism, and it has to be admitted that utopianism has a strong totalizing aspect. This presents problems of varying natures and degrees: first, of course, there's always the danger that the "wrong" utopia might be adopted: that, for instance, my feminism might evolve one day into a sexist totality of its own; that the things of which I accuse patriarchy might simply become inverted in my own ideal world (as is the case in so many of the classic feminist utopias of the 1970s). Angela Carter did an effective satire of this in *The Passion of New Eve*. Evelyn, a man, is kidnapped and castrated by a matriarchal feminist sect that plans to impregnate him with his own semen. Their world-transforming intent includes and inverts a gendered logic of domination, hierarchy, and subordination. Second, at a deeper and more difficult level, I share a belief with some so-called postmodernists that an appropriate object of change is the way we pattern our thoughts: that one thing that lies at the root of all failed attempts at widespread social (left-wing) change is a mistaken affection for and adherence to the mind-set and/or vocabulary and paradigms that are supposedly challenged. I've written about this elsewhere (see *Feminist Utopianism* and *Utopian Bodies*).

So the changes that I might desire to see are less clearly defined than those which you articulate in your letter. They are more about changing the ways in which we think: about thinking our way around alienation, duality, polarizations, competition, separation, and oppositional thinking. And, for me, this is (perhaps) achievable through a utopianism that takes Utopia as a place in which to explore alternatives. This can be in an imaginary space, such as a novel or political theory, or a physical space such as a living community. For me, the exploration of alternatives is a necessary part of the process of transformation. It creates changes in the ways that we think about the world and is an integral part of sustainably changing the way that we behave.

In some ways this gives to Utopia a weaker function than you ascribe to it. In some ways, though, it's far reaching: it asks Utopia to help to *change the way we think.*

You say that "[t]he transformative potential of Utopia depends on locating it in the future, on thinking through the process of transformation from the present, and identifying the potential agents of that transformation"; and, again, I'd like to say "yes" and "no": I see what you mean but disagree strongly with what you say.

Utopian transformation doesn't have to be located in the future, in a far-distant hope for a better place. Rather, it can be part of transformation in the now. Daily life in some intentional communities, for instance, is part of both life-transforming shifts in consciousness *and* incremental changes in daily practice and behavior toward the environment and other people. I'm thinking here of communities such as the Findhorn Foundation which, for all my reservations about New Ageism, I would offer as an example of a place where transformation occurs. The key, I think, is in agency—by living, visiting, or staying in an environment of conscious living (seeking and desiring and practicing personal transformation), people in intentional communities can begin to be part of change on a number of levels. First, with regard to the Green movement, there is a network of communities that are linked, more or less loosely, to Green politics and activism, and so they might be said to be part of a national or global movement. Second, they have tangible impacts on their local environment. I'm thinking here of modest and incremental changes such as the community recycling and compost schemes run from the community at Beech Hill in Devon.[1] Third and no less important, they are places in which individuals begin to change.

I think I'd better close here, but, in summary, I'm trying to say that utopias can be part of change in the here and now and that this change is one that is many, operating at different levels and in different places to varying degree. This may not be changing the world with dramatic and easily observable impact but is, I think, what's required for sustainable and enduring transformation. This is a pluralist utopianism, and it's a utopianism of process. It's empowering in the now and isn't dependent on escapism or distant wish fulfillment, and it takes the way that we think as an essential part of social change.

Dear Lucy,   24 July 2001
Thanks for that. It certainly helps to clarify the extent and nature of our (dis)agreements. I agree that it is useful to think about Utopia as a space in which to explore alternatives. I agree that such exploration is a necessary part of social transformation, and that changes in the way we think are integral to any such transformation. There's a sense in which I also agree that the exploration of alternatives is itself a transformative process—or can be so for the explorers. And I certainly don't "deplore" critical utopianism. Actually, I don't really deplore even the most compensatory forms of utopianism like fantasizing about how to spend a lottery win. I take Ernst Bloch's line that even the most embryonic expressions of wanting the world to be otherwise need to be nurtured and cultivated. I do worry about the apparent current difficulty of articulating positive images of the future.

There are some perhaps quite fundamental disagreements around the issues in your third paragraph. I agree that Utopia is essentially totalizing in that it requires looking at social, economic, political, and spatial processes in a holistic way. That's a very different matter from arguing that utopianism intrinsically leans toward totalitarianism, and I think that the elision between the two that takes place in some anti-utopian discourses is an intellectual mistake (where it is not a deliberate ideological device). I completely disagree that "the way we pattern our thoughts" should be an object of change; and I completely disagree that "one thing that lies at the root of all failed attempts at widespread social (left-wing) change is a mistaken affection for and adherence to the mind-set and/or paradigms that are supposedly challenged." These seem to me to be wildly idealist claims that disregard the structural contexts in which beliefs and practices are produced and reproduced.

Actually, this is undercut in an interesting way by what you say about intentional communities. I see what you mean about their potential for personal change. Unlike utopian novels, which can offer that individual experience which Miguel Abensour has described as "the education of desire," intentional communities provide real rather than virtual spaces for this process (Thompson 790–91). I don't have the firsthand experience of such communities that you have, but it seems to me that the possibilities for change depend on the fact that people are (at least partially and temporarily) removed from the structural relationships of the dominant society, aka global capitalism. The alternative space of the intentional community is not empty, but has rules, structures, constraints, expectations of its own, and it is the positive presence of these, rather than simply the absence of the usual ones, that enables change. (Rather as Erving Goffman argues in *Asylums*, and I think Michel Foucault implies of heterotopia, the self is changed first by stripping away markers of identity, and then by active reconstruction.) The transformation of ways of thinking and of being—since we both would agree, surely, that we are talking about more than a cognitive process here—depends on an alternative *structure* within which another logic of action and understanding makes sense.

If material and discursive practices are so intertwined, can the changes that intentional communities enable survive a move back into mainstream society? Or, given that our ways of being in the world are heavily constrained by and dependent on contexts—contexts which are often so familiar that we are unaware of them—do people simply revert to type when confronted with the pressures of the old world? This is in danger of degenerating into the old chicken-and-egg argument. The kinds of change you look for in individuals, and the "modest and incremental changes" that may be produced in communities are not things I want to dismiss. I am simply pessimistic about these changes adding up to the kind of transformation of global capitalism that is essential to any kind of decent human future. And I do think the question of the future-orientation of Utopia is important, though this need not be a "far-distant" hope for a better place. It seems to me that any utopian space that sets out to be, in Williams's terms, "oppositional" rather than merely "alternative" and that therefore aims to change the outside world must include a view of a transformed future.

The anti-capitalist protests, most recently at Genoa, seem to me to illustrate the strengths of both our arguments. On the one hand, it is quite clear that very large numbers of individuals and groups espouse values and practices that are opposed to the operations of global capitalism. On the other hand, there is, as George Monbiot has said, a dearth of visions of what is to be fought for—and very little sense of how change at this level can be effected. I think there are three main issues that divide us. One, which I've addressed here, is the question of how far the utopias that exist as alternative spaces within capitalism can provide deep and lasting changes in individuals which can be transformative of, rather than erased by, mainstream structures. This is related to the more general questions of the relationship between personal and political, or individual and structural change; how change can be brought about—and what we would each understand by change anyway. These issues may be the ones that really color our different orientations to Utopia, and which account for your (relative) optimism and my (relative) pessimism. Although we should not forget that that too may be materially based, for you are much younger than I!

Dear Ruth,   27 July 2001
On the "when?" of Utopia—should we think of Utopia in terms of the future or the now?—I agree that we should say both. Utopia is forward-looking, yes. Always just around the corner, always on the other side of the horizon, Utopia is "not yet," elusive, glimpsed but never grasped. That's one of the things I love about Utopia. And yet, like you, I want the world to be very different from the way it is now. I want to ride the wave of utopian impulse toward a new now. This all brings to mind Louis Marin's work on the edges of Utopia—the frontier.[2] Utopia has always been here and elsewhere, impossible and desired, imaginable and yet beyond our ken.

Also, and important, I think, utopianism is part of a process and thus is part of the now. That meditative and thoughtful process to which Abensour refers creates something new—albeit fleetingly and imaginatively in the process and moment of reading. This brings me to your interesting and important point about the depth and durability of change in what I've called the utopian space of intentional communities. My research in this area has not directly addressed this question, though I think now that it ought to. I have visited and stayed in some forty communities in Britain and New Zealand, observing and interviewing people who have chosen to live (and sometimes work) together for some common purpose. It is not possible to know from this research about the depth or longevity of change for people who no longer live communally, or "in community" as some prefer to term it. My work has been with communities in process, with people who currently live in communities and their wider locality.

That said, there is an issue I'd like to pursue a little further, as it speaks to those points of difference that have emerged in our dialogue thus far.

This concerns change on the micro level of relations between self and other. This is one level at which utopias affect change, and we have both worked on this in utopian texts. Marge Piercy's *Woman on the Edge of Time* is a case in point. I'm thinking of the way that Piercy takes us with Connie, the visitor to a place in which things are different, into a world where both structures and relations are transformed for the better. This speaks to both of our positions. In the eutopia Connie witnesses and experiences different close interpersonal relations: sexual love, friendships, and parenting are transformed and operated by a dynamic that is not driven by possession. Mattapoisett is as far from the poverty, neurosis, and alienation of Connie's present as is imaginable. Vital factors in this utopia are, I believe, transformed property relations *and* non-hierarchical, non-binary, non-possessive relations of self to other.

Intentional communities around the world experiment with both of these things. Before going further, though, it's important to note that whilst I refer to intentional communities as utopian, they are not utopias in the classic sense of a perfect society (see Davis). In most cases, people established and joined intentional communities because they wanted to live in a way that they believed to be better. Often they express a desire to show by example that another way is possible. They may, as I suggest, operate as utopian spaces of opposition, alternatives, and exploration, but they are not perfect micro societies or communities.

In the communities I have visited, relations of self to other are issues of both contention and celebration. I recently returned from a period of fieldwork in New Zealand, where I surveyed intentional communities across the country, and just about every person I interviewed cited their relationships with others in the community as either (and sometimes both) the best or worst thing about being a part of that community. In some instances, like the Findhorn Foundation in the United Kingdom, the transformation of the self—and of one's relationship with other people en masse and as individuals—is an intention of the community per se. In others, the experience of daily life in close quarters with others effects conflict, contemplation, and change. A different sense of relationship emerges amongst people who live communally. This is most apparent in two areas of life: conflict resolution and personal relationships. Harmonious living in community with others does not involve repressing anger or suppressing annoyance at the seemingly trivial daily events (Who cooked meat in the vegetarian pan? Who left crumbs on the work surface? Why can't you empty the compost bin when it's full?) but rather developing mechanisms for the expression, articulation, and resolution of conflict. Successful intentional communities, be they Christian convents or hippie communes, all have these mechanisms.

Everyday relationships amongst community members are different from collegial, friendship, or marriage relations in mainstream society. People spoke of learning to live in intimacy, acceptance, toleration, and openness in which privacy and the strictly personal are at once diminished and respected. Qualities cited as valuable in this process of learning to be different with people include trust, openness, a willingness to be vulnerable to the other, sensitivity to others, willingness to give without expectancy of reciprocal return, and respect for others. When things are working well in a community it is possible to observe extraordinary relationships between people, both adults and children.

I think it's worth mentioning also that there are dark sides to this. On the one hand, the increased intimacy can and does often lead to complex interpersonal relations and the breakdown of partnerships. Again, this is responded to with innovation; and in some communities, such as Tui in New Zealand, interpersonal conflict resolution has emerged as a speciality, and training courses are now offered to the wider community as income-generating schemes. Also and further, the sense of loss that comes when a person leaves a community is palpable and resembles a form of bereavement. On the other hand, increased intimacy, vulnerability, and trust can and have led to situations of exploitation and abuse. It's interesting that you cite Goffman and Foucault on this as it is the very stripping away of self that is characteristic of the charismatic cult. One former New Zealand community, Centrepoint (closed by the courts in 2000), had as one of its central aims the re-creation of self-other relations. It assumed the form of a religious-spiritual community and tried to create a space in which relationships were not derived from the concept of possession. No private property existed at Centrepoint, and all personal wealth and possessions were donated to the community. Sex was supposed to be free of guilt, and one did not "own" one's partner. Gestalt therapy and EST were employed to strip away the "baggage" of mainstream society in the psyche. Former members, whom I interviewed as new members of other communities, re-called both the overwhelming sense of love and warmth and belonging that Centrepoint gave to them and also the pain and loss when favor was withdrawn. This came in both material and emotional forms of abuse. Questioning the leader might result in the disappearance of one's tooth-brush, for instance, or the sudden unavailability of tampons. One man re-called how, when he objected one day when returning from the shower to find another man in bed with his partner, he was publicly shamed for his possessive impulses and subjected to "punishment" tasks. Others spoke of the pain of receiving coldness where once they had received love.

I appreciate that anecdotes from particular communities do little to ap-proach the magnitude of the subject to which we're referring, but I hope to illustrate both of our points here: that individuals experience transforma-tive processes in communities *and* that rules and structures exist and are connected to material conditions of life (and in particular forms of prop-erty ownership). And yes, this is possible because intentional communities are enclosed and identifiable (if not closed) spaces.[3] This permits a feeling of safety and encourages people to take the risks with themselves that such personal transformations involve.

Dear Lucy,   30 October 2001
What divides us is not, of course, the question of the importance of self-other relations, but the extent to which changes in these can effect changes in the structure and fabric of social life as a whole. This question of how we relate to each other concerns moral philosophers and theologians as well as utopians. In *I and Thou*, Martin Buber (who was all three) talks of the I-Thou relationship, a sort of authentic existential meeting of persons with each other (or God), and only fleetingly and occasionally available. But in *Paths in Utopia*, he also argued for the importance of the kibbutz movement as the necessary economic basis of this. John Macmurray, the Christian Socialist thinker supposedly among the influences on Tony Blair, also argues strongly that relations between persons as ends in themselves rather than means to ends are possible only on the basis of effective material equality. I agree with you that what is important about Piercy's work is that she not only addresses the quality of self-other relations but makes it explicit that she is exploring this in relation to the social structures and property relations that make "good" relations possible. The model of the good relationship with which Piercy works is one that humanistic psychologists would recognize as "separate attachment." A different quality of intimacy is posited, depending on (among other things) the removal of economic dependency between partners. Relationships are no longer held in place by economic necessity, nor indeed by collective expectations that partnerships should necessarily be durable.

I do not for a moment deny that the utopian spaces of intentional communities may allow different, better relations between people, although, as you observe, they may also be sites of oppression and exploitation. But the existence of these spaces does not seem to me to constitute any major challenge to the more generally dystopian character of political culture. Indeed, the emphasis on the self, the individual, and the private seems to me to be linked to a wider political apathy, and a sense that we can really alter *only* this micro-level. The dystopian genre is often critical of capitalism: there's a widespread view that things are not OK, but we live in a culture in which there is no confidence that things can be otherwise, so utopian energies are restricted to very personal levels. Oliver Bennett describes this as cultural pessimism and draws attention to the prevalence of narratives of economic, moral, and ecological decline.

In short, the personal is not political enough. I'm unconvinced about the translation of micro-changes into macro-changes. My quest for Utopia is based on a wish to be different myself, as well as that the world should be otherwise; and I want the world to be otherwise partly because this seems to be a precondition for recovering my own humanity. The danger of this position is that it passes off responsibility for who I am onto external structures and neglects the extent to which, as you say, Utopia is part of the process that must be entered into now, rather than postponed always beyond the horizon. The converse problem is thinking that we can live in what Colin Davis called a Perfect Moral Commonwealth, in which the negative effects of structures are canceled out by individual moral action. Clearly, one must work at both levels. But the general conditions for transformed relations between self and other include a level of material security that capitalism, by its very nature, denies to all but a few.

I was made temporarily more cheerful by reading David Harvey's *Spaces of Hope*. Like you, Harvey is an optimist. The book is a great analysis and critique of globalization and attempts to construct a new "dialectical" concept of Utopia. But Harvey also talks about the need to make connections and alliances across levels, and to understand the relationship between different scales and loci of intervention—in a more complex way than local/global or micro/macro. I almost believed, for a while, that there actually are transformative spaces of hope.

Then came 11 September 2001. This may be a cultural as well as a political watershed. In *The Matrix*, what is needed to break out of the dystopian fiction is simply the recovery of the real. However, the translation of images from disaster movies into grim reality does not provide the conditions for breaking out of dystopia into Utopia. Rather, as you suggested in your first reply, utopian energies have been harnessed to conflicting forces of destruction and annihilation. Despite his hopefulness, Bloch pointed out that "devastatingly, possible Fascist nothing" (197) was as real a possibility for the future as a socialist utopia. In late 2001, the actually very disparate contested politics and cultures of the world are being projected by powerful forces on both sides of the current conflict as great utopias. The West lays claim to civilization and freedom (apparently blind to the irony in calling its military operation "Enduring Freedom"). This is pitted against an anti-modern Islamic view of the good society, which is no more representative of Muslims and Islam than Bush's and Blair's views are representative of yours and mine. But as the military conflict is presented as such a clash of utopias, there seems little space in which any vision of an alternative can be articulated. The effect of the atrocity of 11 September and the military response to it has been to close down the space for hope (see Levitas, "After the Fall"). And the anti-terrorist legislation that has followed in its wake has been so far-reaching that it criminalizes most practical forms of dissent, producing a discursive and material closure that is quite antithetical to utopian exploration and experiment.

Dear Ruth,   8 January 2002
Apologies for the long silence—it's been a long time since I wrote my last letter because I got stuck. Stuck in an uncharacteristic pessimism from which I have yet fully to emerge. We began writing this long before 11 September, and the events of that day are connected to everything that we've been writing and thinking about and they seem to change everything. They change everything, and yet they change nothing. Therein lie the grounds of my newfound pessimism. The impulses behind those actions are not new. They've always existed and are, as Bloch intimates, part of the drive for Utopia.

I've never shied away from acknowledging the dark side of Utopia. We all know that utopianism has its authoritarian aspect. I've argued that this is connected to a totalizing impulse. We all know that horrors have resulted from the drive for Utopia. The murder of European Jews was part of the realization of a certain utopia. Ethnic cleansing, the Holocaust, genocide, and inhumanity have all formed part of the map of Utopia. It has always been important to me—and I know to you—to acknowledge this. It is important not to run away from the dangers and dark sides lest we become naive in our conceptualization of Utopia. That would be irresponsible, sloppy, and dangerous.

But somehow to know this, and even to study it and thus encounter and daily confront it, is not the same as to be called to a television set to see a commercial jet full of passengers being deliberately flown into a building full of people in the name of a cause. It's left me thinking—no, feeling—that perhaps Utopia *is* simply dangerous. Lives *are* affected by idealism. Ideals can, I'm sure, inspire, motivate, and galvanize us to action. But what if those ideals demand the annihilation of other people?

I can see the links to my earlier letter about self-other relations, and I know that the murders on 11 September speak to—and perhaps come from—the desire to consume, eliminate, and destroy the Other. Somehow, though, I don't feel inclined to use it as an illustration of a point.

Well, I do and I don't. I think that this *is* an appropriate interpretation of the events. The events of 11 September *are* an example of the dark side of the utopian impulse and of a certain theory of self-other relations. Perhaps they are also a warning of the dangers of utopianism per se? I can see that there is a trap of anti-utopianism here, but the drive to Utopia has always been dangerous, potentially and actually. Atrocities are enacted daily and globally in the name of various utopias: accumulation of capital, love of God, protection of trade, et cetera ad nauseam. My horror and pessimism stem from the banal fact that ordinary people are capable of horrific acts. Give people an account of the world that legitimizes callousness, cruelty, torture, and murder of other people, and, it seems, they will act accordingly. Utopias can and have historically been built on this.

Dear Lucy,   9 January 2002
I can see that the catastrophic events of 11 September would undermine your feelings of optimism. But you have gone further, and stepped from the critical dystopian mode into the trap of anti-utopianism. The critical dystopia is the dark side of hope, and hopes for a way out; anti-utopia attributes the darkness to Utopia itself, and tells us the exits are ambushed. But the anti-utopian arguments are not proved by acts of genocide. They do not prove that utopias are intrinsically totalitarian or that they can only be imposed by extreme acts of murder and torture. All political movements have utopian elements, insofar as they encompass views of what a good society might be like. Some of these political movements are dangerous and genocidal. *But it is not "utopianism" that makes them so. The problem about totalitarianism is not its utopianism, but its totalitarianism.* The elision of Utopia and totalitarianism is an anti-utopian fallacy that closes off all futures, paralyzes us imaginatively and politically, and says it will never be much better than this. Theologically, I suppose, it would be like saying that because evil enters into the world as a corruption of the good (fallen angels and the like), all pursuit of the good runs the risk of corruption and should therefore not be attempted.

Pessimist though I am, it seems I am less pessimistic than you. The struggle for the future is always the struggle between competing utopias. The problem at the moment is that the competition seems stacked in favor of global capital, which becomes less tolerant when under duress, and makes it even harder to articulate positive alternatives without being marked out as lunatic or terrorist. It isn't grounds for ceding the intellectual and political stage to criminal conspiracies and state terrorism, and allowing dystopia to collapse into anti-utopia.

In any case, all you said before 11 September remains true: that people persist in trying to find better ways of living. And, despite my skepticism about the political effects of these recurrent impulses toward a better life, there are alliances. People are protesting, including protesting about the erosion of civil liberties under the guise of "security." People are prepared to say "not in my name." So that perhaps, in these spaces, there is hope— the hope which Bloch, again, construed "not . . . *only as emotion* . . . but *more essentially as a directing act of a cognitive kind*" (12).

Notes

1. See http://www.diggersanddreamers.org.uk/.
2. Specifically, Marin's "The Frontiers of Utopia" and *Utopics*.
3. It is my observation that closed communities are those in which the dangers of exploitation are the greatest. Lack of interaction and mutual scrutiny with the "outside world" results in an approach to the outside as Other and dangerous, wicked and polluting. Perspectives become twisted and events inside the community appear normal, righteous, and good.

Works Cited

Baccolini, Raffaella. "Gender and Genre in the Feminist Critical Dystopias of Katharine Burdekin, Margaret Atwood, and Octavia Butler." *Future Females, the Next Generation: New Voices and Velocities in Feminist Science Fiction Criticism.* Ed. Marleen S. Barr. Lanham: Rowman, 2000. 13–34.

Bennett, Oliver. *Cultural Pessimism: Narratives of Decline in the Postmodern World.* Edinburgh: Edinburgh UP, 2000.

Bloch, Ernst. *The Principle of Hope.* Trans. Neville Plaice, Stephen Plaice, and Paul Knight. Oxford: Blackwell, 1986.

Buber, Martin. *I and Thou.* New York: Scribner, 2000.

———. *Paths in Utopia.* London: Routledge, 1949.

Carter, Angela. *The Passion of New Eve.* London: Virago, 1977.

Davis, J. C. *Utopia and the Ideal Society: A Study of English Utopian Writing, 1516–1700.* Cambridge: Cambridge UP, 1981.

Foucault, Michel. "Of Other Spaces." *Diacritics* 16.1 (1986): 22–27.

Goffman, Erving. *Asylums.* Harmondsworth: Penguin, 1988.

Habermas, Jürgen. "The New Obscurity: The Crisis of the Welfare State and the Exhaustion of Utopian Energies." *The New Conservatism.* Cambridge: Polity, 1989.

Harvey, David. *Spaces of Hope.* Edinburgh: Edinburgh UP, 2000.

Le Guin, Ursula K. "The Ones Who Walk Away from Omelas (Variation on a Theme by William James)." 1976. *Utopian Studies* 2.1–2 (1991): 1–5.

Levitas, Ruth. "After the Fall." Fifth International Culture Conference, "Culture and Freedom." University of Lisbon. 28–30 Nov. 2001.

———. *The Concept of Utopia.* Syracuse: Syracuse UP, 1990.

———. "For Utopia: the limits of the utopian function under conditions of late capitalism." *Contemporary Review of International Social and Political Philosophy* 3.2–3 (2000): 25–43.

———. "We: Problems in Identity, Solidarity and Commitment." *History of the Human Sciences* 8.3 (1995): 89–105.

Macmurray, John. *Creative Society: A Study of the Relationship of Christianity to Communism.* London: SCM, 1935.

Marin, Louis. "The Frontiers of Utopia." *Utopias and the Millennium.* Ed. Krishan Kumar and Stephen Bann. London: Reaktion, 1993.

———. *Utopics: Spatial Plays.* Trans. R. Vollrath. Atlantic City: Humanities, 1984.

Monbiot, George. "Politics not Parliament." *Guardian* 1 May 2001.

Moylan, Tom. *Demand the Impossible: Science Fiction and the Utopian Imagination.* London: Methuen, 1986.

———. *Scraps of the Untainted Sky: Science Fiction, Utopia, Dystopia.* Boulder: Westview, 2000.

Piercy, Marge. *Woman on the Edge of Time.* London: Women's, 1979.

Rosselson, Leon. "Bringing the News from Nowhere." *Bringing the News from Nowhere.* Fuse Records CFC 390, 1986.

Sargisson, Lucy. *Contemporary Feminist Utopianism.* London: Routledge, 1996.

———. *Utopian Bodies and the Politics of Transgression.* London: Routledge, 2000.

Shenker, Barry. *Intentional Communities: Ideology and Alienation in Communal Societies.* London: Routledge, 1981.

Thompson, Edward. *William Morris: Romantic to Revolutionary.* London: Merlin, 1977.

Williams, Raymond. *Problems in Materialism and Culture.* London: Verso, 1980.

CHAPTER 2

Genre Blending
and the Critical Dystopia

JANE DONAWERTH

The borders of utopia and dystopia as genres are not rigid, but permeable; these forms absorb the characteristics of other genres, such as comedy or tragedy. In this sense, dystopia as a genre is the ideal site for generic blends.[1] Conservative forms are transformed by merging with dystopia, a merge that forces political reconsideration, and traditionally conservative forms can progressively transform the dystopian genre so that its pessimism shifts from being resigned to being militant.

Although the introduction to this volume reviews the current discussion about the nature of the critical dystopia, I need briefly to set out a definition of that genre for my purposes in this essay. Lyman Tower Sargent defines the dystopia as "a non-existent society described in considerable detail and normally located in time and space that the author intended a contemporaneous reader to view as considerably worse than the society in which that reader lived" (9). Gordon Browning argues that the dystopia uses satiric literary techniques, projects the major dissatisfactions of the author with current society onto the dystopian setting, and represents the society as isolated. Ruth Levitas adds the conception that the role of utopia (and, by extension, dystopia) is the "education of desire" (7–8). As Tom Moylan points out (26), Fredric Jameson argues that science fiction (and, by extension, dystopia) lets us apprehend the present as history (151). And Moylan extends these definitions by suggesting that the dystopia, because it, like the utopia, foregrounds setting, articulates a specifically political agency: since it views a sociopolitical system from the viewpoint of a discontented character, it evokes for the reader a "militant pessimism", and it leaves the ending open so that the possibility of a "focused anger" and a "radical hope" remain possible for the reader (155, 157).[2] Finally, Raffaella Baccolini has explained that the crucial turn toward critical dystopias in the last few decades has occurred at least partly because of "blurring borders between genres": "It is precisely the use, re-vision, and appropriation of generic fiction that constitute an oppositional writing practice and an opening for utopian elements in . . . dystopian fiction" (13).[3]

Thus A. M. Lightner's sex role–reversal sf romance *The Day of the Drones* (1969), Samuel R. Delany's epic sf novel *Dhalgren* (1974), and Connie Willis's satiric sf short story "All My Darling Daughters" (1985) fit into the category of critical dystopia. Lightner's, Delany's, and Willis's stories follow the narrative pattern of dystopia, the isolated individual narrator or point of view, from whose perspective rises a critique of society. Lightner's post-holocaust England and Africa, Delany's fictional city Bellona, and Willis's near-future space station create societies significantly worse than the society of the reader, but uncomfortably close to it. And, despite the different decades in which they were written, and the different political purposes of the writers, each offers the reader an education of desire that focuses anger, a view of the present as defamiliarized and historical, and a radical hope for better ways of living.

What I wish to explore here is the blend of genre created in the critical dystopia as matrix and the ways that merging genres open opportunities for radical vision. Let me begin with Lightner's *The Day of the Drones*, a sex role–reversal romance blended with future Earth dystopia. As both Joanna Russ ("*Amor*") and Justine Larbalestier (39–72) have pointed out, the sex role–reversal sf, popular from the 1920s through the 1970s, is a conservative genre that reinforces heterosexual patriarchy as the status quo. Russ argues that these science fictions, often matriarchal and modeled on bee society, follow the pattern of social disorder resulting from women assuming "unnatural" positions of power over effeminized men, and the conflict is resolved through "some form of phallic display" (3): once women taste a kiss or achieve an orgasm with a man, the fantasy of sex role–reversal fictions goes, they give up desire for governing, power, or equality. Larbalestier extends this analysis to show that often the conflict involves four groups: "real women, real men, not-real men, and not-real women" (44). In many of these stories, according to Larbalestier, women are not content with dominance, but are working their way toward extinction of men (although not usually toward lesbianism). All of these stories,

Larbalestier concludes, "lay open the necessity of the heterosexual economy" (72).

Lightner's *The Day of the Drones* revises the sex role–reversal sf by settling the genre firmly in the category of dystopia and by doubling the stakes: the story begins as a race-reversal sf and travels to a sex role–reversal far-future England. Usually reversal is irony, but not in the sex role–reversal sf; there females in dominant positions embody anxieties about possible social change that threatens what the author perceives as a "natural" order. Thus in such a fiction, a "normal" man arrives in a society in which roles are reversed, and his very presence serves as catalyst for reassertion of the "natural" order. The first part of the novel surveys the society, the narrator gradually perceiving the tyrannous mode of government, its savage lack of knowledge and science, its irrational justifications through myth of its existence, and its rigid suppression of social change, the leaders of the society gradually perceiving the threat of the narrator to their position. The leaders then plot to do away with the narrator while one of the female citizens falls in love with him and precipitates immediate reassertion of the "natural" heterosexual patriarchy. This is not a dystopia, however, because the goal is not critique of society or its ills, but rather enforcement of threatened ideology on individuals. There is no potential Utopia opposite to the world where women dominate, as there is in a dystopia, but only the "normal" world that needs to reassert its natural order; so this subgenre belongs, ordinarily, to the family of romance, not dystopia. Lightner changes all that by blending the sex role–reversal sf romance with the dystopia.

Lightner begins the transformation by constructing double post-holocaust societies in *The Day of the Drones*. Five hundred years in the past of this future Earth, there has been a nuclear holocaust that destroyed almost all human beings, animals, and many plants, leaving large portions of the earth poisoned, and only pockets of humanity surviving (22, 43). The story opens in Afria, in an isolated portion of what used to be Africa, in a society where all whites have long ago been destroyed as punishment for the disaster, and where the blacker the skin, the higher up the social hierarchy a person can go (4). The hierarchy is established by educating the smartest and blackest children to the greatest degree, denying light-skinned people college training and reproduction, by destroying light-skinned infants, and by maintaining a very strict monopoly on knowledge (books, machines, and mechanical weaponry) (53). Amhara, very black, very intelligent, and female, is sent away to college, while her cousin, N'Gobi, very light, very intelligent, and male, is denied college education, despite his aptitude for math and mechanics. But N'Gobi finds a duck with a snare on its leg not made by their people, and so earns a right to accompany an exploration team, which Amhara is also invited to join. Five Afrians journey in a helicopter from before the Disaster to find the other remaining humans, where the duck goes when it migrates North. Far north of them in what used to be England, they find another society which is also much worse than that of the readers: a reverse sex–role society, a matriarchy modeled on bee society, which has lost considerably more of pre-Disaster knowledge and which practices human sacrifice of drones, or rebellious young males.

As is clear from this summary, the outlines of the sex role–reversal sf romance remain, but Lightner has merged them with a dystopia: in this grim future, humanity has almost destroyed itself and the world; one remnant in Africa practices a terrible racism; the other in England operates under destructive gender roles. In both societies, the role-reversal sf form allows Lightner to estrange the audience from the biased cultural practices in order to see them more clearly, while the dystopian form enables her to break free from the conservative ideology of "natural social order" that the sex role–reversal form traditionally promotes.

Following the pattern of the sex role–reversal romance, Amhara falls in love with Evan, one of the drones. But there the similarity to other sex role–reversal romances ends. First, the novel is told from the point of view of Amhara, rather than a man, so at first she does not particularly notice the disparities, since the rulers of Afria have sometimes been female. More important, though, Lightner takes pain to show that racial and gender roles are constructed. There are no "natural" or "normal" roles to reassert themselves. In Afria, instead of a right and wrong way to view race, there is a range of responses and prejudices. The Wasan (the Afrian ruler, appointed for life) and Zulli (one of the explorers) demonstrate great bias. When N'Gobi brings the duck to the Wasan, he wonders, in front of N'Gobi, "how much trust can be put in the word of a boy of your color, I would not be too sure" (36). To Amhara, N'Gobi guesses that the Wasan is sending him on the expedition because the radiation poisoning will prevent him from having children and so polluting their race; such "racial purity," N'Gobi sarcastically remarks, is a "fine, idealistic reason" to the Wasan (49). Zulli refuses to eat with N'Gobi on the trip, behavior reflecting the racial segregation in the United States when the novel was published (76). On the other hand, Amhara resists such bias: "Now I could sense his pain and disappointment, and my own feeling of revolt began to boil up in sympathy" (9). In between these extremes, most Afrians passively accept the ideology that their culture has developed concerning race. When Amhara fiercely objects to N'Gobi being denied college, her mother pulls "the curtains and set[s] about putting [her] straight (5).[4] And when Amhara bitterly denounces such prejudice to her favorite teacher—"blind and cruel. The whole state is founded on it!"—Ylma cautions her that out of a terrible disaster, the Afrian state has built a "well-ordered and safe existence" and kept some "knowledge of the past" (41). In addition, Lightner makes room for change. Ylma continues, "[b]ut you must realize that what may be the best wisdom and the best way for one century or even one generation, may not be the best wisdom for the next" (41).

So within Afria, some people see racism as destructive, and many see change as possible. Similarly, when the explorers encounter another civilization, they do not all see the matriarchy as a wrong that should be corrected by their equitable society: while Amhara perceives the society as a "conspiracy of the sexes" and vows to rescue Evan from it, Menasi, the leader of the expedition, calmly points out (when Tadessa complains that "women are in the saddle"), "[t]hat's the situation in the entire insect kingdom" (176, 182). Moreover, neither society has preserved the totality of human knowledge, so neither can be viewed by readers as superior: while Afria has well-developed chemistry and medicine and agriculture, physics and mechanics have been declared taboo (10–12). The bee society, on the other hand, has kept meticulous records of human genetics to prevent their race dying out and has developed the science of beekeeping to high levels (178–79). Nature is reasserting itself in this novel, but not in the form of a template for human interaction and government; instead, the natural world is regrowing after the Disaster, but also evolving, with giant blackberries, and immense dragonflies, spiders, and bees. Lightner emphasizes not tyranny of culture, as in the traditional dystopian critique, nor "natural rights," as in the conservative sex role–reversal romance. The Afrians, at least, make room for difference and change.

The turning point of the sex role–reversal sf, as in many dystopias, is falling in love. In the sex role–reversal romance, falling in love precipitates, in a deterministic fashion, the "natural" order of heterosexual patriarchy. In *The Day of the Drones*, however, falling in love simply promotes recognition in the reader. It is important to recall that in 1969, when this novel was published, many readers would have shared the racial prejudice of many of the Afrian characters, and would have been shocked by the first embrace of Evan and Amhara (193). At this point, the two worlds of the novel meet: the kiss does not restore men to dominance, as in the sex role–reversal romance, but instead gives Evan hope of sexual equality; nor does the kiss undo racial prejudice, for N'Gobi cautions Amhara about the difficulties of such a partnership (142, 193, 157). The kiss rather indicates the possibility of acceptance across cultural divisions and hope of change; although it is quickly countered by fear, for the matriarch discovers Evan and Amhara ransacking the sacred collection of books (for Shakespeare!), and the

Afrian society perceives that the bee society has also perfected a biological weapon, the bees themselves. N'Gobi is killed by the bees.

The ending of the novel, then, is neither the destruction of an unnatural society (the bee society is no different when the explorers escape) nor a triumphant return to a society about to be transformed (we end the story before the explorers are released from quarantine). There is potentially a Utopia, but it is not a return to "normal," which is now seen as falling short of the ideal. Lightner manipulates the dialectical tension between the two worlds to critique both aspects of her own 1960s United States society. The novel ends with Amhara's reflection: "The way is open if we want to take it," acknowledging hope, criticism of the current society (as well as the alien bee society), and the necessity of collaborative social action to achieve change. Lightner's *The Day of the Drones* is thus an early critical dystopia: it offers a critique of gender and racial hierarchies as constructed; it demonstrates the great human cost, both in economic and in psychological terms, of racial and gender bias; and it presents social reform as necessary but not inevitable. But the novel also offers hope: it demystifies gender and racial ideologies and recasts them as problems to be solved.

Now let me turn to an even more complicated case of genre blending. Delany's *Dhalgren* is an epic blended with near-future dystopia and influenced by post–World War II holocaust narratives. The genre of epic may be best defined as a long quest story depicting a search for origins in the service of establishing a national identity, featuring a hero of representative national values and identity, and battle scenes celebrating a people's struggle to give birth to themselves as a nation, defining who constitutes a nation and who does not. Literary characteristics include catalogues (lists that establish the plenitude of the nation and celebrate the spoils of the hero), epithets (that dignify the people), and self-conscious references to preceding epics that reflect emulation and anxiety about precedents as models and rivals.

Delany's *Dhalgren* is a systematic dismantling of the epic within the genre of dystopia.[5] At 801 pages, the novel boasts the length of the epic, but undoes the sense of progress tied to epic length, for the novel is fragmented and circular, beginning with a sentence fragment "to wound the city" that fits with a fragment that ends the novel "I have come to" (801). In addition, the seven sections are headed by titles that proclaim lack of structure and resistance to clear direction: "Prisms," "Ruins," "Plague," "Palimpsest," "Anathemata." As Peter Nicholls explains, "[t]he plot structure is almost invariably that of a quest" in Delany's novels; and especially in *Dhalgren*, while that quest begins as a search for the narrator's identity, it is soon abandoned, as the narrator lives in the present and assembles a new identity as poet and novelist (315). Finally, new forms and new technologies of art suggest alternatives to linear progress, especially Lanya's composition of music through laying down successive tracks on tape, using her harmonica and her friends' sound effects, as well as the Scorpions' holograms, which replace or mask identity (522–23, 646).

As Robert Fox suggests, Kid, the hero, in many ways represents American national identity, for he is a dreamer with a poor memory, indicating American refusal to confront history, and with an ambiguous racial identity (*Conscientious* 98). But elsewhere Fox argues that "Kid's pilgrimage reflects the depletion of the hero myth," for he enters and leaves the city much later "having gained no new awareness that will help to redeem the wasteland" ("You-Shaped" 99). As protagonist, Kid contributes not to establishing but to critiquing American identity. According to Fox, "Kid is a kind of palimpsest of mythic and mundane identities" ("You-Shaped" 103). He never discovers his racial or family identity, although he suspects that he is half Native American. He is bisexual, intent not on reproduction, so necessary to building a nation, but on experience, especially in all forms of sexual pleasure.

There are battles aplenty in *Dhalgren*, but they do not establish a new city, a new order, a new nation, nor do they distinguish between patriots and enemies. Rather than celebrate imperial conquest, the violent encounters examine the civil unrest and street riots of the 1960s civil rights and anti-war protests. The warriors are "bestial watchmen, trammeling the extremities and the interstices of the timeless city, portents of fallen, constellated deities plummeting in ash and smoke, roaming the apocryphal cities, the cities of speculation and reconstituted disorder, of insemination and incipience, swept round with the dark" (*Dhalgren* 646). But Delany nevertheless positions these imperfect heroes in epic contexts, surveying in a Homeric-style description, for example, the parade of Scorpions (596).

The techniques Delany uses to create epic context are the generic techniques of epic language: catalogues and epithets.[6] But again, Delany deconstructs the convention as he employs it. Rather than establish the plenitude of the nation and celebrate the spoils of the hero, his catalogues suggest the immensity of the fall from rational order occurring in Bellona. For example, using a catalogue of elements of architectural design, Delany describes the very buildings of the city as disappearing as Kid approaches them: "Buildings, bony and cluttered with ornament, hulled with stone at their different heights: Window, lintel, cornice and sills patterned the dozen planes. Billows brushed down them, sweeping at dusts they were too insubstantial to move, settled to the pavement and erupted in slow explosions he could see two blocks ahead—but, when he reached, had disappeared" (382). The city, confounded rather than founded, is a "tenebrous city, city without time, . . . generous, saprophytic city" (382). As in this example, epithets render ambiguous rather than dignify. The protagonist does not know his name, but is merely "Kid." The Scorpions are "Nightmare" and "Dragon Lady," but only match such ambitious titles when the switches are turned on for their holograms.

Kid enters the city wearing one sandal, recalling the Greek myth of Jason, whose sandal signifies overthrowing the social order, but Kid finds neither golden fleece nor tragedy during his stay in the city. *Dhalgren* also incorporates allusions to Ovid's *Metamorphoses*, counted by most current critics as an epic: the woman Kid has just slept with runs away, and during pursuit, metamorphoses into a tree (9); a character compares sighting the double moons over Bellona to Oedipus—"when you find out you've killed your father and married your mother after" (454). Bellona, the Roman goddess of war, evokes Roman epic in the name of the ruined city in *Dhalgren*, but it houses no national citizens, only those who fall outside the city, according to Aristotle, "beasts and heroes" (Fox, "You-Shaped" 95).

Besides Greek and Roman myth, *Dhalgren* also refers self-consciously to English and American epic traditions. "Dhalgren," the title, refers to Grendel, the villain and anti-hero of the epic *Beowulf* (Gawron 94–95). The opening, like many epics before it, claims its entitlement to the genre by quite specific allusion, not to the poet-singing and Muse-inspiring tradition, but to the American tradition already revised by Walt Whitman and Allen Ginsberg. "All you know I know," the narrator offers in the opening lines, recasting Whitman's optimistic nineteenth-century catalogue of American interdependence as a bitter twentieth-century admission of human limitation: "careening astronauts and bank clerks glancing at the clock before lunch; actresses cowling at light-ringed mirrors and freight elevator operators grinding a thumbful of grease on a steel handle; student riots" (1). "So howled out for the world to give him a name," pleads the narrator in the second line of the novel, reconstituting the anger of Ginsberg's anguished "Howl" as a much wearier and less authoritative call.

Although published in 1974, *Dhalgren* is thus very much a novel of the 1960s, built on the ashes of a society in ruins. The effects of war linger in the streets of Bellona where *Dhalgren* is set, for it is a strange city, cut off from the rest of society, abandoned by the institutional forces of order, full of burned-out buildings and the smashed debris of consumer culture, still smoking from the disaster destroying it. The setting is surreal, like that which Raymond Olderman finds in the 1960s novels in general, describing "what is fabulous about the actual world we live in" (71). Like many sf near-future dystopias, a favored genre after World War II (beginning with Judith Merril's *Shadow on the Hearth* in 1950), *Dhalgren* allows us to recognize in the ruined city of Bellona parts of the world we readers actually lived in—the burned-out buildings in the corridor left by the 1960s riots in Washington, D.C.; the children adrift and living on food given them by those of us in Madison, Wisconsin, who took them in; the neurotic middle-class housewives who were drugged or warehoused by their husbands in mental asylums in disproportionate numbers in the 1960s in the United States; gang "protection"; depressed middle-management fathers; graffiti; rape; accident; and poetry.

In *Dhalgren*, Delany re-creates the worst parts of 1960s United States—disrupted and traumatized still by World War II, conflicted over civil rights and racism and entering a new war that would further rupture the nation—and aptly names this re-creation, this dystopian city, "Bellona."[7] Bellona, like the U.S. cities of the late 1960s and early 1970s, is a city "of speculation and reconstituted disorder" (646). The only hope of the novel is the simultaneous creation of a self from a memory erased, a new self recorded in a slim over-marketed volume of poetry, *Brass Orchids*, which Kid writes and then carries with him as commentary throughout the novel.

While the traditional epic quite literally builds social order through its deployment of national ideology, *Dhalgren* rehearses epic conventions in order to undo them, and so reflects social disorder. The social trauma of the wider society is reflected in Bellona, and recording Bellona thus becomes social critique of 1960s and 1970s American society. There are large sections of Bellona that are burned out. Racial tension is extreme. Gang members, termed "Scorpions," sell protection and raid warehouses for food and goods, taking over empty houses. There is no apparent government—no mayor, no council, no police, no firefighters. "We have no economy," one character comments. Indeed, social order as we know it has disappeared, and all the people of Bellona live on the wares of the past, the only new product being art, for poems are written and published, and music is composed, taped, and distributed (668). The society of Bellona is an underground that has surfaced, an underground from which surface order, including all business, has fled.

Delany's catalogue of social trauma and decay, which is life in the city of Bellona, includes Kid's puzzled response to, and so a critique of, the meaninglessness of white middle-class life in 1960s America. Early in the novel, Kid, perhaps of Native American descent, visits and then works for the Richardses (whose name, Rich-shards, signifies the meaningless amassing of wealth in Middle America) (73). Mr. Richards leaves the house under pretence of working each day but has no work to do, a hyperbolic representation of the meaningless work of middle-class paper-pushing bureaucracy. When he comes home, he beats his wife and terrorizes his children. Mrs. Richards claims to be making a "real home," but as the increasingly artificial instant foods she prepares signal, her home is actually an escape from the real landscape of the city outside her windows (226). She makes Jello salads and instant coffee and pretends that social order still exists by shutting her doors against the trauma of the city, but the city takes its revenge against her by gradually stealing away her children. Her oldest son has left the family, who do not speak of him (two-thirds of the way through the novel, we find that he runs with a gang); her second son is pushed down an elevator shaft by his sister (a murder that no one but the narrator calls "murder"); her daughter obsessively hunts for a black man who raped her, not for revenge but for the shadow of love. When Kid comes to work for them, he is promised money but never given it. It becomes, at first, an obsession of his—as if, drawn into the middle-class orbit, their values become his center of gravity (219–20). But in truth, the social system has so deteriorated that money is no longer a means of exchange—everything is "free," or rather, scavenged (192, 276). So the status marker that gives middle-class society its meaning and value is now, ironically, an empty symbol.

Especially fraught are white middle-class sexual codes that dictate racial homogeny, monogamy, and heterosexism. *Dhalgren* critiques these social rules by asserting their opposite: sex is frequent, cross-racial, multiple in partners, bisexual, experimental.[8] While the one monogamous married sexual relationship we see is abusive, the many other conjunctions are generally idealized, communal, and portrayed as nurturing. Late in the novel, Kid considers, "Could it be that all those perfectly straight, content-with-their-sexual-orientation-in-the-world, exclusive-heterosexuals really *are* . . . more healthy than (gulp . . . !) us? Let me answer: No *way*! The active ones (of whichever sex) are denser and crueler. The passive ones (of whichever sex) are lazier and more self-satisfied. In a society where they are on top, they cling like drowners to their . . . set-up, not for pleasure . . . but because it allows them to . . . condone any lack of compassion" (720).

Delany returns to the thread of critique of the meaninglessness of middle-class life when introducing many of the public figures of Bellona—Newboy, the poet who pompously mentors Kid (a sympathetic parody of W. H. Auden perhaps?); Roger Calkins, who publishes Kid, lionizes him through his aides, but refuses to read or meet him himself; and Captain Kamp, the astronaut who walked on the moon—only now there are two moons over Bellona and possibly neither one the reality the Captain knew.[9]

Along with this critique of middle-class America, Delany emphasizes scientific relativism. In Bellona, even time is unreliable, and the newspaper is given a date according to the whim of Roger Calkins, the unelected leader of Bellona (377). The elusiveness of knowledge in science is figured in recurring consideration of the cause of Bellona's catastrophe: what has happened to change reality in this city, what has caused this dystopia? Was there an international conspiracy or a major ecological disaster (371)? Was there a bomb (419)? Are they on another planet yet somehow connected to

Earth (461)? Has the sun gone nova, or are they falling into the sun (420, 432)? Are they burning up, or beginning the long freeze of another ice age (448)? Are they simply caught in someone else's narrative, a science fiction (372)? The multiplicity of answers given for the anarchic disarray of Bellona establishes the narrative as paranoid, hinting at terrible fears that cannot be openly acknowledged. It is an extremely effective way to translate for critique the anxiety of the 1960s in the United States, living under threat of the atomic bomb and the knowledge of humans' disastrous effect on earth's ecology, fighting an undeclared war, our own government keeping secret files on any citizen caught in political activity.

The social trauma and disorder mixed with scientific relativism combine in Delany's novel to portray the mysteriousness of fact, the elusiveness of value, in epic proportions. Scientific relativism becomes moral relativism—" 'You meet a new person . . .' Kid mused, 'and suddenly you get a whole new city' " (318). Reality does not hold still long enough in Bellona for anyone to form a moral center or for normative values to crystallize into representative art. At one point in the novel, Lanya composes a symphony for harmonica, playing all the parts herself, laying them down in tracks on top of each other, using her friends' shouts and claps for percussion (522–23). At another point, the novel's narrative itself disintegrates, running on parallel tracks, sending the reader anxiously scanning first one column then another (651–end). Since society is broken, so, too, is mimesis.[10]

Hope rises in Bellona only in fragments, only in individuals, through the merest bodily acts. Upon the thingness of life depends agency and so subjectivity and so poetry in this novel. Kid writes his poems in the john, biting his nails, in between bouts of sweaty sex (90, 277). He is writing himself into existence, hope into existence, desperately. Kid does not know his real name, knows he spent time in an asylum but does not remember his past life except in brief snatches glimpsed as if around corners. Life is insanity, it has no meaning (344). Yet, quite literally, Kid is writing himself an identity. That identity ironically turns out to be tentative and negative: Kid learns, near the end of the novel, that he is not a poet; he discovers, instead, that he is a novelist (although he doubts language as well as his own talent), and the novel he is writing is the novel we are reading (735). The last line of the novel, appropriately a fragment, is completed by the first line of the novel, also a fragment, to come full circle. Life, this novel tells us, is like a novel where, "as one reads along, one becomes more and more suspicious that the author has lost the thread of his argument" (755–56).

Despite the gritty urban reality Kid lives with—the smoke, the hunger, the bad food, the lack of medicine, the loss of memory, the chaos of life—life offers joy. Affirmation and hope come from the certainty that "[e]verybody's somebody's fetish" (324), and in "the intensity of the senses [that] justify this warmth" (587), in homosexual sex (50, *passim*), in heterosexual sex (105, *passim*), in the "fillips and curlicues of light and noise" of the fantasy beast holograms that the Scorpions parade in (610). These moments transform the city: "Kid looked at the warehouses, at the waters between. Joy, sudden and insistent, twisted the muscles of his mouth toward laughter" (374). Figuring forth this affirmation is Delany's style, built as modern sculpture is, out of pieces, but yet making gorgeousness.

Influenced especially by poets—Whitman (patron saint of the American epic), Ginsberg (the novel begins with a howl), and Constantine P. Cavafy (modernist celebrator of city and gay men)—Delany allows language to save the city: "The tenebrous city, city without time, the generous, saprophytic city," a city that is not frozen or sculpted in language but shimmering there, "this timeless city, . . . this spaceless preserve where any slippage can occur, these closing walls, laced with fire-escapes, gates, and crenellations, . . . too unfixed to hold it in so that, from me as a moving node, it seems to spread, by flood and seepage, over the whole uneasy scape" (382). Built on the simple, tried-and-true device of epic catalogue, Delany makes poetry out of the broken landscape, the way 1970s artists made sculpture out of bottle caps and old tires. His long, loose sentences eventually loosen further into broken narrative and multiple typefonts in the Plague Journal section. "What is unrepentantly utopian about the novel," Brian Stableford writes, "is its championing of the conviction that the art of poetry is potentially capable of functioning at the interface of high and low culture, taking a lead in the complex process of myth-making and sociolinguistic reconstruction" (168). Thus *Dhalgren* successfully dismantles the epic as a genre in order to merge it with the dystopia so that the form is opened out to enable questioning of identity (personal and national), and so, radical hope.

Very different from this form of critical dystopia is Connie Willis's fiction, which depends for its operation very much on classical formal satire as a genre. Classical formal satire established very specific conventions, conventions so useful to norm-based social critique that they still obtain in Western satiric literature. Alvin Kernan's summary of these characteristics in his work on Renaissance satire is still helpful.[11] Satire employs plain, blunt language and rough style (especially invective, caricature, burlesque, and disease imagery). In satire, the ideal is only glimpsed, and the grotesque in society is emphasized; narrative is not coherent but fragmented, because social order is decayed; and the scene where satire is set is busy and detailed to give the satirist material to work on. Furthermore, in satire, vices and weaknesses are represented in extreme versions to indicate the necessity of change, which in satire is return to the norm or middle ground. The satirist poses as a simple, indignant person in contrast to the complexly sophisticated, vicious people in society. Plot may be nonexistent if defined as change: the basic plot of satire is good and evil, vice and moderation caught as opposing forces in eternal balance; even if the situation is resolved in a satire, the forces are yet present to continue the battle (Kernan 4–35).

But Willis uses many of the same techniques of satire in her short story "All My Darling Daughters," which is anything but politically conservative.[12] In this short story, dystopia takes the form of an abandoned space station renovated as a boarding school. The target of satire in this story is not capitalist consumerism but patriarchy: "I think fathers are a pile of scut," rails the narrator (95). The satire is signaled by the rough, slangy, invective-filled language of the indignant, rebellious, female adolescent narrator, Tavvy: Tavvy's roommate comes from a "godspit" forsaken colony (82), the dorm mother scares Tavvy "scutless" (84), and a party is dull because there's "Not a bone [penis] in sight" (87). Tavvy is justifiably indignant because her own father "jig-jigged into a plastic bag . . . to carry on the family name" (91) but has refused to see her since, leaving her in the hands of his lawyers, who send her to school, carefully negotiate the penalties for her rebellions with school administrators, and pick a socially useful vacation spot for her.[13]

But "All My Darling Daughters" centers on abuse, not abandonment. First Tavvy, then her friend Arabel, are sexually harassed (and Arabel abused) by a male administrator: "Jig you, scut," Tavvy tells him, "Double" (85, 92). The boys at school, who used to provide Tavvy her addictive escape through sex from the loneliness of school, have new pets—brown, furry, small animals called "tessels" who provide them sadistic sexual pleasure. Tavvy soon figures out "what that big pink hole is for" (98). But she doesn't realize the enormity of the boys' propensity until she herself experiments with one of the animals and hears its scream: "Horrible, awful, pitiful sound. Helpless. Hopeless. The sound a woman must make when she's being raped. No. Worse. The sound a child must make" (102). Here Willis addresses her male readers directly, on a fraught social issue. By defamiliarizing rape, especially child rape, through the medium of animals, she also delegitimizes it.

A parallel in the story lets us see the effects of abuse. Tavvy's roommate, Zibet, is recovering from abuse by her father, and feels terrible guilt that she has escaped while three of her sisters remain at home. Together these young women, although not without suffering severe psychological damage, find solutions to male oppression. Tavvy explains to the dorm mother about the abuse of the animals, and they are outlawed at the school, so some of the boys, at least, will have a chance not to grow up to be sadists. Zibet sends one of the animals, hidden in the baggage, home with her sister, so that the father, becoming addicted to the pet, will leave her sisters alone. This ending is quite bleak, because Zibet is fully aware that she is not strong enough in character to effect the rescue of her sisters (or even her self) from her father, and so is sacrificing the small creature to her lack of courage. To Tavvy she says, full of self-blame, "I told you you didn't know anything about sin" (105).

But the satire of this dystopia also is directed to full-scale radical reform, not simply toward return to a norm. The problem is not individual actions (although they are problem enough in this story), but institutional corruption. The boys are in danger of growing up to be fathers, as Tavvy learns when she complains to Brown about her father, and he assures her, "I'm sure he had your best interests at heart" (87). The ubiquitousness of patriarchy is represented by the voice of Old Man Moulton, the founder of the school, coming over the intercom at lights out, addressing the coeds as "all my darling daughters" (91). Tavvy dismantles the intercom, interrupting the message from the Father. Once Tavvy understands the nature of the tessels, she realizes that because of patriarchy, the control of social institutions by the fathers, she has no recourse, nowhere to seek help: "There was nobody to tell" (104). This moment, before she enlists the dorm mother also to stand against the male administrators, is painful and full of significance for female readers—we have all been there. Still, "All My Darling Daughters" does offer hope, for at least one adult has values that can help to establish a different norm for society: "'Oh, my dear,' [the dorm mother] said, and put her arms around me" (104). The physical expression is especially significant since it is through the physical that the males of this society have refused responsibility and destroyed trust.

Thus in Willis's short story, there is more hope than in Delany's *Dhalgren*, but only marginally so. In many of Willis's fictions, satire carries society back to normative values, and so to security and plot resolution.[14] In some, however, satire pushes over the edge and demands social change. Thus Lightner's renovated sex role–reversal romance set in two dystopias, Delany's postmodern dystopian epic, and Willis's satiric science fiction dystopia are all social critiques. All, surprisingly, are mixed progressive and conservative, politically.[15] They all offer hope, despite the dystopian form and bleak predictions for the future (or for our present). Lightner's romance and Willis's satire require a hope that there is a basic foundation to build on; values in romance are by generic traditions idealized, while values must be normative, by definition, in the satiric form. The disassembled epic, in contrast, as in Delany's *Dhalgren*, results from disruption and trauma, so no stable society exists on which to rest value. Choosing values and hoping become a restorative process; society, value, hope must be constantly rebuilt by individuals out of the rubble of the present. Hope under these conditions is much more tenuous.

While these three novels merge quite different forms with the dystopia, a thread connects all three: representation of sexuality in all three novels works as criticism of affluent mainstream United States culture. In Lightner's *The Day of the Drones*, aberrant, cross-racial sexuality, still criminalized as miscegenation in some states at the time that Lightner wrote her novel, opens the door for hope of a worldwide utopian but diverse culture. In Delany's *Dhalgren*, aberrant bisexuality becomes the basis for a potentially utopian community and a utopian art. In Willis's "All My Darling Daughters," incestuous sexuality and bestiality are exposed as a violation of lost values, which are retrieved by way of utopian cross-generational support from the dorm mother. Willis's fiction as a whole, however, still reinforces the 1960s and 1970s sexual revolution.

From 1950s civil rights to 1960s and 1970s feminism, to 1960s anti-war protests, to 1970s gay rights, United States society questioned its national identity, forcing a renovation, we can see, in traditionally conservative genres. By merging the dystopia with such traditional genres, writers resisted the generic pressure in the genre of dystopia to anti-utopian closure and produced more open, critical dystopian texts.

Notes

1. I am using this term by analogy to linguistic work on "conceptual blends." See, for example, Turner, esp. ch. 5, "Creative Blends" (57–84). On generic blending, see also Delany, "The Gestation of Genres" (63–73).

2. Also helpful is Baggesen's distinction between "utopian pessimism" and "dystopian pessimism," depending on whether or not the fiction portrays evil so as to "leave history open for discussion" (41) and Zaki's adaptation of Baggesen's distinction to feminist writings. In "Breaking the Boundaries," Baccolini argues that women adapt the dystopia to feminist use by presenting language as a means to achieve power and subjectivity. In "Journeying through the Dystopian Genre," she further examines the role of memory of a better time in the past as resistance in dystopias, especially those by women; on women's dystopias, see also Donawerth.

3. Booker, in *The Dystopian Impulse*, argues that the entire twentieth century moves from utopian toward dystopian literature (17). However, his definition of the dystopia is too broad to be very helpful: fiction derived from the utopian tradition, dedicated to social criticism generally referring to real referents, deriving effects from defamiliarization. For a definition of the feminist dystopia, see Donawerth.

4. Contemporary readers would have immediately recognized such issues, as reflected in white skin privilege and interracial mixing. When I told my mother in 1966 that I was dating an African foreign student at college, she sat me down in very similar fashion to make the argument that such unions were hard on the children.

5. For quite a different reading of *Dhalgren* and its genre, see Hassler's essay on Delany's novel as Georgic.

6. Of *Dhalgren* Delany says: "Certainly up through *Dhalgren* one ambition I had for my writing—however wide of the mark it fell—was for it to be a classic prose for its era" (*Silent Interviews* 257).

7. Delany's *Dhalgren*, then, is a critical dystopia after the Holocaust, a science fiction shaped by Holocaust writings. In one of the first passages in which a mysterious "I" narrator takes over the otherwise third-person narrative, the narrator, obviously a writer, muses: "The common problem, I suppose is to have more to say than vocabulary and syntax can bear.

That is why I am hunting in these desiccated streets. The smoke hides the sky's variety, stains consciousness, covers the holocaust with something safe and insubstantial. It protects from greater flame. It indicates fire, but obscures the source. This is not a useful city. Very little here approaches any eidolon of the beautiful" (75). Reflecting on the experience that gives birth to artistic expression, the writer finds that there is not more to say than words can bear in this new age, but rather inability to speak because of the trauma of events, a holocaust that has destroyed not only city and people, but also value and the possibility of beauty. Smoke and fire, the root metaphors of "holocaust," are ubiquitous in the urban setting of Bellona, and Kid compares the streets to "disaster areas after evacuation" (760). Near the end of the novel, the narrator describes even his writing as "the proper ashes of . . . feeling," and another character caustically comments, "Apocalypse has come and gone. We're just grubbing in the ashes" (723, 745). In the middle of the novel, the metaphor of fire in the term "holocaust" is "unmetaphored" (see Colie 11 and 145), turned into literal physical events in the story: George and Kid rescue children from a burning building in the middle of a whole section of the city given over to flames (655), and later the "nest" where Kid and the Scorpions live is destroyed by fire (796). In addition, Holocaust writings have influenced the fragmentation of form in *Dhalgren*. As Ezrahi argues, "Precisely where it is most confined to the unimaginable facts of violence and horror, the creative literature that has developed is the least consistent with traditional moral and artistic conventions. . . . The disjunction between generic memory and conventional forms on the one hand, and 'millennial' subject matter and the literary forms which have evolved to contain the new reality on the other, is a measure of the shifts in the boundaries of art beyond which the imagination becomes inarticulate and form disintegrates altogether" (3). In these ways, Delany avoids the trivialization of the Holocaust that many critics have rightfully condemned: see, for example, Berger (32–33).

8. "Sex is a process to be integrated into one's life over an astonishing range of specific and bodily ways," Delany writes, "[a]nd the frightening, troubling, deeply unsettling insight we all now have to live with is that that range of possibilities *far* surpasses the ones suggested by the oppositions faithful/promiscuous or masturbatory/abstinent that lurk under and finally all but constrain the tripartite division we began with: lover/promiscuous/masturbatory. Questions such as these, I've tried to dramatize in my fiction from various sides, starting with *Dhalgren* or some of the stories" (*Silent Interviews* 219).

9. In his autobiographical account of the period in which he wrote *Dhalgren*, Delany writes of his friendship with W. H. Auden when the poet and the sf writer both lived in Greenwich Village, from 1961 onward; see *The Motion of Light in Water* (141–61), especially. For another autobiographical account of that period in Delany's life, and of the communes with which he was affiliated and which become reflected and refracted in *Dhalgren*, see *Heavenly Breakfast* (and note that one of the key members in Delany's own commune/rock band, "Heavenly Breakfast," is named "Grendahl").

10. My reading of the fragmented form of *Dhalgren* is thus quite different from that of Weedman, who emphasizes Delany's dyslexia, and posits Kid's vision as dyslexic. See also McEvoy's reading of *Dhalgren* as an "overdetermined" use of pieces of information that do not necessarily fit together but are so specific and detailed that the reader is forced to begin trying to fit them together (esp. 113–14).

11. It may seem outdated that I use Kernan to define the genre of satire, but he writes from the heyday of the structuralist era, and the method of these critics lent themselves to defining genre. For a very useful contemporary definition and theory of satire, see Bogel.

12. Of this story, Willis says, "'All My Darling Daughters' is the most powerful thing I've written" (Ingersoll and Kress 100). My thanks to Katie Field for passing this interview on to me. Willis has been judged anti-feminist, but this story is very much a feminist critique of patriarchy; on Willis as anti-feminist, see Kelso. On the issue of feminism, Willis comments, "[f]requently I've been urged to address the themes of feminism in my work, or this or that cause. . . . If I wanted to support nuclear disarmament or ERA, I should be addressing those issues directly, in essays. To address them in fiction is a disservice, because the writer then limits what fiction can do by showing only one side of the issue. In my fiction I want to show that there are thousands of sides to the issues and that in fact it's a problem, not an issue. . . . Historically speaking, women came late to s-f as they came late to everything. As a person, I get some flak, and I have to deal with the problems that any woman does. The key

word for women in the Eighties is not *liberated*; it's *harried*. . . . They want to 'have it all,' find they can't, and then have to decide what to give up. . . . These problems are much more real to me than the problems of men making chauvinistic remarks like 'Women can't really do male viewpoints'" (Ingersoll and Kress 96–97).

13. I thank Katie Field for giving me *Fire Watch*, for sharing fan enthusiasm for Willis with me, and for talking out some of the issues of this essay with me.

14. See, for example, Willis's *Bellwether* and "Miracle," satires that return society to normative values.

15. While Lightner's cross-racial romance signals radical politics in the 1960s, her attribution to Evan of a "natural" talent for mechanics is retrogressive (155, 209). While Delany has suggested that he consciously developed women characters in the 1970s as independent women, *Dhalgren* has been criticized for its biased depiction of Lanya. For Delany's rules of thumb for strong women characters, see *Khatru Symposium: Women in Science Fiction* (participants included Suzy McKee Charnas, Samuel R. Delany, Ursula K. Le Guin, Vonda N. McIntyre, Raylyn Moore, Joanna Russ, James Tiptree, Jr. [Alice Sheldon], Luise White, Kate Wilhelm, Chelsea Quinn, Mog Decarnin, Karen Fowler, Jeanne Gomoll, Jane Hawkins, Gwyneth Jones, and Pat Murphy):

> A good character of either sex must be shown performing purposeful actions (that further the plot, habitual actions (that particularly define her or him), and gratuitous actions (actions that imply a life beyond the limit of the fiction). . . . [T]he character's economic anchors to the world must be clearly shown. . . . Women characters must have central-to-the-plot, strong, developing, positive relations with other women characters. . . . [W]omen and men [must] have some central, non-romantic problem which they must exert their efforts to solve. . . . Do not shirk, avoid, and lie about the ugly when logical story development runs you into it (and with a problem like sexism, one cannot logically walk three steps in any direction without becoming mired down in it). (Smith 28–34)

For criticism of *Dhalgren*, see Joanna Russ's comments in *Khatru Symposium*: "I think *Dhalgren* fails utterly, not only as an egalitarian society (which it obviously is not) but even as an attempt to discuss the question. And one of the betraying signs is the faceless gentleman who is brought in for Lanya to fight. The real fight is obviously between Lanya and Kid; if they could do that, and then eventually make up, and we could see what kind of arrangement the making-up was—now that would be something. But Chip [Delany] doesn't know and neither do I. Yet" (Smith 105). On Willis, see nn. 11 and 13.

Works Cited

Baccolini, Raffaella. "Breaking the Boundaries: Gender, Genre, and Dystopia." *Per una definizione dell'utopia: Metodologie e discipline a confronto*. Ed. Nadia Minerva. Ravenna: Longo, 1992. 137–46.

———. "Gender and Genre in the Feminist Critical Dystopias of Katharine Burdekin, Margaret Atwood, and Octavia Butler." Barr 13–34.

———. "Journeying through the Dystopian Genre: Memory and Imagination in Burdekin, Orwell, Atwood, and Piercy." *Viaggi in utopia*. Ed. Raffaella Baccolini, Vita Fortunati, and Nadia Minerva. Ravenna: Longo, 1996. 343–57.

Baggesen, Søren. "Utopian and Dystopian Pessimism: Le Guin's *The Word for World Is Forest* and Tiptree's 'We Who Stole the Dream.'" *Science-Fiction Studies* 14.1 (1987): 34–43.

Barr, Marleen S., ed. *Future Females, the Next Generation: New Voices and Velocities in Feminist Science Fiction Criticism*. Lanham: Rowman, 2000.

Berger, Alan L. *Crisis and Covenant: The Holocaust in American Jewish Fiction*. Albany: State University of New York P, 1985.

Bogel, Fredric V. *The Difference Satire Makes: Rhetoric and Reading from Jonson to Byron*. Ithaca: Cornell UP, 2001.

Booker, M. Keith. *The Dystopian Impulse in Modern Literature: Fiction as Social Criticism*. Westport: Greenwood, 1994.

Browning, Gordon. "Toward a Set of Standards for Everlasting Anti-Utopian Fiction." *Cithara* 10.1 (1970): 18–32.

Colie, Rosalie. *Shakespeare's Living Art.* Princeton: Princeton UP, 1974.

Delany, Samuel R. *Dhalgren.* 1974. New York: Vintage, 2001.

———. "The Gestation of Genres: Literature, Fiction, Romance, Science Fiction, Fantasy." *Intersections: Fantasy and Science Fiction.* Ed. George E. Slusser and Eric S. Rabkin. Carbondale: Southern Illinois UP, 1987. 63–73.

———. *Heavenly Breakfast: An Essay on the Winter of Love.* New York: Bantam, 1979.

———. *The Motion of Light in Water: Sex and Science Fiction Writing in the East Village: 1960–1965.* New York: Richard Kasak, 1988.

———. *Silent Interviews on Language, Race, Sex, Science Fiction, and Some Comics: A Collection of Written Interviews.* Hanover: Wesleyan UP, 1994.

Donawerth, Jane. "The Feminist Dystopia of the 1990s: Record of Failure, Midwife of Hope." Barr 49–66.

Ezrahi, Sidra DeKoven. *By Words Alone: The Holocaust in Literature.* Chicago: U of Chicago P, 1980.

Fox, Robert Elliot. *Conscientious Sorcerers: The Black Postmodernist Fiction of LeRoi Jones/Amiri Baraka, Ishmael Reed, and Samuel R. Delany.* Westport: Greenwood, 1987.

———. "'This You-Shaped Hole of Insight and Fire': Meditations on Delany's *Dhalgren.*" Sallis 97–108.

Gawron, Jean Mark. "On *Dhalgren.*" Sallis 62–96.

Hassler, Donald M. "*Dhalgren, The Beggar's Opera,* and Georgic: Implications for the Nature of Genre." *Extrapolation* 30.4 (1989): 332–38.

Hill, Christopher. *The English Bible and the Seventeenth-Century Revolution.* London: Penguin, 1993.

Ingersoll, Earl, and Nancy Kress. "A Conversation with Connie Willis." *Riverside Quarterly* 8.2 (1988): 92–100.

Jameson, Fredric. "Progress Versus Utopia; or, Can We Imagine the Future?" *Science-Fiction Studies* 9.2 (1982): 147–58.

Kelso, Sylvia. "Connie Willis's Civil War: Re-dreaming America as Science Fiction." *Foundation* 73 (Summer 1998): 67–76.

Kernan, Alvin. *The Cankered Muse: Satire of the English Renaissance.* New Haven: Yale UP, 1959.

Larbalestier, Justine. *The Battle of the Sexes in Science Fiction.* Middleton: Wesleyan UP, 2002.

Levitas, Ruth. *The Concept of Utopia.* Syracuse: Syracuse UP, 1990.

Lightner, A. M. *The Day of the Drones.* New York: Bantam, 1969.

McEvoy, Seth. *Samuel R. Delany.* New York: Frederick Ungar, 1984.

Merril, Judith. *Shadow on the Hearth.* Garden City, NY: Doubleday, 1950.

Moylan, Tom. *Scraps of the Untainted Sky: Science Fiction, Utopia, Dystopia.* Boulder: Westview, 2000.

Nicholls, Peter. "Samuel R. Delany." *The Encyclopedia of Science Fiction.* Ed. John Clute and Peter Nicholls. 2nd ed. New York: St. Martin's, 1995. 315–17.

Olderman, Raymond M. *Beyond the Wasteland: A Study of the American Novel in the Nineteen-Sixties.* New Haven: Yale UP, 1972.

Russ, Joanna. "*Amor Vincit Foeminam*: The Battle of the Sexes in Science Fiction." *Science-Fiction Studies* 7 (1980): 2–15.

———. "What Can a Heroine Do? or Why Women Can't Write." *Images of Women in Fiction.* Ed. Susan Koppelman Cornillon. Bowling Green: Bowling Green U Popular P, 1972. 3–20.

Sallis, James, ed. *Ash of Stars: On the Writing of Samuel R. Delany.* Jackson: U of Mississippi P, 1996.

Sargent, Lyman Tower. "The Three Faces of Utopianism Revisited." *Utopian Studies* 5.1 (1994): 1–37.

Smith, Jeffrey D., ed. *Khatru Symposium: Women in Science Fiction. Khatru* 3–4 (1975). Rpt. Madison: Obsessive, 1993.

Stableford, Brian. "*Dhalgren.*" *Dictionary of Literary Utopias.* Ed. Vita Fortunati and Raymond Trousson. Paris: Honoré Champion, 2000. 167–68.

Turner, Mark. *The Literary Mind.* New York: Oxford UP, 1996.

Weedman, Jane Branham. *Samuel R. Delany.* Starmont Reader's Guide 10. Mercer Island, WA: Starmont, 1982.

Willis, Connie. "All My Darling Daughters." *Fire Watch.* New York: Bantam, 1985. 81–105.

———. *Bellwether.* New York: Bantam, 1996.

———. "Miracle." *Miracle and Other Christmas Stories.* New York: Bantam, 1999. 10–57.

Zaki, Hoda. "Utopia, Dystopia, and Ideology in the Science Fiction of Octavia Butler." *Science-Fiction Studies* 17 (1990): 239–51.

CHAPTER 3

The Writing of Utopia and the Feminist Critical Dystopia: Suzy McKee Charnas's Holdfast Series

ILDNEY CAVALCANTI

I. The Feminist Critical Dystopia

Situated at the convergence of utopian studies, feminism, and literary theory, this essay aims to provide a definition of the feminist critical dystopia,[1] a subgenre of literary utopianism that has become a major form of expression of women's hopes and fears, and to show the relationship between the dystopian genre in its feminist inflection, utopian desire expressed in literature, and the rhetorical figure of catachresis. Readings of Suzy McKee Charnas's novels of the Holdfast series will provide the ground for the elaboration on a semiotics of the literary utopia, as I move toward the delineation of a catachrestic mode in writing: the writing of utopia, which may be observed in its particular manifestation in contemporary feminist critical dystopias.

To start with the first element, the fictions in focus are *feminist*, but not markedly so in any structural way. Feminist literary criticism has evolved past the belief in an inherently feminist aesthetic. Grouping women's narratives together as *feminist* has to do with "the recent cultural phenomenon of women's explicit self-identification as an oppressed group, which is in turn articulated in literary texts in the exploration of gender-specific concerns centered around the problem of female identity" (Felski 1). Considering the extent to which gender oppression crucially functions as the source of conflict in the feminist dystopias, this articulation finds in them a striking cultural manifestation. It would be misleading, though, to assume that all feminist dystopias express gender oppression to a similar degree. For instance, while the first of Charnas's dystopias in the series, *Walk to the End of the World*, constructs a fictional world where women's subordination to men is thoroughly pervasive, other feminist dystopian texts (including the sequels to *Walk*) render a more nuanced picture of gender imbalance. Although their speculations about gender and power vary in intensity and approach, all feminist dystopias deal with this issue, a factor that marks the connections with contemporary androcentric culture, giving them, to use Charnas's words, a "foothold in reality" (Cavalcanti, "The Profession" 15).

Feminist dystopias are an intrinsically *critical* genre. The term is used in relation to the notion of a "critical utopianism" developed by Tom Moylan, who has dealt with the merging of positive and negative elements in utopias and dystopias.[2] In *Demand the Impossible*, he stresses the revival of a utopian impulse in literature in the late 1960s and 1970s and relates this new wave of utopianism to the reemergence of an oppositional culture "deeply infused with the politics of autonomy, democratic socialism, ecology, and especially feminism" (11). Using the term "critical" in this context may appear redundant (after all, all utopias result from a critique of our present conditions), but in Moylan's conception it implies the important element of textual self-criticism. I have appropriated his theorization in my formulation of the feminist critical dystopia, with "critical" referring to three interrelated factors: the negative critique (of patriarchy as well as certain trends in feminist praxis and theory) brought into effect by the dystopian principle; the textual self-awareness in generic terms with regard to a utopian tradition and concerning its own narrative constructions of utopian "elsewheres"; and "in the nuclear sense of the *critical mass* required to make the necessary explosive reaction" (10), in the sense that the feminist dystopias may have a crucial effect in the formation and/or consolidation of a critical-feminist public readership. This tripartite way of thinking about the critical edge of the feminist dystopias is reflected in the readings.

With regard to the last term, *dystopia* is viewed as a subgenre of literary utopianism (see Sargent). I follow Anne Cranny-Francis's definition of *dystopia* as a literary work featuring "the textual representation of a society apparently worse than the writer's/reader's own" (125); and I find her use of "apparently" relevant, insofar as it hints at the ultimately impossible task of deciding whether a fictional society is worse than our own. Despite this impossibility, the narratives usually referred to as feminist dystopias envision imaginary spaces that most contemporary readers would describe as bad places for women, being characterized by the suppression of female desire (brought into effect either by men or by women) and by the institution of gender-inflected oppressive orders.

As a distinct genre, the literary dystopia appeared at the turn of the twentieth century and acquired a feminist twist in texts like Charlotte Haldane's *Man's World* (1927) and Katharine Burdekin's *Swastika Night* (1937). The late 1960s witnessed the publication of much dystopian writing by women prior to the speculative literature that accompanied second-wave feminism. Anna Kavan's *Ice* and Kate Wilhelm's "Baby You Were Great" were first published in 1967, while Angela Carter's *Heroes and Villains*, Suzette Elgin's "For the Sake of Grace," Pamela Kettle's *The Day of the Women*, Marya Mannes's *They*, Anne McCaffrey's *The Ship Who Sang*, and Alice Sheldon's "The Snows Are Melted, the Snows Are Gone" all came to print in 1969.[3] In very different ways, these texts portray future bad places for women and reveal, to varying degrees, a consciousness perhaps better defined as proto-feminist when seen in relation to the women's critical dystopias of the 1970s, 1980s, and 1990s, among which are Charnas's novels.

II. Building a Hermeneutics: Dystopia, Utopia, and Catachresis

I will discuss the feminist critical dystopia in relation to a figure of speech. In its utopian orientation, the genre can be considered with regard to the rhetorical figure of catachresis. Michel Foucault gives an account of the development of language along the lines of three fundamental figures: synecdoche, metonymy, and catachresis. For him, language itself is catachrestic because literal meanings are not inherent in linguistic signs. Catachresis concerns a link between a thing and a sign marked by concealed resemblances and analogies and has, from its etymology, connotations of misuse or abuse. It is founded upon oblique relations, implying hidden meanings and deviations from normal language usage. Although catachresis underlies the origins and development of language, feminist dystopias strongly and specifically recall this essential figure in the ontology of language (111–14).

As a literary trope, catachresis involves unusual, far-fetched metaphors, being "basic to the figures of rhetoric, since so many of them depend on deviations from 'normal' (non-poetic) usage" (Wales 57). Nevertheless, some literary modes are more closely akin to this figure than others. As speculative writing, feminist dystopias display a more deviant relationship with their referents when compared with realistic (mimetic) literary forms. Without simplifying the problematics of referentiality implicit even in the most literal linguistic utterances, I suggest that in the case of dystopia the relationship between language and referents can only be defined as deviant. This is so to the extent that these fictions portray narrative "novums," to use Darko Suvin's term, which can be of spatiotemporal, social, sexual, technological, and/or linguistic nature. In other words, dystopias are *overtly* catachrestic because they depict fictional realities that are, to different degrees, discontinuous with the contemporary real (although such realities are drawn in relation to, and as a critique of, the world as we know it).

Another way of relating catachresis to the feminist dystopias has to do with the suspension these fictions build around the desired/able utopian object. As I show in my readings, this object remains silent, ineffable, in such a way that the paradox of the "good place"/"no place" carried by the term *utopia* itself can be maintained. It is as if the texts are composed in relation to a central absence: that of the utopian object. Considering another suspension in writing, Roland Barthes calls our attention to the "rhetorical figure which fills [the] blank in the object of comparison whose existence is altogether transferred to the language of the object to which it is compared: catachresis" (*S/Z* 34). He is referring to the process by which beauty is rendered in language: being an absent figure, it exists in literature by means of indirect reference to an object of comparison— that is, by means of catachresis. A parallel can be drawn in the sense that Utopia in the feminist critical dystopia resides in the realm of the ineffable, invisible and silent, that space around which the narrative revolves. In this context, the stories appear as extended figures of catachresis, hiding Utopia in their folds.

Before looking at Charnas's texts, I offer a definition of Utopia. The term is a charged one, with a history that dates back to the title of Thomas More's work about an ideal commonwealth at the dawn of our modernity. Ruth Levitas's is one of the best attempts to clarify its meanings and reconceptualize it. In *The Concept of Utopia*, she proposes an analytical definition of Utopia as "the desire for a better way of being" (198). Expanding her definition in order to incorporate the feminist slant of the texts examined, I address *women's* expression of desire for a different (better) way of being. The distinction between defining dystopia in *formal terms* (i.e., as *narrative*) and utopia in *conceptual terms* (i.e., as *the expression of desire*) is crucial for the present analysis. Fredric Jameson stresses the difference between dystopias and utopias as *texts*: "the dystopia is generally a narrative, which happens to a specific subject or character, whereas the Utopian text is mostly non-narrative and [. . .] somehow without a subject-position" (*Seeds* 55–56).[4] My argument is premised upon a distinction between the dystopia as narrative (on par with Jameson's definition) and Utopia as the critical expression of desire, which serves an anticipatory function, being manifested in the dystopian narrative. I am deliberately moving away from the notion of utopia as a literary genre, toward utopia as a writing mode. In this context, Utopia is the expression of desire manifested by means of writing and located in the workings of dystopian narrative.

I have proposed elsewhere a utopian hermeneutics of the feminist critical dystopia, built from the combination of Ernst Bloch's theories with semiotic approaches to the narrative.[5] Barthes's formulations of an "otherness" in literary language are not at odds with Bloch's conceptualization of the utopian anticipatory consciousness manifested in literary texts. This shared basis allows the creation of a way of reading in search of the utopian element encoded as a textual enigma, or a non-place, that functions as a motivational element of narrative and relates, I argue, to a catachrestic mode.

Cleverly coined, the word "utopia" carries in itself its own contradiction. It refers to a "good" place that is at the same time a "no" place, thus expressing a paradox. In semiotic terms, utopia is a representational "fullness" that carries and exposes its embedded "emptiness" (a deferral in signification), for the sign represents its "non-representability"; the sign itself enunciates its catachrestic nature. Although Bloch never raised this issue from this perspective, his writings show insight into the matter when he discusses the impossibility of defining the utopian object. It is the emphasis on this paradox that allows for his views of Utopia as a changeable and processual *topos*.

In "A Philosophical View of the Novel of the Artist," Bloch detects a motivational narrative element around an enigma, showing that the genre is structured in the "movement forward" toward the Not-Yet: "the artistic process could find its entire self-portrait," that is, the genre portrays "the desire to articulate" (*Utopian Function* 275). Commenting on this insight, Jameson stresses the "emptiness of the work within a work, this blank canvas at the center," which is "the very locus of the not-yet-existent itself" (*Marxism* 132). This representational gap is seen in connection to a utopian Not-Yet. It is in the recognition of the utopian dimension of an absent object whose presence motivates narrative's "desire to articulate" that I locate the thread leading to Barthes's narrative semiotics. While both thinkers discuss the final disclosure of the narrative enigma, they also show an awareness of non-disclosure as a possibility. Bloch locates it in the "blank canvas" that remains as latent utopian possibility in the *Künstlerroman*, as well as in other fragmentary aesthetic forms. Barthes explores the suspension of disclosure by referring to the concepts of "hermeneutic jamming" and the "pensive text." The former relates to the declaration, in discourse, that the enigma it has posed is unresolved; and the latter refers to "suspension" as meaning's "last closure." The "pensive text" is an attempt to "'let it be understood' that it does not say everything; this *allusion* is coded by pensiveness, which is a sign of nothing but itself: as though, having filled the text but obsessively fearing that it is not *incontestably* filled, the discourse insisted in supplementing it with an *et cetera* of plenitudes" (*S-Z* 216–17, emphases original). A discourse that poses its own enigma as unresolved, a "pensive text" that keeps an ultimate meaning in suspension: these formulations evoke the functioning of utopia as a signifier of its own paradox. The writing of utopia may be grasped in relation to such a "supplement of plenitudes." First, because it exists in excess of a textual signifier and, second, because it carries the hopes of perfection and fullness. Hence, the reader's task can be formulated as a search for unresolved enigmas and textual encodings of "pensiveness," more sophisticated elaborations of the textual omissions and elisions identified by Bloch. The feminist writing of utopia is seen as a fiction practice marked by the desire to articulate a good otherness which is, in turn, problematized as a narrative *ou-topos*. The hermeneutics of utopia involves looking for textual strategies that enable the contradictory condition of Utopia to be asserted. Section III tests this way of reading and points toward a theorization of the feminist critical dystopias as emblematic of utopia as semiosis, as a signifying process.

III. In Search of Utopia: Charnas's Holdfast Series

In this section I offer a reading of the Holdfast series, which comprises *Walk to the End of the World* (1974) and its sequels *Motherlines* (1978), *The Furies* (1994), and *The Conqueror's Child* (1999).[6] Centered upon the tale of Alldera Holdfaster, the texts follow her path from slavery in the dystopian patriarchal space of the Holdfast (*WEW*) toward escape into what turns out to be a version of a women's-only "wild zone" (*M*), and finally back to the initial setting for the establishment of a new order in which former women slaves become the Holdfast masters (*F*). *The Conqueror's Child* (*CC*) shifts the focus to the character of Sorrel (Alldera's daughter brought up in the women's land), and tells of her excursion into the free women's Holdfast with a mission. As hinted by this summary, the series takes in the thematic and formal conventions of the quest pattern as found in Greek epic, medieval romance, and the fairy tale, all of which tell of the adventure of a hero to achieve or obtain something. Being motivated by an original "lack" or "insufficiency" (see Propp), quest patterns are inherently utopian. This section aims to highlight this utopian trace and to identify ways in which, to use Bloch's term, the "figures of hope" are allegorized in the series and surface as a historical product of feminism to the extent that the novels reveal a search for a historical otherness marked by a different practice between the sexes. In order to observe how a critical utopianism is both thematically and structurally inscribed (and problematized) in the series, the critical edge will be looked at from the three perspectives mentioned above.

IV. The Critical Edge: Patriarchy and Feminism under Critical Lenses

In terms of narrative technique, feminist dystopias paint an exaggerated picture of the existing power relations between the sexes, as if they were placed under a magnifying glass. Seen through different lenses, and in the process of constructing their fictional worlds, these texts effect what Jameson has termed "world-reduction": an "attenuation in which the sheer teeming multiplicity of what exists, of what we call reality, is deliberately thinned and weeded out through an operation of radical abstraction and simplification" ("World-Reduction" 223). This can be seen in the feminist dystopian focus on gender relations, the main catalyst of narrative conflict. Such an "excision of empirical reality," to use Jameson's apt metaphor, is accompanied by an inverse technique: the compression of forms of gender-polarized oppression belonging to different histories and geographies into certain fictional space-times. These imaginative strategies, more easily achieved in speculative fictional modes, amount to a feminist political stance and a radical critique of empirical power relations. The feminist critique targets both androcentric culture and certain aspects of feminism itself, as illustrated below by looking at *WEW* and *M*.

In its opening lines, using a convention of initiating dystopian literature (i.e., the fictional given that there has been a disaster causing drastic transformation), Charnas sets the post-apocalyptic scene of *WEW*: "The predicted cataclysm, the Wasting, has come and—it seems—gone: pollution, exhaustion and inevitable wars among swollen, impoverished populations have devastated the world, leaving it to the wild weeds. Who has survived?" White men and "fems" have. The latter are reduced to the status of "unmen," and described as "the natural inferiors," "lesser beings" (*WEW* 58). This foregrounds the inferior, relational position occupied by women in the reconstructed society of the Holdfast, where the maintenance of law and order is effected by male domination over women.[7] The depiction of this society has much in common with the social configurations in other dystopias: the mechanisms of exaggerated social control characteristic of strongly hierarchical states, as the word "Holdfast" itself suggests. The space was named after "the anchoring tendril by which seaweed clings to the rocks *against the pull of the current*," thus symbolizing the self-perpetuating quality of the status quo (*WEW* 4, emphasis added). This passage evokes the rigid social mechanisms at work in that space, which include enforced conditioning, censorship, and the manipulative retelling of history. Specifically echoing feminist texts, and marking the gender inflection of the novel is the reduction of women, who are scapegoated by means of a sexual politics of oppression, materialized via spatial confinement, interpellation as permanent slave labor and reproductive machines, denial of access to linguistic expression, and subjection to ritualistic executions and sexual abuse.[8] These forms of violence sound several historical notes and manifest the compression of varied forms of gender-polarized oppression into the novelistic space.

This violent background stages the emergence of Alldera, who gradually becomes a central character and the agent of her own feminist quest. It is her idea that "if any young fems could grow bold enough to dare a concerted and determined break into the Wild . . . , then they themselves might of necessity turn into free fems" (*WEW* 149). At the end of *WEW*, Alldera sets off on a journey that is at once personal and political, individual and collective in its implications, and definitely feminist. In the epilogue, titled "Destination" (which functions as a crossroads and is marked, from its very title, by an anticipatory quality), in the last dialogue with Eykar, Alldera states: "It's just as well that our ways part here. My hope lies in speed, and you can barely hobble" (*WEW* 214). Hope and speed, expectation and agility: more than a clumsy farewell between master and slave, this exchange evokes the radically different political paths implied by a male-centered, decaying culture on one side (represented by Eykar Beck's frailty amidst a crumbling Holdfast), and the forward-moving utopian impulse that underlies the feminist quest for reformulated identities and alternative ways of being (symbolized by Alldera's new journey). Fleeing from a disintegrating order, Alldera departs on her walk to the end of the narrative space (to cross the borders), which is, at the same time, the walk to the beginning of the next novel.

M is what Jameson has termed "an open-air meadow text" ("Science Fiction" 58), but one with a feminist twist. It depicts an all-female pastoral world very much in the fashion of other separatist utopias in which women live in harmony and free from the masculine economy characteristic of the phallocentric order. The absence of the phallus is symbolized by the absence of male characters, in a syntax that initially conflates the male organ with the symbolic significance of the phallus as power. For its portrayal of a society apparently liberated from the rigid constraints of a dystopic order, this novel has been associated with eutopias (rather than dystopias). However, its conflicts and ambiguities reveal the all-female territory to be no easy eutopia and position *M* in the wave of utopianism that has produced highly ambiguous texts.[9]

In *M*, Alldera proceeds with her quest and meets two groups of women in the Wild: the riding women, nomadic tribes of Amazons who have never been to the Holdfast; and the free fems, women who, like Alldera, have fled the Holdfast territory. Descendants of the women survivors of the initial disaster, who developed a parthenogenic form of reproduction enabling the formation of all-female families (the motherlines of the title), the former group constantly patrol their borders, rescuing fugitive fems, forbidding others to return, and killing any man who tries to enter that space. The other group, the supposedly mythical Holdfast escapees, lead their lives in a gypsy style, based on agricultural activity and the exchange of goods with the riding women. Unable to reproduce parthenogenically, the free fems face the prognostic of extinction.

The two groups display distinct cultural identities. The riding women's social organization has abolished power hierarchies: "Where there are no masters, no one can be a slave," states Nenisi, one of them (*M* 248). Political decisions are taken in open councils, and the autonomy of each individual and of the motherlines is respected. Their most cherished values are freedom, a sense of connectedness, and a female-centered version of pantheistic paganism: "We celebrate the pattern of movement and growth itself and our place in it, which is to affirm the pattern and renew it and preserve it" (*M* 386). Through Alldera's point of view, readers are introduced to the women's culture, the elements of which are arguably typical of a feminine economy. However, her ambivalent feelings toward it, "sweet and sour at the same time," function as a constant reminder that this space is no eutopia: "She had wanted the women to be perfect, and they were not" (*M* 294). Examples of the imperfections, "the raw, ugly underside of things," are the warfare and raids among the tribes (*M* 293). It is perhaps the women's inability fully to accept Alldera into their culture, in spite of their initial warmth and nurturing toward escapees, that provokes her strongest feelings of exclusion and mirrors her experience in the phallocratic Holdfast. She is not allowed, for instance, to take part in social rituals (i.e., the Gathers, the festive encounter when matings take place). Unbridgeable cultural rifts had resulted in the creation of a separate camp for the fems, where Alldera seeks refuge after realizing she will always be "a stranger" among the riding women (*M* 297).

Originating from a society with a different power structure and a masculinist value system, the free fems have been unable to reject the Holdfast masculine economy, reproducing its hierarchical model instead. It is again through Alldera's point of view that a critical assessment of the free women's society is made. The teacamp "sometimes seemed just like a big [Holdfast] femhold" (*M* 314), with the repetition of practices of corruption, violent punishment, and the master/slave dichotomy. Alldera voices her dissatisfaction: "I just want to see the free fems break out of the old order, not make it all over again here" (*M* 343). In terms of plot development, the repetition of the Holdfast economy in the free fems' encampment (like the insulation and exclusionary policies of the riding women) provokes Alldera's reiterated criticism and ultimately her dissent. On the symbolic level, both instances hint at the presence of the phallus in the all-women territory.

Depicting a female libidinal economy represents an impossibility, stresses Hélène Cixous. To this effect, she writes: "Men and women are caught up in a web of age-old cultural determinations that are almost unanalyzable in their complexity. One can no more speak of 'woman' than of 'man' without being trapped within an ideological theater where the proliferation of representations, images, reflections, myths, identifications, transform, deform, constantly change everyone's Imaginary and invalidate in advance any conceptualization" (83). The surfacing, in Charnas's picture of an all-female territory, of a masculine economy confirms Cixous's theorizing of the unavoidable "ideological trap" in attempts to reconceptualize "woman" and "man." My reading of *M* shows that the utopia of a woman's land becomes dystopian with the reenactment of a masculine economy in both communities of women, a repetition that shows on a symbolic level that the all-female space has been structurally defined by the phallus. This relates to the paradox of Utopia, the "good place" that is also the "no place," as the depiction of utopia appears as its negation. However, the utopian feminism that underlies Charnas's text prevents it from the stasis of traditional utopian literature.[10] And so the utopian quest continues: Alldera's agency functions as a catalyst for change, with the initiation of an interactional movement between the two groups of women via the negotiation of differences and the preparation for the transgression of the borderlines toward another utopia, in the next novel.

While the critical dystopian focus in *WEW* is on androcentric history and culture, a close reading of *M* suggests the shortcomings of separatism as a political strategy, echoing trends in contemporary feminist thought and action that have questioned separatism as a model to be of use to feminism.[11] The feminist dystopian technique of critically revisiting history reveals its catachrestic quality: whereas the historical echoes of our misogynous culture (*WEW*) and of particular feminist actions (*M*) are fairly obvious, this writing mode constructs an alternative space, thus problematizing the issue of historical referentiality.

V. The Critical Edge: The Critique of Tradition and of Itself

Catachresis is an essential figure of rhetoric because of the deviations it implies from normal language use. One of the ways in which literary texts relate to this figure is indicated by their inter- and intratextual self-awareness. Here, I examine Charnas's novels from such a metafictional angle: observing the ways literary language catachrestically folds over itself enables a better understanding of the engendering of a (self-)critical utopian dimension. A brief discussion of intertextual elements in the series will deal with the critical revision of a literary tradition: the conventions of the quest narrative and of literary utopianism. This will be followed by an analysis of forms of intratextual critique in *F*.

Quest texts in Western culture are traditionally informed by a masculine economy: the hero is usually male, the object searched for being, in most cases, woman herself. Initiating from a quest that conforms to this model and echoes the Oedipal plot, the focus of the series gradually shifts toward a woman character, Alldera. Moreover, the novels break the Oedipal trajectory by keeping the utopian object of the quest in suspension (thus maintaining the original lack, in Propp's terms). Besides revising the conventional quest narrative both in terms of gender and its structure, the series also draws on and revises a tradition of literary utopian writing. The science-fictional element is immediately perceived from the generic self-referentiality of the title of the first novel: its syntactic and semantic parallelism with Jules Verne's *Journey to the Center of the Earth*. Although the quest motif recurs in sf, this is not usually so in conventional literary utopias; typically plot development is secondary to the idea of social betterment and stasis, and the traveler to the utopian space is not invested with the quester's attributes. Charnas's series combines these genres in the construction of a feminist critical dystopia that foregrounds "the political quest of the protagonist" (Moylan, *Demand* 45) in her search for a feminist elsewhere.

In its feminist configuration, the series critically revises the tradition of feminist eutopias and dystopias consolidated throughout the twentieth century. With regard to the latter, I described above the different forms of violence inflicted upon women in *WEW*. Similar elements can be found in dystopian texts such as Burdekin's *Swastika Night*. The higher degree of graphic violence, the centrality of gender, and a stronger critical edge (qualities that will feature in later texts, like Margaret Atwood's *The Handmaid's Tale*) distinguish Charnas's novel from its generic precursors. The apparently eutopian separatism of *M* draws upon earlier feminist eutopias, but this novel differs from texts like Charlotte Gilman's *Herland* in its self-awareness that the women's territory constitutes no blueprint of perfection. Indeed, when compared to Charnas's, even separatist utopias published after *M* still retain a strong degree of feminist naiveté, which suggests that her accurate critique of feminist utopianism was ahead of its time.[12]

I now turn to the third novel of the series in order to explore the issue of intratextual reference. *F* is about the return of the culturally repressed and the overturning of an order: the free fems' return to the Holdfast, led by Alldera, to free the enslaved fems, their conquest of the men, and establishment of a new social arrangement. The sex role-reversal accomplished by overthrowing male domination reinstates violence committed by the women become masters. The novel can be read as an experimental space in which the existing imbalance between the sexes is reversed and indicates the failure of this model: the utopia of reversal becomes dystopic in the same terms as the male-centered Holdfast system.[13] It can also be approached, together with recent critical feminist dystopias like Elisabeth Vonarburg's *The Maerlande Chronicles*, as revisionary of earlier role-reversal eutopias and dystopias.[14] However, the point of interest lies in the question of metafictional self-reflexivity, observed in the ways in which *F* critically revises earlier novels in the series as well as its own construction of a feminist utopian elsewhere.

The sex role-reversal, the central subversion at work in the novel, keeps the binary model but dislocates hegemonic power to the female sex in a symmetrical inversion of the previous power structure. Read by Beck, former master become slave, the runaway fems' cave drawings representing their history of persecution serve the purposes of heightening the dramatic effect of their revenge and refreshing the readers' memory.[15] He reads in such drawings his and the other men's fate:

> He saw spirals, carefully traced shapes of spread fingered hands, counting series of lines in groups of fives—counting days in hiding?
> Then came crude stick figures shown running, or walking bent under heavy loads, or wrapped in each other's arms, or transfixed by barbed slashes, or straining upward to escape the stylized flames that surrounded them. Other figures pursued them, entrapped them, tormented them—squat monsters with rough-drawn, pendulous male genitals, wide mouths full of pointed teeth, and whips in their fists. (*F* 323)

This passage offers a metafictional clue: a representation within a representation. The drawings consist of the fems' representation of women's oppression. In the same fashion, but on a different level, *WEW* is in itself a highly stylized version of real-life women's oppression. The mention of the "crude stick figures," something not refined or drawn in very simple lines, causes a retrospective look at the first novel as an oversimplified representation of the conflict between the sexes (involving the victimization of fems under the persecution of men en bloc), and to contrast this with the more elaborate portrayal rendered in *F*.[16]

The gradual emergence of narrative subtleties, such as the increasing number of groups of women from particular cultural backgrounds and the figuration of complicated bodies challenging the oversimplified biologistic division of the sexes, helps to construct this sophisticated picture.

Regarding the latter, the prominence of certain characters provokes "gender trouble," the subversion of gender identity that undermines the essentialist binary opposition between the sexes (see Butler). One instance is Setteo's embodiment of "something other" in terms of gender, providing a problematic picture of sex and gender: "With his scrotum emptied and withered Setteo was not, strictly speaking, a male. . . . On the other hand, no one could truly mistake him for one of the Blessed [women], either. Other states, between the extremes, must exist. He was curious to discover . . . what those states must be" (*F* 114). This character thus offers one of the clues to the destabilization of the binary model reproduced by the central sex role-reversal plot. His will to discover "other states, between the extremes" of the male/female polarity reinforces gender complications, providing a key to the deconstruction of hierarchical binarisms (upon which sexual difference is construed) at work as a subtext in the novel.

The deconstruction of binary models in *F* can also be approached from the perspective of the differences among women, of the tensions and fractions in and among their communities. The surfacing of such differences acts *against* the homogeneity characteristic of the earlier novels. Replacing the dual sexual differentiation en bloc at work in *WEW*, *M* offers a more complicated picture of women, both individually and in groups. In *F*, this picture is complicated even further. Major ideological clashes among the three communities of women vary in function and effect. The presence of the riding women in Holdfast, for instance, offers us the point of view of a surprised observer (of fems' and men's ways), a recurrent character type in utopian literature. Although these women propose to keep their interference to a minimum by trying to be politically tactful, they ultimately interfere in the fems' affairs.[17] The formation of a dissident group under the leadership of Daya to overthrow Alldera's command illustrates the instances of difference within a particular group of women. Such differences cannot, however, be reduced or itemized. Through Sheel's, a riding woman's, point of view, readers are offered hints of this immeasurability: "[Free fems] seemed to have absorbed power and weight from the earth of their homeland and to have become more alien than ever"; or: "[Fems] were like contrary winds blowing in every direction" (*F* 110, 126). The fragmentation of the women characters' desires and motivations substitutes multiplicity for the more homogeneous orientation of the earlier novels and of the beginning of *F* itself. The narrative acquires an increasingly dystopian tone in proportion to the transformation of desirability into undesirability. Alldera's dissatisfaction with the new order gradually becomes noticeable: "And she understood well the longing for something fresh, innocent and hopeful to arise from the welter of bloody struggle in which they had all been living; something around which all of [the fems'] own differences could be centered and resolved" (*F* 243). The issue is given further stress by Eykar's interpellation: "Haven't you come back to be something else than our own creation? Something new, something of your own not crippled by those old times?" (*F* 268).

The narrative subtleties discussed above reveal ever-shifting subject positions and gender identities liable to construction and reconstruction. In terms of the definition of utopia as the expression of women's desire, the novel problematizes the issue of the women's utopian desire, the object of which (the search for another practice of the sexes) is both textually constructed and negated. *F* extrapolates its own content and perpetrates a formal vengeance by means of its open-endedness. Appropriately titled "A Traveler," the final part of the novel anticipates still another story to be told, another journey to be started, which enables the utopian dimension of the women's quest to be kept. This leaves the Utopia of a radical feminist elsewhere alive. Finally, Charnas has accomplished no small task by melding form and content together whilst leaving her readers expectant of more storytelling. I would call such expectation a reader's desire *for* narrative, generated by the characters' desire at work *in* her narrative. The following section takes all novels of the series into consideration, emphasizing *The Conquerer's Child*, in an investigation of its critical utopianism from the third angle.

VI. The Critical Edge: The Formation/Consolidation of Critical Utopian Subjectivities

Fedeka, the healer, says the following about Alldera: "Nothing suits her, she has no place else to go, but she can't seem to accept herself and the life around her. It's a sickness I have no medicine for" (*M* 346). These words epitomize dissatisfaction and longing, feelings that can be associated, both thematically and formally, with the whole sequence of novels, with the utopian movement, and with the feminist quest. I argued above that the misogynist machine shown in *WEW* functions as a dystopian narrative space where points of resistance and political hope are started and feminist utopias envisaged. *M* and *F*, in turn, project two feminist utopias: an autonomous all-female society situated outside the phallocratic order of the Holdfast and a utopia of sex-role reversal. However, these alternative societies provide no unproblematic pictures of eutopias, the conflicts emerging in them indicating their dystopian quality. The effect achieved by this textual mirror game, especially by means of narrative parallelisms (oppressive sexual politics, exclusionary practices, territorial disputes, border transgressions, slavery), is the projection upon readers of the characters' feelings of dissatisfaction, "a sickness" Charnas herself offers "no medicine for."

Shifting to this feeling of dissatisfaction, which finds correlations in utopian thought and in feminist theory, I read *CC* in terms of the analogy that can be drawn between the critical positionality of its main character, Sorrel, "conceived by customary Holdfast rape but born and raised in a Grassland camp" by the riding women, and the female feminist reader (*CC* 22). The latest (last?) novel of the series shows her journey to the New Holdfast to meet her mother and find a safe haven for Veree, a boy child rejected by the riding women. Through this character, "not a fem and not a Woman but a misfit," readers are presented with detached critical assessments of both the riding women's land and the New Holdfast (*CC* 87). Sorrel decides to leave the Grassland after her realization that her "uniqueness" actually meant foreignness (*CC* 22). Her dissatisfaction with the practice of the sexes in the New Holdfast is perceptible throughout the novel in her attempts to guarantee a better fate to Veree than that of Holdfast men. Such discontent is also expressed by some fems: "*This life is so much better, but it's not yet good enough. It's not what I joined you for . . .—a state of permanent enmity between us and the men, between us and our own sons*" (*CC* 45, emphasis original). The first-person narration through which Sorrel's affective perspective is conveyed helps to construct the female feminist reader's critical response.

A feeling of dissatisfaction is close to the expectant feelings central to Bloch's writings about utopianism. Besides, the women characters' unfinished quest (hence their dissatisfaction) fits what the German philosopher has described as "the still unattained aspect in the realizing element." He identifies "a deficit in *the act of realization*," responsible for dissolving the traditional connection of the act of concretion of a utopian goal with a finished idea. This aspect of human action is anchored in the notion of the Not-Yet: "*in the realizing element itself there is something that has not yet realized itself*" (*Principle* 190, 193, emphasis original). This idea crucially underlies his philosophy of Utopia as never-ending process, marked by a correcting element when Utopia is realized, becoming a "topia." My reading of the series discloses precisely this lack of congruence between the women's achievements and (what had been) the utopian goal-images motivating their actions. This generates a suspension in what Propp called a conclusive "liquidation of misfortune."

Also relevant in this context is Bloch's concern with an aesthetic of fragmentation and its utopian potentials. Cultural forms privileged by Bloch include expressionist paintings characterized by the technique of montage, the open-ended novel of the artist, artistic fragments, and unfinished works of art. They illustrate his association of lack of closure with the utopian function, which allows formal parallels with Charnas's series of unfinished novels, each sequel being a fragment in a larger picture. On the issue of artistic fragments, Bloch discusses a characteristic "exploding crack," a "hollow space" that marks the central "un-finish-ability" of certain cultural works. According to him, fragments denote a utopian mode in the sense that they shatter the myth of "roundness" and "enclosedness" and open up a horizon of interpretative possibilities. Following Bloch, I suggest that each novel of the series can be seen as a "belated fragment" of a larger work, separated by the utopian "hollow spaces" in between stories. Such spaces effect a break in the narrative flow, causing critical thought to emerge (*Principle* 217–22).

Of course, there are sequels and sequels. Aesthetic elaboration, a critical take on utopianism, and a radical feminist perspective distinguish Charnas's series from the wave of literary and filmic sequels produced and marketed each year. Whereas the latter tend to rewind the narrative to a zero degree with the resolution of a conflict at the end of each episode so that the same story can be repeated for easy consumption, each novel of the Holdfast series is told from a different perspective, avoiding closure and consolatory endings.[18] The anticipatory spaces in between novels provide important shifts so that each tale of the quest offers a renewed glance at a particular feminist utopian vision. An analogy with painting may illuminate this point. The series can be compared to thematic sets of impressionist works (e.g., Monet's cathedrals or his water lilies) that portray the artist's impressions of the same object in different canvases, from different angles, in different lights, at different times. Similarly, Charnas's Holdfast novels seem to concentrate on one subject matter—the search for a feminist utopia, for an alternative economy of desire that does not objectify women as the signifier of a male desire—which is explored in each novel from a different perspective and chronology. The possibilities are endless.

VII. The Writing of Utopia

> *Perhaps the ultimate motive for metaphor, or the writing and reading of figurative language, is the desire to be different, to be elsewhere.*
> —Harold Bloom, *The Western Canon*

Although Harold Bloom places semioticians and feminists among the "School of Resentment," his remarks set the stage for my final comments on a semiotics of utopia in relation to the feminist critical dystopias, as it locates the protagonists of the story of reading and writing (authors, texts, readers) in a perspective of a motivating desire, a desire to be elsewhere. Charnas's dystopias are a narrative practice that responds to our social environment in a way that is self-consciously critical and feminist. This writing, triggered by the author's desire for an elsewhere, is in itself an act of hope, in the sense that Isabel Allende uses this phrase.[19] As a specific signifying practice, the dystopian fictions are symbolic materializations of desire. In addition to this, they are centered upon the women characters' oscillation between the (problematic) affirmation of their own desire and the education of this desire into political hope, thus promoting the engendering of female feminist subjectivities. In an extremely self-reflexive way, they articulate female desire on three levels: desiring women (authors) portraying desiring women (characters) which may, in turn, trigger women's (readers') desire. This is one sense in which the feminist critical dystopias are emblematic of utopia as semiosis: they are a specific symbolic system motivated by, an expression of, and able to trigger, female feminist desire.

I argued above that the feminist critical dystopias offer a privileged domain for theorizing utopia as semiosis. In semiotic terms, the morphology of the word *utopia* indicates a representational fullness that carries in itself and exposes an embedded emptiness: the word being the signifier of an absent signified. I expanded this idea by bringing together Bloch's and Barthes's elaborations on narrative enigmas, which enabled the understanding of the contradictory condition of utopian discourse and the formulation of a utopian hermeneutical approach. In my readings, I propose that these narratives are emblematic of utopia as a signifying process to the extent that feminist dystopian fictions are textual signifiers pointing toward a utopian signified that is deferred. The feminist good place exists in the feminist dystopias as the no place, as a space off-narrative—the unresolved narrative enigma. Just as the "good place" (*eu-topos*) and the "no place" (*ou-topos*) are contained and expressed by one sign, so too feminist dystopias are texts that dream with the good otherness while being aware of the impossibility of their ever expressing it.[20] They are a utopian discourse to the extent that the narrative workings are directed toward that supplement of plenitudes which exists in excess to a textual signifier (i.e., it exceeds narrativization) and carries hopes of perfection and happiness. My readings of Charnas's novels show that the hidden, final feminist Utopia both generates and motivates the dystopian narratives, which can now be grasped as a utopian writing mode.

In the dystopian narrative machine, the presence of the writing of utopia is equivalent, to borrow Barthes's metaphor, to "the rustle [which] is the noise of what is working well" (*Rustle* 76). If the rustle stops, plot stops flowing and narrativity stops. Therefore, this negativity in utopian writing (manifested by the figural evasion of the space of women's desire) is, in the last analysis, a positivity. First, because it is the very condition of narrativity. This understanding of the writing of utopia relates to the issue of language struggling to say the unsayable, whose major figural expression is catachresis. This leads back to the proposition that this figure offers an appropriate way of thinking about the feminist critical dystopia. Each novel in Charnas's series keeps the promise of the dreamed utopian space by taking readers into a narrative detour, which is the work of catachresis. Second, such space of negativity in the writing of utopia is a positivity in that it opens up a supplementary relationship to meaning (the cultural surplus, for Bloch), driving readers to anticipate utopian significance that is not yet there. Barthes terms this anticipation "the rustle of language": "just as, when attributed to the machine, the rustle is only the noise of an absent noise, in the same way, shifted to language, it would be that meaning or—the same thing—that non-meaning which produces in the distance a meaning henceforth liberated from all the aggressions of which the sign, formed in the 'sad and fierce history of men,' is the Pandora box" (78). As textual signifiers, feminist dystopias epitomize, perhaps more than any other literary genre, the inextricable relation between the sign and the "sad and fierce history of men." My readings trace the functioning of this compromised fiction practice and the dream of liberated meaning it anticipates. This is encoded, I argue, in the articulation of the desire for an elsewhere, which is also the writing of utopia.

I will conclude by commenting on the role of the reader, one of the protagonists in the stage set by Bloom. For him the act of reading is motivated by the reader's subjective desire to be elsewhere. Dystopian texts effect a radically different response when compared to literary eutopias. While the latter can trigger a compensatory response to the extent that it offers a momentary bracket from the social evils, the dystopian novum offers no such consolation. From the perspective of a feminist reading, this is crucial in terms of promoting affective identifications and raising readers' political awareness. In other words, the reading position constructed by feminist dystopias denies the satisfaction of desire and reinforces readers' initial position as desiring subjects.

With regard to the deferral of the moment of utopian fulfillment, a recurrent pattern of feminist critical dystopias, its major function is that it adds a self-critical and processual element of utopianism. Working on Barthes's speculations regarding "the rustle of language," I will focus on the role of the utopian subjectivity in this process, foregrounding the crucial role of the reader's desiring subjectivity and utopian imagination in engendering such critical utopian meaning. Vonarburg's *The Maerlande Chronicles* offers an interesting example, as this feminist dystopia is as much about reading and deciphering as it is about alternative socio-sexual configurations and gender-inflected oppression. Besides, the passage quoted below shows the female protagonists engaging with interpretative practices involving a semiotic interplay between a textual fullness and emptiness:

> One day Mooreï had shown [Lisbeï] a black and white engraving, a cube seen in perspective. "Is it hollow or full?" Full, of course, since the purpose of drawing it from an angle was to create the illusion of a free-standing object. "Look carefully." She studied the engraving, puzzled. Was it full or empty? And sud-

denly, in an invisible but instantaneous transfer, the black and white surfaces changed perspective and the cube was hollow. After several tries, she understood: *a kind of deliberate mental twist* enabled you to see the hollow cube. She burst into delighted laughter. (121, emphasis added)

The cube passage is reiterated later in the narrative. In the second instance, Lisbeï receives a gift in a box whose decorative pattern causes her to remember the drawing of her childhood. These passages can be considered as a metaphor for the role of the utopian subjectivity in approaching feminist dystopias. This is so to the extent that a utopian hermeneutics depends on a deliberate mental twist from the reader to see the text/cube/box in its full utopian meaning. This holds true for every individual act of reading, but acquires greater relevance in cases like the present, in which reading becomes not only a public affair, but also, one hopes, a shared political stance, and a utopian statement in itself. What may be learned during a voyage throughout the realms of the feminist dystopia is that if you look long enough and engage with the texts in their full potentialities, you will see the picture of utopia forming.

Notes

1. Although this implies the idea of a distinct subgenre, literary genre is approached here in a dynamic way as a set of cultural relationships involving the repetition and/or the redrawing of conventions of the writing, marketing, and reception of literature. Hence, the provisionality of the definition that follows. In fact, the sheer diversity of feminist dystopias pulls against any conclusive mappings. Although, for analytical purposes, they may be grouped together, these fictions are a hybrid mode, and some could easily be claimed as, for instance, modern fairy tales (e.g., Angela Carter's *Heroes and Villains*); thrillers (e.g., Elizabeth Wilson's *The Lost Time Café*); science fiction (e.g., Doris Lessing's *Canopus in Argos* series); romance (e.g., Anne McCaffrey's *The Ship Who Sang*); or heroic sagas (e.g., Charnas's Holdfast series). Baccolini examines some generic intersections, finding in them the opening up of utopian elements in feminist dystopias ("Gender and Genre").
2. See also Moylan, *Scraps*.
3. For bibliographical sources see Relf, Mahoney, and Cavalcanti, "Articulating."
4. He clearly refers to the classical utopian text.
5. See Cavalcanti "Articulating." See Bammer for Blochian readings of feminist utopianisms.
6. The titles are abbreviated to *WEW, M, F* and *CC*, followed by page numbers.
7. Although this analysis emphasizes the oppressed position of women, there are other groups of ex-centric subjects in the novel: children, male youths, and rovers (men who fail the Holdfast ritual of initiation). Bartkowski aptly defines the Holdfast social structure as a "male gerontocracy" in her reading of *Walk to the End of the World* (84).
8. In Burdekin, "reduction of women" refers to the act that establishes the lower status of women. The metaphor inspired Lefanu's chapter on dystopias, which offers a commentary on *WEW*.
9. *M* can be and has been read as a feminist (e)utopia (see Bartkowski; Barr, *Lost in Space*) and as a critical utopia, being characterized by a mixture of eutopian and dystopian elements (see Moylan, *Demand*). However, the series is approached here as predominantly dystopian in formal terms. There is a difference between reading *M* separately and as one text in a mosaic composed of a series of four novels when the whole picture turns out to be more dystopian than utopian.
10. The danger of stasis is suggested metaphorically by the fact that both groups are generative dead ends, thus presenting no viable option.

11. Looking at this text as a critique of the general feminist utopia, as well as actual localized practices, of separatism is an approach sometimes ignored by feminist readers.

12. See Sally M. Gearhart's *The Wanderground* (1979) and Katherine V. Forrest's *Daughters of a Coral Dawn* (1984).

13. In this sense, it allegorizes the feminist philosophical debate concerning women's access to power.

14. See Kettle's serious *The Day of the Women* (1969) and Gerd Brantenberg's satirical *Egalia's Daughters* (1977).

15. It also has the strategic function of filling a gap for those who have not read the first novel.

16. For Charnas, "*Walk* was and is a sort of barometer of a certain moment and level and tone of feminism among middle-class, white, thirtyish feminists . . . that is now long gone" (Cavalcanti, "The Profession" 7). Published twenty years later, *F* is clearly attuned with the multifaceted feminisms of the 1990s, and the drawings may also function as an allegory for the (no longer either possible or desirable) univocity of the North American feminism of the 1970s.

17. This is usually the case in static literary utopias. The visitor's agency is a trait in critical utopias. One way the visitor interferes is, for example, by instigating an illegal mating without consent and arranging for a pregnant fem to escape to the Grasslands to give birth to a child, a fact that provokes outraged reaction. Another confrontation occurs between free fems and bond fems. During the invasion of the Holdfast, some of the slaves resist siding with the invaders: the co-opted Matris and their followers.

18. A utopian element is observed in such cultural narratives: they satisfy readers' hopes of a happy end and longing for a sense of collectivity. But these are usually fulfilled by the affirmation of a simplistic (white, male, heterosexual, middle-class, capitalist) consensus concerning the common good. This dangerous utopia provides an escape through entertainment, helping to maintain the status quo.

19. For Allende, writing is an "act of hope, a sort of communion with our fellow [wo]men. The writer of good will carries a lamp to illuminate the dark corners. Only that, nothing more—a tiny beam of light to show some hidden aspect of reality, to help decipher and understand it and thus to initiate, if possible, a change in the conscience of some readers" (48–49).

20. The fact that both meanings are juxtaposed in the same prefix (i.e., the Greek *ou* and *eu* are synthesized in the *u*) stresses the point that one signifier contains its own contradiction.

Works Cited

Allende, Isabel. "Writing as an Act of Hope." *Paths of Resistance: The Art and Craft of the Political Novel.* Ed. William Zinsser. Boston: Houghton, 1989. 41–63.

Baccolini, Raffaella. "Gender and Genre in the Feminist Critical Dystopias of Katharine Burdekin, Margaret Atwood, and Octavia Butler." Barr 13–34.

Bammer, Angelika. *Partial Visions—Feminism and Utopianism in the 1970s.* New York: Routledge, 1991.

Barr, Marleen S., ed. *Future Females, The Next Generation: New Voices and Velocities in Feminist Science Fiction Criticism.* Lanham: Rowman, 2000.

———. *Lost in Space: Probing Feminist Science Fiction and Beyond.* Chapel Hill: U of North Carolina P, 1993.

Barthes, Roland. *The Rustle of Language.* Trans. Richard Howel. Oxford: Blackwell, 1986.

———. *S/Z.* Trans. Richard Miller. London: Jonathan Cape, 1975.

Bartkowski, Frances. *Feminist Utopias.* Lincoln: U of Nebraska P, 1989.

Bloch, Ernst. *The Principle of Hope.* 1959. Trans. Neville Plaice, Stephen Plaice, and Paul Knight. Cambridge: MIT, 1995.

———. *The Utopian Function of Art and Literature: Selected Essays.* Trans. Jack Zipes and Frank Mecklenburg. Cambridge: MIT, 1993.

Bloom, Harold. *The Western Canon.* New York: Harcourt, 1994.

Butler, Judith. *Gender Trouble: Feminism and the Subversion of Identity.* New York: Routledge, 1990.

Cavalcanti, Ildney. "Articulating the Elsewhere: Utopia in Contemporary Feminist Dystopias." Diss. U of Strathclyde, 1999.

————. "The Profession of Science Fiction 52: 'A Literature of Unusual Ideas,' Interview with Suzy McKee Charnas." *Foundation* 72 (1998): 5–19.

Charnas, Suzy McKee. *The Conqueror's Child*. New York: Tor, 1999.

————. *The Furies*. London: Women's, 1994.

————. *Walk to the End of the World* & *Motherlines*. London: Women's, 1974/1978.

Cixous, Hélène & Catherine Clément. *The Newly Born Woman*. Trans. Betsy Wing. London: Tauris, 1996.

Cranny-Francis, Anne. *Feminist Fiction: Feminist Uses of Generic Fiction*. New York: St. Martin's, 1990.

Felski, Rita. *Beyond Feminist Aesthetics: Feminist Literature and Social Change*. London: Hutchinson Radius, 1989.

Foucault, Michel. *The Order of Things: An Archaeology of the Human Sciences*. London: Routledge, 1966.

Jameson, Fredric. *Marxism and Form: Twentieth-Century Dialectical Theories of Literature*. Princeton: Princeton UP, 1974.

————. "Science Fiction as a Spatial Genre: Generic Discontinuities and the Problem of Figuration in Vonda McIntyre's *The Exile Waiting*." *Science-Fiction Studies* 14 (1987): 44–59.

————. *The Seeds of Time*. New York: Columbia UP, 1994.

————. "World-Reduction in Le Guin: The Emergence of Utopian Narrative." *Science-Fiction Studies* 2 (1975): 221–30.

Lefanu, Sarah. *Feminism and Science Fiction*. Bloomington: Indiana UP, 1989.

Levitas, Ruth. *The Concept of Utopia*. Hempstead: Philip Allan, 1990.

Mahoney, Elisabeth. "Writing So to Speak: The Feminist Dystopia." Diss. U of Glasgow, 1994.

Moylan, Tom. *Demand the Impossible: Science Fiction and the Utopian Imagination*. New York: Methuen, 1986.

————. *Scraps of the Untainted Sky: Science Fiction, Utopia, Dystopia*. Boulder: Westview, 2000.

Propp, Vladimir. *Morphology of the Folk Tale*. 1928. Trans. L. Scott. Austin: U of Texas P, 1996.

Relf, Jan. "Rehearsing the Future—Utopia and Dystopia in Women's Writing, 1960–1990." Diss. U of Exeter, 1991.

Sargent, Lyman Tower. "The Three Faces of Utopianism Revisited." *Utopian Studies* 5.1 (1994): 1–37.

Suvin, Darko. *Metamorphoses of Science Fiction: On the Poetics and History of a Literary Genre*. New Haven: Yale UP, 1979.

Vonarburg, Elisabeth. *The Maerlande Chronicles*. Trans. Jane Brierley. Victoria: Beach Holme, 1992.

Wales, Katie. *A Dictionary of Stylistics*. London: Longman, 1989.

CHAPTER 4

Cyberpunk and Dystopia:
Pat Cadigan's Networks

DAVID SEED

I

In his discussion of utopian subgenres, Lyman Tower Sargent describes dystopia as a "non-existent society described in considerable detail and normally located in time and space that the author intended a contemporaneous reader to view as considerably worse than the society in which that reader lived" (9). The more the dystopian text includes a dimension of debate, by characters and within the narrative structure itself, about the values and directions of its future society, the more justified we would be in reading the narrative as a *critical dystopia*. The regimes of *classical dystopias* like George Orwell's *Nineteen Eighty-Four* and Ray Bradbury's *Fahrenheit 451* are rationalized by leading institutional figures—O'Brien and Beatty—whose explanations challenge the protagonist's (and, by implication, the reader's) capacity to identify the faults of those regimes. The protagonist's defeat in argument can lead to physical submission, as happens in Orwell, or to the physical destruction of the *raisonneur* figure followed by a symbolic relocation of the self outside the confines of the regime, as in Bradbury. Although such extreme consequences do not occur in Pat Cadigan's science fiction, debate over the nature of her near-future societies is integral to her works. When asked in an interview whether she was utopian or dystopian, Cadigan replied: "I don't think adhering to either extreme is realistic. There is a middle-ground and that's where I see myself: on the cautionary but plausible line of thinking. . . . Human beings are neither utopian nor dystopian so that's what I choose to reflect in my books" ("Pat Cadigan: She's Nobody's Fool" on line). Cadigan's sentiments have been echoed by William Gibson who has stated similarly: "I don't think I'm dystopian at all. No more than I'm utopian. The dichotomy is hopelessly old-fashioned really. What we have today is a combination of the two" (Johnson on line). In the first of these statements, Cadigan gives the reader advice not to expect generic purity or even homogeneity in her fiction. However, dystopian, even critical dystopian, elements inform her novels, particularly when she transforms familiar American locations in order to dramatize changes in social and mental life brought about by shifting economies and new technologies. Cadigan's characteristic narrative pattern traces the efforts of her protagonists to understand the structures of their society. Typically, her plots center on and gain impetus from investigations that gradually bring about a new awareness in her protagonists of their own social locations.

Cadigan's sf grows out of a specific set of material conditions in 1980s America (the consolidation of business conglomerates, the increasing sophistication of electronics in the entertainment industry, and above all the growth of virtual reality technology). One of the writers who, by Cadigan's account, helped shape her view of science fiction was Gardner Dozois, whose essay "Living the Future" opens a profitable line of inquiry into her novels. He argues that sf is particularly able to show the "*interdependence* of things" (115) and to offer a holistic image of the connectedness of our lives: "You live in an organic surround, an interlocking and interdependent gestalt made up of thousands of factors and combinations thereof: cultural, technological, biological, psychological, historical, environmental" (116). We shall see how Cadigan expresses this notion of surround as a technologically dominated socioeconomic system that, to a greater or lesser extent, entraps her characters. Her fiction is packed with tropes of connectedness that foreground the problematic nature of such connections.

Cadigan has become saddled with the label "Queen of Cyberpunk," which relates her to that body of sf, but which does not explain her complex attitude toward the technology she describes. Introducing the cyberpunk anthology *Mirrorshades*, Bruce Sterling characterizes the 1980s as a period when technology had become all-pervasive, declaring that "its influence has slipped control and reached street level" (xii). Cyberpunk engages with a new critical phase in the relation between humanity and technology. The only female writer to be represented in *Mirrorshades*, Cadigan has described the central concern of her writing as being the "impact of technology on human beings," particularly its liabilities ("An Interview" on line). In a 1993 interview, she took this notion in a more critical direction: "A lot of times, a culture almost seems to float on top of its own black market, and things from that filter up through the culture. I get the feeling that this law-abiding peaceful thing that I live in now is almost never-never land" ("Interview, 1993" on line). The example she cites is of Hallmark Greeting Cards, her former employer in Kansas City, which promoted an image of sweetness and light while using Asian sweatshops to manufacture its products.

In her fiction, Cadigan constantly probes the promotional claims of the technology of VR to explore its human costs. Thus, she stresses its unpredictable applications: "We may develop a technology for a particular purpose and it ends up being used for something that no-one foresaw" ("How Cyberpunk" on line). And she tends to focus on the consumption phase of production because "most people who are on the inside of a technology have no idea what it's like to look at from an end user's point of view" ("How Cyberpunk" on line). Cadigan's treatment of this technology marks one of the differences between her novels and those of the leading initial practitioner of cyberpunk, William Gibson. Although Gibson is credited with an imaginative depiction of the new technology, critics have been arguing with cogency that he is not interested in dystopian issues. David Tomas, for example, proposes that Gibson refers to dystopian urban centers but very quickly moves on to representations of cyberspace (121). Peter Fitting has adopted a similar position in seeing Gibson as an heir of Raymond Chandler: "The most striking aspect of William Gibson's characters . . . lies in the borrowings from the repertory of *noir* film and what could only be called the glamorizing of petty crooks and data thieves" (8). In other words, the personnel and commodities might have changed, but the power structures and crimes have remained traditional. At greater length, Tom Moylan has demonstrated that Gibson's trilogy contains oppositional elements but avoids anything approaching dystopian critique by "containing that radical vision within the limits of a caper plot" (*Scraps* 197).[1]

These comments on Gibson help to explain why famous passages like the following from *Neuromancer* remain local descriptions isolated from the action of the narrative: "Night City was like a deranged experiment in Social Darwinism, designed by a bored researcher who kept one thumb personally on the fast-forward button. Stop hustling and you sank without a trace, but move a little too swiftly and you'd break the fragile surface tension of the black market" (14). The contradiction here between Social Darwinism, used to explain the absence of social planning, and the notion of controlled experimentation could have produced a real tension in the novel over the nature of agency (i.e., are characters the playthings of forces or the subjects of technological exploitation?). Essentially, the passage explains the compulsive activity of Gibson's characters, to establish a narrative tempo rather than a critical perspective on socioeconomic conditions.

II

When looking back on the sf which influenced her early writing, Cadigan stressed the importance of Ron Goulart's Chameleon Corps stories. The hero of the latter, Ben Jolson, "was always changing his face," she recalled, "and in *Mindplayers* characters] were always changing their minds, literally" ("Japan Futures" on line). In his preface to *The Chameleon Corps*, Goulart explained his concerns as deriving from popular culture inflected by his reading of Erik Erikson and R. D. Laing: the stories "make up a series of miniature psychodramas kicking around the idea of self, and contemplating the masquerades and impersonations we sometimes try to pass off as our real identities" (vii). Goulart's hero is a special agent from the Political Espionage office of the home planet Barnum who sorts out crises like that in "Chameleon," in which a dispute is raging over the promotion of zombies throughout the planets. Goulart's names foreground circus (Barnum), film (Keystone), and music (Jolson). In short, artifice at every point. Jolson maneuvers his way through every crisis by his ability to impersonate versions of the stories' main characters. For example, like the Plastic Man prototype recognized by Goulart, Jolson can change shape at any point by transforming himself into a bird or by fantastically extending his limbs.[2] The effect of these transformations is to make him invulnerable. Plastic Man offers a way for Goulart to evade social fixity and to find freedom through mobility—a need expressed by other American novelists of the 1960s, such as Richard Farina and Ken Kesey. Jolson's capacity to change at will gives him an endless repertoire of forms without the dread of formlessness as discussed by Tony Tanner in *City of Words*, but Goulart draws on the Plastic Man comics in other ways that affect his narrative methods (18). The Chameleon Corps stories typically move quickly. The reader is plunged into situations with a minimum of explanation; sudden reversals take place which, despite Goulart's references to Erikson and Laing, are not mental sequences; and stories close abruptly with an ending to Jolson's particular "job." By drawing attention to his artifice, Goulart reminds his reader not to take too solemnly the narratives which deal lightly with 1960s themes like student protest, covert government experimentation, and economic imperialism. In other words, the world of the stories remains a recognizable version of the reader's present, and the narratives enact a conservative sequence of actions since Jolson is professionally committed to preserving the status quo.

Cadigan's first novel, *Mindplayers* (1987), draws on Goulart's theme of transformation but uses a totally different narrative method to establish a dystopian future America. In her *Locus* interview, she has stressed the need in fiction to "give it that vividness, that 'you are there' feeling for a reader," and she does this by using a first-person narrator who assumes the reader understands new terminology (4). Unlike the utopian device of a visitor returning home, Cadigan gains a dystopian effect of "embedding" from the very start by situating the reader in an already existing situation with a minimum of explanation. Among the new terms the reader has to confront in *Mindplayers* are *madcap* (a headset for entering the "system"), *pathosfinder* (a kind of psychotherapist), and *mindsuck* (a form of murder in which the mind is extracted from the body, leaving it an empty shell).[3] It should immediately become obvious that such terms are lexical constructs from familiar contemporary English and not terms implying abstruse technology as found in "hard" science fiction. *Mindplayers* opens with the following statement: "I did it on a dare. The type of thing where you know it's a mistake, but you do it anyway because it seems to be Mistake Time" (4). The explanations naturalize what is to come as a normal sign of human weakness and at the same time defer the immediate referent of "it." When we are told that the mistake was to go along with a friend in the theft of a "madcap," the concrete usage of a descriptor takes us nearer to an explanation, but only comparatively. Such terms are used by Cadigan to hook our curiosity and encourage us to construct by inference a society of sophisticated computer technology where traditional crimes are still punished. The self-conscious tone of Cadigan's narrator becomes another critical dystopian characteristic of her fiction. It implies a member of a futuristic society who nevertheless has only partial knowledge of her world and as such embodies the typical sf characters who, for Cadigan, should be "ordinary people who are thrust into bizarre situations" ("Transforming the Familiar" 68).

The crime that opens *Mindplayers* sets in train a sequence of events with its own momentum. The protagonist, Allie Haas, is pushed to the wrong side of the law by her friend's theft. At the very beginning of the novel, she is subjected to the indignities of a total recording of her self by the Brain Police: "You lose consciousness when you're dry-cleaned: afterward, you dream or you drift. When the fog cleared, I was lying naked on a slab in a boxy gray room while the Brain Police photographed everything inside and out. I could see the mug-holo taking shape in the tank on the ceiling. Unbelievable. My first offence and they were taking a mug-holo as though I were a hardcore mind criminal" (6). Although Cadigan's immediate source for the Brain Police was a Frank Zappa song, the name has an Orwellian resonance in suggesting a dystopian regulation of thought. "Drycleaned" displaces a familiar mechanical process onto mind control. The term's very familiarity performs a dystopian function in implying a reduction of the thinking human subject into an object that can be socially "cleaned." This metaphor screens a more sinister one made explicit later in the novel when we are told that the "Mental Strip Search is just one step removed from brainwashing" (41). The repressive possibilities in the new technology of *Mindplayers* are declared; laws have been put in place to forbid a "full wash" of the mind to "prevent the government from correcting people into obedient robots" (41). Despite these laws, the intertextual echoes of Orwell and the references to brainwashing set up a sinister context for Allie's experiences. From the very first page, she finds herself at odds with the state legal apparatus.

The process Allie endures, and correspondingly the institutions lying behind it, are naturalized through terms and images already familiar to the reader, but then defamiliarized through their unusual application. Thus, a naked body on a slab suggests a morgue as if Allie were undergoing a symbolic death at this point. The traditional mug shot, limited to the face, has now been extended into all areas, inner and outer, of the self. While we recognize a totalization of police monitoring procedures, at the same time we wonder about the technological means for achieving this. This query arises out of a casual collapse of distinctions between inner and outer that makes up one of the major themes of the novel. Similarly, a dry-cleaning of the mind sounds like an oxymoron conjoining physical and mental processes, but again it proves impossible rhetorically to separate the two.[4] Cadigan constantly demonstrates a dependence of the mind on the body and its wider technosocial environment.

Cadigan's references to the Brain Police mark an important difference between her novel and Orwell's. In *Nineteen Eighty-Four*, the action of the novel builds to a climax that confirms Winston Smith's dread of the Thought Police. The positioning of his arrest makes manifest the state apparatus. Cadigan, however, places the equivalent episode at the beginning of *Mindplayers* so that it can function as a springboard into the main narrative, which takes place against a background of the commercial redesigning of the personality. For ten years up to 1987, Cadigan's job at Hallmark was that of designing greeting cards, and *Mindplayers* extrapolates that packaging process. It expresses, as Cadigan has stated, an "attempt to project the commodification of human emotion into the future" (Jenssen on line). She has commented on contemporary consumerism in ways directly relevant to her first novel: "We collect icons now, in this more or less Outdoor reality. Only the icons have names like Gucci, Ann Klein, Sony, VW." And she has shared the insight that fed into *Mindplayers*: "I realized that what most people really desire when they decide they want clothes, or a car, or even a soft drink, is a certain status or cachet that is promised to them by the commercial urging them to buy it" ("Transcript" on line). In the novel, the social self becomes the commodity that can be acquired through a system of franchising: "Getting franchised involved an overlay on the core personality, the mental equivalent of a mask, if a bit more complicated. The physical surgery wasn't absolutely necessary but most people seemed to prefer going the whole route. Rampant brandname-ism. They wanted everyone to know which designer personality they had" (94). The full meaning of Cadigan's "dry-cleaning" should now be emerging. Through an analogy with cosmetic surgery introduced later, she extrapolates a commodified version of the selves presented in everyday life. It is a process of display, of conspicuous consumption.

Here Cadigan may be drawing on James Tiptree/Alice Sheldon's 1973 story, "The Girl Who Was Plugged In," which she has named as an important pioneering narrative in cyberpunk. P. Burke, the girl who attempts suicide, is offered the chance of a new life by being connected to a simulacrum that embodies a reified form of female beauty. Paradoxically, she is offered a kind of freedom and self-realization by becoming connected to a worldwide electronic network (hence the story's title). A grotesque disparity emerges between P. Burke's reshaped self-image and the cybernetic alterations to her body: "The disimprovement in her looks comes from the electrode jacks peeping out of her sparse hair, and there are other meldings of flesh and metal" (48). The cost of this transformation is that P. Burke, through her public "waldo" self, has to promote commercial products in a world where advertising has become virtually outlawed. Her release from the prison of a hated body results in her commodification as a public televised image. Cadigan also evokes a screening of the "core" self which implies a dissatisfaction with the latter so widespread as to be a social neurosis. Since these "selves" are worn like clothes, it becomes increasingly difficult to conceive of a single stable and authentic self. As the novel progresses, tension develops between representations and references to the real. The latter is never quite lost, but becomes problematized in ways Cadigan was to develop in her subsequent novels.

The commercial system of mindplaying forms the backdrop to the action of the novel, in which Allie is offered the chance of avoiding prison by becoming a "pathosfinder," a kind of psychotherapist enabled by VR. The presence of a device for inducing amnesia called the "belljar" makes an unmistakable reference to Sylvia Plath's narrative of psychotherapy. Allie herself enters the multidimensional space of VR through her eyes, which are repeatedly described as entrances. The physical act that corresponds to the cyberpunk trope of jacking into the network requires the removal of the eyeballs and insertion of electronic connections in the sockets (a term that straddles the human and the technological). Eyeballs become gemlike objects in their own right, a bizarre reification of point of view. Again and again, the organ of the gaze becomes the object of the gaze in *Mindplayers*. Thus, Luke Jackson's comment on Cadigan's *Fools* (1992) applies equally well to her first novel: "characters are subjected to external reality rather than autonomous objects." Instead of using the "assaultive gaze" for visual appropriation, the subject "becomes assaulted by reality through his/her gaze" (on line).

Before she can function as a pathosfinder, Allie must first explore her own psychospace, and much of the novel's action describes her navigation of her own and her clients' inner spaces. Or rather, we should say that she explores virtual spaces that are inflected but not owned by any individual. Cadigan has reported that her original plan was to show Allie entering other characters' minds, but that would have placed a kind of telepathy at the center of the narrative and introduced an irrelevant resemblance to a novel like Alfred Bester's *The Demolished Man*. Virtual space for Allie and her clients is, as Cadigan has stated, "neutral territory that neither had control over" (Jenssen on line). Allie's astonishment at her experiences is contextualized through a series of imagistic allusions to the Alice books (hall with locked doors, pool, fall down a hole, etc.) which recur in Cadigan's other novels and provide dramatic immediacy to her narrative. Allie's very name could be taken as a part-echo of Alice or as signifying a conduit (alley) of communication; she herself earns the nickname of Deadpan Allie by her masklike concealment of surprise. Allie wanders through labyrinths where dimensions and locations shift unpredictably; hence the appropriateness of the Alice references. Her first shock is one of size when she sees a cathedral within her own psychospace. As she pursues her explorations, in a process that closely resembles psychoanalysis, but in which blockages and repressions are given tangible form, the analogy that presents itself is with dream. Indeed, Cadigan has often described dream as humanity's first artificial reality.

Allie as narrator and protagonist gives a strong continuity to *Mindplayers* since her disorienting experiences compel her to engage in continuous dialogue with others about the nature of the mind. The text is punctuated with statements like the following: "*The mind is a dynamic thing. It will go on and on, changing, reshaping itself*" (90). And if the mind can somehow create its own landscape, then it follows that no single image is ever fixed or static. Thus an apparently stable object like a cathedral can mutate unpredictably. Again and again, we see Allie struggling for expression through similes or temporarily giving up: "There is no way to describe being thought" (164). She even "witnesses" the oscillations in perception of a composer as a to-and-fro movement between mind and world: "There was never any point of stability or equilibrium; he teetered back and forth between perceiving first the outside world and then the inside of his mind as dominant. The remaining eye remmed occasionally with dreams cannibalized both from actual vision and the mind" (251). The language is heavily evaluative according to norms of perception. This character's failure to orient himself toward reality—still only partly problematized in Allie's commentary—is demonstrated through a lack of coordination between his eyes. There is a muted irony as Allie's diagnosis comes shortly before a crisis in her subjectivity where she experiences increasing difficulty in reconciling her fragmentary experiences with any concept of a unified whole self.[5] She is warned: "The mind is a very capricious thing! You've begun talking about it as though it were a suit of clothes. You think you can have that much control over it?" (274). The novel presents an extended dialogue on the mind and on the conditions of perception. By questioning one of its initial metaphors, *Mindplayers* shows the mind able to resist any definition or explanation. This self-reflexive nature of Cadigan's novel further explains how it can be viewed as a critical dystopia. Central metaphors and figures are destabilized and their possible meanings critiqued, as we shall see in her next and still most famous novel.

III

Synners is set in Los Angeles, a city that Mike Davis has shown to occupy a problematic position in American culture. Davis extrapolates on L.A.'s building program, which detaches sites from nature and history. Thus, "to move to Lotusland is to sever connection with national reality, to lose historical and experiential footing, to surrender critical distance, and to submerge oneself in spectacle and fraud" (18). With hardly any modification, this indictment could stand as a summary of Cadigan's characters' experience of VR. More important for this discussion is Davis's characterization of the symbolic meaning the city has come to assume: "The ultimate world-historical significance—and oddity—of Los Angeles is that it has come to play the double role of utopia *and* dystopia for advanced capitalism" (18). Although he suggests a balance between the two, it is particularly the dystopian pole of interpretation that Davis stresses in his account of representations of L.A. in postwar *noir* fiction and film. From Chandler onward, he identifies a tradition that extends into sf through Bradbury, Leigh Brackett, and Philip K. Dick (including *Blade Runner*).[6] For Davis, "*noir* everywhere insinuated contempt for a depraved business culture while it simultaneously searched for a critical mode of writing or filmmaking within it." The cumulative effect of these works was therefore to bring about a "dystopianization of Los Angeles" (21).[7]

Davis tends to conflate *noir* style with dystopian themes rather easily. In fact, Leighton Grist argues that in *Blade Runner* the *noir* elements pull awkwardly against the sf features (275). Nevertheless, this conflation helps to explain many of the effects in Cadigan's early fiction. The *noir* problems of subjectivity and orientation experienced by the protagonist; the ordinary nature of the latter's identity and her position as victim within a corrupt world; and the negative use of urban milieux all inform Cadigan's fiction to varying degrees. They further characterize one of the bleakest depictions of L.A. in cyberpunk, Richard Kadrey's *Metrophage*. Here the city is going though an entropic decline sardonically signaled in the city's new name as "Last Ass."[8] In a context of rationing, some humans have separated into different castes: the Piranhas living in the ruined buildings on street level, the Croakers (anarchists and doctors performing illegal medicine) in the sewers. The spatial separation of the social groups gives direct physical expression to their respective socioeconomic positions. Within this context, we encounter Jonny Qabbala, a street dealer. Despite his name, Jonny's function throughout the novel is to act as a witness to the decay of the city. It is an ironic measure of Jonny's social ignorance that so much has to be explained to him; his whole life is described as a series of "dull, terrifying discoveries" where he is "trying to find some point of reference, finding it and having it swept away at the next moment" (130). Kadrey stresses the physical cost of the city's decline through the trade in body parts, the volunteers for paid medical experimentation, and the paucity of accommodation. The Golden Age of Hollywood Pavilion, a complex of Teflon-coated tents, houses some 2,000 vagrants. And there is a clear continuity between the trade in drugs—Kadrey at one point quotes William Burroughs's famous "algebra of need"—and medical trafficking. Indeed the city itself comes to resemble a gigantic diseased organism: "The sewers, laced within the body of the city, were the corroded veins of a sick addict" (42). The nineteenth-century tropes of the city as labyrinth and organism are used by Kadrey to hint at the near chaos of L.A., which is inefficiently administered by the "Committee." Conspiracy enters the narrative when a mysterious virus, suspected of being man-made, starts sweeping the city. It proves to be the last (and uncontrollable) result of NATO biological warfare experimentation in the L.A. area. A final irony emerges as this biotechnological weapon becomes a domestic source of death. Kadrey concludes this series of ironies by describing a revolution by the Croakers, which results in the apocalyptic destruction of sections of the city by fire but leaves the power structure untouched. As with the later critical dystopias, *Metrophage* and *Synners* move from a single *noir* cyberpunk hero to a collective agency figured through tropes of an urban body and disease.

IV

Metrophage and *Synners* echo a strategy similar to that of Burroughs's 1960s Nova trilogy in his usage of the metaphor of virus to suggest a complex variety of meanings. *Nova Express*, the last volume, is punctuated with apocalyptic calls for revolution within a state of extended crisis. *Metrophage* moves toward an end point of revolutionary upheaval that proves to be inconclusive. *Synners* also concludes at a point of breakdown and resistance in L.A. after describing the "entertainment industry in the future" (Dery 113). The novel describes the trade in brain sockets, which provides the "direct interface for input-output with manufactured neural nets. Computers" (*Synners* 171). This technology offers the possibility of reifying the brain's activities into commercial commodities and resembles Sterling's "optic television" described in "Twenty Evocations" as TV wired directly into the optic nerve (156). As in her other novels, Cadigan registers the critical dystopian political consequences of this technology through brief allusions to Orwell and Yevgeny Zamyatin (whose name emerges from the computer toward the end of the novel). However, where those writers saw the state apparatus as a monolith, Cadigan shifts her dystopian focus to economy and culture. She traces a process of hegemonic expansion in the entertainment colossus Diversifications Inc., which, like the Tyrell corporation in *Blade Runner*, presides over L.A. as if with a mind of its own: "The computer-run wheels of the complex mechanism known as Diversifications Inc. continued to turn as reliably and smoothly as ever, unaffected by new developments. It had accommodated an intelligent entity before, and though it knew this one was different, it had no reason to care" (255).[9] Briefly, Cadigan raises a series of questions in this description: those of control, singular activity as against the multiplicity in its title, machine consciousness, and transformation through absorption. Diversifications takes over a video company called Eye Traxx, and one character notes how the style of the individual entrepreneur changes accordingly to fit a new corporate image. In a novel packed with the discourse of linkage—system, wiring, and so on—the "mechanism" of Diversifications can be read as a self-expanding structure of connections. Early on, we are given the grotesque image of a man with a "thick black cable" entering his skull, which actualizes such connections (38). One of the most satirical sections of *Synners* follows the production of a video spectacular called *The Last Zeppelin* from "concept" to hyperbolic marketing. By the time it is released, the video has lost what was even initially a tenuous connection with history.

Synners is held together by what Laura Chernaik calls a "mosaic narrative form" (76). As such, the novel invites a reading across sections that ironically comment on each other. The formal construction of the novel thus parallels its critical themes. The segmented narrative obstructs the reader's construction of any grand narratives, and in that sense *Synners* resembles Pamela Zoline's story "The Heat Death of the Universe," which, Moylan argues, pursues a dystopian critique of gendered cultural practices

(*Scraps* 180).[10] Drawing on modernist montage, Cadigan produces a complex multifocal novel of segments in which juxtaposition invites the reader to speculate about possible analogies between images and episodes. To name but two instances, in one chapter a character has a tattoo printed and later another character notes that a hotsuit's needles leave a pattern of lines on the body; in another, Mark dreams of escape from the "prison" of the flesh as a figure watches a TV program discussing relationships with prisoners. Especially as many minor characters are never named, Cadigan implies that urban experiences are common and shared. The examples cited shift our perspective temporarily to the local subject, frequently reversing point of view. One of the novel's main themes revolves around a conversion of activities into video representations. The constant changes of perspective deny the reader any objective access to the narrative. In this respect, *Synners* exemplifies a characteristic of contemporary sf that Scott Bukatman has explained: "The constant meditation on the mediation of the real" has produced a special self-consciousness in which the "science fiction of the spectacle, even in its more diluted instances, acknowledges its own complicity with the spectacularizing of reality" (30). This produces a textual condition of rapid perspective shifts and allusions to sf novels and films that also recurs in Cadigan's latest novel.

The scrutiny of the real partly takes place through dialogue between characters who are to varying degrees complicit in the very system they are criticizing. Looking back on her composition, Cadigan has stated: "When I was writing *Synners* I realized I was delineating two different types of people. One type, like Visual Mark, wanted to crawl into VR and have the door shut behind him. The other, like Gina, wanted to climb out and pull it all out with her. Display it outside. So there are the inner-directed and the outer-directed" ("An Interview" on line). Cadigan thus identifies two poles of a broad spectrum of response in *Synners* to VR.

Gina Aiesi, at one pole, performs an important linking function between characters and possesses one of the strongest, most critical voices in the novel. She articulates a clear hostility to the emerging ideology of the synthetic as she attacks pop videos: "I want it to come out of human—fucking—*beings*" (199). Gina constantly challenges the displacement of physical human presence by synthetic representations, the casual disposal of employees by Diversifications as expendable material, and the bodily cost to Mark and others of the new technology. Not surprisingly, she develops a reputation within the company as a troublemaker, but this merely confirms to the reader the importance of her voice. However, she is also a compromised figure. At one point in the novel, a woman is, or rather *seems*, about to commit suicide. TV cameras appear so as not to miss the "show," but when she jumps it is revealed that she is wearing a harness and merely making a new video. The woman is none other than Gina. The fact that she herself works for Diversifications does not invalidate her critical role in the novel, but rather demonstrates the impossibility of taking a stance outside the system. For the activities of Diversifications extend into every area of experience, even dream.

As the opposite locus of response, Visual Mark is so called because the visualizing center in his brain has hypertrophied. This has turned him into a commercial property because technology makes it possible to tap into his images and market them as videos. Mark is a VR junkie who constantly tries to escape the materiality of his own body: "He'd just lie here now and watch the pictures. The video show that ran endlessly in his head . . . was coming up to where he could see it better—that, or he was going down to where it was, it didn't matter to him one way or the other" (87). Like Gibson's Case who tries to escape the "prison of his own flesh," Mark dreams of an Emersonian expansion of consciousness into limitless space, an escape from his "box" (Gibson 12). His recurring mental image of a shore represents this desire as a launch into non-definition. Already in the lines quoted, we can see his confusion over spatial location, and in fact his very name reflects thematically on a willed loss of direction with "no mark to point the way" (*Synners* 89). Mark's dream is one of ideal motion "where no limits applied, no boundary conditions were enforced, and he could fly through the universe if he wanted to" (233). Even here he cannot escape his material condition since he depends on the "wire," the technological hook-up to the system, in order to realize his dream. Toward the end, Mark appears to die of a seizure, but his consciousness persists as a disembodied voice within this electronic system. He approaches the condition of pure information, and Cadigan shrewdly puns on the ambiguities of his fate by revising his name into Markt. Simultaneously, Mark has become part of the past (Marked), tricked by the system (another meaning to *mark*), and synonymous with the very *market* that was exploiting him.

Visual Mark responds addictively to what Darko Suvin has described as the utopian potential of cyberspace: "In a world laced with pills and drugs, cyberspace is itself a kind of super-drug vying in intensity with sexual love" (44). Kevin Robbins has similarly shown that much early discussion of VR was utopian in its hopes of transcendence through a cyberspace which commentators like Howard Rheingold took to open up an ideally accessible virtual community.[11] Cadigan's continuing fascination with VR, by contrast, has not blinded her to its potential costs.[12] In *Metrophage*, apocalypse is triggered by a would-be revolution. In *Synners*, Cadigan stays true to her central metaphor of the diseased body and presents it as a form of seizure. The columnist Val Schaffner has made two points about L.A. that converge in Cadigan's ending. First, he declares that the city is "arranged to facilitate oblivion. The space around the freeways can be ignored. It is like outer space" (61). Then he notes a pre-apocalyptic temper to L.A. life which thinly "masks a premonition of catastrophe" (62). In *Synners*, Mark supplies one link between the multiple interlocking systems of his body and those of anyone else connected by the sockets, the computer network, and the traffic system of the city. Mark's fear of the "Big One" getting into the system is realized in his apparent death, and then a number of others with implants start keeling over from strokes. An electronically transmitted virus apparently causes the deaths. In addition, it penetrates the computerized traffic control system and produces a massive failure. "GridLid" becomes gridlock. As usual for Cadigan, the cause can never be defined, as one character insists: "It's not a virus or a bomb" (357). Again, the event becomes instant spectacle: "The machinery of the city was melting down, and they were all just watching it happen on TV" (321). One of the striking transformations of the city that takes place is a temporary restoration of the street to pedestrians. As Davis, Schaffner, and others have pointed out, the city term "freeway" encapsulates a double identification between the motor car, the road, and unfettered movement. Extraordinarily, since he ignores the structured and guided nature of the freeway system, Jean Baudrillard argues that L.A. offers the ideal freedom of movement only to be found in the desert (53). At the same point, he argues that driving in L.A. involves participating in an essentially collective propulsion. Cadigan would endorse this second point, but critically. At the end of *Synners*, the identification between vehicle and free movement is dramatically disrupted as more and more characters circulate on foot. However, traditional apocalypse usually implies ultimate transformation: the destruction of one order and the coming into being of a new one, as happens at the end of Bradbury's *Fahrenheit 451*. Both Kadrey and Cadigan deny such total transformation. It is a measure of their political skepticism that apocalyptic change is both temporary and partial.

Criticism on *Synners* to date has tended to concentrate on questions of gender and the body. Jenny Wolmark has taken Cadigan to task for not addressing gender sufficiently (125); whereas Anne Balsamo has argued that Cadigan never allows her technological themes to exclude consideration of their consequences for the body (138–46). Cadigan herself has been somewhat contradictory in her statements on gender. In the 1993 interview she states: "Women have been invaded by technology for ever, like birth control," but then adds that men have too ("Interview, 1993" on line). *Synners* demonstrates that technology can take its toll on both genders.

V

Synners puns in its title on a number of concerns partly anticipated in Raymond F. Jones's *Syn* which also interrogates the notion of the synthetic. The earlier novel makes a useful contrast with *Synners* as it helps to demonstrate how Cadigan transforms the traditional narrative methods of a dystopia. *Syn* describes the experiences of Arthur Zoran who returns to Earth after several years on a planet colony. He finds that Earth has suffered a nuclear war and then been turned into a security state where travel is banned and every citizen is subject to monthly EEG tests to prove their humanity. The reason for this is the proliferation of synthetic beings ("Syns") who are indistinguishable from humans except by computer testing. An officer of Central Security declares: "The avowed purpose of the Syns is to replace humanity with themselves. They consider themselves a completely superior form of life" (10). Whereas at first they were content merely to reproduce and build up their numbers, now they have gone on the offensive. The officer warns travelers returning to Earth that it is an us-or-them situation: "The mission of the Syns is to destroy and replace mankind. Ours must be to destroy the Syns first" (10). Zoran's return is thus to a transformed Earth from which he feels more and more estranged. The officer's declarations collapse possibilities into stark alternatives and in effect essentialize political loyalty into a question of genes. To Zoran, the new situation resembles historical periods like seventeenth-century New England as he exclaims that he is witnessing a "gigantic, world-wide witch hunt!" (33). The search for Syns can only be carried out through the state super-computer, which, coincidentally, Zoran helped design. When he engages in dialogue with this computer, he discovers that the story of the Syns had been invented to destroy human pride. And so the narrative turns into parable, and the evocation of a police state strengthened by a computer is a means toward the end of dramatizing the dangers of political fanaticism.

How then does this subject reveal itself through the puns in the title? The moral meaning in the term makes a satirical comment on fanaticism. In their attempts to destroy the supposedly alien Syns, humans are committing the collective sin of barbarism, and historical echoes (as Syns are destroyed in gas chambers) show how little has been learned from earlier epochs. The pseudo-category of Syns represents an attempt to externalize a hated aspect of humanity itself. There is no way—no sign—to differentiate Syns from humans other than through a sine wave within a computer-generated EEG, which the limitations on scientific knowledge prevent humans from recognizing. The ultimate irony of the novel, then, is that the category of Syns is purely synthetic in that it has no basis in observable reality. The regime promoting the ideology of difference proves to be manipulable by its own technological creation—the state computer. Jones's novel engages with a subject similar to Dick's *Do Androids Dream of Electric Sheep?* but lacks the sophistication of the latter's sustained questioning of criteria for recognizing humanity. Jones is too eager to describe a repressive state apparatus, whereas Dick filters the official account of how the replicants were created through a series of question-and-answer scenes in which Rick Deckard interrogates his own humanity.

Similarly to Jones's novel, Cadigan's title puns on technology and ethics.[13] The pun is first used by Cadigan in "Rock On." Gina, in a world similar to that of *Synners*, has become a human "synner" or channel for substitutes for the live performance of rock. Through brain terminals, she works as a mixer combining and improving on the sounds desired by individual bands. The result is entrapment by exploitation, gendered because her band is called Man-O-War and commercial since it is termed a "conglomerate." Gina, like her analog in *Synners*, protests against the displacement of live performance. Thus, technological connections actually break previous physical ones. Similarly in *Synners*, the human synthesizer extends the technology of instrument simulation through a combination of sound and image. As one character declares, "We're gonna take that stuff provided by the bands—images, pictures, shit like that—and work it around into some form. . . . We're *real* synthesizers now. Real synners" (218).

The first commercial meaning of "synner" is thus someone who through the new technology combines electronic sound production and rock video. Chernaik glosses this meaning: "In the slang used by many characters in the novel, a 'synner' is someone who uses a synthesizer in his or her work. . . . The 'synners' are not dialogizers or marxist synthesizers; they are cyborgs" (70). As she states, "synner" indicates a process in which the human autonomy of characters is constantly brought into question. In effect, "synners" are hybrid entities whose ambiguous physical status reflects their shifting ambivalence toward technology. However, we should recognize that the term itself recedes into the collective past of the novel, and toward the end, synthesis is rescued from commodification and revived as a collective action, a putting together of selves rather than a displacement. When Gabe has sex with Gina, they "synthesize something together" by sharing the pleasure of their bodies (389). By the same token, characters get together to "synthesize" a means of resisting the spread of the computer virus.

VI

VR as depicted in *Fools* and *Tea from an Empty Cup* fractures the self and destabilizes the self's location. In *Tea*, VR spaces which the protagonists enter mutate unpredictably. Within VR, dimension and substance lack the stability we presume in reality, with the result that the VR self or POV (point of view, as in cinema) is constantly disoriented. The root term *topos* in dystopia, of course, refers to place, but place itself becomes destabilized here, shifting the reader's attention from things to process, asking the question how these changes occur. As noted earlier, this question is one of control. Although VR has its protocols and icons whereby Cadigan's characters negotiate their way forward, there is a constant ambiguity over how much they are in control. Cadigan's original title for this novel was to have been *Bunraku*, the name of the Japanese puppet theater, which would have explicitly foregrounded this issue.

The fragmenting of the self became apparent as early as *Mindplayers'* references to acting. Cadigan develops this process further in *Fools* as she combines a performatory notion of the self as a repertoire of social roles similar to that outlined in Erving Goffman's *The Presentation of Self in Everyday Life*, research into multiple personality disorder, and the perception that cyberspace is a "theatrical medium, in which people participate in events that have dramatic structure and emotions" (Rheingold 190). Cadigan has stated that she sees "more acting in the world today," and she weaves this perception into the narrative of Marva, a Method actress who loses control of the roles she has to play ("Exchange" on line).

This proliferation of roles disorients the reader more radically than elsewhere in Cadigan's work. Earl Jackson has helpfully unravelled the complexity of the opening chapter, but with a clarity that does not match the experience of reading *Fools* (on line). Cadigan signals shifts between the consciousness of Marva, Mersine (a Brain Police officer), and their alter egos through changes in typeface. In Joanna Russ's *Female Man*, the protagonists' names all begin with the letter J, and each has a clearly defined role. In *Fools*, by contrast, designations (it would be anachronistic to talk of names here) are used sparingly so that the reader has to cope with sudden shifts in subjectivity from observer to observed. As Elisabeth Kraus has also shown, in "Just Affix My Reality," the novel further develops the separation of the self into segments and episodes, which we saw in *Mindplayers*, and draws on pop performance and Stanislavsky's acting techniques to obscure any concept of originating agency. *Fools* is a claustrophobic narrative because it undermines its characters' capacity to verify their experiences. The most recurrent image is that of the mirror, which solipsistically throws the observer's image back at her or opens up further Alice-like worlds for her to enter. Because each "self" exists on the same narrative level, consciousness becomes segments or bytes of narration.

The dystopian dimension of *Fools* emerges in its paranoid evocation of the self as the passive subject of external controlling agencies. All the processes glanced at in *Mindplayers*, like "dry-cleaning" or "mindsuck," recur as more imminent threats. A repeated crisis of agency keeps occurring as characters are "steered," quantified into salable personae, or have their consciousness constructed like a "bad splice in an ancient film" (228). Cadigan indicates the sf context of her narrative when a character realizes with horror: "I'd been bodysnatched," a moment that resonates throughout the novel in further undermining the reliability of appearance (97). The alienation of modern urban life is thus given expression here as total uncertainty over *whose* life any "self" is living. Unlike the 1950s narrative to which "bodysnatched" alludes, Cadigan blurs the boundaries between the self and an alien other.

In her most recent novel, *Dervish Is Digital*, Cadigan returns to this motif of body-snatching, which supplies a backdrop to a crime narrative. The protagonist, Konstantin, is investigating the "technocrimes" of Dervish in defrauding VR users. Although she is a member of a law-enforcement agency, and therefore positioned within a state apparatus, Konstantin is another of Cadigan's innocents, learning as her investigation brings her into contact with arms dealers and professional gamblers. The action oscillates between Hong Kong and America through networks that are transnational, like VR itself. In her investigation, Konstantin discovers evidence of brainwashing and body-snatching; the terms overlap. As in the first *Invasion of the Body Snatchers*, a character suspects that what is being witnessed is "one of those mass hysteria things" (53). These terms and this comment sound pointedly old-fashioned in the context of the latest VR technology, but Cadigan shows that dystopian fears of total surveillance and control are becoming realized. As Konstantin looks at the city which embodies contemporary society, she reflects: "It was a profile that, outwardly, had changed very little in the last seventy years. The changes took place on the inside now . . . having little if any effect on the exteriors. As if, Konstantin thought suddenly, there was some hostile, omniscient observer that humans were trying to fool into believing that absolutely nothing was happening. . . . Maybe this was the standard learned behavior of a society that had put itself under permanent surveillance" (46). The ironic twist comes at the end of this passage as the Orwellian image of external monitoring is reversed into self-imposed surveillance. Here we encounter yet another shift from a traditional to a critical dystopia in which the polarity between self and state has collapsed. In interviews, Cadigan has expressed her misgivings about the emerging mind-set in America that electronic surveillance is justified. The novelist David Brin's study, *The Transparent Society*, addresses the same fears, again with bearings from Orwell, of electronic surveillance through CCTV, hacking, commercial taps, and so on (see chapter 3). *Dervish Is Digital* shows a society where the interlock between government, business, and crime networks has become so complete that the three are inseparable. This is one of Konstantin's discoveries, but it is not enough for her to realize it in the abstract. A drug triggers a paranoid hallucinatory sequence in which she fears that "they're monitoring your vitals," at which point surveillance shades into a form of body invasion (189).

Pat Cadigan's characters typically find themselves embedded in technological networks that operate from economic imperatives and exact their human cost. As Mark Dery has shown, Cadigan, along with writers like John Shirley and Norman Spinrad, resists the displacement of the body in postmodern economy and culture: "They inveigh against the supersession of the authentic by the synthetic, of the visceral by the cerebral: the supplanting of human performance by computer-controlled MIDI instruments; of 'real' sounds by digital samples or synthesized substitutes" (105). Cadigan's wariness over the new technology does not take the form of strident polemics, however. Instead, she creates dialogues wherein rival perspectives emerge through an examination of technology and its operations on the human body. The reader cannot forget the critical implications of such examinations as they grow from her use of dialogue, deconstruction of metaphor, and allusion to traditional dystopias. Throughout her work, Cadigan dramatizes a systemic crisis of agency that results from technological incursions on the body. But whereas in her earlier novels she allows for a degree of individual and collective response, in her later novels she increasingly foregrounds her protagonists' loss of autonomy.

Notes

1. See also Moylan's "Global Economy, Local Texts." In contrast, Hefferman argues that Gibson undermines the utopian/dystopian opposition traditional to sf by presenting a post-holocaust world "in exhilarating and euphoric language and images" (25).
2. Goulart has written extensively on the history of comic books; see his *Great History of Comic Books* and *Encyclopedia of American Comics*.
3. The original title of the novel was *The Pathosfinder*.
4. For a helpful comment on this kind of discourse, see Siivonen.
5. See Kraus on the exteriorizing of forms of the mind in Cadigan: "Lived experience becomes so rare that it is turned into a commodity with utilitarian value" ("'Just Affix My Reality'" 110).
6. In his later study of L.A., *Ecology of Fear*, Davis flatly denies the futuristic dimension to *Blade Runner*, describing the film as presenting the "ghost of past imaginations" (361). For a discussion of L.A.'s "hyperreality" according to Baudrillard and others, see 392–93.
7. Of the examples that could be cited to show this process, Wylie's *Los Angeles: AD 2017* follows a Wellsian "sleeper awakes" pattern to dramatize the critical pollution of the environment. The publisher hero sees the signs of impending crisis, then falls asleep for 46 years, only to discover that the survivors have moved into a massive underground complex beneath the streets of the city. Wylie follows a formulaic sequence of estrangement, disaster (the deserted and ruined streets), culminating in an explicitly dystopian description of the "craven new world" of a planned genetic hierarchy rationalized by the needs of the crisis.
8. Jurek glosses the title to mean the "ceaseless transformation of the city into the post-human" (86).
9. For comment on the packing of urban space in *Blade Runner*, see Jarvis (142–43).
10. Kraus also argues that Cadigan's fiction could be compared to the indeterminacy of quantum mechanics in "Real Lives."
11. The U.S. edition of Rheingold's *Virtual Community* had the folksy subtitle of *Homesteading on the Electronic Frontier*.
12. In Cadigan's second novel, *Tea from an Empty Cup*, a VR addict dies while on a "trip" and the sections concerning the investigation of his death are titled "Death in the Promised

Land." The utopian promise historically attached to America has been displaced onto a nationally promoted technology. Entry into VR is signaled by the message "WELCOME TO THE LAND OF ANYTHING GOES" (75).

13.   Characters in *Synners* confront the following syllogism: Information is power; power corrupts; therefore the age of fast information is a very corrupt one. References to sin, however, are flip asides that reveal nothing of characters' values.

Works Cited

Balsamo, Anne. *Technologies of the Gendered Body: Reading Cyborg Women*. Durham: Duke UP, 1996.

Baudrillard, Jean. *America*. Trans. Chris Turner. London: Verso, 1988.

Bester, Alfred. *The Demolished Man*. 1953. London: Gollancz, 1999.

Blade Runner. Dir. Ridley Scott. 1982.

Brin, David. *The Transparent Society*. Reading: Addison, 1998.

Bukatman, Scott. *Terminal Identity: The Virtual Subject in Postmodern Science Fiction*. Durham: Duke UP, 1993.

Burroughs, William. *Nova Express*. 1964. New York: Grove, 1992.

Cadigan, Pat. *Dervish Is Digital*. London: Macmillan, 2000.

————. *Fools*. London: Harper, 1994.

————. *Mindplayers*. London: Gollancz, 1989.

————. *Synners*. London: Harper, 1991

————. *Tea from an Empty Cup*. London: Harper, 1998.

Chernaik, Laura. "Pat Cadigan's *Synners*: Refiguring Nature, Science and Technology." *Feminist Review* 56 (1997): 61–84.

Davis, Mike. *City of Quartz*. New York: Vintage, 1992.

————. *Ecology of Fear: Los Angeles and the Imagination of Disaster*. London: Picador, 1999.

Dery, Mark. *Escape Velocity: Cyberculture at the End of the Century*. London: Hodder, 1996.

————, ed. *Flame Wars: The Discourse of Cyberculture*. Durham: Duke UP, 1994.

Dick, Philip K. *Do Androids Dream of Electric Sheep?* New York: Ballantine, 1968.

Dozois, Gardner. "Living the Future: You Are What You Eat." *Writing and Selling Science Fiction*. Ed. C. L. Grant. Cincinnati: Writer's Digest, 1976. 111–27.

"Exchange with Pat Cadigan: Queen of Cyberpunk." 1998. Available at http://media-in-transition.mit.edu/science_fiction/transcripts/cadigan.html

Fitting, Peter. "Beyond the Wasteland: A Feminist in Cyberspace." *Utopian Studies* 5.2 (1994): 4–15.

Gibson, William. *Neuromancer*. London: Grafton, 1989.

Goulart, Ron. *The Chameleon Corps and Other Shape Changers*. New York: Macmillan, 1973.

————. *The Encyclopedia of American Comics*. New York: Facts on File, 1990.

————. *Ron Goulart's Great History of Comic Books*. Chicago: Contemporary, 1986.

Grist, Leighton. "Moving Targets and Black Widows." *The Movie Book of Film Noir*. Ed. Ian Cameron. London: Studio Vista, 1992.

Hefferman, Nick. *Capital, Class and Technology in Contemporary American Culture*. London: Pluto, 2000.

"How Cyberpunk Lit Influenced Technology: Interview with Cyberpunk Author Pat Cadigan." Available at http://www.theregister.co.uk/content/7/17517.html

"An Interview with Pat Cadigan." Available at http://www.t0.or.at/pcadigan/intervw.htm

"Interview with Pat Cadigan, May 1993." Available at http://www.avnet.co.uk/home/amaranth/Critic/ivcadign.htm

Jackson, Earl, Jr. "Extrapolating Plot Lines from Deep Undercover in Pat Cadigan's *Fools* (one version)." Available at http://www.anotherscene.com/suspense/cadigan/ foolsgd.html

Jackson, Luke. "The Creation of Subjects in Pat Cadigan's *Fools*." Available at http://www.anotherscene.com/suspense/cadigan/lukefp.html

"Japan Futures, Cadigan's Future." Available at http://www.wmin.ac.uk/~goffinl/pat_cadigan_iz.html

Jarvis, Brian. *Postmodern Cartographies: The Geographical Imagination in Contemporary American Culture*. London: Pluto, 1998.

Jenssen, Stephanie. "Talking with Pat Cadigan." Available at http://www.ii.uib.no/~bjornts/ICW/PR2/PR2_3.html

Johnson, Antony. "Waiting For The Man." Available at http://www.spikemagazine.com/0899 williamgibson.htm

Jones, Raymond F. *Syn.* New York: Belmont, 1969.

Jurek, Thom. "From *Straight Fiction.*" McCaffery 85–86.

Kadrey, Richard. *Metrophage.* London: Gollancz, 1988.

Kraus, Elisabeth. "'Just Affix My Reality': Pat Cadigan's Constructions of Subjectivity." *Simulacrum America: The USA and the Popular Media.* Ed. Elisabeth Kraus and Carolin Auer. Rochester: Camden, 2000. 107–21.

———. "Real Lives Complicate Matters in Schroedinger's World: Pat Cadigan's Alternative Cyberpunk Vision." *Future Females, The Next Generation.* Ed. Marleen S. Barr. Lanham: Rowan, 2000. 129–42.

McCaffery, Larry. *Storming the Reality Studio: A Casebook on Cyberpunk and Postmodern Fiction.* Durham: Duke UP, 1994.

Moylan, Tom. "Global Economy, Local Texts: Utopian/Dystopian Tensions in William Gibson's Cyberpunk Trilogy." *minnesota review* 43-44 (1995): 182–97.

———. *Scraps of the Untainted Sky: Science Fiction, Utopia, Dystopia.* Boulder: Westview, 2000.

"Pat Cadigan: She's Nobody's Fool." Available at http://www.harpercollins.co.uk/voyager/inter-vws/200596/cad2.htm

"Pat Cadigan: Transforming the Familiar." *Locus* 35.1 (1995): 4, 68–69.

Rheingold, Howard. *Virtual Reality.* London: Secker, 1991.

Robbins, Kevin. "Cyberspace and the World We Live In." *Cyberspace/ Cyberbodies/ Cyberpunk: Cultures of Technological Embodiment.* Ed. Mike Featherstone. London: Sage, 1995. 135–56.

Sargent, Lyman Tower. "The Three Faces of Utopianism Revisited." *Utopian Studies* 5.1 (1994): 1–37.

Schaffner, Val. *Lost in Cyberspace: Essays and Far Fetched Tales.* Bridgehampton: Bridge Works, 1993.

Siivonen, Timo. "Cyborgs and Generic Oxymorons: The Body and Technology in William Gibson's Cyberspace Trilogy." *Science-Fiction Studies* 23.2 (1996): 227–44.

Sterling, Bruce. "Twenty Evocations." McCaffery 154–61.

———, ed. *Mirrorshades: The Cyberpunk Anthology.* New York: Ace, 1988.

Suvin, Darko. "On Gibson and Cyberpunk SF." *Foundation* 46 (1989): 40–51.

Tanner, Tony. *City of Words: A Study of American Fiction in the Mid-Twentieth Century.* London: Cape, 1976.

Tiptree, James, Jr. *Her Smoke Rose Up Forever.* Sauk City: Arkham, 1990.

Tomas, David. "The Technophilic Body: On Technicity in William Gibson's Cyborg Culture." *New Formations* 8 (1989): 113–29.

"Transcript of Chat with Pat Cadigan on December 10, 1998." Available at http://www.eventhorizon.com/sfzine/chats/transcripts/pages/121098.html

Wolmark, Jenny. *Aliens and Others: Science Fiction, Feminism and Postmodernism.* Hemel Hempstead: Harvester, 1993.

Wylie, Philip. *Los Angeles: AD 2017.* New York: Popular Library, 1971.

CHAPTER **5**

Posthuman Bodies and Agency in Octavia Butler's *Xenogenesis*

NAOMI JACOBS

I. Introduction

Although science-fiction novelist Octavia Butler claims to avoid "all criti-cal theory" (Potts 331), the issues at play in her *Xenogenesis* trilogy are essentially those of the postmodern critique of the humanist subject: the critique of the individual as a rationally self-determining, self-defining being, and of individual identity as the source of agency.[1] In these novels, Butler confronts humanity with an impossible choice: either extinction, or transformation through a genetic "trade" with an alien species, the Oankali. In this context, the human race stands for the human being as we once knew it, facing a seemingly horrifying posthuman future. Like those films that Kelly Hurley classifies as "body horror," Butler's narrative tells of a "human subject dismantled and demolished: a human body whose in-tegrity is violated, a human identity whose boundaries are breached from all sides" (205). Yet Butler's critical dystopia suggests a resource for hope in these very violations and ruptures—indeed, in the evolution of the human toward a posthuman body, posthuman subjectivity, and posthuman form of agency.

Butler's trilogy works through a series of perspectives on posthumanity, with each volume's central consciousness being increasingly distanced from the human. In the first volume, we see the Oankali through the eyes of a human who regards metamorphosis with horror. But the second and third volumes are narrated from the perspectives of Human/Oankali hybrids or "constructs," who embody the utopian possibilities of post-humanity. Her representations of Oankali sexuality, epistemology, communication, and politics suggest that the fluidity and openness of the posthuman body might enable new forms of subjectivity and agency, grounded in relation rather than separation. As is characteristic of the critical dystopia, the terms of her critique shift in such a way as to destabilize the dystopian genre itself. Butler proffers—and problematizes—two of the "utopian possibilities" (Moylan 105) found in the critical dystopia. The more conventional and, I will argue, the less central to her project is that offered by a group of humans who choose to attempt a settlement on Mars rather than to lose their species identity in becoming part of the posthuman hybrid. The other is to be found in the radically changed relation to difference, identity, and agency exemplified by that new hybrid itself, which figures both the utopian possibilities and the dangers of the posthuman. On the whole, although contradictions in Butler's work expose her own ambivalence about such a future, it is the posthuman alternative that provides the more compelling image of hope.

II. Agency, Dystopia, the Posthuman

Much of the repulsive force of classical dystopia comes from its portrayal of a world drained of agency—of an individual's capacity to choose and to act, or a group's capacity to influence and intervene in social formations. Theorists usually define agency as including both the capacity to choose for oneself and the capacity to act upon one's choices; both capacities are compromised in dystopia because the spheres of thought and of action are so severely constrained. The citizens of dystopia are gripped in a social formation so powerful, a web of control so densely woven, that at worst they do not even know they are not free; at best, they might attempt a rebellion, but it will be mercilessly crushed. Whether dystopia is an Orwellian place of fear and deprivation or a Huxleyan one of vapid contentment and plenitude, the individual who would choose or act "otherwise" (see Messer-Davidow) will be reprogrammed, exiled, or killed, so that the social fabric may maintain its impenetrability. The ideal citizen of dystopia is fully integrated with the social formation and has no self to express. The regimes of power in these classic dystopias understand free agency as based in individuality, and they use every means available to destroy any kind of identity that is separable from and potentially at odds with the collective. The realm of subjectivity is such a regime's primary locus of social control; without a clear sense of self, a citizen of dystopia will feel no need to rebel, even if means of rebellion were available.

The classic dystopian text thus speaks from and to the humanist perspective, in which the unique, self-determining individual is the measure of all things. Against the perversions of dystopia is set the model of a "truly human" life in which self-expression and self-determination are relatively unconstrained. Indeed, such self-determination is sometimes offered as a characteristic that sets human beings apart from (other) animals. This notion of the human assumes individual subjectivity as a natural essence rather than a social construct. The humanist subject asserts the incommensurate desires and thoughts of a particular self located in a particular body/mind. Agency is then seen as most authentic when the self asserts itself against some opposing social force or will; agency is enabled by the individual's separateness and independence from the social. The term "has been used to celebrate the victory of the individual not just over technology, or structure, or biology, but over all naturalistic causal accounts of action, however rich and complex" (Barnes 105). While the claims of the body may be considered in such an agent's process of choice, that process is intellectual, not physical, emotional, or intuitive. As is suggested by the association of agency with "integrity," a word connoting both wholeness and honor, the free agent is thought to be complete in himself, impenetrable; his boundaries are inviolable. I use the masculine pronoun advisedly here, as a reminder of the extent to which this humanist self has been conceptualized in masculine terms.

self critical

The understanding of subjectivity that informs this notion of agency has come under rigorous critique by a number of contemporary thinkers, most notably Michel Foucault, Louis Althusser, and their later interpreters. It is a critique that has taken both dystopian and utopian forms. In the most pessimistic versions of this argument, the modern subject is seen as thoroughly decentered, multiple, and fluid; its desires are entirely the product of social forces. There is no self to act or to be expressed. Although individuals may believe they are freely choosing and freely acting from a position of integrity, their choices and actions merely duplicate subject positions to which they have been "called." A person may believe herself to be bounded, complete, and independent; but this sense of unity or self-identity is itself a mark of the extent to which the subject exists in a state of subjection and is penetrated through and through by Otherness.

The loss of identity and agency that accompanies this version of the posthuman subject has become ever more entwined with issues of embodiment in recent decades, for the development of biotechnologies and cybertechnologies has given rise to the very concrete likelihood of significant changes in the human body as we have known it. The posthuman subject will be concretized in a posthuman body, whose individuality can be modified by appearance-altering surgeries, cyber-prostheses, and even the repair of defective genes. Many fear that a new servitude awaits the product of these new technologies, which augur the obsolescence of the "natural" human. The possibility of free agency seems to disappear if the embodied self becomes endlessly variable or if it is reduced to a particular configuration of genetic code, accessible to surveillance and manipulation by those in positions of social and financial power. Even the erasure of the physical limitations of the human body can seem to entail the erasure of humanity itself, or at least of some fantasized essence for which despite ourselves we feel a desperate nostalgia. The posthuman body, like the posthuman subjectivity it concretizes, seems to bode a self so vulnerable, so permeable and unstable, that it will be incapable of agency.

However, the posthuman subject and body can also carry a more utopian valence. Writes Susan Squier, "Posthumanity is not only oppressive (though it can be that), but can also affirm linkages: to other psyches, other species (animal and vegetable), and other agencies, from the technological to the multiple and intrapsychic" (128). The work of feminist theorists has been instrumental in developing this positive analysis. Such a concept of subjectivity as multiple and fluid opens spaces for transformative encounters with difference. Difference may represent a threat to the unified humanist subject, who is defined in and exercises agency through opposition to some Other; but the posthuman subject, a location where differences intersect in unstable configurations, can always make room for more. If the boundaries of the self are permeable, selfhood can be understood as bearing endless potential for changes more fundamental than the organic "unfolding" or realization of some essential self in the humanist model. Donna Haraway has famously heralded the prospect of the new "cyborg," embodying the liberatory potential of the posthuman subject and body. Her much-cited essay "A Cyborg Manifesto," though far from uncritically celebratory of technoscience, argues for "pleasure in the confusion of boundaries" between human and animal, human and machine, male and female, self and other (150). In the cyborg, the old human imperfections are prosthetically corrected; psychotropic technologies reconcile the spirit that is willing with the flesh that is weak. The loneliness and rigidity of the humanist body are eased. The posthuman body need no longer be confined to one gender, one sexuality, one race, one subjectivity; no longer even confined to what William Gibson terms the "meat" of the organic, as the body melds with machines (6). In its cyborg wisdom the posthuman body refuses fixity, definition, boundaries.

Other feminist theorists have also presented the multiplicity of the posthuman subject as a source of political resistance. In some cases they have argued that the fissures in this decentered self can bring an epistemological advantage to members of disadvantaged groups. Black feminists such as Deborah King and Kimberle Crenshaw find that the "intersections" of their conflicting identities make it possible to develop powerful critiques of the interactions of subordination and domination in each of their various grounds for identity. Gloria Anzaldúa develops *mestizaje* (mixed-race consciousness) or border-dwelling as a flexible version of selfhood, one less likely to lead to the oppression of others. And Rosi Braidotti proposes "nomadism" as a transdisciplinary, polyglot style of thought involving "an acute awareness of the nonfixity of boundaries" and "the intense desire to go on trespassing, transgressing" (37). For Braidotti's nomad, identity is serial; many different styles of being or thinking may be used as needed and then set aside. The parallels with Butler's universe-roaming, hybridizing, shape-shifting aliens are not difficult to trace.

Feminist theorists such as Susan Hekman and Diana Meyers have also done important work in formulating new understandings of agency that are compatible with this more positive approach to the posthuman subject.[2] When power is understood not as a monolithic structure that immobilizes all within its reach, but rather as a constantly shifting interplay of forces and tendencies, the self must be seen as a hybrid of many conflicting discursive formations; as a result of those very conflicts, spaces can open up for resistance, spontaneity, self-creation. According to Paul Smith, the very contradictions among the subject positions we inhabit give rise to the possibility of resistance; agency begins in a "*disturbance* in self-certitude and epistemological cernment" (78, emphasis added). And as Judith Butler puts it, "one is . . . in power even as one opposes it, formed by it as one reworks it, and it is this simultaneity that is at once the condition of our partiality, the measure of our political unknowingness, and also the condition of action itself" (241). The subject is always constituting discourse as well as constituted by it, and can act only out of this dialectic process. If this is so, agency cannot be entirely a matter of individual autonomy. In accord with such an understanding, Ann Donchin writes, "Autonomy in the strong relational sense is both reciprocal and collaborative. It is . . . not solely an individual enterprise but involves a dynamic balance among interdependent people tied to overlapping projects. Moreover, the self-determining self is continually remaking itself in response to relationships that are seldom static. . . . the self exists fundamentally in relation to others" (239). Such a relational self, unlike the self-contained humanist self, does not premise its free agency upon uniqueness or separation, and thus is capable of forging a posthuman autonomy.

In *Xenogenesis*, Octavia Butler explores both the dystopian dangers and the utopian potential of this imbrication of selfhood, agency, and the posthuman. She posits an alien race whose very nature is premised upon metamorphosis and boundary-crossing by way of its practice of gene-trading. The Oankali's goal is not to preserve an essential species identity, but always to be transforming themselves into something else. For them, restriction to an unchanging shape or a fixed identity would mean the end of life. They have roamed the universe for millennia, hybridizing themselves with life forms they encounter; the process involves their own irrevocable evolution as well as that of their trading partners. Thus in many ways, for Butler's readers, coming to terms with these aliens involves coming to terms with the posthuman. As Eric White has noted, the trilogy "can be said to intervene in and reverse a tradition of paranoiac responses to evolution in which Nature in effect persecutes Culture," and it succeeds in "exorcising the spectre of 'human nature'" (400, 407) as a cherished essence that needs only to be purified, not transcended. The name of the Oankali recalls the Hindu goddess Kali, emblem of creative destruction; adorned with skulls and dancing upon dead children, she kills in order to bring about renewal and rebirth. Successfully challenging the humanist linkage between humanity and freedom, between identity and agency, Butler's trilogy conveys both the beauty and the horror of a future in which the self-determining humanist self has dissolved and the human body as we know it will have changed or even disappeared.

III. Decentering the Human: *Dawn*

In the first volume of the trilogy, Butler evokes and then places into question our fears of the posthuman body and faith in "the human" as a locus of transcendent value. The opening of *Dawn* employs many of the common tropes of dystopia—and indeed, of alien abduction accounts. Humankind has all but destroyed itself in a nuclear exchange, from which a few survivors have been rescued by the Oankali. The protagonist, Lilith, is held captive by inscrutable, invisible beings who keep her under constant surveillance. She is "awakened" from and returned to suspended animation as they determine, without her knowledge or consent. She is isolated from her kind. She is interrogated. Her own questions are met with silence, for power need not explain itself to the powerless. She is refused reading matter and writing materials. Eventually, she learns that her captors have chosen her for a function she would not have chosen for herself: to select and to "mother" a group of other humans whom she must persuade to participate in the Oankali gene-trade. To her own wishes, the Oankali appear entirely indifferent. If she refuses to cooperate, she will be returned to suspended animation. In physical terms, she is reasonably comfortable and well cared for. Once her isolation is broken by contact with an Oankali, the worst aspect of her situation is the loss of choice and agency. She is infantilized, unable to obtain food for herself or to leave her room without assistance. She is "adopted" by an alien family without having been consulted.

Not "permitted even the illusion of freedom," no longer capable of directing her efforts toward her own goals, she feels she has become nothing more than a "useful [tool]," an "experimental animal" (56, 58, 60).

Furthermore, her physical integrity has been broken, her boundaries penetrated. The Oankali's powers of surveillance extend to a level never conceived of by George Orwell; they have "read" not simply Lilith's face and voice, but also her DNA, like a book, and "done a certain amount of rewriting" (135). She vehemently objects to this tampering with her essential self, even when the changes are to her advantage. For instance, her genetic tendency to cancer has been "repaired," but she feels this to have been a violation, for "she did not own herself any longer. Even her flesh could be cut and stitched" (6). And when her Oankali companion Nikanj wants to increase her memory capacity so that she can better understand the Oankali language, she protests, "I don't want to be changed!" (76). Lilith clings to her limitations, even to a disease that will kill her, rather than give up her sense of self-control and independence, or her belief in an inviolate self. The "trade" initially offered by the Oankali does not include a constituting role for humans, except in the sense that their genetic materials will constitute elements of the new species. The humans are deployed by the aliens toward an end they have not chosen and cannot participate in shaping. Foucault argues that resistance to oppressive power becomes possible at cultural nodes where contradictory discourses come into conflict; "points of resistance are present everywhere in the power network" (76). But the humans face in Oankali culture an apparently seamless form of power. The humans' genetic codes (discourses that the Oankali deploy and even plunder) are not accessible to their own manipulation. Simply put, the humans are outclassed by the aliens' greater capacities. Benevolent tyrants, the Oankali believe that their greater powers and knowledge give them the right to choose what is best for the humans and to act accordingly. Though Lilith does agree to participate in the Oankali plan, she continues to think about how she might escape their power, once she has been returned to Earth. Lilith's objection to any change in her essential self, however beneficial, is writ large in the opposition of all the humans to the prospect of "trading" genetic material with the Oankali and producing children who are no longer human. Altogether, this seems at first to be the classic dystopian plot in which an oppressive hegemonic reality—the Oankali and their project—is opposed by a narrative of human resistance and liberation (see Baccolini).

But here is where Butler begins to shift the ground of judgment by casting into doubt the legitimacy and even wisdom of the quest for human survival. Though the humans understand themselves to be free agents, their actions bear out the Oankali view that human beings are driven by a fundamental "contradiction" or genetic flaw: a combination of intelligence and hierarchical behavior that leads to competition and violence in political as well as personal spheres. Throughout the trilogy, those human beings who hold most tightly to their human identities are also the ones who exhibit the worst elements of humanity. Whether out of stupidity or calculation, they rape, steal, mutilate, and murder, all in the name of keeping intact their supposedly superior species identity. Nevertheless, the ideal of the "human" remains a standard and a refuge. In one telling exchange, after Lilith has rescued Alison from a rape attempt, Alison asks, "Are you really human?" and Lilith replies, "If I weren't human, why the hell would I care whether you got raped?" (180). These human beings would all be dead, as a result of human actions, if they had not been rescued by the aliens. Yet they persist in believing the human superior to any new form into which they might evolve—no matter how evidently superior their "oppressors" might be. With most of them, their opposition appears more an irrational psychological resistance than a true desire for liberation.

One source of this resistance is certainly anxiety about the permeability and fluidity of a posthuman body without firm boundaries. Butler vividly evokes the visceral terror the humans initially experience upon seeing the Oankali. Even when more accustomed to the physical appearance of the aliens, they find the thought of having children who "won't be human" deeply repellent. In this particular manifestation of their constantly evolving identity, the Oankali have a humanoid form but are covered with sensory tentacles (247). From these sensory organs they shoot out "filaments" that can probe and "taste" the very genetic structure of another being or substance. In this way, the Oankali can also communicate directly with each other's neurological systems; truly they are "wired" for a kind of virtual reality. The Oankali are constantly penetrating and being penetrated, dramatizing a terrifyingly limitless intimacy. The Resister humans call the Oankali "worms"—a term emphasizing the qualities of softness, shapelessness, and permeability which seem to them so disgustingly inhuman, and which are so at odds with the humanist conception of the self. "Worm," as it happens, is also the epithet used by the Terrans to describe their Tlic captors/partners in "Bloodchild," another of Butler's explorations of the horrors and attractions of accommodating the posthuman.

The humanist ideal of rational self-determination is similarly challenged by the Oankali's driving need to find and merge with newness. This need is described as a hunger; to be separate from others is to starve. Their processes of perception and learning are most often characterized as "tasting," and in a very real sense they "feed upon" the organisms whose genetic imprints they so voraciously take into their memories. The English language tends to characterize knowledge in terms of more ethereal senses: we come to "see" a new idea or to "hear" what someone teaches us. Sight and hearing are both forms of sensation that can be experienced at a great distance from what is sensed. Even when we say we "grasp" a concept, the buried metaphor is of taking something into our hands so as to be able to possess it, or to use it as a tool. The Oankali, by contrast, literally take knowledge into themselves, make it a part of themselves, and pass it on to others in the intimate exchanges of linked neurological systems. Their delectation of the strange must happen at close range; it is not possible without a literal merging of self with otherness; nor is it a "taste" they can choose not to exercise. It is a "certainty of the flesh" that literalizes the impossibility of isolated individual agency and consciousness (476). By thus creating "bodies that know," writes Stacy Alaimo, "Butler radically challenges the oppositions between body and mind, nature and culture" (53). This hunger must qualify any characterization of the Oankali as all-powerful slavemasters; their own freedom is curtailed by the instincts which drive them—as is the case for humans, Butler has said (Potts 332). It is clear that the humans feel that to lose their species identity by merging with the Oankali would mean the loss of the independent agency that they see as essential to humanity. At one point Lilith advises Nikanj that the humans who have attempted an escape should not be forced to return: "Otherwise people who decide later to come back will seem to be obeying you, *betraying their humanity* for you. That could get them killed" (246, emphasis added). Here in a nutshell is the ludicrous illogic of the human thinking about humanity. To choose otherwise than solidarity with other humans, against all others, is perceived as a betrayal of humanity; the punishment for this betrayal is a violent death at the hands of one's own kind. Where is the free agency in such a "choice"? And what is there, in such a vengeful and xenophobic humanity, to which any rational being would wish to remain loyal?

The humans' fear of the loss of self-determination is also evident in their reactions to the seductiveness of the ooloi, the "third sex" of the Oankali, who mediate all mating and reproduction. Giving off a pheromone that is irresistibly seductive, they lure humans into neurophysical linkages that are exquisitely pleasurable yet involve complete loss of agency and a terrifying dissolution of the boundaries of the self. It is more than once described as like "drowning" (454). The filaments of the ooloi's tentacles penetrate to the very nervous system, creating a state similar to cyberpunk accounts of being directly plugged into a computer. When two humans are linked through an ooloi, they feel each other's sensations as well as their own and those of the ooloi, and their pleasure is multiplied.

This coupling—or rather, tripling—is a virtual experience, an out-of-body experience; the humans plugged into the ooloi are unconscious, passive, not actually touching each other, yet more perfectly joined than is possible through the human sensorium. In ways much inflected by the issue of agency, the humans feel dirtied and shamed after having given in to this seduction. The men find the experience particularly humiliating, for once penetrated by those filaments, they feel they have been feminized. After his seduction, one man is angry because he was "not in control of what his own body does and feels. He's taken like a woman. . . . Someone else is pushing all his buttons" (203). Another feels his "humanity was profaned" and "manhood . . . taken away" by the coupling (192). As Dorothy Allison characterizes their feelings, the attraction of the ooloi seems to be that of enslavement, "as if the slavemasters had gotten under their skin" (478). Perhaps this is why Butler imagines the humans as unable to touch each other in loving ways once they have bonded chemically through an ooloi. The exquisite pleasures of posthuman sexuality make human pleasures obsolete. And if "love is chemical," suggests Frances Bonner, "the element of choice has disappeared" (54).

These alluring ooloi, with their capacity to manipulate DNA and their pressing upon the humans a metamorphosis into something no longer human, serve as a figure for the power and attraction of biotechnologies and cybertechnologies that offer us unimaginable gains at unpredictable costs. These humans have already benefited from such gains: their genetic tendencies to disease have been corrected, any injuries are quickly repaired, their strength and memory have been increased, and their lifespan has been increased to 500 years. The children who result from the exchange will be able to enter into symbiosis with living and self-aware environments; to generate food and shelter without labor; to communicate directly with others, to merge completely, to know the "flavor" of another's DNA more intimately than one human being can ever know another through the human senses. Although one of the Oankali asserts that through the gene-trade the humans will become not better, only different, it is clear that the Oankali have amassed ever-greater powers and sophistication through their long history of gene-trading. Free of both self-destructive and violent tendencies (unless one considers their "trading" itself to be a form of violence), extremely long-lived and healthy, brilliantly intelligent, capable of mind-melding and many other superhuman feats, the Oankali represent a state of being that matches point by point many utopian fantasies of a better human future, an improved human type. And yet, because to merge with the Oankali would bring the disappearance of the human type and the diffusion of the humanist subject, such metamorphosis is regarded with horror by the human beings to whom it is offered.

The Oankali, by contrast, feel no species loyalty. With every "trade," they too will be transformed, not simply augmented. The best qualities of each group will be combined into something new. As Nikanj says to Lilith, when she objects to his prediction of a changed family structure once the genetic trade is complete, "Trade means change. Bodies change. Ways of living must change. Did you think your children would only *look* different?" (260). While the Humans desperately hold to a sense of individual integrity which they believe to be endangered by species change, the "Oankali seek difference and collect it. They need it to keep themselves from stagnation and overspecialization" (329). It is in their nature to be eternally changing their nature. Their hunger for the new is one characteristic that persists through each trade.

In *Dawn*, then, two narratives are established and placed into conflict— that of the aliens, justifying their practices; and that of the humans who attempt to resist those practices and cling to their human identity. As in many classical dystopias, we encounter an oppressive, nearly omnipotent, ubiquitous power from the perspective of a resistant consciousness, a rebellious soul. That human beings are stripped of agency, and that humanity itself is threatened, should signify the negative pole of the book's moral universe. But unlike classical dystopias, it is not clear which of these narratives is to be preferred. Though we might expect the resistant humans to represent a lost ideal to be recuperated or an endangered essence to be preserved, most of these human beings exercise agency in only the most brutal forms. The "human" world that we might expect to be posited as the hopeful alternative, the locus of value, here promises little more than a return to barbarism. The true horror has already occurred, and not as a result of predatory aliens: human beings themselves have already nearly succeeded in wiping out the species. Thus, the humans are imprisoned and enslaved most irrevocably by their own species nature. The actions of most of Butler's fictional humans bear out the Oankali's judgment that if human beings do not evolve toward posthumanity, their innate aggressiveness will destroy them. The genetic "contradiction" that drives humans to commit atrocities can thus be understood as the hegemonic reality that oppresses them, in which case the extinction of humanity in the genetic trade becomes the narrative of hope for escape from that oppression.

The second and third volumes of the trilogy achieve no satisfactory resolution of these ambiguities. Both further develop, in positive ways, the tremendous powers of the Oankali/Human hybrids, as well as the rewards of their intersectional subjectivity and relational autonomy. Yet *Adulthood Rites* asserts the justice of allowing humans to continue a separate existence in an only slightly modified form; and *Imago* portrays the intersectional or relational self, characterized in such positive terms by some feminist theorists of agency, as subject to terrible devolutions in the absence of stabilizing others. As is typical of Butler's work, this trilogy will arrive at only a qualified resolution of the problems it raises.

IV. Inhabiting the Posthuman: *Adulthood Rites* and *Imago*

As *Adulthood Rites* opens, some years have passed. Some humans have been returned to a rehabilitated Earth to carry out the gene-trade. Those who refuse to parent the hybrid offspring created with their genetic material have been allowed to escape and to found their own villages. Rendered infertile by the Oankali, who consider human beings too dangerous to be allowed to breed freely, these Resisters are described as having little to live for, other than the hope that somehow they will be able to breed among themselves or with "construct" children kidnapped from the trade villages where Humans and Oankali live, work, and raise families together. Their behavior continues to bear out, for the most part, the wisdom of the Oankali judgment, further destabilizing the meaning of the resistance plot. In *Dawn*, we looked through the eyes of Lilith, who comes to accept the inevitability of her situation, but never entirely to reconcile herself to the expected disappearance of her species. In this volume, we see both Oankali and Human life from the perspective of Akin, a construct child who combines traits of both species. Each Human/Oankali construct is the product of five parents. The genes of one Oankali and one Human male-female pair are mixed by an ooloi, who contributes the "organelle" that inhabits every cell of an Oankali, driving and enabling its capacity for metamorphosis (544). The resulting "seed" is implanted in one of the female parents. The construct children vary a great deal in appearance and capability; to some extent, they are experiments, the outcome of which is not assured. Here is another aspect of Butler's account that makes it inaccurate to see the Oankali as all-powerful oppressors. Despite the enormous detail and range of the ooloi's knowledge of those individuals with whom it bonds— knowledge that extends to the level of cell structures and DNA strings— just what the product of a mixing will look like, or how it will behave, cannot be entirely predicted. The constructs are protean, metamorphic, monstrous, like the posthuman bodies described by Judith Halberstam and Ira Livingston as "no longer part of 'the family of man' but of a zoo of posthumanities" (3). Like Haraway's cyborg, a construct is the product of symbiosis, boundary-crossing, merging with other beings; the structure of Oankali family life and biology assures that such boundary-crossing will permeate the construct's experience. Through Akin, Butler begins to explore just what it might mean to replace the human phenotype and sensorium with another more fluid and relational.

From before his birth, Akin embodies an intensely relational form of subjectivity. Even in the womb, he is touched by the sensory filaments of his family members, and after birth he experiences "[b]ody to body understanding." He comes to "perceive himself as himself," but also "to know that he was also part of the people who touched him—that within them, he could find fragments of himself. He was himself, and he was those others" (255). Furthermore, like the empaths of Butler's *Parable* books, he can directly experience any pain that he causes to others. His ability to "taste" the genetic makeup of his parents and siblings gives him a visceral understanding of the extent to which his identity overlaps with theirs. The close genetic and chemical bonds between family members are so powerful that siblings are "not complete without each other" (362). To a large extent, Oankali society is a structure made up not of individuals but of "groups of two or more people," starting at a very early age with the "paired siblings" who share a most intimate connection (437). Thus when Akin, still an infant in Oankali terms though talking and thinking at a very high level, sees one of his human kidnappers dying of an illness that an ooloi might have healed, his reaction is that it is "utterly wrong to throw away a life so unfinished, unbalanced, *unshared*" (326, emphasis added). His captor no doubt considers himself a free agent, acting in opposition to Oankali tyranny, but to Akin he is pathetically incomplete, because so thoroughly deprived of relation to others. To the Oankali, to "share" is to complete oneself, not to endanger oneself. In Haraway's words, "the aliens live in the postmodern geometries of vast webs and networks, in which the nodal points of individuals are still intensely important" ("Biopolitics" 228). To link with others is to enter into wholeness, not to lose oneself. This assumption is reflected in their complicated names, which are unique to each individual yet contain the names of their kin groups and their home "entity," as well as their ooloi parent and birth parent.

The merging of identities between Oankali is paralleled by their symbiotic relationship with the "entities" in which they live and travel. The Oankali create no machines, always preferring to "share" rather than to use. Holding all life sacred, they eat no animal food, although they have "assembled" animals called "tilio" to serve as transports. The very ships in which the Oankali travel are living and growing beings capable of communicating and of receiving pleasure, as are the larval forms of these "entities" which the trade villages inhabit. Aspects of villages that appear to be trees, grasses, houses, and so on, are actually parts of the larval ship that have been trained to grow in these ways, for the use of the inhabitants. The ability to work with the ships is one characteristic the Oankali "never trade away" (441). In an intriguing variation on the prospect of a cyborg future in which humans merge with machines, or machines replace the organic,

Butler envisions machines being replaced by organic, self-aware entities, whose own teleology is in symbiosis with that of the Oankali. A number of Butler's critics have addressed the persistent presence of the African-American history of slavery as a back-narrative to her stories.[3] One could, no doubt, characterize the ships and the construct animals as "slaves," in that they are controlled by those they were created to serve. I believe, however, that such a reading distorts the tone and flavor of Butler's descriptions, as well as her own statement that she is generally more interested in issues of "symbiosis" than of slavery (McCaffery 57). Both the ships and the tilio receive pleasure from the exchange of sensory information that occurs with any contact with the Oankali. Whatever their origin, there is no implication that these conscious beings experience any oppression in their service to their creators, or that the relation is exploitive.

Like other aspects of Oankali life, the Oankali political process involves a merging of subjectivities that resembles what Katherine Hayles calls the "distributed cognition of the emergent human subject" (290). We encounter this process when Akin, who has spent a good deal of time with Resister humans, comes to believe that a group of "Akjai" humans should be allowed to colonize Mars with Oankali help and to continue in their original form, just as the Oankali always keep an unchanged "Akjai" form in case a trade fails. Akin's empathic abilities have enabled him to share the grief of these humans, cut off from the purposefulness of caring for their own children or perpetuating their species. And combining both Human and Oankali qualities as he does, Akin feels that the uniqueness of the human being should be preserved. Even though he believes that human beings "are not free," that they are "held" by their contradiction, he feels they should be allowed to "be bound in their own ways," to have the "freedom" to fail (467, 468). His situation is one Diana Meyers describes as central to posthuman agency, in which "the tensions between the different dimensions of intersectional identity introduce a wedge of optionality that authorizes individual reflection and choice" (164). His intersectional identities, Human and Oankali, create in Akin an understanding that requires and enables action. But he can exercise no direct agency in a form we would recognize. In order to act toward his goals, he must enter the political process by merging with others.

First, through neurological linkage, he shares with an Akjai the experiences that informed his views, conveying "on an utterly personal level what he had suffered and what he had come to believe" (468). The Akjai then speaks to the "people" and asks for a consensus on the issue. Linked through the ship entity, adult Oankali and constructs engage in simultaneous transmission of their thoughts and feelings. Most Oankali believe that to allow the human species to continue and to reproduce in its present form would be "profoundly immoral, antilife," and that it would be a "cruelty" to condemn them to repeat their brutal history (475). But they change their minds when the Akjai conveys to them what it had experienced through Akin and also links them directly to Akin, so that they can feel his bewilderment and his conviction that Resister humans "must survive as a separate, self-sufficient species" (471). Having directly linked to Akin's consciousness, having felt what his "flesh" knows, they grant him the right to act on that "knowledge" (470). Thus, as in humanist models of agency, Akin as lone individual does bring about change in the collective. Yet, he does so through direct sharing of experiences, an opening of himself to others.

While acknowledging the utopian dimensions of the Oankali political process, Hoda Zaki has seen their "fusion via the creation of a group mind" as uncomfortably resonant with ideologies such as fascism, and it is true that individual identities seem to be erased or subsumed in the consensus-seeking process (243). Unnamed individuals "speak" at some points; and at others, "[m]any answers blended through the ship into one" (470). But the Oankali process does not erase difference. "Confusion, dissension" characterize the discussion before consensus is reached, and even though the People's ultimate decision is to allow and enable the Mars colony, most of them still believe the project is doomed (471). Thus, an individual has powerfully moved the collective to acknowledge an alternative view and to assist a dissenting group to achieve its wishes. A truly fascist consensus would brutally repress dissent to achieve a fully unified collective; but although the Oankali link their minds for purposes of decision making, the individual mind is never unaware of itself in this complex relation, nor must any individual give up an independent view once the decision has been reached. After a later group exchange, Akin describes the process as being "like Lilith's rounded black cloud of hair. Every strand seemed to go its own different way, bending, twisting, spiraling, angling. Yet together they formed a symmetrical, recognizable shape" (742). This resembles the form of agency described by Ellen Messer-Davidow as "neither a capacity of the individual nor a function of the social formation, but the co-(re)constitution of individual practices and social processes"; it is a "recursive" process which takes into account the claims of others on the self, as well as the self's claims on others (30).

Michelle Green has argued, on the basis of this successful project for human survival, that the *Xenogenesis* novels "illustrate how human agency can triumph over prejudice, violence, and essentialism" (187). By contrast, I see the Martian project as affirming neither the human nor human agency in any straightforward way. First, human nature as Butler portrays it does not appear to be particularly worthy of preservation. When Akin is kidnapped as a child, his kidnappers treat him roughly, drink to excess, and fight. He observes a revenge shooting in which several people are killed. Violent raids are common and there is a trade in kidnapped women and stolen construct children. Some of the villagers even want to cut off the tentacles of construct children to make them look more human—an action that Akin compares to cutting out someone's eyes. Despite some exceptions, such irrational fear, resentment, and brutality also characterize human behavior as Akin observes later in life. And although the volume ends with the apparent triumph of the Resisters' project, its final scene is one of refugees fleeing a village set on fire by looters—hardly a hopeful indication that the human "contradiction" can be overcome.

Ultimately, it is not human agency, but posthuman agency, that makes possible the survival of something like the human. Akin's intervention was necessary for the settlement project to be approved, and the project can be achieved only with the aid of the Oankali, who will terraform the planet and provide assistance in the initial stages. Furthermore, if nothing but confronting new survival challenges will put into abeyance humanity's violent tendencies (a view also dramatized in Butler's *Parable* series), they will be doomed to roam space for eternity, ever seeking out new places in which to escape their own natures. There can be no permanent home, only endless struggle, unless humanity changes in fundamental ways. At one point, Akin holds out the hope that chance, or random mutation, could resolve humanity's fatal contradiction. Ultimately, the Oankali decide that only carefully selected humans will be allowed to join the settlement project; and at least at first, they are to reproduce through ooloi, who will modify their genetic makeup so they can "breed their way" out of violence (497). Thus, although Butler's Resisters see their goal as to preserve the Human, they must become more like the Oankali in order to survive; and this evolution will not be one they themselves control or carry out. Already the Oankali "organelle," the element that carries the capacity for genetic change, is in every one of their cells. Although they disdain their fellow humans who have agreed to participate in the gene-trade and contribute to the next generation of Oankali, even the Martian colonists must evolve toward the posthuman or die.

In *Imago*, human characters and the fate of the human species become less and less central to the story. We encounter the posthuman yet more intimately in the first-person voice of Jodahs, another of Lilith's children and the first construct ooloi. At this point the human emigration to Mars has been under way for fifty years. But the evocation of the Mars colony as a utopian alternative has become peripheral to the drive of the narrative and is mentioned only occasionally from this point forward. In insect development, the "imago" is the perfected type; and the trilogy culminates not with an image of the colonists' life, "fully human and free," but with the completion of the new species, as well as the reconciliation of the participant Humans to this joining (531). Jodahs, Butler's most radical instance of the posthuman, is "the most extreme version of a construct—not just a mix of Human . . . and Oankali characteristics, but able to use [its] body in ways that neither Human nor Oankali could. Synergy" (549). Both its powers and its vulnerabilities inform Butler's exploration of the posthuman body and subject.

As the novel opens, Jodahs is entering its first metamorphosis and gaining the increased powers and sensory awareness of an ooloi "subadult." The fact that Jodahs develops as ooloi comes as a disturbing surprise to the Oankali, who had planned not to create construct ooloi in this generation of the trade. The combination of ooloi powers with human volatility is seen as extremely dangerous. Because the Oankali have harnessed the cell-growth power of the human "talent for cancer," Jodahs has "regenerative abilities" that enable it to quickly repair damaged tissue, even to grow new limbs for damaged beings. It can also change itself, to "create new forms" (547). Along with these increased powers, however, comes an increased vulnerability, a porosity of self. The construct ooloi's shape and scent, indeed its very existence, are dependent upon the presence of others. After linking with and healing a wounded human, Jodahs sometimes looks more like that person, sometimes takes on characteristics that it senses would please that person. So for instance, with the hostile Joao, who accuses, "You treat all mankind as your woman!" Jodahs begins to look like a woman Joao "used to dream about when [he] was young" (599, 604). This mutability means that without mates—without any permanent relation to others—Jodahs has no stable self. When wandering in the forest, it takes on traits of trees or animals, at one point developing webbed fingers and toes, at another finding its skin becoming "green, scaly" (610). It must return to its siblings in order to recover a coherent self. "It's easier to do as water does," says Jodahs, "allow myself to be contained, and take on the shape of my containers" (612). Only after finding human mates is Jodahs able to harness its powers and retain a coherent self. The price of its powers, then, is interdependence, to the point that an ooloi will die if one of its mates dies. As Roger Luckhurst comments, "openness, othering, 'radical' difference, brings its own terrors, its own peculiar depredations to perceived integrities of the self" (37).

The potential terrors of such interdependence are illustrated yet more dreadfully by Jodahs's paired sibling Aaor, another mateless ooloi. In the absence of any "container" to hold it, Aaor devolves to "a kind of near mollusc, something that had no bones left . . . it no longer had eyes or other Human sensory organs. . . . It could not speak or breathe air or make any sound at all" (674). In a provocative comment, one of its parents says, "it almost lost itself. It was becoming more and more what it appeared to be" (675). Where the humanist self is sometimes represented as endangered by the demands of relation with others, this posthuman self drifts "toward a less complex form" in the absence of such relation (681). Its body, starving for the intimate contact of neurosensory linkage available only to mates, undertakes a kind of suicide. Like Jodahs, Aaor must find mates before it can be "stable and secure in itself" (712). In the devolutions of her human/alien hybrids, Butler places into question any wholly utopian account of boundless posthuman subjectivity and mutable posthuman bodies.

Nevertheless, she concludes her trilogy with what is clearly meant to be a happy ending. Out of love rather than fear or capitulation, a group of Humans have agreed to mate with Jodahs and other constructs, and the Oankali collective has given its permission for the next stage of evolution to occur, the stage that will bring about the new species in its achieved form. Jodahs tenderly constructs and plants the seeds for the new town that will feed this new community. In the last line, Jodahs feels the seeds "begin the tiny positioning movements of independent life" (746). Jim Miller reads this phrase as an indication that "the humans have lost the worst elements of their xenophobia, and the Oankali have come to recognize the importance of individual autonomy. The seeds of a community based on collective cooperation that respects 'independent life' have been planted" (342). It does not seem to me, however, that this new community will be significantly different in character, structure, or culture from the community originally envisioned by the Oankali. The "independent life" of this seed is no different from that of the parent cells from which it was developed—cells unmodified by the genetic trade with humans. It is true that the Martian alternative, as Rebecca Holden observes, "makes it possible for many of the other humans to choose to stay . . . with Oankali mates without betraying, in their own eyes, the rest of humanity and thus themselves. . . . the recognition of the human view of reality and self-definition keeps the choice from being completely restricted and allows them to enter into their new cyborg positions with a clearer sense of themselves" (55). However, neither choice is achievable without collaboration, interdependence, and accommodation with the posthuman.

V. Conclusion

Where, then, are we left in Butler's ambiguous work? In her depiction of selves whose boundaries are both established by and overlap with those of others, Butler suggests the possibilities and the problematics of posthuman subjectivity and bodies. The rewards of the posthuman are ecstatic joinings, augmented consciousness and knowledge, the expansion and extension of self. In the Oankali pentangle of lifelong mates and in the extended families of children produced year after year for centuries there exists a harmony and security unknown to humanity. In the group process of consensus-making is a form of politics more intimate, more immediate, and more stable than any human structure could be. The costs of the posthuman are an intensified dependence and an apparent loss of individual identity and autonomy. But feminist theorists of agency would suggest that the entirely independent and self-determining subject was never more than a fantasy—and a destructive one at that. Although it is Butler's posthuman bodies that show most vividly the impossibility of a wholly integral self and the powers of a relational one, even her resistance plot underscores the need to overcome our allegiance to this fantasy.

On a literal level, Butler's biological essentialism does require biological evolution as the solution to the problems of human life, and thus would seem to eliminate politics from the equation, as Zaki argues. However, if we read her work as a metaphor rather than a manifesto, a different kind of political use might be made of it. Her extreme depictions of the humanist self, violently defending its integrity against the threatening Other, and of the posthuman self, struggling to maintain any coherence in the absence of constituting Others, might both be read as cautionary accounts of the excesses of humanist and posthumanist thought. In a sense, her work sets up and then blurs the false dilemma between integral and dispersed subjectivities, between an identity politics incapable of coalition-based action and an uncommitted postmodernism allowing itself to be shaped by, "contained" by, whatever opposition it encounters. In so doing, *Xenogenesis* certainly fulfills the role that Moylan has described for the critical dystopia: "making room for and giving voice to emergent forms of political consciousness and agency that speak to the conditions of the times" (192). In these novels, Butler ultimately asks her readers to set aside their fears of difference and of change, and to enter willingly into less absolutist, more relational ways of being and acting in the world.

Notes

1. For their questions, suggestions, and editing assistance, many thanks to Raffaella Baccolini, Tom Moylan, Nathan Stormer, and audience members at meetings of the National Women's Studies Association and the Society for Utopian Studies.
2. See also Gardiner; Mackenzie and Stoljar.
3. See especially Boulter, Helford, and Peppers.

Works Cited

Alaimo, Stacy. "Displacing Darwin and Descartes: The Bodily Transgressions of Fielding Burke, Octavia Butler, and Linda Hogan." *ISLE: Interdisciplinary Studies in Literature and Environment* 3.1 (1996): 47–66.

Allison, Dorothy. "The Future of Female: Octavia Butler's Mother Lode." *Reading Black, Reading Feminist: A Critical Anthology.* Ed. Henry Louis Gates, Jr. New York: Meridian, 1990. 471–78.

Anzaldúa, Gloria. *Borderlands/La Frontera: The New Mestiza.* San Francisco: Spinsters, 1987.

Baccolini, Raffaella. "'It's Not in the Womb the Damage is Done': Memory, Desire, and the Construction of Gender in Katharine Burdekin's *Swastika Night.*" *Le trasformazioni del narrare.* Ed. E. Siciliani, A. Cecere, V. Intonti, A. Sportelli. Fasano: Schena, 1995. 293–309.

Barnes, Barry. *Understanding Agency: Social Theory and Responsible Action.* London: Sage, 2000.

Bonner, Frances. "Difference and Desire, Slavery and Seduction: Octavia Butler's *Xenogenesis.*" *Foundation* 48 (1990): 50–92.

Boulter, Amanda. "Polymorphous Futures: Octavia E. Butler's *Xenogenesis* Trilogy." *American Bodies: Cultural Histories of the Physique.* Ed. Tim Armstrong. New York: New York UP, 1996. 170–85.

Braidotti, Rosi. *Nomadic Subjects: Embodiment and Sexual Difference in Contemporary Feminist Theory.* New York: Columbia UP, 1994.

Butler, Judith. *Bodies That Matter: On the Discursive Limits of "Sex."* New York: Routledge, 1993.

Butler, Octavia E. "Bloodchild." *Bloodchild and Other Stories.* New York: Four Walls, 1995. 3–29.

———. *Lilith's Brood.* Compilation of *Dawn,* 1987; *Adulthood Rites,* 1988; *Imago,* 1989. New York: Warner, 1989.

Crenshaw, Kimberle. "Beyond Race and Misogyny: Black Feminism and 2 Live Crew." *Words That Wound.* Ed. Mari J. Matsuda. Boulder: Westview, 1993.

Donchin, Anne. "Autonomy and Interdependence: Quandaries in Genetic Decision Making." Mackenzie and Stoljar 236–58.

Foucault, Michel. *The History of Sexuality.* Vol. 1. New York: Vintage, 1980.

Gardiner, Judith Kegan, ed. *Provoking Agents: Gender and Agency in Theory and Practice.* Urbana: U of Illinois P, 1995.

Gibson, William. *Neuromancer.* New York: Ace, 1984.

Green, Michelle Erica. "'There Goes the Neighborhood': Octavia Butler's Demand for Diversity in Utopias." *Utopian and Science Fiction by Women: Worlds of Difference.* Ed. Carol A. Kolmerten and Jane Donawerth. Syracuse: Syracuse UP, 1994. 166–89.

Halberstam, Judith, and Ira Livingston. "Introduction." Halberstam and Livingston 1–19.

———, eds. *Posthuman Bodies.* Bloomington: Indiana UP, 1995.

Haraway, Donna J. "The Biopolitics of Postmodern Bodies: Constitutions of Self in Immune System Discourse." Haraway 203–30.

———. "A Cyborg Manifesto: Science, Technology, and Socialist-Feminism in the Late Twentieth Century." Haraway 149–81.

———. *Simians, Cyborgs, and Women: The Reinvention of Nature.* New York: Routledge, 1991.

Hayles, N. Katherine. *How We Became Posthuman: Virtual Bodies in Cybernetics, Literature, and Informatics.* Chicago: U of Chicago P, 1999.

Hekman, Susan. *Moral Voices, Moral Selves.* University Park: Pennsylvania State UP, 1995.

———. "Subjects and Agents: the Question for Feminism." Gardiner. 194–207.

Helford, Elyce. " 'Would you really rather die than bear my young?': The Construction of Gender, Race, and Species in Octavia E. Butler's 'Bloodchild.'" *African American Review* 28.2 (1994): 259–71.

Holden, Rebecca J. "The High Costs of Cyborg Survival: Octavia Butler's *Xenogenesis* Trilogy." *Foundation* 72 (1988): 49–57.

Hurley, Kelly. "Reading Like an Alien: Posthuman Identity in Ridley Scott's *Alien* and David Cronenberg's *Rabid.*" Halberstam and Livingston 203–24.

King, Deborah K. "Multiple Jeopardy, Multiple Consciousness: The Context of a Black Feminist Ideology." *Signs* 14.1 (1988): 42–72.

Luckhurst, Roger. "'Horror and Beauty in Rare Combination': The Miscegenate Fictions of Octavia Butler." *Women: A Cultural Review* 7.1 (1996): 28–38.

Mackenzie, Catriona, and Natalie Stoljar, eds. *Relational Autonomy: Feminist Perspectives on Autonomy, Agency, and the Social Self.* New York: Oxford UP, 2000.

McCaffery, Larry. "An Interview with Octavia E. Butler." *Across the Wounded Galaxies.* Ed. McCaffery. Urbana: U of Illinois P, 1990. 54–70.

Messer-Davidow, Ellen. "Acting Otherwise." Gardiner 23–51.

Meyers, Diana Tietjens. "Intersectional Identity and the Authentic Self." Mackenzie and Stoljar 151–80.

———. *Self, Society, and Personal Choice.* New York: Columbia UP, 1989.

Miller, Jim. "Post-Apocalyptic Hoping: Octavia Butler's Dystopian/Utopian Vision." *Science-Fiction Studies* 25.2 (1998): 336–60.

Moylan, Tom. *Scraps of the Untainted Sky: Science Fiction, Utopia, Dystopia.* Boulder: Westview, 2000.

Peppers, Cathy. "Dialogic Origins and Alien Identities in Butler's *Xenogenesis.*" *Science-Fiction Studies* 22.1 (1995): 47–62.

Potts, Stephen W. "'We Keep Playing the Same Record': A Conversation with Octavia E. Butler." *Science-Fiction Studies* 23.3 (1996): 331–38.

Smith, Paul. *Discerning the Subject.* Minneapolis: U of Minnesota P, 1987.

Squiers, Susan. "Reproducing the Posthuman Body: Ectogenetic Fetus, Surrogate Mother, Pregnant Man." Halberstam and Livingston 113–32.

White, Eric. "The Erotics of Becoming: *Xenogenesis* and *The Thing.*" *Science-Fiction Studies* 20.3 (1993): 394–408.

Zaki, Hoda. "Utopia, Dystopia, and Ideology in the Science Fiction of Octavia Butler." *Science-Fiction Studies* 17.2 (1990): 239–51.

CHAPTER 6

"A useful knowledge of the present is rooted in the past": Memory and Historical Reconciliation in Ursula K. Le Guin's *The Telling*

RAFFAELLA BACCOLINI

Il tempo mi appare come una cosa corpulenta, da quando lo spazio non esiste più per me. . . . Il tempo è la cosa più importante: esso è un semplice pseudonimo della vita stessa. . . . E' vero che ora per me il passato ha una grande importanza, come unica cosa certa della mia vita, a differenza del presente e dell'avvenire che sono fuori della mia volontà e non mi appartengono.[1]
—Antonio Gramsci, *Lettere dal carcere*

I. Introduction

The Telling, the long-awaited new novel by Ursula K. Le Guin, is the first full-length Hainish series novel in more than twenty years. Prior to this, Le Guin had in fact written mostly short stories and novellas set in the Hainish universe, of which the most recent is *Four Ways to Forgiveness*. Her new novel is a continuation of this collection in terms of both themes and genre. Like *Four Ways*, *The Telling* is concerned with history and with the portrayal of a dystopian world. The novel also represents her first full-length exploration of dystopia since *The Word for World Is Forest*. Like that novella, it is, once again, a story of cultural contact, the kind of anthropological science fiction that is characteristic of Le Guin's work. Like *Word*, the new novel deals with the survival of culture and is related to historical facts—the Vietnam War (*Word*) and the Cultural Revolution in China as well as the rise of religious and secular fundamentalism (*Telling*). Furthermore, they are both, more or less overtly, critical dystopias.[2] But besides being a story of cultural contact, *The Telling* presents a quest for identity for its protagonist, one rooted in knowledge of history, memory, and acceptance of responsibilities. Given these themes, it is useful to read the novel in the context of the following debates: the relationship between the utopian genre, history, and memory; and the thorny issue of historical forgiveness. Any discussion of the past and memory, in fact, seems to be connected to the issue of reconciliation (reparation and/or compensation). Le Guin's novel centers on such issues, and in the course of her narrative she provides insights into these themes, ultimately suggesting that if happiness and despair are the conditions of the citizens of utopia and dystopia, respectively, knowledge and awareness are those of the protagonists of the critical dystopia. And it is memory and the recovery of history that lead to this more open and critical condition.

II. History and the Utopian Genre

All utopias and dystopias are dependent on their historical context for understanding, and yet the relationship between the utopian genre and history has always been controversial. The utopian society, normally located in time and space, entails by its very definition (*ou-topos* = no place; *eu-topos* = good place) a suspension from real time and space. The utopian space, especially in sf, is generally located elsewhere, both spatially and temporally. It often takes place on another planet and in the future. In the classical utopias, it is also located in a separate place, often an island, and its actions take place in a separate, but not really parallel time. According to some critics, such as Raymond Ruyer, Utopia entails the end of history: by representing perfection and, consequently, stillness, Utopia is a way to free humanity from the constraints of time. However, as Lyman Tower Sargent has repeatedly observed, very few utopias aspire to perfection, while most look back to an idealized or romanticized past that is then projected into the future.[3] Therefore, far from being an escape from history, Utopia is in fact a product of history and of the periods in which it has been created. Utopia, then, offers an alternative to the problems of a specific time and space. And yet, by its very nature, it is "forward-looking," thus contributing to the notion that it may sound paradoxical to speak of history and Utopia.[4] At the same time, by employing the convention of the journey, most classical utopias avoid historical process while supporting the idea that history is progressive.

Similarly, dystopia shows a complex relationship to history. On the one hand, like utopia it is normally located in time and space and requires a similar suspension from them; on the other, even more than utopia, it is immediately rooted in history. Its function is to warn readers about the possible outcomes of our present world and entails an extrapolation of key features of contemporary society. Dystopia, therefore, is usually located in a negatively deformed future of our own world. In this respect, it clearly appears as a critique of history—of the history shaping the society of the dystopian writer in particular. In order to do this, as Jean Pfaelzer says, dystopia often portrays a "historical collapse," almost "a regression" to a previous time (62). Thus, dystopia shows how our present may negatively evolve, while by showing a regression of our present it also suggests that history may not be progressive. Paradoxically, then, dystopia depends on and denies history. This feature, among others, has contributed to the categorization of dystopia as a conservative genre—as well as to its conflation with the anti-utopia. Moreover, dystopias show a profound interest in history and, more precisely, in its control, which often implies its revision and even erasure. Even such a statement as "History is bunk," from Aldous Huxley's *Brave New World* (22), discloses the dystopian government's attempt to mask its fear of the power of history by ridiculing it as irrelevant gibberish. And it is George Orwell's *Nineteen Eighty-Four*'s (in)famous Party slogan that more aptly summarizes dystopia's relationship to history: "Who controls the past ... controls the future: who controls the present controls the past" (32). From Katharine Burdekin's *Swastika Night* to Orwell's *Nineteen Eighty-Four* to Margaret Atwood's *The Handmaid's Tale*, information about the past and the present is strictly controlled and manipulated by those in command. History, its knowledge, and memory are therefore dangerous elements that can give the dystopian citizen a potential instrument of resistance. But, whereas the protagonists, in classical dystopia, usually do not get any control over history and the past, in the critical dystopia the recovery of history is an important element for the survival of hope.

Despite this connection of history with hope and resistance, after 1989, with the fall of the Berlin Wall and the "end of ideologies," thinkers such as Francis Fukuyama announced the end of history and, consequently, the end of utopias. In his controversial essay "The End of History?" Fukuyama argues that society has entered a new and lasting phase and that this change is so dramatic that it might be best represented as the end of history. The twentieth-century battles of ideologies (between Western liberalism, communism, fascism; and between capitalism and socialism) came to an end with the fall of communism in 1989, when, according to Fukuyama, free-market liberalism universally triumphed. Such an argument suggests that history seems to derive only from struggle; once the struggle between political ideologies has ceased, history comes to an end.[5] Similarly, for Russell Jacoby, the end of history entails the end of ideologies and of utopianism, so that "radicalism now lacks historical force or future" (9). For him, "it is clear that radicalism and the utopian spirit that sustains it have ceased to be major political or even intellectual forces" (7). The end of history, then, brings with it the end of Utopia. Once humanity's desires are replaced by consumer demands and, thus, are fulfilled by the ideology of free-market liberalism, there is no more space for utopian longing, or utopian longing is co-opted. Consequently, Fukuyama laments an inability of our present to foresee a better future: "In our grandparents' time, many reasonable people could foresee a radiant socialist future in which private property and capitalism had been abolished. . . . Today, by contrast, we have trouble imagining a world that is radically better than our own, or a future that is not essentially democratic and capitalist. . . . We can also imagine future worlds that are significantly worse than what we know now. . . . But we cannot picture to ourselves a world that is *essentially* different from the present one, and at the same time better" (qtd. in Jacoby 10).

Despite Fukuyama's and others' predictions, "spaces of hope"—to quote the title of David Harvey's book—continue to be imagined in the critical dystopias of this turn of the century. It is precisely the combination of utopia/dystopia and history that appears as one of the characteristics of the critical dystopia. History, together with memory, in fact, figures prominently in the critical dystopia of the 1980s and 1990s at the level of genre and theme. And the recovery and knowledge of history appear to be necessary elements to promote a utopian space. These critical dystopias read like *almost-historical novels*—novels in which history figures significantly and its recovery becomes a pivotal element both for the narrative structure of the critical dystopia and for the protagonist's quest.[6] In the classical dystopia, on the other hand, the recovery of history is often accompanied by a nostalgia for the past—its authors apparently forgetting that it is from that very past that the dystopian future originates—and it is never fully attained; and yet, it is presupposed that history, without the authoritarian state's interference, could be known objectively. In the critical dystopia, on the other hand, history is central and necessary for the development of resistance and the maintenance of hope, even when it is a dystopian history that is remembered. These novels, then, promote historical consciousness. In fact, the critical dystopian character is less naïve about the nature of historical knowledge and certainly is less nostalgic. A particular use of memory and history in dystopia, then, can reveal a critical or a nostalgic attitude toward the past.

III. History, Memory, and their Value for Utopia

> *We speak so much of memory because there is so little of it left.*
> —Pierre Nora, "Between Memory and History"

Although history did not become a separate discipline until the Enlightenment, its value has always been recognized. Yet, it was not until Friedrich Nietzsche that the discourse about history was problematized. In *The Use and Abuse of History*, he argues that the past, and therefore memory and history, is functional and of use; yet he concludes his remarks with the recommendation to learn to forget.[7] Nietzsche, however, did not question the value of history per se; rather, he questioned belief in a historical past from which individuals might learn only a single truth. For him, writes Hayden White, "there were as many 'truths' about the past as there were individual perspectives on it. . . . Nietzsche divided the ways in which men looked at history into two kinds: a *life-denying* kind, which pretended to find the single eternally true, or 'proper,' way of regarding the past; and a *life-affirming* kind, which encouraged as many different visions of history as there were projects for winning a sense of self in individual human beings" (332, emphasis added). The division between a life-denying and a life-affirming value of history is similarly made for memory, and I would argue that an alternative way to spell out this distinction—one that will prove useful to my discussion of the value of history and memory to utopia—is to distinguish between anti-utopian, or conservative, and utopian, or progressive, features of history and memory.[8]

Indeed, like history—or, better, a certain attitude toward history—memory began to be questioned at the end of the nineteenth century. Whereas for ages memory had been an indispensable guide to life, by then societal transformations were occurring so rapidly that memory alone could not serve as a model of behavior (Gross 369).[9] After Nietzsche, thinkers and philosophers who dealt with the issue of memory did not attack the value of memory per se; rather, they identified different kinds of memory. They distinguished between a less valuable memory, like habits that tend to hinder individual growth rather than aid it, and a highly functional one—a distinction that, to a certain extent, had always been present in the debate on the art of memory.[10] Indeed, Western philosophical tradition has always identified two kinds of memories, distinguishing *recall* from *recognition*: Plato, Aristotle, Aquinas, and Augustine, for example, have all identified two types of memories, of which the second involves judgment and leads to knowledge (Yates 1–81).

Among the philosophers whose ideas about memory are relevant for utopian discourse is Ernst Bloch, who distinguishes "*anamnesis* (recollection) from *anagnorisis* (recognition)" (Geoghegan 58). For Bloch, recollection is conservative and precludes new knowledge because all knowledge lies in the past. In contrast, *anagnorisis* "involves recognition . . . [in which] memory traces are reactivated in the present, but there is never simple correspondence between past and present, because of all the intervening novelty. The power of the past resides in its complicated relationship of similarity/dissimilarity to the present" (Geoghegan 58). Bloch's value for a utopian theory of memory lies in his recognition of the importance of memory as a repository of experience and value. In order for memory and history not to hinder progress, and Utopia, there has to be room for novelty in memory, and history must not be cyclical (Geoghegan 59). Memory is therefore necessary to an understanding of oneself and of the past, but also of the present and the future, and acquires thus a social dimension.

This line of thought emphasizes the connection between memory and emancipation and forgetting and loss, another common trope of Western culture.[11] Theodor Adorno, in stressing memory as an act of resistance, warns us against the liquidation of memory that is taking place: "The spectre of man without memory . . . is more than an aspect of decline—it is necessarily linked with the principle of progress in bourgeois society. . . . This means no less than that the advancing bourgeois society liquidates Memory, Time, Recollection as irrational leftovers of the past" (qtd. in Marcuse 99). Similarly, Marcuse suggests that the erasure of memory leads to the one-dimensionality of the modern world, where remembrance is perceived as dangerous and subversive as "a mode of dissociation from the given facts, a mode of 'mediation' which breaks, for short moments, the omnipresent power of the given facts" (Marcuse 98). Memory, then, helps to break hegemonic historical discourse, the master narratives that have "managed to erase historical memory so that it is almost impossible to see that what is going on around us was not always the same" (Moylan, *Scraps* 26).

Thus, memory has a redemptive power that, according to Walter Benjamin in his "Theses on the Philosophy of History," also associates remembrance with hope: "To articulate the past historically does not mean to recognize it 'the way it really was.' . . . It means to seize hold of a memory as it flashes up at a moment of danger" (VI, 247). For Benjamin, "the past can be seized only as an image which flashes up at the instant when it can be recognized and is never seen again"; that is why memory is important, "for every image of the past that is not recognized by the present as one of its own concerns"—and thus is not remembered—"threatens to disappear irretrievably" (V, 247). Thus a society that is incapable of recollection, recognition, and remembrance is without hope for the future, as it shows no concern for the often silenced histories of the oppressed, the marginalized, the dispossessed: "it is only for the sake of those without hope that hope is given to us," Benjamin reminds us (qtd. in Marcuse 257). Historical amnesia therefore leads us toward Anti-Utopia and, together with nostalgia, it creates a false sense of the past as a better time. By leaving out "embarrassing" memories of an unjust past, official commemorations offer a sanitized version of history and thus extend injustice into the future and foreclose the possibility for change.

Therefore, the utopian dimension of memory, highlighted by Bloch, Benjamin, and others, cannot be separated from its ethical dimension. A link between memory, choice, responsibility, and action is also suggested by Adrienne Rich who, in "Resisting Amnesia: History and Personal Life," stresses the importance of recognizing the limits of white, middle-class feminism. For Rich, knowledge of the past is fundamental for resistance and change: "If it is the present that calls us to activism, it is history that must nourish our choices and commitment" (152). By analyzing the painful but instructive dialectic between change and continuity, she also stresses our responsibility and accountability in the choices we make:

> But you do have a choice to become *consciously* historical—that is, a person who tries for memory and connectedness against amnesia and nostalgia, who tries to describe her journeys as accurately as possible—or to become a technician of amnesia and nostalgia, one who dulls the imagination by starving it or feeding it junk food. Historical amnesia *is* starvation of the imagination; nostalgia is the imagination's sugar rush, leaving depression and emptiness in its wake. Breaking silences, telling our tales, is not enough. . . . Historical responsibility has, after all, to do with action—where we place the weight of our existences on the line, cast our lot with others, move from an individual consciousness to a collective one. But we all need to begin with the individual consciousness: How did we come to be where we are and not elsewhere? (145, emphasis original)

Such a theory of memory also acquires an ethical dimension. Only those who choose to remember are capable of taking responsibility for their actions and being accountable. Choosing to ignore or forget what was or what we did ultimately means avoiding responsibility and may lead to political paralysis.

Thus, by combining these different versions of memory and history, I would argue that their value for Utopia rests precisely in a theory of remembrance that is an important step for a political, utopian praxis of change, action, and empowerment, in that our reconstructions of the past shape our present and future. Memory, then, to be of use for Utopia, needs to disassociate itself from its traditional link to the metaphor of the storage, and identify itself as a process. As Utopia is a process, so memory needs to be perceived as a process, not fixed or reachable but in progress.

IV. History, Memory, Reconciliation

> *I don't think we ought to focus on the past. I want to focus on the future.*
> *I want to put that history behind me.*
> —Ronald Reagan

Any discussion of memory cannot avoid considering the theme of forgetfulness that is increasingly intertwined with the issue of reconciliation. In order to move beyond past conflicts, a widespread call for reconciliation is going on everywhere, so much so that Roy L. Brooks has claimed that "we have clearly entered what can be called the 'Age of Apology' " (3).[12] What is happening is certainly a complex and fascinating phenomenon that wavers between what seems to have become "contrition chic," on the one hand, and the recognition of guilt, the possibility of atonement and mourning accompanied by the possibility of settlement (rather than reparation) without apology, on the other. This raises the disturbing doubt that all this may be nothing more than a superficial operation to boost a nation's self-image. And beyond this very disturbing suspicion, the issue reveals the complex relationship between the need to remember and the need to forget in order to build the future.[13]

Many think that it is not necessary to hold on to the past because the past is an unnecessary burden, an obstacle to progress toward the future. U.S. President Reagan's comment during his visit to Bitburg Military Cemetery on 5 May 1985—the cemetery where SS soldiers are buried— suggests just that: a desire to move beyond the past, a desire for forgetfulness. Similarly, Australian Prime Minister John Howard said that while he was in power there would be no formal apology to Aboriginal Australians and that it was best to focus on the future: "It is time that we stopped this business about who was to blame for what may or may not have happened in the past" (Gordon on line). Prior to the establishment of the "Truth and Reconciliation Commission" in South Africa, the old regime had urged that the time had come "to forgive and forget" (Siebert on line).[14] Such positions of denial are obviously problematic and do not contemplate the possibility of contrition. Reagan, like the South Africans politicians, just wanted to get on and forget the whole thing, without even asking the victims if such a move is appropriate or even desirable. In so doing, he silences the victims, and secures for himself a power he does not and should not have. In his case, forgetfulness is the answer. And Howard is even more adamantly against the business of apology.

When contrition is part of the agenda, however, the issue becomes more complex. Episodes of contrition have certainly represented important moments in that they have marked a significant understanding and admission of responsibilities—an act of recognition. At the same time, not all acts of contrition for past wrongs have a practical follow-up in present-day life and politics.[15] The gesture of contrition does not lead to a substantial change in everyday life, but it certainly helps to revive pride in a nation's or a group's self-esteem. Therefore, one is left to wonder whether these often "empty gestures" are mostly done to make those who apologize feel good and to reaffirm the status quo. Even if they are not, but are nonetheless ineffective for a real change, what good are they—to the victims and in general? What is the value of repentance without some form of redress, whether monetary or non-monetary? How popular have these gestures become? To what extent have they been commodified and co-opted?[16]

Of all the recent requests for forgiveness, the Roman Catholic Church's document "Memory and Reconciliation," issued on the occasion of the Jubilee in 2000, is certainly unparalleled. Yet because of its language and argumentation, Rome's apology remains puzzling and problematic. In the history of the Church "there are no precedents for requests for forgiveness by the Magisterium for past wrongs" (International Theological Commission, 1.1 on line). However, the document makes a distinction between the Church, which is always "holy and immaculate" and therefore never wrong, and individual Catholics, who can and do make mistakes (1.2). It also argues that "sin is ... always personal," which means that today Catholics cannot be blamed for errors of the past, and, even more, that the Church is not responsible for personal sins (1.3). Furthermore, the "determination of the wrongs of the past" implies "a correct historical judgment" (4). Only when there is "moral certainty" that what was done individually by certain "sons and daughters" of the Church was perceived by them as wrong "can it have significance for the Church of today to make amends for faults of the past" (4). Moreover, in every form of repentance and in specific gestures connected with it, the Church "addresses herself in the first place to God" and not to actual victims (Conclusion), so that the purpose of the document is not "to examine particular historical cases but rather to clarify the presuppositions that ground repentance for past faults" (Introduction). Finally, in calling for the "purification of memory... [that] aims at liberating personal and communal conscience from all forms of resentment and violence that are the legacy of past faults," the document claims that "[t]his should lead to a corresponding recognition of guilt and contribute to the path of reconciliation" (Introduction). But the very use of the term "purification" seems to imply forgetfulness—that is, once the sin is atoned for, the memory of it is purified or cleared, and no trace of it is left. Therefore, the document, although unprecedented, makes apology a rather vague, if not outright ambiguous, and difficult process.

What these acts of contrition have in common is that church and state share a religious language and follow a script of guilt, atonement, and forgiveness that too often implies forgetfulness, thus doing very little to address the issue of reconciliation. Political leaders often insist on the need to overcome the contradiction between justice and memory, on the one hand, and reconciliation, on the other, with a form of negotiated reconciliation that, by erasing the past, cleans the slate for a new beginning and a new identity. For it is true that, as Maurice Halbwachs has argued, collective memory is one factor shaping a group's identity.[17] Thus, if too close an adherence to the past on either part may lead to a stall in the path to reconciliation, a reconciliation that does away completely with the memory of the past may very easily lead to denial and self-deception. The language employed and, consequently, the outlook and actions taken may well represent the difference between a superficial and a successful reconciliation. *Religious* forgiveness should not be a part of the discourse of *political, secular* reconciliation. Whereas reconciliation implies mutual acceptance that the past wrongs have happened and, in turn, acceptance of responsibilities followed by political and legal measures—thereby combining individual and collective action—forgiveness belongs to an individual, religious plane and cannot be requested or enforced as a political goal.

Le Guin's *The Telling* addresses the issue of reconciliation and offers an example of resistance to such a religious script. Against a superficial notion of individual forgiveness, the novel identifies a utopian process of memory and telling that leads to individual moral responsibility and awareness (a way of finding one's place in a historical context, of living in the present and past simultaneously) and possible individual and collective action (a way of building one's future). Such a process, which occurs in the exchange between the protagonist, Sutty, and her antagonist, Yara, opens a utopian horizon within the critical dystopia, one in which knowledge and awareness are fundamental to resistance. This horizon also encourages an acceptance of responsibilities—not a nostalgic, static condition but a vital, critical process of memory and knowledge that does not dwell on denial and guilt and is therefore also instrumental for an active sense of identity.

V. Le Guin's *The Telling*: "Conclusions led to new beginnings"

The Telling addresses the recent shift to the Right which Tom Moylan has summarized as "a shift to religious fundamentalism alongside a shift to a secular emphasis on individual entrepreneurial gain and an increase in physical and psychological violence against the non-privileged sectors of the population (with an accordant rise in racism and xenophobia, sexism, homophobia)" ("New Ground" 234–35). In the novel, Sutty, a young Anglo-Indian woman from Terra trained on Hain to be an Observer for the Ekumen, is sent on her first mission to the planet Aka. Because of the relative difference in time spans occasioned by travel in a Near-As-Fast-As-Light ship, Sutty arrives expecting simply to study the language and literature of Aka. However, she finds that Aka, now dominated by the new regime of the Corporation, has become a restrictive society dedicated to science and consumerism. She also learns that an ancient spiritual belief system, known as the Telling, has been banned and that the cultural history of that planet has been suppressed. Sutty, who has fled from religious intolerance and fundamentalism on Terra, ironically finds herself in a system that is equally intolerant (of religion) and fundamentalist with regard to profit and science. Assigned by her Ekumen Envoy to investigate, Sutty travels upriver to a remote mountain region, where she finds the remnants of the suppressed culture. She learns of this pocket of resistance at first through small details in behavior and ambience: use of outlawed words, and gestures, disregard for Corporation rules, and the stubborn resurfacing of the old writing on walls that shows through the faded paint. After winning the confidence of the clandestine culture and seemingly evading the surveillance of a Monitor, a Corporation agent, she joins a pilgrimage to the sacred mountain, Silong, where the last repository of books and historical treasures stands. Sutty's official, albeit covert, mission to find and record lost traces of the planet's past also becomes a private and personal quest. In order for her to understand the Akan past, she must come to terms with her own history and with her painful memories, particularly the death of her lover Pao at the hand of Terran religious fundamentalists. In her search to recover and preserve an endangered history, she discovers that she needs to do her own telling. In a series of challenging meetings, Yara, the agent who has followed her to Silong, and Sutty reveal to one another their painful pasts and are thus able to maintain their positions with respect and understanding. The novel ends on the critical question of how she and the Ekumen might intervene to save the old culture, the destruction of which may have been precipitated by her own planet, Terra.

In several interviews, Le Guin has stated that the initial impetus of the book was "what happened to the practice and teaching of Taoism under Mao," "a 2500-year-old body of thought, belief, ritual, and art" that was "essentially destroyed within ten years" (Gevers on line). However, the novel's themes and its open and fragmentary structure provide a larger commentary on the paradoxical and global rise of materialism and fundamentalism in the last few decades. *The Telling* reflects a similar shift in both the societies the author describes—the suppression of an ancient belief on planet Aka, and the dominance of a fundamentalist religion and the suppression of politics on Terra. Such dark visions of religious and secular fundamentalist worlds "have been fuelled by the rise, during the last two or three decades, of the fundamentalist side of every world religion, and the willingness of many people to believe that fundamentalism is religion" (Gevers on line). *The Telling*, therefore, with its combination of a religious fundamentalist society driven by the pursuit of materialist and scientific growth provides an extrapolated dystopia of our world.

Against this bleak scenario, Le Guin juxtaposes a fragmentary and open narrative, which, with the theme of Sutty's quest for history and memory—hence identity—counters dystopian pessimism with hope and responsibility.[18] The novel offers a powerful story of utopian resistance in the face of oppression. The unresolved ending of the novel with the bargaining meeting among representatives of the Ekumen, the Telling, and the Corporation opens a possible door toward utopia.[19] Le Guin has stated, in fact, her dislike for "conclusive conclusion" and has said that she prefers, instead, "to leave doors open" (Gevers on line). Such a strategy, together with the fragmentary nature of the novel, provides a "utopian" resistance, also at the level of form, to the dystopian fundamentalism of the events narrated. In fact, in Sutty's recovery of the Telling, the novel's events are enriched with stories, almost parables, that resist a traditional pattern of reading and explication. The central element of the stories is their ambiguity, as they problematize both Sutty's and the readers' certainties. The "Dear Takieki" story and, consequently, the book's open ending offer an example.[20] The story, like most in The Telling, leaves Sutty and readers puzzled as it lacks what we would recognize as a traditional conclusion, and its telling is not accompanied by any official exegesis. It serves, though, to confirm the idea that Aka is "a cash, not a credit, economy," where the reward, whether spiritual or material, is immediate and not deferred to an afterlife (171). Such a concept is what allows Sutty to tweak the Ekumenic principle of non-interference: because Terran missionaries have exchanged technological information for spiritual conversion—to the Akans a form of usury—the Akans "have been waiting for decades for [Terrans] to tell them what they owe [them]" (263). Akan mercantile culture—which has become more important with the new capitalist religion and which, up to that point, has been questioned by Sutty and the readers alike—lies also at the basis of the final bargaining and, therefore, is the very thing that produces the hopeful open ending. The structure and the events suggest, then, that there is no single truth, and that we are in real danger when we allow one idea to become the *only* idea. Paradoxically, it is through an economic view of society, otherwise criticized in the book, that such a point is made: every story, every event has at least two sides, a positive and a negative. While there is never *the* right way, there is equally no room for an indecisive relativism, for as the actions of the protagonists show, there is always an alternative. With Sutty, we are invited to remember that "Conclusions [lead] to new beginnings" (103).

VI. "Belief is the wound that knowledge heals": History, Literacy, and Memory

> *The first step in liquidating a people is to erase its memory.*
> *Destroy its books, its culture, its history.*
> —Milan Kundera, *The Book of Laughter and Forgetting*

Memory and the past are recognized as important elements in dystopia by both the regime and the individual citizen trying to understand and escape his/her condition.[21] As the quotation from Kundera suggests, in order to fabricate a single, true, hegemonic discourse, which citizens will unquestioningly follow, it is necessary to erase memory. Such a step was clear for Burdekin, who in *Swastika Night* describes the "erasure of memory," and for Orwell, who in *Nineteen Eighty-Four* describes the manipulation of history. Memory and the past are such important parts of dystopia because, paraphrasing Antonio Gramsci, the conditions of the dystopian citizens are not so different from those of a prisoner, who, having no control over space nor over the present and the future, can reside only in the past. This is also true for Le Guin's protagonist: in order to have a say over her present and future, Sutty needs to know the past. In her quest, then, she needs to bring her past into a living relationship with her present. In this utopian process of memory, history and the past—both official and personal—are fundamental elements in her double quest. She needs to recover, preserve, and study the culture of Aka and to come to terms with her own past and sense of self.

Both societies described in the book have gone through the erasure of memory. The Unists on Terra have proclaimed and initiated "The Time of Cleansing," when "Only one Word, only one Book" will remain, "all other words, all other books [being] darkness, error" (4–5). Similarly, on Aka, art and culture have been destroyed, all the temples and libraries blown up, and religion outlawed. Thus, Sutty has left behind "Terra and its holy terrorism" only to find on Aka a situation all too familiar to her, since the inhabitants of Terra "are living the future of a people who denied their past" (15, 12). The result, she thinks, is the same: "secular terrorists or holy terrorists, what difference?" (62).

Sutty's journey upriver to the town of Okzat-Ozkat allows her to find traces of "tattered remnants of the old way of life" (64). As her stay continues, she discovers fragments of what once was "a way of thinking and living developed and elaborated over thousands of years[,] . . . an enormous interlocking system of symbols, metaphors, correspondences, theories, cosmology, cooking, calisthenics, physics, metaphysics, metallurgy, medicine, physiology, psychology, alchemy, chemistry, calligraphy, numerology, herbalism, diet, legend, parable, poetry, history, and story" (98). In short, the Telling is "a religion of process" which is "very different from Terran religions, since it entirely [lacks] dogmatic belief, emotional frenzy, deferral of reward to a future life, and sanctioned bigotry" (102, 121). The transmission of such a heterogeneous system relies on the work of the "maz," professionals whose essential work is "telling: reading aloud, reciting, telling stories, and talking about the stories" (115). Thus, the very nature of this system and the fact that it has been destroyed make the connection between storytelling (language and history) and memory (literacy and education) even more important. Both have always been and still are extremely valuable for the survival of the culture and its people. The stories tell the world, but telling does not mean explaining (139). As Sutty discovers fragments of a lost "world made of words," memory assumes an even more central role for the preservation of such world—a principle that is clearly stated in *The Arbor*, one of the texts of the Telling: "the leaves of the Tree perish but always return so long as we see them and say them. . . . 'Mind's life is memory'" (127, 131). Every story that is not told and is not recognized as valuable by the present risks disappearing irretrievably, as Benjamin says.

The importance of storytelling for one's sense of self and for one's future is made clear in a pivotal scene, an encounter between Sutty and maz Elyed Oni: "It's all we have. . . . It's the way we have the world. Without the telling, we don't have anything at all. . . . Our minds need to tell, need the telling. To hold. The past has passed, and there's nothing in the future to catch hold of. . . . So what we have is the words that tell what happened and what happens. What was and is" (142). Language is then fundamental to one's identity, but once more Le Guin is careful to resist a Western insistence on "logos," the Word, and portrays a system that values difference and plurality, not one Word but many. The Telling can be said to offer a revision of Cartesian "I think, therefore I am" with "We tell, therefore we are." Only by telling the world may we get to know it; hence history and its knowledge are a major element of *The Telling*, just as they were in *Four Ways*, because learning is intrinsically linked with hope and change.[22]

History, memory, and the telling of tales are subversive elements in that they promote hope and the potential for change. In living their culture, the people of the Telling challenge the hegemonic discourse of the Corporation and create for themselves a way to attain freedom. By preserving knowledge and choice, crucial elements of change, they preserve the process of the Telling and save the nearly-utopian enclave of the library of Silong. Utopia then is maintained in the very choice to make memory and history the central subjects of the book. Knowledge, as awareness of the past and of who we are, also becomes a step to build change or a utopian possibility for the future. At one point, Sutty makes clear that knowledge— teaching Terran history to the Akans—could change their political situation (205). This idea is associated with Utopia, since sharing knowledge is one of the principles of the Ekumen, the utopian League of All Worlds (214). History and memory then represent an alternative to the hegemony of the social order, tools to dismantle the singleness of its discourse, while remaining attuned to the plurality of visions and limits of the past. There is no notion of a perfect, idealized past, just as there is no insistence on a single, true history, but only on the necessity of knowing the past as a way to attain freedom. History and the Telling are "ways of holding and keeping things sacred" (199). Asked about the importance of stories for remembering who we are, Le Guin has said:

> To remember, if my Latin is correct, actually means to put the parts together. So that implies there are ways of losing parts. Kundera [in *The Book of Laughter and Forgetting*] talks about this aspect of storytelling, too. In fact, he says that history, which is another kind of story, is often deliberately falsified in order to make a people forget who they are or who they were. He calls that "the method of organizing forgetting." History is one way of telling stories, just like myth, fiction, or oral storytelling. But over the last hundred years, history has preempted the other forms of storytelling because of its claims to absolute, objective truth. Trying to be scientists, historians stood outside of history and told the story of how it was. All that has changed radically over the last twenty years. Historians now laugh at the pretense of objective truth. They agree that every age has its own history, and if there is any objective truth, we can't reach it with words. History is not a science, it's an art. (Jonathan White on line)

Against the false, imposed, and singular story of the regime, memory, historical knowledge, and storytelling are instruments of resistance that create the utopian dimension of Le Guin's book. They do so because, unlike in classical dystopia, where the *art of memory* remains trapped in an individual, regressive nostalgia, in *The Telling* and in other critical dystopias the *culture of memory* allows for the formation of a collective resistance.[23]

VII. Reconciliation and Forgiveness in *The Telling*

> *Words are actions and they make things happen.*
> —Hanif Kureishi, *Intimacy*

In a recent interview, Nick Gevers has observed that Le Guin's newest works have "a strong reconciliatory air" (on line). In her answer, Le Guin stresses her preference for reconciliation over compromise. Although reconciliation as a coming to terms with the Other has always been one of her anthropological sf concerns, her recent fiction unequivocally addresses the issue of reconciliation. If forgiveness is the central element of her collection of novellas *Four Ways*, it is less overtly so in *The Telling*. Moreover, in *The Telling*, Le Guin moves away from forgiveness toward reconciliation. Consistent with its description of a system that is not a traditional religion, the novel similarly does away with the religious connotation in the notion of forgiveness and moves toward a more secular reconciliation. Hence, the closing meetings between Sutty and Yara propose understanding and acceptance of the past and of responsibility without the need for either forgiveness or forgetfulness. Sutty and Yara engage in a utopian process of memory and telling that leads to awareness and an acceptance of individual moral responsibility and possible individual and collective action. Such a process opens a utopian horizon within dystopia, of which resistance, liberating knowledge, and awareness are main elements. Having fulfilled the first part of her quest—the partial recovery of the Telling—reconciliation is what allows Sutty to complete the second: to come to terms with her past and, in so doing, to attempt to preserve the old culture. In order to enact a positive change in the system, she needs to accept also a transformation in her sense of self.

Through the story, Sutty's character evolves from the insecure Observer who feels she is failing because of her lack of detachment to a self-aware woman who takes responsibility for her actions. Despite the fact that the Envoy Tong Ov chooses her as the best suited Observer for the mission because she is a child of violence and conflict, Sutty keeps wavering between feelings of being all-mighty and all-powerless. But in her journey, she eventually learns to apply the underlying Hainish element in Ekumenical thinking: to "take responsibility" without cultivating guilt (19). Such a change makes her a good observer and listener, but also a good teller, even if initially a reluctant one. The lesson Sutty learns is one the Hainish share with the people of the Telling: "dharma without karma," or having a sense of duty, of doing right without necessarily believing in an afterlife—or taking responsibility in the here and now (102). The recovery of the Telling interwoven with Sutty's own telling of her traumatic past and her learning of Yara's painful recollections sets in motion a memory process that is essential for the utopian element of the novel.

In their meetings Sutty and Yara both acquire a liberating knowledge about themselves and their respective worlds. Despite her reluctance to meet with the Monitor, Sutty nonetheless faces her responsibility and conducts what initially sounds like a cross-examination. Things change with the second meeting, when, influenced by what she has learned from the Telling, she and Yara replace interrogation with dialogue. The macro- and micro-histories they learn allow them to transcend prejudice, to share their different and yet similar pasts, but most of all to challenge fundamentalist thought and open a path toward change. In this process, both share the burden of untold and painful stories whose telling becomes liberating and enacts a possible change. Sharing their stories allows them to move from pain, hatred, and misunderstanding to mutual respect, with no need for absolution of the crimes and the violence experienced: "The silence they shared after their words was peaceful, a blessing earned" (240). Their shared histories become a "dark foundation" for their new knowledge (242).

Only through this reconciliation can Sutty also reach healing and a personal balance. She needs to come to terms with her past, not to deny it, in order to accept her responsibility and find a fuller sense of self. Similarly, Yara accepts his responsibilities and chooses to take his life rather than betray Sutty and the others. Thus balance and reconciliation can be said to be one: reaching an understanding, acceptance of past and present rather than forgiveness between parties. History, memory, and knowledge, then, are the forces that allow such process: by knowing one's past and one's relationship to it we shape our sense of identity and we give ourselves the choice of acting on our present and future. What I have called the "utopian process of memory" is further suggested by the image that closes the novel. In the meeting at which the Ekumen representatives, the Corporation, and the people of the Telling bargain for the survival of the library at Silong, it is the memory of Pao and Yara that sustains Sutty: "But it was not the Monitor's, it was Yara's face that she held in her mind as the bargaining began. His life, Pao's life, that was what underwrote her bargaining" (264).

VIII. *The Telling* as a Critical Dystopia

> Hope is Memory that Desires.
> —Honoré de Balzac

In an article on the feminist dystopia of the 1990s, Jane Donawerth identifies two main features of recent women's sf writing: a) the urban apocalyptic spaces, repressive governments, dysfunctional families, problematic sex, prominent machines, and liberated gender roles that are "symbols for the dangers and possibilities of women's freedom"; and b) a nonlinear, fragmented, postmodern form that is often modeled on the slave narrative (49). Without calling such works "critical" dystopias, Donawerth recognizes in these novels a "place of birth" for hope and "political renewal" (62). To Donawerth's fine reading of these texts, I would add another feature that seems to be fundamental to defining such texts as critical dystopias: the presence of memory and history. Recovery of history and literacy, and individual and collective memory become instrumental tools of resistance for the (often female) protagonists of sf women writers' recent dystopias. Because authoritarian, hegemonic discourse shapes the narrative about the past and collective memory to the point that individual memory has been erased, individual recollection becomes the first, necessary step for a collective action. Whereas, in the classical dystopia, memory remains too often trapped in an individual, regressive nostalgia, Le Guin's novel and the other critical dystopias show that a *culture of memory*—one that moves from the individual to the social and collective—is part of a social project of hope.

My reading of Le Guin's novel, however, adds yet another element to the features of the critical dystopia, one that is also present in other novels such as Burdekin's *Swastika Night*, Atwood's *The Handmaid's Tale*, Octavia Butler's *Parable of the Sower*, and Marge Piercy's *He, She and It*. As I have argued elsewhere, these novels resist closure, and in so doing they allow their protagonists and readers to hope.[24] But they also suggest that happiness is not necessarily the condition of the citizen of a critical dystopia. The ambiguous, open endings of these novels maintain the utopian impulse *within* the work, for characters and readers alike, whereas in classical dystopia, utopian hope is available only to the reader *outside* the story. By rejecting the traditional defeat of the individual, these critical dystopias open up a space of contestation and opposition for those groups (women and other "ex-centric" subjects whose subject position is not contemplated by hegemonic discourse) for whom subjectivity has yet to be attained. But they also suggest that awareness and responsibility are the conditions of their protagonists. Thus, in the critical dystopia, even in the presence of utopian hope there is not much room for happiness. Rather, a sense of regret and of missed opportunity accompanies the awareness and knowledge that the protagonists have attained. Instead of an easily compensatory and comforting happy ending, the critical dystopia's open ending leaves its protagonist dealing with his or her choices and responsibilities. Although such a move may seem to move the dystopian text toward a more realistic framework, it is another radical element that contributes to the creation of the text's utopian horizon. It is in the acceptance of one's responsibility and accountability, often worked through memory and the recovery of the past, that we bring the past into a living relationship with the present and may thus begin to lay the foundations for a utopian change.

Notes

1. "Time appears to me as a huge thing, since space does not exist any longer for me. . . . Time is the most important thing: it is a simple pseudonym for life itself. . . . It is true that now the past is very important to me, as the only certainty in my life, differently from the present and the future that are beyond my will and do not belong to me."

2. Baggesen has already pointed to Le Guin's utopian pessimism in *Word*.

3. Among others, Suvin also argues that perfection "just does not exist as a requirement of the genre. . . . A radical change from the author's situation is clearly implicit in utopias, but it is not necessarily a final one that cannot be improved upon" (111).

4. Roemer, for instance, has persuasively demonstrated that many late-nineteenth-century American utopias are informed by a radical forward-looking perspective.

5. In order to work, Fukuyama's thesis must disregard a number of factors, for example, the revival of nationalisms in countries like Italy, France, Germany, and in eastern Europe, as well as what westerners often term the "rest of the world." These factors, together with the recent "clashes" that have led to the events of 11 September 2001 and beyond, seem a tragic but obvious refutation of Fukuyama's argument.

6. Although the historical novel is, by definition, set in the world that existed before an author's time, sf novels such as Piercy's *He, She and It* and Butler's *Kindred* are very much concerned with history—1600 Prague and the slave past, respectively. Jameson, after all, has already argued that "science fiction as a genre entertains a dialectical and structural relationship with the historical novel" and that both create "formal and narrative dislocation" in representing past or future in order to restore "our capacity to organize and live time historically" (523).

7. Nietzsche identifies three attitudes toward the past, which he calls monumental, antiquarian, and critical. Monumental historical awareness views the past as a source of models; it turns to the past for imitation of heroic action, thus risking mythologizing the past and looking at it with nostalgia. The antiquarian approach shows an indiscriminate reverence for the past, while the critical attitude criticizes the past in the name of the present in an attempt to free oneself from its claims. For Nietzsche we must first learn the past and then forget it.

8. Geoghegan has best explored the relationship between memory and utopianism. Questioning whether memory can have a utopian function, he notes that what "is most desired is missing in the often uncontrollable present but can be present in a controllable, if, in varying degrees, mythic, past," and claims that for many people "memory has a built-in utopian function" (54). It is important, however, to point out that not all desires automatically fit the notion of Utopia and that desire per se is not enough to qualify as Utopia.

9. Moreover, the past began to be linked to habits and conventions, which could become sources of paralysis in the modern world. The twentieth-century attack on memory is, then, really an attack on the value of habit, the repetition and remembering of something from the past or, in other words, a "remembering embodied in acts which have become automatic" (Gross 369). Though nineteenth-century philosophers expressed unconditioned support for the value of habit, modern writers and philosophers have not hesitated to show contempt for it. For a discussion of supporters and detractors of habits, see Gross.

10. Memory, for example, is of two kinds in Augustine: archaeological and processual. By the first, he means memory thought of in spatial terms: levels, layers, deposits of memory. Memory is something fixed and static, a site where the archaeologist of memories can dig down through layer after layer of deposits to recover what s/he seeks. By the second, he means a temporal rather than spatial metaphor. Memory is therefore instrumental for an understanding of the present and the future alike, and the memory that is brought forth is always different as one weaves memories. At the turn of the twentieth century, Bergson distinguished between a limited and a spontaneous memory, anticipating Proust's distinction between voluntary and involuntary memory. An analogous distinction between kinds of memories is also present in Freud. Like Nietzsche, Freud believed the past could be a burden on the present; like him, he worked toward the assumption that the past could be known and transcended—in a certain way forgotten, done away with—through psychoanalytic cure. And yet, the disturbing suspicion that we cannot altogether be free of the past is present in Freud. An altogether different distinction is made by Halbwachs, who separates individual from collective memory, thus adding a social and cultural dimension to memory. For him, individual memory is always influenced by collective memory.

11. For the Greeks, memory was inextricably linked with imagination and identity, thus creating a profound link with the artistic imagination. Mnemosyne, the goddess of memory, was the mother of the Muses and the patroness of intellectual and artistic efforts. Through her daughters, she granted the power to "tell of what is, and what is to be, and what was before now" (Hesiod l. 38), so that memory became, in a sense, the source of creativity. Conversely,

to be bereft of memory was equivalent to losing oneself. The link between memory, imagination, and identity is a founding element of Western culture, and frequently recurs in much literature, including the utopian tradition.

12. To give a sense of the popularity of the acts of (more or less) contrition, we have recently witnessed a plethora of apologies: Queen Elizabeth to the Maori; French Premier Lionel Jospin on the execution of French deserters during WWI; Italian Premier Massimo D'Alema on Italian colonialism in Libya; Japanese Premier Keizo Obuchi to Dutch living in Indonesia during WWII; Polish President Aleksander Kwasniewski to Jews about the 1941 killings; President Bill Clinton to many groups; South Africa's President F. W. de Klerk to victims of apartheid; German President Johannes Rau about the Nazi killings in Marzabotto (Italy). Consider also the requests for reconciliation between Italian fascists and Resistance members; the project Apology Australia; as well as more problematic acts of contrition on the part of the Catholic Church regarding Giordano Bruno, the Crusaders, and sexual abuses.

13. On memory and forgetfulness, see Rossi.

14. Instead, the Commission has been established in order to wrestle with the past, remember it, and move forward. As Father Michael Lapsley says, "there is no evidence in the history of the world that societies were able to successfully bury their past. Evidence shows that what they've attempted to bury came back to haunt them" (Siebert on line).

15. See, for example, the Church's crusades against "new" groups—like gays and lesbians—or the ongoing racist and xenophobic incidents against citizens of Asian descent in the summer 2001 in England. Likewise, contrition on the part of the Church for the persecution of Bruno or for its members' behavior during the Crusades seem to bear little relevance to present-day life.

16. See, for instance, the "I'm Sorry" T-shirt and the Sorry Song CD currently on sale in Australia ("Apology Australia Project" on line). Some of these issues have been discussed by Jack E. White with regard to the issue of slavery. He claims that "without some form of reparations, apologizing for a historical wrong is an empty gesture" (on line).

17. And collective memory constructs its past according to the needs of a given group. See Halbwachs.

18. Le Guin's structure has met with disappointment on the part of some reviewers. See Jonas, Stumpf, and Saunders. Yet Le Guin, when asked why she has turned to a "contemplative and discursive rather than plot-driven" type of narrative, stated that she has "never written a plot-driven novel. . . . My stories are driven (rather slowly and erratically, with pauses to admire apparently irrelevant scenery) by a different chauffeur" (Gevers on line).

19. In interview, talking about America's "war on terrorism," Le Guin said, "Don't call me utopian. Utopia is always something you can't get to because it doesn't exist. I prefer to be called hopeful" (Newitz on line).

20. It tells the story of a foolish man who, upon the death of his mother, is left with only a sack of bean meal. He meets several people who offer him different things for his bean meal, but the man always refuses to exchange it, even when he meets a couple of maz—the professional performers or storytellers of the Telling—who offer him a farm in return (168–70). For Sutty, it is an indication of Akan cash mentality: "reward, whether spiritual or fiscal, was immediate" (171).

21. For more on the function of memory in dystopia, see Baccolini, "Journeying."

22. On the importance of history and literacy in Four Ways, see Donawerth; on how history is made, see Byrne.

23. Similarly, nostalgia, traditionally regarded as "the expression of a regressive wish to retreat to a less complicated moment in history or personal experience" (Rubenstein 3), can assume in the critical dystopia a progressive value, provided that its cure, to return home, is not considered its solution. Feminist critical dystopias, in fact, have shown that there cannot be return if there is awareness and knowledge of the past, since home is a place that has never been as it was, and past is the root of our present. On the different awareness about the past in classical and feminist critical dystopia, see Baccolini, "Journeying." Nostalgia may have a liberating or compensatory dimension: evoking nostalgia or longing is a way to enable characters and readers "to confront, mourn, and figuratively revise their relation to something that has been lost, whether in the world or in themselves. . . . Narratives that engage notions of home, loss and/or nostalgia [can] confront the past in order to 'fix' it"

(Rubenstein 6). Thus, Le Guin's novels use nostalgia "to represent not a place or a time but a longing for balance. In this book, it is the stories, and their tellings, that carry the weight required to restore balance" (Ruvinsky on line).

24.   See Baccolini, "Gender and Genre."

Works cited

"Apology Australia." Available at: http://apology.west.net.au/events.html

Atwood, Margaret. *The Handmaid's Tale.* 1985. Boston: Houghton, 1986.

Augustine. *The Confessions.* Trans. F. J. Sheed. New York: Sheed, 1943.

Baccolini, Raffaella. "Gender and Genre in the Feminist Critical Dystopias of Katharine Burdekin, Margaret Atwood, and Octavia Butler." Barr 13–34.

———. "Journeying through the Dystopian Genre: Memory and Imagination in Burdekin, Orwell, Atwood, and Piercy." *Viaggi in utopia.* Ed. Raffaella Baccolini, Vita Fortunati, and Nadia Minerva. Ravenna: Longo, 1996. 343–57.

Baggesen, Søren. "Utopian and Dystopian Pessimism: Le Guin's *The Word for World Is Forest* and Tiptree's 'We Who Stole the Dream.'" *Science-Fiction Studies* 14.1 (1987): 34–43.

Barr, Marleen S. *Future Females, the Next Generation: New Voices and Velocities in Feminist Science Fiction Criticism.* Lanham: Rowman, 2000.

Benjamin, Walter. "Theses on the Philosophy of History." *Illuminations.* Trans. Harry Zohn. London: Fontana, 1992. 245–55.

Bergson, Henri. *Matter and Memory.* 1896. Trans. N. M. Paul and W. S. Palmer. London: Allen, 1912.

Brooks, Roy L. *When Sorry Isn't Enough: The Controversy over Apologies and Reparations for Human Injustice.* New York: New York UP, 1999.

Burdekin, Katharine. *Swastika Night.* 1937. Old Westbury: Feminist, 1985.

Butler, Octavia E. *Kindred.* 1979. London: Women's, 1995.

———. *Parable of the Sower.* New York: Warner, 1993.

Byrne, Deirdre. "Truth and Story: History in Ursula K. Le Guin's Short Fiction and the South African Truth and Reconciliation Commission." Barr 237–46.

Donawerth, Jane. "The Feminist Dystopia of the 1990s: Record of Failure, Midwife of Hope." Barr 49–66.

Freud, Sigmund. "Remembering, Repeating and Working-Through." 1914. *The Standard Edition of the Complete Psychological Works of Sigmund Freud.* Vol. 12. Trans. J. Strachey. London: Hogarth, 1958. 147–56.

Fukuyama, Francis. "The End of History?" *National Interest* 16 (1989): 3–18.

Geoghegan, Vincent. "Remembering the Future." *Utopian Studies* 1.2 (1990): 52–68.

Gevers, Nick. "Driven by a Different Chauffeur: An Interview with Ursula K. Le Guin." *SF Site.* Available at: http://www.sfsite.com/03a/ul123.htm

Gordon, Michael. "Apology Back on the Agenda." Available at: http://www.age.com

Gramsci, Antonio. *Lettere dal carcere, 1926–1937.* Ed. Antonio A. Cantucci. Palermo: Sellerio, 1996.

Gross, David. "Bergson, Proust, and the Revaluation of Memory." *International Philosophical Quarterly* 25 (Winter 1985): 369–80.

Halbwachs, Maurice. *On Collective Memory.* Ed. and trans. Lewis A. Coser. Chicago : U of Chicago P, 1992.

Harvey, David. *Spaces of Hope.* Berkeley: U of California P, 2000.

Hesiod. *Theogony.* Trans. Richmond Lattimore. Ann Arbor: U of Michigan P, 1984. 123–86.

Huxley, Aldous. *Brave New World.* 1932. New York: Harper, 1969.

International Theological Commission. "Memory and Reconciliation: The Church and the Faults of the Past." Dec. 1999. Available at: http://www.vatican.va/roman_curia/congregations/cfaith/cti_documents/rc_con_cfaith_doc_20000307_memory-reconc-itc_en.html

Jacoby, Russell. *The End of Utopia: Politics and Culture in an Age of Apathy.* New York: Basic, 1999.

Jameson, Fredric. "Nostalgia for the Present." *South Atlantic Quarterly* 88.2 (1989): 517–37.

Jonas, Gerald. "Science Fiction." *The New York Times on the Web.* 1 Oct. 2000. Available at: http://partners.nytimes.com/books/00/10/01/reviews/001001.01scifit.html

Kundera, Milan. *The Book of Laughter and Forgetting.* New York: Harper, 1999.

Kureishi, Hanif. *Intimacy.* London: Faber, 1998.

•

Le Guin, Ursula K. *The Eye of the Heron. The Word for World Is Forest.* 1972. London: Victor Gollancz, 1991.

———. *Four Ways to Forgiveness.* New York: Harper, 1995.

———. *The Telling.* New York: Harcourt, 2000.

Marcuse, Herbert. *One-Dimensional Man: Studies in the Ideology of Advanced Industrial Society.* Boston: Beacon, 1966.

Moylan, Tom. "New Ground: US Dystopias, Nation, and State." *Utopianism/Literary Utopias and National Cultural Identities: A Comparative Perspective.* Ed. Paola Spinozzi. Bologna: COTEPRA, 2001. 233–44.

———. *Scraps of the Untainted Sky. Science Fiction, Utopia, Dystopia.* Boulder: Westview, 2000.

Newitz, Annalee. "In Utopia." Available at: http://www.sfbg.com/SFLife/tech/78.html

Nietzsche, Friedrich. *The Use and Abuse of History.* Trans. Adrian Collins. Indianapolis: Bobbs, 1957.

Nora, Pierre. "Between Memory and History: *Les Lieux de Mémoire.*" *Representations* 26 (1989): 7–25.

Orwell, George. *Nineteen Eighty-Four.* 1949. New York: Signet, 1961.

Pfaelzer, Jean. "Parody and Satire in American Dystopian Fiction of the Nineteenth Century." *Science-Fiction Studies* 7 (1980): 61–71.

Piercy, Marge. *He, She and It.* New York: Fawcett, 1991.

Rich, Adrienne. "Resisting Amnesia: History and Personal Life." *Blood, Bread, and Poetry. Selected Prose 1979–1985.* London: Virago, 1987. 136–55.

Roemer, Kenneth. *The Obsolete Necessity: America in Utopian Writings, 1888–1900.* Kent: Kent State UP, 1976.

Rossi, Paolo. *Il passato, la memoria, l'oblio.* Bologna: Il Mulino, 1991.

Rubenstein, Roberta. *Home Matters: Longing and Belonging, Nostalgia and Mourning in Women's Fiction.* New York: Palgrave, 2001.

Ruvinsky, Morrie. "To Tell the Truth." *Los Angeles Times* 24 Sept. 2000. Available at: http://www.latimes.com

Ruyer, Raymond. *L'Utopie et les Utopies.* Paris: PUF, 1950.

Sargent, Lyman Tower. "The Three Faces of Utopianism Revisited." *Utopian Studies* 5.1 (1994): 1–37.

Saunders, Christopher. "The Telling." Available at: http://www.bookreporter.com/reviews/0151005672.asp

Siebert, Hannes. "Healing the Memory." *CCR* 6.3–4 (Dec. 1997). Available at: http://ccrweb.ccr.uct.ac.za/two/6_34/p46_skills.html

Stumpf, Edna. "Touching Down Again on Another Planet." *Inquirer.* [Philadelphia] 10 Sept. 2000. Available at: http://inq.philly.com/content/inquirer/2000/09/10/books/TELL10.htm

Suvin, Darko. "The Riverside Trees, or SF and Utopia: Degrees of Kinship." *minnesota review* 3–4 (1974): 108–15.

White, Hayden. *Metahistory: The Historical Imagination in Nineteenth-Century Europe.* Baltimore: Johns Hopkins UP, 1975.

White, Jack E. "Sorry Isn't Good Enough: A Simple Apology for Slavery Leaves Unpaid Debts." *Time* 30 June 1997. Available at: http://www.cnn.com/ALLPOLITICS/1997/06/23/time/slavery.html

White, Jonathan. "Coming Back from the Silence." *Whole Earth Review* 85 (1995). Available at: http://www.snowlight.com/ursula_le_guin.htm

Yates, Frances A. *The Art of Memory.* Chicago: U of Chicago P, 1966.

CHAPTER 7

"The moment is here . . . and it's important": State, Agency, and Dystopia in Kim Stanley Robinson's *Antarctica* and Ursula K. Le Guin's *The Telling*

TOM MOYLAN

And through it all moved the Iron Heel, impassive and deliberate, shaking up the whole fabric of the social structure in its search for the comrades, combing out the mercenaries, the labor castes, and all its secret service, punishing without mercy and without malice, suffering in silence all retaliations that were made upon it and filling the gaps in its fighting line as fast as they appeared. And hand in hand with this, Ernest and the other leaders were hard at work reorganizing the forces of the Revolution. The magnitude of the task may be understood when it is taken into
—Jack London, *The Iron Heel*

Well burrowed, old mole!
—Karl Marx, *Eighteenth Brumaire*

I

From Yevgeny Zamyatin's OneState to Margaret Atwood's Gilead, the state is a major target of critique in the classical dystopian narrative. Yet in the dystopian turn of the closing decades of the twentieth century, the power of the authoritarian state gives way to the more pervasive tyranny of the corporation. Everyday life in the new dystopias is still observed, ruled, and controlled; but now it is also reified, exploited, and commodified. From Tyrrel in Ridley Scott's *Blade Runner* (1982) to Kagimoto, Stamm, Frampton in Octavia Butler's *Parable of the Sower* (1993), the corporation rules, and does so more effectively than any state, as its exploitive tentacles reach into the cultures and bodies of the people who serve it and who are cast aside by it.

This said, the ruling force in Jack London's "proto-dystopia," *The Iron Heel,* is not yet limited to that of the state, party, or corporation.[1] The Iron Heel that sweeps through London's naturalist narrative and transforms it before our readerly eyes into what will soon be known as the literary genre of *dystopia* is an encompassing representation of the machinery of the economic-political-cultural power of modern capitalism by way of an anticipation of its extreme form in fascism. As well, E. M. Forster's 1909 short story "The Machine Stops" proffers a narrative of social domination by a force not reducible to that of the authoritarian state. The eponymous Machine, which rules so totally that it even names itself the deity of the society, could well be a representation of the modern bureaucratic state, but it could also, or simultaneously, be regarded as the manifestation of the economic logic, managerial technology, and commodified culture of the new regime of Fordism. Indeed, these early literary gestures both teach the primary lesson of the dystopian imaginary: namely, that it is the totalizing political-economic machinery of the hegemonic system (and not simply the state, party, corporation, religion, or other undemocratic power) that brings exploitation, terror, and misery to society.

And yet, the well-known works that follow Forster and accumulate in the intertextual matrix of the classical dystopian mode zero in on the *state* as the primary form of that totalizing power. In this sense, the early dystopias share at best an anarchist or at worst a liberal fear and loathing of the state that sidesteps the economic rule of capital and conflates the bureaucracy and social engineering found in fascist, socialist, and, in some works, liberal or social democratic states. The critical logic of the classical dystopia is therefore a simplifying one. It doesn't matter that an economic regime drives the society; it doesn't matter that a cultural regime of interpellation shapes and directs the people; for the social evil to be named, and resisted, is nothing but the modern state in and of itself. Even as late as Ray Bradbury's *Fahrenheit 451,* the state-run fire company that burns books and executes readers is foregrounded, not the processes of the reification and commodification that characterize the controlled society of Bradbury's America.

A fuller discussion of the politics of representation of the state in the classical dystopia must wait, for what I am examining in this essay are the *shifts* that occur in the political imaginary of dystopian writing from the 1980s to the last years of the century.[2] Initially, the dystopian science fiction of the early to mid-1980s changes the central power structure from the state to the corporation; but then, the later critical dystopias move to a fresh consideration of the role of the state, eventually examining its relationship to the oppositional movements within the dystopian societies.[3]

Having said that, again the pattern is not neat and tidy. Indeed, exceptions arise immediately in the two works of print fiction that establish, if not launch, this dystopian revival: William Gibson's *Neuromancer* (1984) and Margaret Atwood's *The Handmaid's Tale* (1985).[4] Reminiscent of London and Forster, Gibson dispenses with the state as the center of social control, but he then locates that power in the figure of twinned AIs ruling the matrix (while both corporate and shadowy governmental players are implicated). Thus, even as Gibson portrays an abstract totalizing force, the groundwork for a linkage of cybernetic technology to the actions of transnational corporations is established, a move already nihilistically portrayed in *Blade Runner* and later to be challenged by cyberpunk sf such as Bruce Sterling's *Islands in the Net* (1989) or Pat Cadigan's *Synners* (1991).[5]

Atwood, on the other hand, continues in a more classical dystopian mode with her portrayal of the religious fascist state of Gilead; and yet *Handmaid* (in my reading) *anticipates* the emergence of a critical dystopia or (in the analyses of others) *begins* the trend of critical dystopias as it offers a social map that traces both the depredations of state power and possible vectors of hope within the ambit of that hegemonic force.[6] In addition to mapping Gilead, Atwood charts the linkage between desire and domination in ways that go beyond Orwell or even Huxley; and she explores the imbrication of state, economy, and culture that produces contemporary consumer society more fully than does Bradbury's prescient tale. Significantly, she does both with a self-reflexivity that develops through her focus on language and her framing narrative as she brings a *critical* dystopian sensibility not only to the content of her text but especially to its form.

Gibson and Atwood, then, begin to move away from the classical dystopian privileging of the power of the state in favor of a focus on the extensive and intensive power of the economic-cultural system, and on the potential for resistance to it. Another key text that contends differently with the state in this period is Kim Stanley Robinson's *The Gold Coast* (1988). Robinson's deceptively normal narrative (appearing, in an example of genre blurring, more as a realist coming-of-age story than a dystopia) is fully a dystopian text of its time; but it does not attain this status by portraying a society dominated by a singularly authoritarian state.[7] And yet the state is present: as the particular integration of the economic and the political that developed in the military-industrial complex of the postwar United States. Writing in the latter years of the Reagan era, Robinson captures the logic of that regime's military Keynesianism, which preserved big government for the defense establishment as it eliminated the hard-won protections, benefits, and entitlements of the social welfare state. Thus, it is specifically the power found in the *partnership* of state and corporation (as between the Pentagon and defense firms such as Laguna Space Research and Argo AG/Blessman Enterprises) that encloses the society in which the protagonist Jim, his family, and friends struggle to survive. In addition, Robinson exposes the "bread and guns" aspirations of this system as he describes the related economic mechanisms producing the commodity culture and labor regime that shape the quotidian of the inhabitants of this future California. In *Gold Coast*, therefore, the post-Vietnam era state is decentered, but it is also thriving in its linkage with corporate America as it becomes but one element in the power grid of the U.S. political economy.[8]

In many works of the dystopian turn, however, portrayals of the state disappear. In Cadigan's *Synners* or Richard Kadrey's *Metrophage*, for example, the narratives' conjunctural and personal crises are produced by corporations, not the state. However, in the critical dystopias by Butler (*Parable of the Sower, Parable of the Talents*) and Marge Piercy (*He, She and It/Body of Glass*) new meditations on the state return to the dystopian intertext.

In Butler's southern California of the twenty-first century, the fledgling corporate hegemony seen in Robinson's very-near-future Orange County has moved several stages further in dominating and finally (in a nightmare replay of Ronald Reagan's and Margaret Thatcher's dreams) destroying the viability of society itself. Serving as a reminder of what a socially responsible state might once have meant to its citizens, a shadowy version of the former U.S. government exists; but, under neoliberal discipline, it has become a minor adjunct, if even that, to the corporations that ravage the environment, privatize towns and public services, and enslave people as indentured servants. Regulation and support once provided by the progressive welfare state for the protection of the population has disappeared, and even the accommodationist role of the liberal and early neoliberal state in nurturing and protecting corporate development has disappeared as corporations (i.e., Kagimoto, Stamm, Frampton) become strong enough to look after their own infrastructural development and military protection. Privatization prevails in *Parable of the Sower*'s full-fledged neoliberal regime, and the minimalist government stands as a sign of the failure of the state to prevent the forward surge of an economic logic driven by free-market ideologies and globalizing dreams. In *Parable of the Sower*, the presidential election arouses little interest amongst the deprived and defeated populace; while in *Parable of the Talents* the religious-political Earthseed community regards the reformist coalition contesting the election against the Christian Identity government as an insufficient effort and concentrates instead on its preparations for flight to a utopia in the stars.[9]

In *He, She and It*, Piercy creates a similar scenario of neoliberal hegemony as she focuses on the power of one of the twenty-three megacorporations that have "divided the world among them," occupying protected enclaves "on every continent and on space platforms" (35, 5). However, this author of one of the influential critical utopias of the 1970s breaks new ground as she speculates on possible forms of oppositional grassroots and state power. Writing twenty years after *Woman on the Edge of Time* and within the new dystopian imaginary, Piercy highlights the exploitive logic of the corporations that has rendered the entire globe an environmental and economic wasteland wherein the only lives of comfort are those enjoyed by the enhanced citizens of the corporate enclaves. While regional state formations continue in this twenty-first century dystopian world in the form of entities such as Norika or Europa, these descendants of the supra-state structures of the 1980s and 1990s are but feeble remains of those units and of "the old UN," now functioning only as a weak "eco-police" that has little power against the megacorporations. Even more absolutely than in Butler, there is no indication at all of anything resembling the nation-state (5).[10] And yet, beyond the privileged corporate localities (which suggest today's gated communities) and the weak regional entities, there are other spaces of hope to be found in Piercy's dystopian world.

To be sure, the labor pools of the Glop (before the movement catalyzed by Riva and the gangs creates at least the conditions for a trade union consciousness and local governance) are urban working-class landscapes not yet exercising autonomous power; but the radical community of Jewish and Palestinian women in the devastated Middle East and the embattled city-state of Tikva represent forms of state power that already work as sites of opposition rather than co-optation or accommodation.[11] The woman's community of the Black Zone is a liberated area that (as an amalgam of the best traditions of historical revolutionary states, anarcho-syndicalist models, and lived and imagined feminist communities) transcends contemporary instances of state power and provides a utopian locus *and* horizon, however sketchily drawn, of an organized political structure committed not only to its own development but also (after a period of separatism during which it struggled into existence from literal ashes) to playing a leading role in mounting a global revolutionary challenge to megacorporate power. Indeed, Piercy's political protagonist, the radical organizer Riva, could not move forward in her clandestine work without the backing of the new post-state formation of the Black Zone and its agent, Nili.

Additionally, the progressive Jewish city-state of Tikva stands in a historically evocative location in Massachusetts as a more familiar speculation on a form of oppositional state power that draws on ancient Greek and colonial American predecessors as well as more recent instances such as the kibbutzim, intentional utopian communities, and perhaps even those rare examples of U.S. city governments that (for an election or two) were in the hands of progressive political leadership (Berkeley and Chicago come, sadly because of their passing, to mind). While the Black Zone community provides vision and muscle to the entire global struggle, the state apparatus of Tikva (fighting for economic and literal survival as well as for the goals of the anti-corporate movement) serves as the immediate base for the emergent alliance with its multiple strategy of state power, mass movement, and direct action that defeats the Yakamura-Steichen campaign to steal the android Yod and, in doing so, gains time and space for continued resistance and organizing in the Glop, the city-states, and perhaps in the more isolated Rural Zones.

II

In reality, however, the state is nothing but a machine for the oppression of one class by another, and indeed in the democratic republic no less than in the monarchy; and at best an evil inherited by the proletariat after its victorious struggle for class supremacy, whose worst sides the proletariat, just like the Commune, cannot avoid having to lop off at the earliest possible moment, until such time as a new generation, reared in new and free social conditions, will be able to throw the entire lumber of the state on the scrap-heap.
—Frederick Engels, Introduction to *The Civil War in France*

Given the dominance of neoliberalism in the historical conjuncture of the 1980s and especially the 1990s, the dystopian shift from representations of the state as the locus of dominant power is not surprising. If indeed the ruling ideas of an era are those of its ruling forces, then the narrative step from state to economy as the motor of society can be read at its least self-conscious register as a symptomatic echo of neoliberal hegemony. Like it or not, the success of the attacks on the welfare and regulatory state by the ideologues of the "free market" has legitimated a general suspicion of the state as a mechanism for delivering social justice and democratic and ecological well-being. Sincere and opportunistic leaders alike, most tellingly in liberal and social democratic circles, have been all too willing to relinquish any semblance of oppositional, or even alternative, state power in order to accommodate restructured corporations. The claims of neoliberal thinkers that the interference of the state will inhibit the growth of the market have clearly prevailed in a broader ideological sphere than that of its adherents—in spite of the fact that, as Fredric Jameson puts it, "the creation of any genuinely government-free market involves enormous governmental intervention and, de facto, an increase in centralized government" ("Globalization" 58). This, then, is the contradictory secret of neoliberalism: economic viability is not a matter of eliminating the state but rather of restricting its activities to those that aid capital and not society. Indeed, *more* state intervention (to protect trade, subsidize infrastructure development, bail out failing firms, and deliver military protection) is required by the neoliberal order, not less.[12]

In this regard, the shift in the dystopian imaginary from state to economy is at the very least a passive reflection of the hegemonic line on government. However, for many of the new dystopian writers, who are generally opposed to neoliberal ascendancy, the new perspective has a more pressing political meaning. At this register, the marginalization or defeat of the socially responsible state stands as an indictment of reformist left and center-left governments that failed to challenge and indeed went on, in a more traditional vein, to assist the resurgence of transnational capital in the 1980s and 1990s. As well, in the realm of actually existing socialism, analysts such as Eric Hobsbawm and Jameson argue that the collapse of the USSR "was due, not to the failure of socialism, but to the abandonment of delinking by the Socialist bloc" ("Globalization" 56).[13] That is, the Soviet failure can also be traced to the efforts of its own state apparatus to come to terms with the world capitalist market rather than to build a delinked alternative. Further, the failure of revolutionary parties either to take state power or, having done so, to use it effectively adds to the critical doubt concerning the oppositional role of the state within anti-capitalist, anarchist, and even socialist praxis.

Finally, at the most self-conscious register of critique (no longer under the ideological shadow of neoliberalism, but now adamantly against it), the critical dystopian displacement of the state implies a stance that accords with the vision of the contemporaneous anti-capitalist movements.[14] Here, the recognition of the shift of the dominant agency from state to economy takes on an initial utopian valence as some dystopian texts reject anti-utopian despair and opt for a militant, collective, grassroots opposition that will proceed without compromising itself in the halls of state systems. At this register, the critical dystopian counter-narrative assumes its most powerful meaning: as the anti-corporate alliance engages in a confrontation, and, in some cases, secures a utopian enclave that, at its most productive, supports an oppositional vector within and against the dystopian society. In texts such as Cadigan's *Synners*, Kadrey's *Metrophage*, and Butler's *Parable* books, there is a shared expression of this pattern of utopian spatiality and process working its way through the dystopian text.

In each, the alliance makes no use of the existing state apparatus but rather grows out of its various members' suffering and labor, develops strategies from its own diverse subject positions, and thus deploys its own expertise to build a counter-force that defeats, if briefly, the corporate power.

In this alliance formation that goes beyond the identity-based politics of the 1980s yet embraces its lessons and desires, the critical dystopias portray a politics suited to the moment, one that refunctions the sense of "combination," as Jameson reminds us, in a collective action that achieves a unity-in-diversity capable of fighting simultaneously on economic, political, and cultural terrains.[15] While there is no overt connection between the political imaginary of this counter-narrative and that of the anti-capitalist movement, there is a structure of feeling that informs both, one that has grown out of the conditions of the societies in which both have flourished. Here lies the social value of the critical dystopia as it becomes part of the oppositional culture engendered by the combination of environmental, labor, human rights, anti-racist, and other activists demonstrating in Seattle, London, Washington, Prague, Quebec City, Genoa, Brussels, Barcelona, Kananaskis, and elsewhere.

Yet, in this shared imaginary, a newer moment of political challenge has appeared: one that the anti-capitalist movement (and its precursors and allies) needs to come to terms with, and one that shows up in the critical dystopian intertext by the end of the 1990s. That is, while the energy produced by the demonstrations has grown, and while these primarily *cultural* battles against neoliberal hegemony are gaining legitimacy, the pressing question facing those who oppose transnational capital (and its state and semi-state minions such as the G-8, the World Bank, the IMF, the WTO, as well as "Third Way" collaborators in states such as Britain and the United States) is just what type of *structural* strategy can bring the victories on the cultural front to bear on the process of transforming political and economic structures.

Part of the answer lies in just how the new opposition will again take up the vexed question of the role of the state in that radical process. As intellectuals and activists alike have argued, the movement must find a way to engage on the terrain of the state as well as the street. Contrary to the argument of Michael Hardt and Antonio Negri, the state cannot readily be set aside in an unmediated challenge to what they call "Empire." While Hardt and Negri rightly identify the globally exploited "multitude" as the progressive, even vanguard, force that is driving the new opposition, the stages between the current situation and the transformative victory of that multitude must necessarily involve dealing with local, national, regional, and global formations: at the very least, to stem the harm of capitalist rule and begin to win back the lost ground of social welfare and environmental protection, but also to move forward to restructure society in the interests of its people and not of the corporations draining its lifeblood.[16] The question, therefore, is just what are the appropriate strategies that this international movement can adopt in order to move from a successful politics of gesture to a politics of contestation carried out within and without the space of the state.

The answers to this question will only be forged in the historical crucible, but some initial speculation can be found in Piercy's *He, She and It*, as the utopian entities of the Black Zone and Tikva play a crucial role in the new alliance politics. Both express a concrete utopian vision legitimated by the secured political space of their own formation, and both provide a base from which new action can be mounted. Piercy's thought experiment therefore breaks new ground in the oppositional sensibility generated by the critical dystopian imagination. And yet, even here a strategic step is missing, for the Black Zone and Tikva are *achieved, utopian* formations forged from previous struggles (however much internal debate continues in both). What is absent is the further consideration of how the movement can move forward within *existing* state formations, at an initial stage to protect people and the environment from corporate actions, at an intermediate stage to gain more state power for social transformation, and in the long run to move toward the very post-state alternatives that are prefigured in imagined communities such as the Black Zone or Tikva (or, in the critical utopias, in Piercy's Mattapoisett, Ursula K. Le Guin's Anarres, Joanna Russ's Whileaway, or Kim Stanley Robinson's El Modena).[17]

Even before Hardt and Negri's intervention, political intellectuals and activists had been reconsidering this question of strategic engagement with state power; and they have offered commentaries that point to possible directions—even as those commentaries and subsequent actions will themselves shift the horizon of engagement and thereby raise new questions as the political situation continues to develop. However, for the purposes of this essay, a useful beginning to this interrogation during the period of the critical dystopia can be found in Pierre Bourdieu's arguments for deploying the power of the state in the battle against the neoliberal onslaught. Writing as a public intellectual and aligning with the French strikes of 1995, Bourdieu calls, in his *Contre-feux* (1998), for a Left involvement with state power as a component of the concerted action against neoliberalism. As put in the English translation *Acts of Resistance*, he insists that "dominated groups in society have an interest in defending the state, particularly its social aspect" (41). Thus, the "left hand of the state, the set of agents of the so-called spending ministries which are the trace, within the state, of the social struggles of the past" must stand against the "right hand of the state, the technocrats of the Ministry of Finance, the public and private banks and the ministerial cabinets" (2). In taking this position, Bourdieu is in accord with Jameson, who argues that "the nation-state today remains the only concrete terrain and framework for political struggle" ("Globalization" 65). Both seek an engagement with the state that recalls Marx's caveat in *The Civil War in France*, which notes that fighting on the ground of the state is a process of occupying and realigning (and sometimes "lopping off," as Engels says) sectors in the interest of a total social transformation, and not simply a one-dimensional act of laying hold of "the ready-made state machinery" and wielding it for its own purposes (362–63). Fighting on the terrain of the state does not, in short, mean fighting on the state's, or capital's, terms.

Further refusing the limitations of ethnic nationalism in favor of the ideological scope of what he sees as "civic" nationalism, Bourdieu calls for a battle against the "*involution of the state*, in other words, the regression to a penal state, concerned with repression and progressively abandoning its social functions" (34, emphasis original). Such a contest will aim to restore "an enlightened, reasonable definition of the future of the public services, of health, education, transport and so on" (26). However, his strategic vision breaks beyond the confines of national boundaries, as he calls for regional and international engagement that draws the actions of any given state into the wider scope of global contestation. He argues, first, that the struggle for the state should be carried out "in coordination with those who, in the other countries of Europe, are exposed to the same threats," and he then states the "need to reinvent internationalism" (26, 59).[18] Finally, both Bourdieu and Jameson base their call for an engagement with the state in the context of a mass politics. Bourdieu develops his assessment in light of the 1995 strikes and (before the demonstrations in Seattle took the situation further) connects his political vision with the "vanguard of world struggle against neoliberalism" (59); while Jameson looks for a localized but necessarily international opposition that is not reducible to the parameters of state, religion, or other singular formation ("Globalization" 67).

This, then, is an emerging strategic perspective on the place of the state in the fight against neoliberal hegemony. However, before turning to later critical dystopias that explore this new ground, it is worth noting two areas that will require further attention as this strategy unfolds. The first, as Alex Callinicos observes in his generally positive discussion of Bourdieu, is the related question of just how much can be won with direct state power in a capitalist order. While, like Nicos Poulantzas, Bourdieu works from a conception of the state as a set of interconnected institutions relatively autonomous from one another and the economy, there are still "structural limits to the state's responsiveness to pressures from below" (Callinicos 93). The power of corporate interests is such that only so much can be gained by progressive action within a state apparatus before steps are taken to shut it down—as prefigured as early as London's novel and seen in the efforts in Germany to deflect the Green Party in government in the late 1990s. Recognition of these limits should not stop radical work within the state, but it could alert activists to realize that only so much can be gained within the parliamentary framework without a base in mass, community politics.

The second area of concern is the issue of political leadership. As Callinicos notes, Bourdieu, along with many on the Left, "rejects Gramsci's conception of the revolutionary party as the organic intellectual of the working class" (101). While a rejection of an orthodox vanguard leadership may be justified in this historical moment, there is still the matter of who will lead the political movement. And while the record of revolutionary parties in taking the struggle forward without falling into sectarian purity or opportunistic accommodation is not promising, spontaneous revolution alone is not sufficient to defeat global capital. Thus, the question of leadership remains open; promising models, however, can be found in examples as diverse and contradictory as the Zapatistas, the Brazilian Workers' Party, the German Greens, the Irish Sinn Fein, or the South African Communist Party.[19] What *is* clear is that collective leadership is needed; but, as the international movement has learned, an effective leadership must be non-privileged, non-teleological, diverse, open, and yet capable of mobilizing an entire alliance.

With these caveats in mind, it is still possible to recognize an emerging strategy of opposition that refuses reformist "marginal improvements inflated with self-deceiving rhetoric" and strengthens "the forces capable of challenging the structures of capitalist domination" (Callinicos 101). This long-term agenda is concretely utopian, working with tendencies and latencies in the current conjuncture and resisting both romantic fantasy and opportunist co-optation. Like Utopia itself, it has an asymptotic quality that stays open to modification as conditions change. It therefore strives not to be blinded by a pre-determined telos nor deflected by pragmatic achievement but seeks to expand its very sense of horizon and agency as history itself unfolds.

III

What is true in Antarctica is true everywhere else.
—Kim Stanley Robinson, *Antarctica*

"The margin between collusion and respect can be narrow," Tong said.
"Unfortunately, we exist in that margin here."
—Ursula K. Le Guin, *The Telling*

By the end of the century, these questions of political leadership and the oppositional potential of state intervention had been addressed in new works by Robinson and Le Guin. In *Antarctica* (1997), Robinson explores a political movement that effectively engages with existing state power in order to turn it against the hegemonic order it supports. As with *Gold Coast*, his account of daily life and structural crises set in the microcosm of the "science continent" appears as a realist treatment of a fairly "normal" slice of contemporary life (albeit here in a hybrid and self-reflexive sf text that draws on a variety of modes, from the mystery, love story, and survival adventure to discourses of science, law, history, and critical theory, and opening out into poetry). Indeed, it is only gradually (in a process that catches the very truth of dystopian narrative) that the reader breaks through that apparent normality and begins to "put together the pieces of the puzzle" so as to discover the nature of corporate and state power at work in this near-future world (*Antarctica* 259).

As the deeper subject of Robinson's text, that of society itself, emerges in a dystopian reading, it becomes apparent that the one place on Earth meant to be preserved for "pure" research has become a contested terrain on which the global struggle is replicated in the actions of several competing interests. On a continuum that ranges from the exploitive designs of transnational corporations, to the understandable needs of nearby South American nations for natural resources, to the on-site requirements of the scientists and service workers, to the desires of the "feral Antarcticans" for a new life as residents and stewards of a continent, and obliquely to the concerns of the ecological activists who engage in sabotage to protect the "last pure wilderness on earth," the players in this struggle over the future of this unique social space (and, by metonymic implication, of the entire planet) reach a crisis point when two key events occur in a context that is simultaneously local and global (49). On one hand, the government contract for the service company that maintains McMurdo base for the National Science Foundation is due for renewal. After initially taking over with the blessing of the government's privatization policy, corporate interests are eager to continue exploiting the facility as a profit-making enterprise; but the workers in McMurdo, fed up with sweatshop conditions, are moving toward submitting a competing bid to run the company as a cooperative. On the other hand, the renewal of the international Antarctic Treaty is blocked in a congressional committee by a Republican administration more attuned to accommodating those corporate interests than to protecting the land and the workers. These two events thus generate the crisis that blasts away the ordinariness of the everyday (for readers and protagonists alike) and reveals the deeper contradictions in the world system.

In the words of Carlos, who identifies himself as a "true Antarctican," Robinson casts this conflict as one between capitalism, "the dominant economic order [that] tends to subsume everything else," and science, "the great outsider . . . [that] tries to make a utopia within itself, in the rules of scientific conduct and organization, and . . . also tries to influence the world at large in a utopian direction" (183, 299). And yet, the quests by the feral Antarcticans and the protagonists (Val, X, and Wade) to find ethically and creatively fulfilling lives suggest that science, if it *is* to fulfill this macro-utopian potential, must be self-critically open to many dimensions and possibilities to keep from closing in on a fixed stance and strategy. The scope of this counter-force of human and ecological possibility is further enlarged by the poetry that runs through the text. Written by Ta Shu, a video/performance artist (on site through an NSF Artists and Writers Grant, as Robinson actually was in 1995), the poetic interludes contribute a surplus consciousness that helps to keep all elements of the utopian counter-narrative open. In this spirit, Ta Shu's commentary on post-Treaty Antarctica concludes, significantly in the subjunctive, that "[t]his could be a good place" (534); and this poetic anticipation is then given a more directly political dimension as the legal language of the new Treaty asserts (now materially as well as metonymically) in its last clause that "[w]hat is true in Antarctica is true everywhere else," which implies a provocative possibility of a radical horizon rather than a homogenizing blueprint (539).

As in the other critical dystopias, the process that leads to the progressive resolution of the crisis involves an oppositional movement based in the concrete tendencies and latencies of the moment and not simply in abstract desire. Thus a cross-class, cross-gender, and international alliance develops: one that consists of the workers (including their leader, Joyce, and X) who want to form a cooperative; the scientists who want to continue their, pure and utopian, research; the feral Antarcticans (including their spokesperson, Mai-Lis, and Val) who want to be citizens of the continent; the South American nations (with Carlos as their representative) that seek energy resources for sheer survival; Sylvia, the local NSF administrator who is sympathetic; and Wade, the staff expert on Antarctica for Phil Chase, the radical senator from California, who simply wants to do the right thing in his job. The needed breakthrough in the contest between McMurdo and Washington occurs when the disastrous sabotage perpetrated by the northern eco-activists (here Robinson manages to stay provocatively open on the question of the action's worth or danger) damages communication and endangers personnel; for only then do the discrete players combine to fight for the common goal of securing a radically revised Treaty that can resolve the crises and create a new economic, political, and cultural horizon, for them all.

It is at this point that Wade plays a catalyzing role within the state apparatus. He persuades Phil to fight for the award of the contract to the workers and for ratification of the now radically revised Treaty. As he puts it: "The moment is here, Phil, and it's important. . . . We're at an unstable point in history, the teeter-totter is wavering there in the middle, co-opification versus the Götterdämmerung, they've got the guns but we've got the numbers! The time is ripe . . . for you to come falling down out of space onto our side of the teeter-totter and catapult them out of there!" (545). Of course, without the political agitation and organizing by the workers, ferals, and South American allies, the conditions for this uncompromised intervention would not have developed. And yet, it is that very intervention that furthers the utopian aims of the alliance. As a result, local transformation gets under way, and the global balance of power is also significantly altered, for the Treaty implicitly gives Antarctica, as a "site of special scientific interest," the status of a liberated zone which becomes an actually existing utopian space that is at least partially delinked from the capitalist system. Within this utopian locus, scientific research can co-exist with a regulated natural resource extraction (reserved primarily for the needs of the Latin neighbors), the workers cooperative can develop its radical alternative, and the feral citizens can lead more ecologically viable lives. In addition, as with Piercy's enclaves, Antarctica itself stands as a new form of autonomous political space that provides a radical horizon for the rest of the world as well as a base from which vectors of transformation can be encouraged and supported (539).

In the spirit of William Morris's concern for the steps people need to take as they change a society, Robinson's thought experiment gives its own provisional answers to the questions of state intervention and leadership. Certainly, Phil and Wade could only hold to an uncompromised legislative position in the context of their connection to the collective leadership of the allied movement. Thus, from a more radical democratic position than Callinicos might like, Robinson suggests that a preordained leadership body is not necessary, for such leadership will develop as individual figures emerge from the various interest groups and forge a common agreement on immediate tactics and long-term strategies. In the Antarctic event, there is no vanguard entity, but certain people (X, Wade, Val, Mai-lis, Joyce, Carlos) draw on previous knowledge and experience, grasp the immediate situation, and articulate strategies that shape the overall trajectory of the movement.

Le Guin's *The Telling* (2000) also gives us a dystopian narrative that focuses on a hegemonic social order (in this case on a planetary scale) that is opposed by a counter-force, again in the form of an alliance: but now one that is backed by the utopian power of her well-known Ekumen (that galactic version of a revolutionary post-state administration). In this work, which intertextually extends the vision of *The Dispossessed* (but, like Piercy's, revisits utopian politics and poetics in a dystopian mode), Le Guin spins a self-reflexive political fable that draws on discourses of science, religion, history, and storytelling to invoke the oppressive realities of Aka and Terra alike.

With critical echoes of the Chinese Cultural Revolution and occupation of Tibet, the repression of fundamentalist religious and secular regimes, and the rigidity of some post-revolutionary states, the rationalist Corporation State has banned and suppressed the earthly spirituality and culture of a people who have built their entire way of life around the practice of the Telling. Since it is by means of this extended ritual of communal storytelling that its adherents live, the government's move toward total suppression threatens to eradicate the culture. However, this genocidal policy begins to be disrupted when the newly arrived Ekumen Observer, Sutty, is sent out from the capital at Dovza City by the on-planet Ekumen Envoy, Tong, to the remote town of Okzat-Ozkat to investigate rumors that this suppressed culture ("a fragment population") survives on the margins of Corporation rule (13). Coming from Terra, where her own secular Commonwealth culture was destroyed by theocratic rulers, Sutty is ironically drawn into a sympathetic accord with the people of the Telling who have continued their old ways in spite of the government actions. With them, she treks to the mountainous refuge at the Lap of Silong to visit the remaining library where the last books that nourish the Telling are kept. Over several months, she immerses herself in learning the culture; and, as the possibility of government discovery and final elimination increases, she decides to help the people of the Telling by using her Ekumen technology to copy and preserve the rare documents.

The event that sparks the change in this dystopian situation occurs when a Corporation State Monitor, Yara, crash-lands near the library and is nursed back to life by the residents of the caves (with Sutty as a reluctant participant). In the heated exchanges between Sutty and Yara (which echo the Chinese Red Army's "speaking bitterness" experience), the Ekumen agent gains the spy's confidence, and he chooses to die rather than betray his rescuers; but before he does so he, in turn, provides Sutty with knowledge that will enable her to help the people of the Telling. She resolves to do so once their spiritual leaders, the maz, make it clear that they want such help, and by extension that of the utopian power, the Ekumen. Thus, Sutty's observation segues to intervention, as her political decision is ethically reinforced by the "underlying Hainish element in Ekumenical thinking: *Take responsibility*" (19).

The next steps toward liberating the culture and hence the people of the Telling are taken when Sutty reestablishes contact with Tong, and the two of them convince the Ekumen leadership that action is necessary. The galactic Ekumen respond with a twofold change of local policy: on one hand, they step in to protect the library at the Lap of Silong; and, on the other, they put a price on the information and "less exploitive" technology that they had been freely transferring and then threaten to end all such transmission unless the Corporation State changes its policy on the Telling (262). "Tat for tit," as Tong inelegantly summarizes the bargain—albeit a bargain which the mercantile culture of Aka could endorse as valid (263). This reformist intervention, which grew from Sutty's fieldwork and the resistance of the people of the Telling, then promises to provoke deeper changes that can restore Aka's "base culture" to its earlier non-hierarchical condition (261).

What we get in Le Guin's millennial fable, therefore, is a critical dystopia with a strong utopian presence, one found not only in the actions of yet another oppositional alliance but also (again, as in Piercy) in the power of a successful utopian post-state formation. However, we then move another step further into the question of oppositional engagement with existing state power as Le Guin, like Robinson, closes her tale with the account of successful maneuvers between the (local and galactic) opposition and the ruling state (an example of radical intervention that can speak to both Callinicos's and Hardt and Negri's concerns about the dangers of compromise or co-optation). It is, therefore, not only Sutty and the people of the Telling but also Tong and the Ekumen leadership (and here is also an answer that perhaps comes closer to Callinicos's call for an organized leadership while preserving the radical democratic intention of Hardt and Negri's intervention) who collectively bring about the transformation on Aka. In the Envoy's action, in particular, we get a condensed signifier of the sort of contestation within a state apparatus that can achieve not only a degree of reformist protection (rather than amelioration) but can also lead toward social transformation (in this case, as Aka shifts from a vertical to a horizontal power structure). The risk of stepping into such an action within the state apparatus is summed up by Tong when he admits to Sutty that he necessarily works at the "margin between collusion and respect," but it is a risk that is minimalized and deflected by the degree to which his work is protected from opportunist or defeatist compromise by the Ekumen's leadership and utopian power (21).

In these turn-of-the-century fictions, Robinson and Le Guin bring new life to the progressive political imaginary as they work within a dystopian structure of feeling necessary to their time, but their texts may also signal another moment of exhaustion for dystopian writing because both push the genre to its limits as they bring a fresh infusion of utopian vision to the pages of their texts. Perhaps the time has come for another creative and critical turn: just now in the direction of a revival of *eutopian* narratives that speak a directly transformative truth to global, capitalist power. As David Harvey puts it in his call for the regeneration of such an authentic, concrete utopianism in the face of the "degenerate utopianism of neoliberalism": "There is a time and place in the ceaseless human endeavor to change the world, when alternative visions, no matter how fantastic, provide the grist for shaping powerful political forces for change. I believe we are precisely at such a moment" (195).

Notes

1. The last paragraph of *The Iron Heel* ends with the unfinished sentence cited in the epigraph that opens this essay; see 224. I borrow the term "proto-dystopia" from Beachamp and am also indebted to his reading of London. See also Wegner; and Moylan, *Scraps.*
2. Such a discussion would, among other things, need to examine the role of anti-communism in the evolution of the dystopian narrative.
3. In "Locus, Horizon, and Orientation," Suvin discusses the difference between the "classical dystopia" and the diffused dystopian quality of sf, especially in the postwar "maps of hell" (as Kingsley Amis put it). He designates the science fictional versions as "simple dystopias" (171). Using this terminology, the cyberpunk fiction of the early 1980s that contributes to the dystopian turn can best be understood as "simple dystopia" as opposed to the self-reflexive "critical dystopia" that begins to appear by the mid-to-late 1980s.
4. Fitting identifies Zoë Fairbairn's 1979 novel, *Benefits*, as one of the first in the new line of dystopias (see 143).
5. For more on Gibson's trilogy, see Moylan, "Global Economy, Local Texts."
6. For more on the literary and political connotations of the term *critical* as I use it, see Moylan, *Demand*, 41–52. Perhaps the classical dystopias that get closest to Atwood's degree of analysis of desire and power are Aldous Huxley's *Brave New World* and Katharine Burdekin's *Swastika Night.* See also the discussion in *Scraps* (163–66) of *Handmaid* as a precursor of the critical dystopia. While sympathetic to the formal maneuvers and political substance of Atwood's work, I end up calling her text, in a play on Le Guin's *The Dispossessed*, an "ambiguous dystopia"; and in my reading of her closing chapter, I question the extent of Atwood's critique, seeing it as an instance of a detached and ironic liberalism rather than an expression of radical contestation. Many of my colleagues, however, see *Handmaid* as a critical dystopia in its own right. See the discussions of Atwood by Baccolini ("Gender and Genre" and "Journeying"), Cavalcanti, Sargent, Wolmark, and—in this volume—Fitting.
7. On genre blurring, see Baccolini, "Gender and Genre," and Moylan, *Scraps* 189.
8. For more on the relationship of the political economy and the state in *Gold Coast*, see *Scraps* 203–22.
9. For more on Butler's two *Parable* books, see *Scraps* 223–46.
10. For more on *He, She and It*, see *Scraps* 247–72.
11. Piercy's account of radical alternatives developing from the long and tragic history of the Middle East has become even more timely and tragic as conditions have deteriorated under Israeli and American rule.
12. In *Seeds*, Jameson performs one of his typical interpretive moves when he makes the argument that the ideological opposition to big government (in liberal democratic as well as "communist" societies) is, in the political unconscious of people on the populist Right who have themselves been betrayed by the neoliberal hegemony, a displacement of antagonism to the corporation rather than the socialist or liberal state: "But this anti-institutionalism can only secondarily be identified as anti-socialist or anti-Stalinist, since the more funda-

mental object at which it is directed is corporate capitalism itself, with its sterile language and made-up structures, its invented hierarchies and simulated psychologies. This is the only experience people in the West have had of omnipotent and impersonal power structures, and it is an experience over which late capitalism works, far more subtly and shrewdly than any left or populist movements, systematically redirecting such energies against fantasies of 'big government' and 'bureaucracy,' as though the corporations were not themselves the fundamental site of everything bureaucratic in First World capitalist countries" (63).

13. See Jameson, "Actually Existing Marxism" and Hobsbawm.
14. With others, I use the designation *anti-capitalist* rather than *anti-globalization* as a descriptor of the oppositional movement that emerged in Seattle in 1999. What people seem to be fighting for is an alternative form of globalization rather than a refusal. The demand for ecological sanity, economic justice, and universal human rights is an indicator of this direction.
15. "*Combination*, the old word for labour organization, offers an excellent symbolic designation for what is at issue on this ultimate, social level; and the history of the labour movement everywhere gives innumerable examples of the forging of new forms of solidarity in active political work" (Jameson, "Globalization" 68).
16. See *Empire*, especially part 2 and part 4. Unfortunately, the extensive debate on Hardt and Negri's work had just begun as I completed this essay. My comments here should be read as an initial contribution to that debate.
17. As in Le Guin's *The Dispossessed*, Piercy's *Woman on the Edge of Time*, Russ's *The Female Man*, and Robinson's later work, *Pacific Edge*.
18. Jameson puts the argument this way as he calls for an internationalism that goes beyond the limits of particularized nationalism: "And this is, perhaps, the deeper, philosophical reason why the struggle against globalization, though it may partially be fought on national terrain, cannot be successfully prosecuted to a conclusion in completely national or nationalist terms—even though nationalist passion, in my Gaullist sense, may be an indispensable driving force" ("Globalization" 66). His argument accords with Marx's insistence on the "emphatically international" character of the larger struggle; see *Civil War in France*, 373.
19. See, for example, Harvey, 186–88. When this book was going to press the Workers Party had just won national elections in Brazil by an overwhelming majority, and the European Social Forum was debating entry into parliamentary politics at its meetings during the November 2002 anti-globalization gathering in Florence.

Works Cited

Atwood, Margaret. *The Handmaid's Tale*. Boston: Houghton, 1985.
Baccolini, Raffaella. "Gender and Genre in the Feminist Critical Dystopias of Katharine Burdekin, Margaret Atwood, and Octavia Butler." *Future Females, the Next Generation: New Voices and Velocities in Feminist Science Fiction*. Ed. Marleen S. Barr. Lanham: Rowman, 2000. 13–34.
———. "Journeying through the Dystopian Genre: Memory and Imagination in Burdekin, Orwell, Atwood, and Piercy." *Viaggi in utopia*. Ed. Raffaella Baccolini, Vita Fortunati, and Nadia Minerva. Ravenna: Longo, 1996. 343–57.
Beauchamp, Gorman. "Jack London's Utopian Dystopia and Dystopian Utopia." *America as Utopia*. Ed. Kenneth M. Roemer. New York: Burt Franklin, 1981. 91–107.
———. "The Proto-Dystopia of Jerome K. Jerome." *Extrapolation* 24.2 (1983): 170–81.
Blade Runner. Dir. Ridley Scott. 1982.
Bourdieu, Pierre. *Acts of Resistance: Against the Tyranny of the Market*. Trans. Richard Nice. New York: New, 1998.
Bradbury. Ray. *Fahrenheit 451*. New York: Ballantine, 1953.
Butler, Octavia E. *Parable of the Sower*. New York: Warner, 1993.
———. *Parable of the Talents*. New York: Seven Stories, 1998.
Cadigan, Pat. *Synners*. New York: Bantam, 1991.
Callinicos, Alex. "Social Theory Put to the Test of Politics: Pierre Bourdieu and Anthony Giddens." *New Left Review* 236 (1999): 77–103.
Cavalcanti, Ildney. "Articulating the Elsewhere: Utopia in Contemporary Feminist Dystopias." Diss. U. of Strathclyde, 1999.
Engels, Frederick. "Postscript to Introduction to the Civil War in France (1891)." Available at: http://www.marxists.org/archive/marx/works/1871/civil-war-france/postscript.htm

Fitting, Peter. "The Turn from Utopia in Recent Feminist Fiction." *Feminism, Utopia, and Narrative.* Ed. Libby Falk Jones and Sarah Webster Goodwin. Knoxville: U of Tennessee P, 1990. 141–58.

Forster, E. M. "The Machine Stops." *Oxford and Cambridge Review* 8 (1909): 83–122.

Gibson, William. *Neuromancer.* New York: Ace, 1984.

Hardt, Michael, and Antonio Negri. *Empire.* Cambridge: Harvard UP, 2000.

Harvey, David. *Spaces of Hope.* Berkeley: U of California P, 2000.

Hobsbawm, Eric. *The Age of Extremes.* London: Verso, 1994.

Jameson, Fredric. "Five Theses on Actually Existing Marxism." *Monthly Review* 47.11 (1996): 1–10.

———. "Globalization and Strategy." *New Left Review* 4 (2000): 49–69.

———. *The Seeds of Time.* New York: Columbia U P, 1994.

Kadrey, Richard. *Metrophage.* New York: Ace, 1988.

Le Guin, Ursula. *The Dispossessed.* New York: Harper, 1974.

———. *The Telling.* New York: Harcourt, 2000.

London, Jack. *The Iron Heel.* New York: Macmillan, 1908. Edinburgh: Rebel, 1999.

Marx, Karl. *The Eighteenth Brumaire of Louis Napoleon.* 1852. Available at: http://www.marxists.org/archive/marx/works/1852/18th-brumaire/index.htm

Moylan, Tom. "Global Economy, Local Texts: Utopian/Dystopian Tensions in William Gibson's Cyberpunk 'Trilogy'." *minnesota review* 43–44 (1995): 182–97.

———. *Scraps of the Untainted Sky: Science Fiction, Utopia, Dystopia.* Boulder: Westview, 2000.

Piercy, Marge. *He, She and It.* New York: Knopf, 1991.

Robinson, Kim Stanley. *Antarctica.* New York: Harper, 1997.

———. *Blue Mars.* New York: Harper, 1996.

———. *The Gold Coast.* New York: Tor, 1988.

———. *Green Mars.* New York: Harper, 1993.

———. *Pacific Edge.* New York: Unwin, 1990.

———. *Red Mars.* New York: Harper, 1992.

Russ, Joanna. *The Female Man.* New York: Bantam, 1975.

Sargent, Lyman Tower. "The Three Faces of Utopianism Revisited." *Utopian Studies* 5.1 (1994): 1–37.

Singer, Daniel. *Whose Millennium? Theirs or Ours?* New York: Monthly Review, 1999.

Sterling, Bruce. *Islands in the Net.* New York: Ace, 1989.

Suvin, Darko. "Locus, Horizon, and Orientation: The Concept of Possible Worlds as a Key to Utopian Studies." *Not Yet: Reconsidering Ernst Bloch.* Ed. Jamie Owen Daniel and Tom Moylan. London: Verso, 1997. 122–37.

Wolmark, Jenny. *Aliens and Others: Science Fiction, Feminism and Postmodernism.* Iowa City: U of Iowa P, 1994.

CHAPTER **8**

Unmasking the Real? Critique and Utopia in Recent SF Films

PETER FITTING

I

The present discussion of the critical dystopia flows from Lyman Tower Sargent's call for a rethinking of the concept of the dystopia. The addition of the term critical, to my mind, is connected to a decline or at least a transformation of utopian writing in the 1990s. I will argue that, rather than understand "critical dystopia" as a work that combines utopia and dystopia, we should see it first of all as a *dystopia*. The term *critical dystopia* should be understood as referring to a concept that offers engaged critics, those of us interested in more than the strictly formal qualities of the literary utopia, a tool for evaluating recent dystopias. Margaret Atwood's *The Handmaid's Tale* is a classic example of a dystopia, and, as I shall explain, it is a *critical* dystopia (although obviously, not all dystopias are critical dystopias). An often-cited example of a work that combines utopia and dystopia is Marge Piercy's *He, She and It* (published in Britain as *Body of Glass*) where the utopian city-state of Tikva fights for survival in the midst of a larger dystopian future United States. Thus insofar as Piercy's novel presents us with the rudiments of a utopian society, however threatened, and because this is the central driving force of the novel, I would still tend to classify it as a eutopia (or positive utopia), and not as a critical dystopia.[1] The focus in Piercy's novel is on a utopian struggle within a larger dystopian context, a struggle that is not limited to the embattled city-state of Tikva but includes glimpses of other attempts at utopian communities within the Glop as well as the hidden community of Jewish and Palestinian women in Israel to which Malkah goes at the end of the novel. The larger dystopian setting does not take away its utopian import, and in fact utopias have often included a dystopian counterpart that is sometimes contrasted to the utopian society (as in Ursula K. Le Guin's *The Dispossessed*), or that may threaten it (as in Piercy's *Woman on the Edge of Time*), or that may in fact represent the past (as in Joanna Russ's *The Female Man*).

What is important in the critical dystopia and distinguishes it from other dystopias is to be found in the adjective *critical*, which implies an explanation of how the dystopian situation came about as much as what should be done about it. Thus, to take two extreme examples, a comparison between the dystopian society of Gilead in Atwood's novel and the explanation of how it emerged from our present is very different from the explanation of the dystopian future given in of the *Terminator* movies. In *The Handmaid's Tale*, the description of the dystopian society contains an implicit warning that this may be where we are heading, as well as an account of those elements in our present that have produced this future. The future of the *Terminator* films, on the other hand, is not important in itself, but serves rather to provide a justification for the films' events. Thus Atwood's novel is a *critical* dystopia while the films use a dystopian setting because of the narrative advantages of that context, like the lawlessness of the frontier for the western or the "Time of Troubles" for the Japanese samurai film. In this context, I could also cite the role of the energy crisis that precipitates the social and economic collapse depicted in the *Mad Max* films. Again, the narrative does not include an examination or critique of those elements in the present that contribute to that crisis.

This contrast may be seen in terms of *foreground* and *background*: Gilead is the *subject* of Atwood's novel, while the decaying and devastated landscapes of so many science fiction movies of the past few decades provide the backdrop for the adventure. This device of setting events in a dystopian future feeds on collective anxieties (like the threat of nuclear destruction in *Terminator 2*), without attempting to elucidate or understand them and without offering collective solutions or political strategies for dealing with them. Yet, in addition to pointing out that these dystopian settings work as a device for motivating the adventures and special effects of recent sf films, I note that the increase in such settings has occurred at the same time as a pause in utopian writing and thinking. It is my contention that this pause is significant insofar as so many people seem to be aware that they are living in an increasingly threatened world (in which inequity and exploitation are on the rise), and yet they remain paralyzed, unable or unwilling to act, convinced that the electoral system and politics in any form are shams. In such dystopian times, then, the critical dystopia will do more than simply depict the accommodation with or the flight from that world.

In the midst of this contemporary political paralysis, I have become interested in how popular films represent the crisis, and specifically in the rise of new configurations of conspiracy theory (as can be seen in the related television success of *The X Files*) which explain the ineffectiveness of conventional political activity in terms of hidden forces that control and manipulate us. More specifically, in the context of the critical dystopia, I am interested in films that critique the present by depicting our reality as a comfortable but artificial world which screens a much more frightening "real" reality "behind all this" (a theme epitomized in the fiction of Philip K. Dick).

In this light, I want to look at four films from the end of the twentieth century—*Pleasantville* (1998), *Dark City* (1998), *The Truman Show* (1998) and *The Matrix* (1999)—which portray illusory, constructed realities that are inhabited by people (or in *The Truman Show* by a single character) who are deliberately kept unaware of the artificial nature of their worlds. I will argue that the motif of a pseudo reality shifts attention away from the concrete features of the traditional dystopia to the mechanism that produces the illusory reality and to what is hidden behind it. In the popular imagination, this theme—the sense that our "reality" is somehow false—is often explained in terms of conspiracies and cover-ups. I will explain it rather in terms of ideology—as a trope or figure for the many ways in which government and media collude to obscure any significant discussion of the real economic workings of contemporary society, a process that leaves us confused and unsure of how to act to change that situation.

These films are all different in their presentation of an artificial reality and the "real" reality lying behind it. In *Dark City* and *The Matrix*, the constructed realities are explained in science fiction terms; while *The Truman Show* and *Pleasantville*—set more or less in the present—focus on television's role in the production of an illusory reality. Moreover, in *Dark City* and *The Matrix*, the discovery that the characters' somewhat dystopian reality is false leads to the uncovering of a truly dystopian real reality; while in the other two films there is a juxtaposition of a false utopian world and our own (not very dystopian) present. But these contrasts and complications are what make these films so fascinating.

II

The Truman Show presents a world very much like our own. The unknowing hero of a television show since birth, twenty-nine-year-old Truman

Burbank lives in a fabricated reality, surrounded by hidden television cameras. All his friends and neighbors, and even his wife, are actors fed their lines, and anyone who attempts to deviate from the scripted story is quickly written out of it. On a first level, the film has been understood as a critique of television, and especially of "reality culture," through the film's depiction of a television audience now bored with the revelations of Jerry Springer and *Most Dangerous Police Chases*, and eager for "real TV" at its most extreme (a phenomenon observable already today in the growing popularity of live webcams, hidden surveillance cameras, or television shows like *Survivor* and *Big Brother*).[2] More than fifty years ago, Walter Benjamin, in "The Work of Art in the Age of Mechanical Reproduction," commented on the impact of mechanical reproduction and the resulting loss of aura. Today, in a world in which new technologies have made it impossible to tell the real from the copy or the simulacrum, this loss of aura can be seen in the ever-increasing demand for images of the "real" that can somehow be verified as authentic, because it is "live," for instance; the emblem of such authenticity is, I suppose, the "money shot" in pornography (the moment of ejaculation which—at least with current technology—cannot be faked).[3] Yet the link between our craving for authenticity and the artificiality and shallowness of the reality we are offered through the media is not explained or examined in this film—to satisfy the viewer, it suffices that Truman escapes.

Moreover, his gradual suspicion that his world is a construct and that its purpose has been deliberately hidden from him is not accompanied by any larger self-realization or discovery—as epitomized by the puerility of his discussions with his friend Marlon. Nor is there a deeper meaning for the film audience: like the TV audience of *The Truman Show*, who can enjoy their voyeurism even as they cheer for Truman's escape, we the film audience are even more co-opted, but to an even greater extent, because we are shown Christof and his crew as they manipulate Truman and then attempt to deal with his escape—an insider's view that the show's television audience does not see.

In opposition to the illusory utopia of Seahaven Island, *The Truman Show* offers only an equally false alternative: Truman's desire to leave and go to Fiji to find the young woman with whom he fell in love as a teenager and who was removed from the show. We are not shown what happens after he escapes, for of course he will have escaped (back) into our own world. This is the film's central contradiction, for the illusory world of Seahaven from which he must escape is in fact more desirable than the real but rarely seen world of the television audience who cheer on his escape. Thus, while the film apparently values independence over an artificial life of comfort and ease, it lacks even John the Savage's pleading—in an earlier rebellion against planned happiness in Aldous Huxley's *Brave New World*—that he wants "the right to be unhappy" (187).[4] In contrast to the critique of a similar false utopia of small-town life in *Pleasantville*, Truman is not actually rejecting this world. What he really wants is the girl he met at a dance and not the submissive, boring wife provided him by the show's producer. Truman provides a displaced figure of escape for an audience who crave deliverance from their own deadening existence, while the causes of the inadequacies of their existence are concealed and denied. The contradiction, then, lies in that fantasy of escape not *from* Truman's world, but *to* it, for it is his world's comfort and its absence of contemporary urban cares and problems that so absorb the audience. In this way, the film reaffirms rather than critiques the present, suggesting by means of his escape that the only real "utopia" is our own world, thus negating the utopian project itself.

III

Unlike the sunny but false utopian present of Truman's world, *Dark City* is set in a strange, dystopian 1940s film noir metropolis which, as the spectator learns in the opening sequence, is not what it seems. Again we are in on the secret, although in contrast to the complicity of the television watchers in *The Truman Show*, our knowledge is one of confusion, not collusion, as we try to understand what is going on. Unlike the actors in that film, who were all aware of the artificial character of Seahaven, here the characters are "in the dark," unaware that their world is not real; and, indeed, this is a city of perpetual night, a fact that no one even seems to notice. Again, it is the hero's attempts to understand what is going on that drive the narrative. Unlike *The Truman Show*, however, this is sf, and the explanation for this illusory world is at once more far-fetched than a television producer's ambitions and his sponsors' desire for profits and more threatening because everyone is equally confused.

Here alien "Strangers" have captured some humans and transported them to the artificial world of Dark City to try and understand—through experiment—why they, the Strangers, are dying. They conduct their experiments by means of "tuning," a continuous telepathic reshaping of this simulated world. Every night at midnight the clocks stop, and humans are rendered temporarily unconscious; they awaken with new implanted memories in an adjusted reality. When the protagonist, Murdoch, awakes at the beginning of the film, he does not know who he is, even as he discovers that he has the ability to resist this induced sleep and to telepathically change reality itself. As he tries to recover his past, he discovers too that this is not Earth, but an island floating in space, and he turns to his own dream world, that of an apparently implanted childhood memory of Shell Beach, which he begins to reconstruct.[5] The film ends not with the struggle against the Strangers nor with an attempt to awaken the other humans, but—like Truman's desire to go to Fiji—with Murdoch's escape into another artificial world, albeit one of his own making.

Like Truman's friends and neighbors, here everyone is again an actor, although they do not know that they are only playing roles, that they are being manipulated and controlled through the use of implanted memories. The scenes in which characters try to explain to Murdoch how to get to Shell Beach are chilling illustrations of an older definition of ideology as "false consciousness." Although people "know" how to go there, their experience contradicts this, for they cannot find the way, even as they continue to believe that Shell Beach is just outside of town; and their thoughts—like the directions they give Murdoch—lead only to puzzling dead ends. Interestingly enough, the inability to leave the closed worlds implicit in *The Truman Show* and *Dark City* is made explicit in *Pleasantville*; there it is a geographical given, taught in school, and everyone knows there is nothing outside Pleasantville. In *Dark City*, the characters think they can leave, but the roads do not go where they remember; and Truman is prevented from leaving Seahaven Island, first because of his imprinted fear of water—stemming from his father's faked drowning—and then, when he does manage to cross the bridge, because a series of bizarre, obviously staged accidents (a forest fire and a nuclear incident) force him back to Seahaven.

Since there is no obvious "literal" interpretation of the situation in *Dark City*—as opposed to seeing *The Truman Show* as a criticism of the manipulative power of television and its willingness to cater to the public's voyeuristic tastes—it is the conflicting thought processes of the inhabitants whose memories and knowledge are contradicted by practical experience that I find significant because they reflect the confusion and helplessness of people frustrated and discouraged with the political system today. In the film, unfortunately, the only way offered out of this gloomy prison is strictly an individual one, as Murdoch sets out to create the Shell Beach of his memories. We do not know what will happen to the others or whether Murdoch will be able to make Dark City over into his own solipsistic utopia.

IV

In *The Matrix*, people are again living in a false reality that looks like our present. Actually, this is a future Earth where humans are only dreaming that they are awake and living at the end of the twentieth century, for they are in fact all wired into a vast computer-programmed virtual reality which maintains them as an energy source for the machines that now control the planet. Unlike the previous two films, this one presents a hero whose quest to understand and find "real" reality moves from the desire for individual escape to a collective struggle. The protagonist, Neo, breaks out of the virtual reality of "our" present into a bleak, devastated future Earth where he joins Morpheus and his crew in a lonely fight against the overwhelming force of the machines and their deadly programs, the Agents.[6] While the estranged figures of humans and machines, by their very distance from our reality, have prompted a variety of interpretations of this film—as a facsimile of capitalism itself, for instance, one in which workers are vampirically drained of surplus value through the labor process—I am more impressed by a reading that focuses on the representation of collective struggle, which, however dystopian the context of these efforts, is a utopian feature that is not found in the two previous films. Here the goal is not a question of an individual escape from a stifling, false reality into a personal fantasy world, but the success of a collective struggle to free the human race from oppression. Thus, however vague or fanciful the film is in terms of its depiction of the causes of human suffering, it presents a more utopian form of struggle and resistance, a welcome correction to the myth of the solitary hacker of so much cyberpunk, for the hackers here are working collectively. And how far off the mark, really is *The Matrix* in its depiction of today's world? How is the virtual reality of our present as offered by the machines different from the imaginary satisfactions of the illusory false utopias offered us by the media, which, like the machine dreams of the film, acclimatize and blind us to the growing immiseration of so many Americans? This actual reality is captured in Cipher's filmic decision—after nine years of "boring struggle" (his words)—to sell out Morpheus and the others in exchange for the illusion of his choice (fine wines and food in luxury restaurants), a cynical echo of the choices made by the heroes at the end of *Dark City* and *The Truman Show* as they opt for escapes into fantasy worlds.[7]

V

While I have tried to show a range of critical stances and explanations of the meaning of these illusory realities (from *The Truman Show*, which offers little in the way of critical thinking; through *Dark City*, which with its presentation of the trope of false consciousness at least offered a glimpse of the contradictions in the concept of the illusory reality; as well as some possible progressive readings of *The Matrix*), my explanation may be further clarified through an examination of *Pleasantville*. This film goes in the opposite direction to the other films considered here, as the hero moves from the present of today to the imaginary small town of 1950s television shows like *Ozzie and Harriet* or *Father Knows Best*. Bud and his sister, Mary Sue, are transported into a black-and-white 1950s world out of some neoconservative advertisement for family values. Unlike the previous films, *Pleasantville* offers a critique of the ideological fantasy of small-town America as well as offering a way of testing the concept of the critical dystopia. At the very beginning, the film frankly acknowledges the dystopian aspects of our present, by taking us inside three high school classrooms: in the first, the students are being told that their job prospects are poor and getting worse; in biology class, they are being warned about sexually transmitted diseases and AIDS; and, in the third class, they are given an alarming account of ozone depletion, global warming, and the imminent prospect of a worldwide famine. Despite the terrors and risks of the present, however, this film explicitly rejects the all-too-familiar solution of a return to an earlier, happier time, showing instead how Bud grows up and out of his desire to live in the fantasy world of Pleasantville as he learns actively to live in the present. The film does this by restaging in miniature the transition to the 1960s, a time that social-conservatives see as the moment of the destruction of the right-wing American utopia. The film does this not in terms of the discovery of poverty in the United States or of opposition to the Vietnam War, but very explicitly in response to current attacks on equity and equal rights.

With the introduction of two teenagers from the present into this black-and-white world, Pleasantville begins to change, first of all under the impetus of Mary Sue's sexual preoccupations. In a triumph of special effects, bits of color begin to appear here and there in this black and white film, first in a flower, and then in bodies. But there is a backlash against the coming of color, especially after Bud's mother discovers the emptiness of her life as a model housewife and decides to leave her husband. The introduction of color into the film, as a special effect that reflects the transition to color from the black-and-white television of the 1950s, is a powerful symbol of, and makes specific allusion to, positive change. A first reference is to the use of the word "colored," for in the 1950s American blacks were politely referred to as "colored" people, and the second is to the civil rights movement. The scenes of harassment of "coloreds" and the attack on the soda fountain in the film are an eerie and troubling reminder of the racism at the core of the social-conservative utopia of the 1950s and of the television footage of the violent resistance to attempts to integrate stores and restaurants in the 1960s in the South.

The allusion to feminism through color is done by linking sexual awakening with Bud's sister and mother. Not only are there no bodily functions in Pleasantville, as illustrated by the absence of a toilet in the girls' washroom at the soda fountain, but everyone seems completely ignorant of sex. Fires do not exist, and the fire department serves instead to rescue cats from trees. Sex is explicitly linked to color, and more spectacularly to fire. When Bud's mother discovers masturbation—following Mary Sue's instructions—her orgasm in the bathtub is shown from outside the house as an exploding fireball that sets a tree on fire, in full color.[8] Then, after Bud has gone to the fire station and yelled "cat" (to get the fire department to the house), he has to show firefighters how to work the fire hose: "so that's what that's for," one says as water begins to shoot from his hose.

For some time, the 1950s have been used as an emblem of happier times, when family values and small-town America were concrete manifestations of the triumph of capitalism and the "end of ideology." But as the film reminds us, this is an unreal, false vision that paints over and denies a number of repressed realities of the time which exploded into public awareness in the 1960s. Moreover, the critical purpose of the film is furthered by the ability of some of the characters, most explicitly Bud and Mary Sue, and Mr. Bill Johnson at the soda fountain, to think about what is happening and to reflect on what constitutes meaning and happiness—a level of self-awareness and introspection that seems almost completely lacking in *The Truman Show* and *Dark City*.[9]

VI

There are numerous objective explanations for the apparent failure of the utopian moment of the 1960s, a crisis that is today reflected in a seeming paralysis of the political process in which fewer and fewer people even bother to vote, and—on the part of people involved in the utopian politics of the 1960s—in a fragmentation of those utopian projects into local issues and identity politics. What I have tried to do in discussing these films is to suggest that *The Truman Show, Dark City*, and (to a lesser degree) *The Matrix* reflect this paralysis, by turning back to an earlier stage of political awareness. For in these three films the very possibility of any critique of existing social reality—the necessary first step in utopian action—has been supplanted by a vague, uncertain perception that at the end of the twentieth century the workings of social reality are no longer visible to us.[10] More important, in their preoccupation with artificial, illusory worlds we can detect a growing awareness that something is wrong with the reality offered us by the media. Like the directions to Shell Beach, however, thinking about these issues produces only confusion. Instead of a *critical* look at the present, then, these films offer the inadequate but nonetheless satisfying explanation that reality is not what it seems or, worse, that we are living in an artificial or false reality as victims of sinister forces that control and manipulate us, and for which the only solution lies in personal escape (except for *The Matrix*), as summed up in the lottery ticket or in the television show *Who Wants to Be a Millionaire?*

While the rising popularity of conspiracy theories may reflect a growing distrust of what we are told by politicians and the media, both increasingly in the control of large corporations, a critique based on the demand that the government open the Roswell Files, for example, will not produce any real understanding of the present and certainly will not lead to the transformation of society. *Pleasantville*, on the other hand, does offer a critical deconstruction of our own myth of the Golden Age, that of some happier, simpler time offered by small-town America in the 1950s.[11] While *Pleasantville* does not offer any instructions for political action, it serves as a powerful rejection of one of the most influential ideas in the arsenal of those opposed to change. Instead of attempting to escape, the film's central characters acknowledge and confront the dystopian aspects of the present. This film certainly does not resolve these contradictions or propose any utopian avenues of struggle (fundamental, I think, to the critical dystopia), but it does suggest yet another way of understanding the concept of the critical dystopia: as a work that rejects false utopian solutions to the dystopia of the present.

We can hope that our attention to the critical dystopia is misplaced. Perhaps we have not seen the last of Utopia. The demonstrations against globalization that began in Seattle and spread around the globe suggest a new alignment of those who are opposed to the status quo and disgusted with conventional electoral politics but are also unwilling to abandon the political arena. Perhaps we are at the dawn of a new form of utopian political struggle.[12]

Notes

1. Moylan reviews the arguments for considering *He, She and It* as a critical dystopia (247–72). Sargent does not actually call Piercy's novel a critical dystopia, but writes that its combination of dystopia and eutopia undermines "neat classification schemes" (7). There is already a category for dealing with and categorizing works in which a utopian sequence or episode is set within a larger, often dystopian, narrative: the "micro-utopia," as developed, for instance, in Racault's discussion of some classic French texts (like Prévost's *Cleveland* or the El Dorado episode of *Candide*). See his extended discussion of *Cleveland* and *Candide* (597–690).

2. The pleasure of looking, of spying or watching someone unaware, is at the basis of much recent film theory. For a discussion of the earliest films and this pleasure, see Williams, *Hard Core*, as well as her anthology, *Viewing Positions*. For a close analysis of some of the earliest films about looking, see the studies of a group of early films collected in Gaudreault. The best known example of a live webcam broadcast began in 1995 when an art student, Jennifer Ringley, began to broadcast twenty-four hours a day an uncensored live feed from her apartment, and then, after she moved, from her bedroom (www.jennicam.org).

3. For a discussion of the "money shot" in pornography, see Williams, *Hard Core.*
4. Huxley's dialogue goes as follows:
    "But I don't want comfort [John the Savage tells the Controller]. I want God, I want poetry, I want real danger, I want freedom, I want goodness. I want sin."
    "In fact," said Mustapha Mond, "you're claiming the right to be unhappy."
    "All right then," said the Savage defiantly, "I'm claiming the right to be unhappy."
    "Not to mention the right to grow old and ugly and impotent: the right to have syphilis and cancer; the right to have too little to eat; the right to be lousy; the right to live in constant apprehension of what may happen tomorrow; the right to catch typhoid; the right to be tortured by unspeakable pains of every kind." There was a long silence.
    "I claim them all," said the Savage at last. (Huxley 163)
5. Of course this memory of Shell Beach may also be a buried, somehow unerased childhood memory from before humans were taken to Dark City. Like Deckard's photos of his childhood in *Blade Runner,* Murdock's memories may or may not reflect real events; their emotional power is undiminished in either case.
6. The lethal "agents" of the Matrix are an interesting twist on the deadly black "ice" ("Intrusion Countermeasures Electronics") of Gibson's cyberpunk novels that protects the fields and towers of data in the matrix: "Ice that kills. Illegal, but then aren't we all? Some kind of neural-feedback weapon, and you connect with it only once. Like some hideous Word that eats the mind from the inside out. Like an epileptic spasm that goes on and on until there's nothing left at all" (182). The reference to the Jefferson Airplane (when Morpheus offers Neo the choice of two pills, the film is quoting the song "White Rabbit": "one pill makes you larger, and one pill makes you small") provides another allusion to 1960s rebellion, and the sound track, which includes the well-known contemporary political band Rage Against the Machine, makes the link between the 1960s and the present. At the same time that it plugs into the rebelliousness of the 1960s, the film is notable insofar as it is not fixated on the "youth" aspect of the 1960s, portraying instead a cross-generational resistance to the numbing machine dreams fed to the inhabitants of the Earth. For younger viewers, there is of course another level of meaning in the film insofar as it resembles a video game: not only in the fight sequences, but in the questions and choices that initiate Neo's quest (which pill?), the safe points (telephone booths), and the anonymity of the evil monsters who return again and again after they are "killed" (the agents). Not since Arnold Schwarzenegger's portrayal of a robot in the first *Terminator* (1984) has there been such an effective description of a cold, humanoid killing machine. Of course this is hardly an original interpretation, given that the agents and the world in which Neo and the others fight them are simply computer programs and the virtual world they generate.
7. The poverty of desire in consumer society is epitomized for me in Godard's film *Le Weekend* (1967) when Joseph ("the son of God and Alexandre Dumas") offers the couple their heart's desire if they will drive him to London. In response they can only come up with a list of designer-name consumer goods:
    Roland: A Mercedes . . . a big sports Mercedes?
    Joseph: O.K.
    Corinne: A Saint-Laurent evening dress?
    Joseph: O.K.
    Roland: A hotel on Miami beach?
    Joseph: Hmmm . . .
    Corinne excitedly: Turn me into a blonde—a real one, O.K.?
    Roland: A fleet of Mirage IVs like the yids used to wipe out the wogs?
    Corinne: A weekend with James Bond?
    Roland with a glean in his eye: Yeah, me too . . .
    Joseph: Is that really all you want?
    Roland: Sure, it'll do . . .
    Joseph contemptuously: You poor goons! What a pair of bastards! You won't get a thing from me. (Godard 47)
8. This suggests another 1960s reference: the Rolling Stones song "She's a Rainbow" (*Their Satanic Majesties Request* 1967), with its refrain "she comes in colors everywhere." In conversation, Raffaella Baccolini has pointed out that the potential feminist message of the film is seemingly contradicted by Mary Sue's decision to remain in the 1950s.

9. Compare Truman's moments of reflection when he talks to his best friend, Marlon. Consider, too, that the most poignant of Marlon's speeches is directly fed to him by Christof, another example of the film's cynicism which makes the spectator complicit with a world in which, using a television metaphor, it is implied that we are intelligent enough to change the channel—i.e., television is only giving people what they want.

10. My comment that the "workings of social reality are no longer visible to us" is based on the work of Jameson, and in particular on his description of what he calls the "problem of representation" in post-industrial society:

> The technology of contemporary society is therefore mesmerizing and fascinating not so much in its own right but because it seems to offer some privileged representational shorthand for grasping a network of power and control even more difficult for our minds and imaginations to grasp: the whole new decentred global network of the third stage of capital itself. This is a figural process presently best observed in a whole mode of contemporary entertainment literature—one is tempted to characterize it as "high-tech paranoia"—in which the circuits and networks of some putative global computer hook-up are narratively mobilized by labyrinthine conspiracies of autonomous but deadly interlocking and competing information agencies in a complexity often beyond the capacity of the normal reading mind. Yet conspiracy theory . . . must be seen as a degraded attempt—through the figuration of advanced technology—to think the impossible totality of the contemporary world system. (37–38)

11. This nostalgia for the past is reflected today in architecture and urban planning in the so-called New Urbanism movement. See Shibley.

12. See in particular Hardt and Negri.

Works Cited

Atwood, Margaret. *The Handmaid's Tale.* Toronto: McClelland, 1985.

Blade Runner. Dir. Ridley Scott. 1982.

Dark City. Dir. Alex Proyas. 1998.

Gaudreault, André, ed. *Ce que je vois de mon ciné.* Paris: Méridiens Klincksieck, 1988.

Gibson, William. *Burning Chrome.* 1986. New York: Ace, 1987.

Godard, Jean-Luc. *Weekend and Wind from the East: Two Films by Jean-Luc Godard.* New York: Simon, 1972.

Hardt, Michael, and Antonio Negri. *Empire.* Cambridge: Harvard UP, 2000.

Huxley, Aldous. *Brave New World.* 1932. New York: Bantam, 1958.

Jameson, Fredric. *Postmodernism, or, The Cultural Logic of Late Capitalism.* Durham: Duke UP, 1991.

Mad Max. Dir. George Miller. 1979.

Mad Max beyond Thunderdome. Dir. George Miller. 1985.

The Matrix. Dir. Andy Wachowski and Larry Wachowski. 1999.

Moylan, Tom. *Scraps of the Untainted Sky: Science Fiction, Utopia, Dystopia.* Boulder: Westview, 2000.

Piercy, Marge. *He, She and It.* New York: Knopf, 1991.

Pleasantville. Dir. Gary Ross. 1998.

Racault, Jean-Michel. *L'Utopie narrative, 1675–1761.* Studies on Voltaire and the Eighteenth Century 280. Oxford: Voltaire Foundation, 1991.

The Road Warrior. Dir. George Miller. 1981.

Sargent, Lyman Tower. "The Three Faces of Utopianism Reconsidered." *Utopian Studies* 5.1 (1994): 1–37.

Shibley, Robert. "The Complete New Urbanism and the Partial Practices of Placemaking." *Utopian Studies* 9.1 (1998): 80–103.

Terminator. Dir. James Cameron. 1984.

Terminator 2: Judgment Day. Dir. James Cameron. 1991.

The Truman Show. Dir. Peter Weir. 1998.

Williams, Linda. *Hard Core: Power, Pleasure and the "Frenzy of the Visible."* Expanded ed. Berkeley: U of California Press, 1999.

———. *Viewing Positions: Ways of Seeing Film.* New Brunswick: Rutgers UP, 1995.

CHAPTER 9

Where the Prospective Horizon Is Omitted: Naturalism and Dystopia in *Fight Club* and *Ghost Dog*

PHILLIP E. WEGNER

Everything living, says Goethe, has an atmosphere around it; everything real in general, because it is life, process, and can be a correlate of objective imagination, has a horizon. An inner horizon, extending vertically as it were, in the self-dark, an external one of great breadth, in the world-light; and the regions behind both horizons are filled with the same utopia, are consequently identical in the Ultimum. Where the prospective horizon is omitted, reality only appears as become, as dead, and it is the dead, namely naturalists and empiricists, who are burying their dead here. Where the prospective horizon is continuously included in the reckoning, the real appears as what it is in concreto: as the path-network of dialectical processes which occur in an unfinished world, in a world which would not be in the least changeable without the enormous future: real possibility in that world. Together with that Totum which does not represent the isolated whole of a respective section of process, but the whole of the subject-matter pending in the process overall, hence still tendential and latent. This alone is realism, it is of course inaccessible to that schematism which knows everything in advance, which considers its uniform, in fact even formalistic, stencil to be reality. Reality without real possibility is not complete, the world without future-laden properties does not deserve a glance, an art, a science any more than that of the bourgeois conformist.
—Ernst Bloch, *The Principle of Hope*

I

The epigraph is taken from Ernst Bloch's monumental inquiry into the ir-repressibility of the utopian impulse (223). According to him, the naturalists and empiricists, with their careful schematic mappings of an apparently fixed and closed social reality and their a priorist assumptions about the law-governed structure of human nature, deny the presence of history, of the real possibility of change, located within any present. Although Bloch is referring to a much larger philosophical and aesthetic debate, the oppo-sition he sets up here—that between naturalism and utopia—also usefully recalls an important event in the literary history of the latter part of the nineteenth century. Fredric Jameson argues that the dramatic reemergence of utopian fiction in the late nineteenth century needs to be understood, at least in part, as a response to the asphyxiating historical closure of the then-reigning literary naturalism (*Political* 193).[1] This is as much the case for William Morris, whose *News from Nowhere* is a reply to the work of the English naturalist writer George Gissing, as it is for Morris's other primary interlocutor, Edward Bellamy, the latter decrying the "profound pessimism of the literature of the last quarter of the nineteenth century," and writing his hugely influential narrative utopia, *Looking Backward*, as an attempt to provide an alternative to it (194).

If this latest manifestation of the literary utopia represents a dialectical negation of the vision of literary naturalism, might we then be able to speak of what Hegel names the "negation of the negation," a third form that recapitulates and subsumes elements of both aspects of what might now be understood as an initial contradiction?[2] In other words, what hap-pens when the thoroughgoing pessimism about the present moment is suddenly transported into the "otherworldly" space of the utopian fiction? It is precisely such a negation of the negation, I want to argue here, that gives rise in the late nineteenth and early twentieth centuries to perhaps the most influential and productive subgenre of the modern narrative utopia: that of the *dystopia*.

Any discussion of the dystopian form must now come to grips with the history of its development and transformation in the course of the last century offered in Tom Moylan's *Scraps of the Untainted Sky*. Challenging many of the conventional assumptions about these works, Moylan argues that dystopian fictions are not "texts that temperamentally refuse the pos-sibility of radical social transformation"—and in this they could be under-stood to be as dialectically other to what Bloch and Jameson see as the "Anti-Utopianism" of literary naturalism as they are to their more properly utopian predecessors. "Rather," Moylan maintains, "they look quizzically, skeptically, critically not only at the present society but also at the means needed to transform it" (133). His focus then moves from the more general category of the dystopia to what he calls the "critical dystopia," a textual practice first emerging in the late 1980s in response to the conservative political retrenchments of the Reagan-Thatcher era, and exemplified for him by Kim Stanley Robinson's *Gold Coast*, Octavia Butler's *Parable* novels, and Marge Piercy's *He, She and It*. The "strongly, and more self-reflexively 'critical'" stance of these texts, Moylan crucially maintains, does *not* signal the emergence of "an entirely new generic form but rather a significant retrieval and refunctioning of the most progressive possibilities inherent in dystopian narrative" (188). He then concludes that such texts "negotiate the necessary pessimism of the generic dystopia with an open, militant, utopian stance that not only breaks through the hegemonic enclosure of the text's alternative world but also self-reflexively refuses the anti-utopian temptation that lingers like a dormant virus in every dystopian account" (195).

There are two crucial points that I would like to take from Moylan's reading. First, he helps us recognize a difference between the utopian and dystopian forms that goes deeper than the familiar "good place–bad place" opposition. Of the new critical dystopias, he notes, "[a]s an anticipatory machine in that new context, the critical dystopias resist both hegemonic and oppositional orthodoxies (in their radical and reformist variants) even as they refunction a larger, more totalizing critique of the political economy itself. They *consequently inscribe a space for a new form of political opposition*" (190, emphasis added). Such an "inscription" of a new space for political opposition is in fact, I would argue, following Moylan's lead, characteristic of *all* dystopias (something only "formally and politically foregrounded in the recent works" [189]). In short, the subject of utopian desire in the dystopia is *politics* itself—of agency and of a kickstarting of the engine of history in a moment when it seems to many to be terminally stalled. To put this another way, Utopia is always already a politics *in potentia*, what Slavoj Žižek, in turn drawing upon Alain Badiou, names an Event: "an intervention that cannot be accounted for in the terms of its pre-existing 'objective conditions,'" and indeed whose success (pace Bellamy) or failure in "seizing the masses" then helps to define these very conditions (164). On the other hand, the dystopia, and especially the recent critical dystopia, defiantly holds open, in the conditions of dimmest radical political possibility (as in the years of global neo-liberal onslaught), precisely the hope that such a politics might reemerge. In this way, the critical dystopia becomes a self-consuming text, one that narrates the desired abolition of the very conditions of its own emergence, such that politics once again replaces the desire for politics. Indeed, dystopia after dystopia—from Moylan's ur-classical dystopia, E. M. Forster's "The Machine Stops" (1909) to his most recent critical dystopia, Marge Piercy's *He, She and It* (1991)—tells the story of a growing resistance and ultimate opposition to the "considerably worse" social and historical conditions that it portrays. The very presence of critical dystopian fictions thus tells us a great deal about the historical situation, as they struggle to maintain "militant pessimism" in the face of very great odds—and it is in this effort, as Moylan demonstrates, that their real significance lies.

And yet, while these works consistently help us locate a horizon of political contestation in any present, their ultimate conclusions concerning the viability of such actions vary tremendously; or as Moylan puts it, "the dystopian genre has always worked along a contested continuum between utopian and anti-utopian positions: between texts that are emancipatory, militant, open, and 'critical' and those that are compensatory, resigned, and quite 'anti-critical'" (188). Later, he continues, "contemporary dystopian examples that are anti-critical can be identified as texts that more readily remain in the camp of nihilistic or resigned expressions that may appear to challenge the current social situation but in fact end up reproducing it by ideologically inoculating viewers and readers against any form of anger or action, enclosing them within the very social realities they disparagingly expose" (195–96). In such texts, the "dormant virus" of the "anti-utopian temptation," haunting as it does the very corpus of the dystopian form, springs to life once again.

In what follows, I want to suggest that the line between these two poles often remains a hazy one, as any particular dystopian vision can pass back and forth between them—something very much the case in the two recent film dystopias I will examine in the next sections of this paper. Such an instability is, I would further maintain, a consequence of the particular patrimony of the form itself—for rather than a virus, such a tendency toward the Anti-Utopia should be conceived of as a *genetic* inheritance in the very formal structure of the dystopia, a legacy of its roots in the traditions of literary naturalism. Interestingly, most of the dystopian fictions remembered best today come from authors who understood their politics to be left of center, if not explicitly socialist—something equally the case, as Jameson's discussion of Gissing makes evident (Emile Zola and Theodore Dreiser also come to mind), for the nineteenth-century practitioners of literary naturalism. In all of these cases, we see emerging a fundamental and often irresolvable contradiction between the author's or the text's explicit political orientation and what Jameson calls the "ideology of form"—that is, "'form' apprehended as content . . . formal processes as sedimented content in their own right, as carrying ideological messages of their own, distinct from the ostensible or manifest content of the works" (*Political* 99).

As I noted above, Moylan locates the paradigmatic expression of the modern dystopia in Forster's short story "The Machine Stops," showing in great detail precisely how this text sets the formal pattern that will be taken up by the works following it. In a long footnote near the beginning of his discussion of this particular text, Moylan explains why he views Jack London's earlier *The Iron Heel* (1908), "though politically preferable to Forster's" work, as outside the bounds of the subgenre of the dystopia proper: "It is *almost* a dystopia, or perhaps a 'proto-dystopia.' . . . to put it more formally, the dystopian genre (complete with its eutopian surplus of the future Brotherhood of Man, encoded, as in Orwell and Atwood, in the textual apparatus of the text—in this case a footnote) is born within the pages of this text" (307). While the dialectical history I outlined above would relocate works like *The Iron Heel* squarely within the tradition of the modern dystopia (which is not the same thing as denying Moylan's insights into the role Forster's story plays in the later formal codification of the subgenre), it is precisely its status as such a liminal case, wherein the seams between its various components are still evident on the surface, that makes it so useful for my purposes here. For the tension Moylan notes in London's fiction makes evident the contradiction between London's left-wing socialist political impulses and the despairing claims of his naturalist form—a naturalism even more readily apparent in the fictions *The Son of the Wolf, The Call of the Wild*, and *White Fang*, by which the turn-of-the-century American author is best remembered today. This contradiction manifests itself in terms of a formal dislocation in the text, the utopian space literally located on the narrative's horizons, in a series of footnotes written by the future historian Anthony Meredith to the older rediscovered manuscript narrating the adventures of Avis and Ernest Everhard. Utopia then becomes no more than a ghostly frame to the detailed naturalistic portrait of the world located in the main body of the text.

However, an even more significant absence in *The Iron Heel*, and one which will also be a central part of the subgenre to which London's text helps give rise, is any vision of *revolution*, either as a specific punctal event or a series of tendencies within the near future, by which the radically other human situation haunting the borders of the narrative might become material. Indeed, I argue elsewhere that the radical party on which London pins so much hope resolves itself into a figure for the emergent corporate and state bureaucracies that would come to cast such deep shadows across the history of the then new century.[3] Vanishing in London's text then is any mediatory link between the dystopia and absent present utopian future—indeed, as the former becomes ascendant during the course of the narrative, the latter resolves itself into little more than a formal placeholder, an expression of desire rather than hope, for something n finds increasingly unimaginable. (A similar predicament is one of the other most influential dystopian visions of the ...tury, Yevgeny Zamyatin's *We*, as the text's utopia is located in ...c norizon "world" of the "infinite revolution.")[4] A dawning realization of the terrible power of the narrative apparatus he sets into motion here is indicated by London's inability, or unwillingness, to complete his central narrative, the text literally breaking off in midsentence: in order to do so, he necessarily would have to show the imminent defeat of the global alliance of socialist parties, the final victory of the Iron Heel, and the full emergence of a three-hundred-year "dystopian" future of oligarchical rule. Indeed, such a narrative completion would sunder utterly the link between the utopian and naturalist tendencies at work in the text.

The link between dystopia and the formal properties of naturalism is also made explicit by London's and Zamyatin's direct descendant, George Orwell, who, in a May 1947 letter to F. J. Warburg, who soon would publish *Nineteen Eighty-Four*, writes, "I will tell you now that this is a novel about the future—that is, it is in a sense a fantasy, but in the form of a *naturalistic novel*. That is what makes it a difficult job—of course as a book of anticipations it would be comparatively simple to write" (*Collected Essays* IV, 329–30). Moreover, Orwell already had acknowledged a deep admiration for the work of Gissing, and there is even evidence that he had his English predecessor in mind when developing his vision of Oceania.[5] In one of his last essays published before his most famous novel, Orwell describes the Victorian England pictured in Gissing's fiction in terms that bear an uncanny resemblance to the "future" dystopian world of *Nineteen Eighty-Four*. "The grime, the stupidity, the ugliness, the sex-starvation, the furtive debauchery, the vulgarity, the bad manners, the censoriousness—these things were unnecessary, since the puritanism of which they were a relic no longer upheld the structure of society. People who might, without becoming less efficient, have been reasonably happy chose instead to be miserable, inventing senseless taboos with which to terrify themselves" (*Collected Essays* IV, 430).

While their socialism teaches Gissing, London, and Orwell that such a situation must always be viewed as the consequence of human "choice," and hence open to the possibility of change, their fascination with the dark cynicism of naturalism threatens to blot out this realization altogether, grounding the present catastrophe in human nature itself, something expressed in both London's and Orwell's cases as a deep human lust for "power" that will inevitably derail any project of radical transformation. Of course, Orwell will push these tendencies to their final conclusions, making *Nineteen Eighty-Four* for so many of its readers a full-blown formal *anti-utopia*—"a non-existent society described in considerable detail

and normally located in time and space that the author intended a contemporaneous reader to view as a criticism of utopianism or of some particular eutopia" as Lyman Tower Sargent usefully defines the practice (9). I
wonder, though, if Anti-Utopia is a position that any human being can inhabit for very long, and if such a pure form of an assault on the utopian
imaginary exists. For indeed, most anti-utopias upon further inspection
turn out to be—and this is something very much the case in *Nineteen
Eighty-Four*—what Karl Mannheim calls "conservative utopias," a form of
"counter-utopian" thinking wherein "not only is attention turned to the
past and the attempt made to rescue it from oblivion, but the presentness
and immediacy of the whole past becomes an actual experience" (235).[6]
In works such as Orwell's, it is these nostalgically longed for past utopias
that are likewise located on the textual horizons—think of Winston Smith's
childhood, his golden country, the sanctuary above Mr. Charrington's
shop, and the glass paperweight containing the Indian Ocean coral—while
the naturalist vision remains the dominant note in the text.

Equally significant is that these later dystopias betray another deep formal link to the traditions of nineteenth-century naturalist fictions, and
this turns on the figuration of radical political agency itself. Does anyone
anymore (or indeed ever) really find I-330's calls for "infinite revolution"
or Winston Smith's dogged faith in the Proles—the latter devastatingly
named by Raymond Williams a "stale revolutionary romanticism" (79)—
an effective rebuttal to the deeply naturalist visions of the essential vicious-
ness, selfishness, and cowardice of human nature offered by Zamyatin's
Benefactor or Orwell's O'Brien? These classical texts thus establish a pattern that will haunt the tradition of dystopian writing throughout the
twentieth century: desirous of a radical change of affairs but unable to
imagine any mechanism or agency by which such a change might come
about, these dystopias oscillate between the radical openness of Utopia and
the asphyxiating closure of naturalism. Indeed, as we shall see, it is exactly
this dilemma that marks the two popular film dystopias that I will examine
in the pages that follow.

II

What make the two 1999 films—David Fincher's surprise hit *Fight Club*
and Jim Jarmusch's *Ghost Dog*—so interesting is the way they adopt the
formal strategies of the dystopia, as well as its precursors in naturalist
fiction, to the new situation of what has been variously described as an
emergent global, post-industrial, Post-Fordist, or service economy. To be
precise, both narratives are located on the horizons of dystopia proper—
Fight Club is more akin to what Moylan calls the "proto-dystopia," focusing

on the emergence of a truly dystopian (and perhaps, even utopian) near-future situation, while *Ghost Dog* is part of the more recent subgenre of the dystopia, the superhero comic book narrative.[7] However, in this way, these two films express a particular kinship to one of the currently dominant strands of dystopian fiction, what Jameson describes as the postmodern "dirty realism" of cyberpunk, in which "what is implied is simply an ultimate historicist breakdown in which we can no longer imagine the future at all. . . . Under those circumstances . . . a formerly futurological science fiction . . . turns into mere 'realism' and an outright representation of our present" (*Postmodernism* 286).[8] (The great literary example of this kind of realist critical proto-dystopia is Leslie Marmon Silko's *Almanac of the Dead*). The blasted urban landscapes of both films are very much those of cyberpunk fiction: post-industrial urban cores, filled with abandoned buildings, decaying factories, and the waste products and "throwaway" populations of twentieth-century capitalist culture. *Ghost Dog* is shot in a decaying and nearly empty Jersey City; and we learn that the decrepit Victorian home of the central characters in *Fight Club* has "no neighbors, just some warehouses and a paper mill." Moreover, both films share a deeply critical view of the bankruptcy of our modern corporate and consumer culture. And finally, like the critical dystopias examined by Moylan, both films work to move beyond this negative critical gesture, and (re)imagine history in the form of the collective political agencies that would lead us beyond the present impasse.

I want to begin my discussion of *Fight Club* elsewhere, however, with an image that has been very much on the minds of many people since September 2001: that of skyscraper towers falling down. In the final movement of the film, members of the paramilitary terrorist organization Project Mayhem, under the direction of the film's protagonist, the schizophrenic "Tyler Durden" (whether this is actually his name or simply that of his fantasy double is never made clear), have planted explosives in the corporate skyscraper towers of the credit card companies. This task is undertaken in the belief that the destruction of the global debt record—read finance capital—will eradicate the current order and open up history to the possibility of a new beginning. In the one direct statement of a utopian vision in the film (and bearing out Moylan's point that these texts always contain such a horizon), Brad Pitt's Tyler Durden tells his double, the injured and recumbent Edward Norton—in a scene whose visual presentation recalls the interview with a T. S. Eliot-quoting Colonel Kurtz in *Apocalypse Now*—that he dreams of a world where the skyscrapers are overrun with vines, cornfields have been planted in the city plots, and where we all wear leather clothes meant to last a lifetime: a primitivist utopia not unlike that found in the "scraps of the untainted sky" seen at the end of Forster's "The Machine Stops," the Mephi garden world of Zamyatin's *We*, Winston Smith's mythic golden country, the Uganda of Ignatius Donnelly's *Caesar's Column*, the post-apocalyptic landscape of George R. Stewart's *Earth Abides*, or the various reverse evolutions of J. G. Ballard's dystopias (to which the film's vision seems especially indebted). All of these examples raise some interesting questions about the persistence of primitivist nostalgia in the dystopian narrative form. Indeed, we might ask to what degree dystopias, like their naturalist predecessors, are responses first and foremost to the modern urban condition, and an expression of a desire to move beyond this particular social formation.

In the film's final scene, Edward Norton's character stands holding hands with his girlfriend, Marla Singer (Helena Bonham Carter). Together they watch from their urban skyscraper perch the buildings around them imploding and falling to the ground. Oddly enough, at this moment, we get a brief flash of a penis, a film still image apparently crudely spliced into the main narrative action. This recalls Pitt-Tyler's earlier confession that he used his employment as a theater film reel changer as an opportunity to splice into Disney and children's animation pictures still images from pornographic movies: the audience does not consciously *see* these images, but they do have the powerful effect of upsetting their consumerist slumbers, if only for the briefest of moments.

Interestingly, both the image of the skyscraper "coming down" and the strategy of *detournement* represented by Tyler's guerrilla action (we also see him urinating into the soup at the upscale hotel at which he works as a waiter) are figures that have become something of mainstays of contemporary cultural studies analysis. Indeed, one of the classic texts of cultural studies, Michel de Certeau's "Walking in the City," opens with an image not unlike that seen in *Fight Club*'s narrative frame. In his essay, de Certeau imagines the intellectual critic standing on the 110th floor of the World Trade Center. In this privileged location, he is "lifted out of the city's grasp" and transfigured into a voyeur, consuming the abstract image of the city as "a universe that is constantly exploding" (91–92). The intellectual fiction at work in this scene is, according to de Certeau, that we can be transformed into "a viewpoint and nothing more," a passive witness to the ongoing catastrophe that is modernity. Such a position, however, is one that makes politics unimaginable. Thus, de Certeau issues a call for intellectuals to come down from these heights, and into the space of the "ordinary practitioners of the city," those who "make use of spaces that cannot be seen" from the perspective at the top of the system, and those to whom the book is dedicated—"To the ordinary man" (93 and v).

In an incisive reading of de Certeau's essay, as well as a range of other cultural studies texts, Meaghan Morris notes that this now commonplace "intellectual ritual of renouncing the heights" bears a striking parallel to what she calls a populist art of comic reduction (comparing corporate towers to penises and dildos in order to "deflate" their pretensions), and indeed betrays the *populist* political resonances of so much current cultural studies work, ranging from the nuanced analyses of postmodern "organic intellectuals" in Andrew Ross's *No Respect* to the celebration of "the people" and their consumerist "resistances" in John Fiske's *Understanding Popular Culture*. Such gestures, she goes on to argue, more often than not miss "the point about the role of the 'urbanization of capital' in creating economic and social inequalities, precisely at a time when its operations in our cities are reaching new heights of intensity and savagery, directly affecting our lives" (128).

That the political identifications of Fincher's film are deeply populist as well is made explicit early on. We have two veterans of popular neo-populist cinema at work here: Fincher, whose earlier *Aliens 3* contains an assault on a Japanese-identified corporate power, and Edward Norton, Jr., who until this film was best known for his chilling portrayal of a young, demagogic Southern California white supremacist in *American History X*. Moreover, the Chuck Palahniuk novel on which the film is based also makes clear its links to an earlier tradition of populist skyscraper fictions. The climactic scene in the novel differs from that in the film in that we find our protagonist *on* the roof of the world's tallest building (in this case, the single structure Project Mayhem plans to destroy); his apparent suicide attempt is then interrupted by the appearance of Marla Singer and a group of his supporters—a scene that recalls the climax of Frank Capra's populist classic *Meet John Doe* (see Palahniuk 12–15, 203–05).

Crucially, however, Fincher's film offers us a new kind of populist mass, one produced by the particular conditions of the service economy: the members of the Fight Club are, as Tyler describes them, "an entire generation waiting tables and pumping gas—slaves with white collars . . . working jobs we hate so we can buy shit we don't need." Later, he informs the police chief who dares to challenge this nascent revolutionary collective: "The people you are after are the people you depend on. We cook your meals, we haul your trash, we connect your calls, we drive your ambulances, we guard you while you sleep." Thus, while the endless cycle of consumerism that was so central to the post–World War II Fordist cultural revolution continues unabated, the older "guaranteed" and high-wage positions that had also been such a fundamental part of this mode of regulation and regime of accumulation have disappeared without a trace.[9] The depths of alienation and dissatisfaction of these men have thus drawn them first into the cult of sensation represented by the Fight Clubs, and then into the organized, highly disciplined, and lethally effective terrorist organization Project Mayhem. That the Fight Clubs themselves draw upon some of the central tropes of naturalist fiction, especially in its U.S. manifestations, is borne out by Henry Giroux in his deeply critical analysis of the film: "Violence in *Fight Club* is treated as a sport, a crucial component that lets men connect with each other through the overcoming of fear, pain, and fatigue. . . . Violence in this instance signals its crucial function in both affirming the natural 'fierceness' of men and in providing them with a concrete experience that allows them to connect at some primal level" (36).

Yet the film itself is finally not really about these men: they remain throughout largely nameless presences, classically naturalist representatives of what Georg Lukács calls social types rather than full characters. Indeed, after the shooting death of one of the organization's founding members, a new mantra arises in the group: "Only in death does a member of Project Mayhem have a name." Our protagonist, on the other hand, does have a name—at least one for his followers—and, even more important, a history. He is, when we first meet him, firmly ensconced within the young urban middle class, working as a "recall coordinator," one of the new Post-Fordist information managers, traveling across the country investigating gruesome automobile crashes and evaluating the cost effectiveness of general recalls for the auto manufacturers. However, he too is trapped in the deepest depths of modern alienation: an insomniac, finding no reward or pleasure in his work, detached from everyone around him (he becomes addicted to support groups because "when people think you're dying they really listen to you instead of just waiting for their turn to talk"), and, most important, deeply dissatisfied with the consumerist ethos in which he lives. He is someone who, as his schizophrenic double tells him, is "looking for a way to change [his] life." He, or rather his double, accomplishes this by blowing up his upper-floor condo dwelling, as well as all of his material possessions (he later tells an investigating detective, "this wasn't just stuff, it was me"), moving into an abandoned structure in the city's decrepit and nearly abandoned industrial district (another sign of the Post-Fordist reality they inhabit), and ultimately launching the Fight Club movement. Norton's character thus replicates de Certeau's gesture of coming down from the tower's heights. And indeed, the film opens with Norton's character and his Tyler Durden persona already in the tower, the main body of the narrative taking the form of an extended flashback of his movement down from these former heights. In this way too, he appears to become one with the very different alienations of the "common man."

This populist gesture of "coming down" into the world of the "people" is a central one of both naturalist and dystopian fiction: think of Frank Norris's or London's regular evocations of "the People" (and the last line of

Meet John Doe is, "There they are Norton, the People; try and lick that") or Orwell's romanticization of the Proles. However, this gesture is a deeply ambivalent one that finally maintains an unbridgeable gap between the "us" of the middle-class protagonist and the "them" of the People. In his discussion of Gissing's *The Nether World*, Jameson argues that the "conceptual and organizational framework" of naturalist fiction "is not that of social class but rather that very different nineteenth-century ideological concept which is the notion of 'the people,' as a kind of general grouping of the poor and 'underprivileged' of all kinds, from which one can recoil in revulsion, but to which one can also, as in some political populisms, nostalgically 'return' as to some telluric source of strength" (*Political* 189). The same combination of fascination and revulsion—a schizophrenia of the naturalist populist form as deep as that of the film's protagonist—is evident in *Fight Club*. For precisely when the original Fight Clubs metamorphosize into Project Mayhem, that is, from a therapeutic movement of "de-alienation" to a political one of collective action and social change, the film's attitude towards it changes dramatically as well. Suddenly, the sympathetic image of a deeply alienated public becomes one of a secret underground fascist organization, threatening to consume society in a maelstrom of violence and destruction. It is from this reality—one that he is responsible for—that our protagonist then rapidly retreats, slaying his populist double and returning to his old middle-class self (the concluding pages of Palahniuk's novel are in fact far more ambiguous about the nature of this return). In a symbolic reversal of de Certeau's gesture, he has returned to the heights of the tower, and from there bears witness to an aestheticized destruction of the city.

It is at this point then that we finally arrive at the real political center of this film. The protagonist's schizophrenia is a classic example of the narrative device Sigmund Freud names, in his discussion of E. T. A. Hoffmann's "The Sandman," "splitting." But here we have moved from Freud's individual psychoanalytical framework into a larger social and cultural one, where the Other serves as the screen image onto which Norton's character, as well as the film's audience, can project their deepest and most dangerous political desires. Indeed, his double, Tyler Durden, tells him, "you were looking for a way to change your life. You could not do this on your own. All the ways you wished you could be, that's me."

And yet, the film remains fundamentally divided in its view of these desires. In a way, then, critiques of the film such as those advanced by Giroux miss a crucial point about *Fight Club*. To say that the film "mimics fascism's militarisation and masculinization of the public sphere with its exultation of violence as a space in which men can know themselves better" and to critique its blatant "misogynistic representation of women, and its intimation that violence is the only means through which men can be cleansed of the dire effect women have on the shaping of their identities" (which would make Fincher's most recent film, *The Panic Room*, appear as an attempt to redress these shortcomings) is in fact to ignore the fundamental disavowal of these representations, and politics, that occur not only in the climactic scene in the tower, but throughout (36, 37). The film is as easily seen as a parody of exactly this hyper-masculine and protofascist imagery as it is of all other forms of "self-help" discourse. In other words, any such approach which imagines that the film takes its own vision seriously heals the division that structures both the psyche of its protagonist and its larger narrative vision.

Thus, the general assault on social and cultural alienation which has been the focus of much of the conversation about this film actually serves as a mere pretense for investigating a far more troubling issue plaguing our present: our fundamental sense of *political* alienation, the radical sense of otherness that too many feel when faced with the prospects of their own potential for action. The fundamental structure here is an ethical rather than a political one—and it may be this ethical stance which is part of the legacy of naturalism to dystopian fictions, a legacy that the best of the critical dystopian fictions must work to overcome.[10] Locating these political desires within the fundamentally alien other, the film can conveniently also maintain its disavowal of them. Moreover, by conveniently taking up the existential burden of (political) action, the fundamentally Other populist underclasses of this film—alien invaders not unlike those in *Independence Day*, a film to which *Fight Club* often bears an uncanny resemblance, or, indeed, even those in our real-world recent history—do the dirty work of "beginning" history once again, fusing a new collective in opposition to them.[11] The real fascism hinted at in this film is thus not that found in Project Mayhem, but in the state reaction that would surely arise as a response to its appearance. After the events of September 2001, this dystopian fantasy may have begun to become something of an actuality.

III

Although there are no towers in *Ghost Dog*, this film also opens with an invocation of the scopic view, as we "see" the landscape of the city from the aerial perspective of a pigeon flying overhead. The viewer then once more comes down from this distanced viewpoint, diving back into the urban texture of the city and meeting this film's central protagonist, the African-American ninja warrior, Ghost Dog (Forest Whitaker). This gesture of taking the viewer/reader into the lives of the "other half" is, of course, also very much part of the tradition of literary naturalism (Stephen Crane's

Maggie: A Girl of the Streets is exemplary in this regard), and the decayed urban setting of this film, as well as the brutally violent contest between two opponents, meets some of the basic expectations of the form as well.

The film makes its links to the original historical context of naturalism explicit in a number of other ways. *Ghost Dog* is the second part of a diptych by Jim Jarmusch exploring the environmental, social, and cultural consequences of industrial modernization in the United States. The first installment, *Dead Man* (1996), is set in an 1870s U.S. West being dramatically transformed by modern industrialism, and follows the adventures of an eastern clerk, "William Blake" (Johnny Depp), and his Native American companion, Nobody (Gary Farmer), as they encounter the "dark Satanic mills," violence, cannibalism, and other destructive energies of the emerging industrial and mercantile economy. *Ghost Dog* takes us to the other end of both the continent and this history, as the factories of the first film now lie in silent ruin. The central protagonists of this film too are very much like those in *Ghost Dog*, cultural hybrids caught between worlds in which they have no place (and the character of Nobody also makes a brief cameo appearance in *Ghost Dog* as well).[12] Together, both films offer a devastating revisionist commentary on the violences—environmental, racial, and cultural—of both capitalist modernization and dominant popular cultural forms, unveiling both as terrible dystopias in their own right.

However, *Ghost Dog*'s connection to the traditions of literary naturalism is even more direct: for this film can be read as an adaptation of London's classic work of naturalist fiction, *The Call of the Wild*. Ghost Dog is, after all, the name the former sled dog Buck is given by the Alaskan Yeehat Indians in the novel's concluding pages: "They are afraid of the Ghost Dog, for it has cunning greater than they, stealing from their camps in fierce winters, robbing their traps, slaying their dogs, and defying their bravest hunters" (87). Such a description is equally apt for this film's central protagonist, as he engages in a brutal war of extermination with the local Mafia, the Vargo family, after they have turned on him, their former contract employee (labor flexibility in the realm of organized crime), in order to cover up the execution they ordered of one of their members. His technological, military, and strategic prowess is truly staggering: Ghost Dog effortlessly penetrates every crevice of the Mafia crime network, even invading the family's countryside estate and murdering all the senior bosses and their bodyguards. Later, in one of the film's most clever scenes (adopted from an earlier Japanese film) Ghost Dog shoots another Mafioso through the drainpipe in his bathroom sink. Both Ghost Dogs too are caught in a desperate struggle with their deep sense of loyalty to the "master" who saves them from near death: Buck is rescued by John Thorton from his cruel amateur gold-hunting owners, shortly before they sink to their deaths under a sheet of ice; and the film's protagonist, as we learn in two crucial flashback scenes, was saved eight years earlier by the Mafia soldier Louie as he was being beaten by two white youths in an alleyway (whether Louie meant to save him, or was just protecting himself, the film's multiple flashbacks make unclear—interestingly, the film also refers directly to the Japanese classic of multiple points of view, *Rashomon*). Ghost Dog then vanishes for four years, and upon his return presents himself to Louie as his dedicated servant.

In his discussion of London's novel, Jonathan Auerbach shows how Buck serves as a figure for the author London himself. Auerbach argues that Buck's achievement of a place for himself within the natural order serves as a fantasy narrative of London's own successful establishment of himself as a writer—that is, as a full-fledged member of an emerging professional middle class: "London thus manages in his naturalist masterpiece to dramatize vividly his position as a writer in capitalism's mass market without having to recognize himself as such" (112–13). A similar kind of displacement occurs in the film: this latest "Buck," the African-American samurai warrior, emerges as the quintessential fantasy image of the contemporary professional (a figure also popularized in 1980s cyberpunk dystopian science fiction). What is central for both London's novel and this film is the issue of the "call." This is not, however, the call of the wild, or of the natural world, but of a fundamental self-making through one's work, one's "calling": the work of the trail in the original, and that of the disciplined training and focus of the samurai warrior.

However, it is here that the two narratives diverge in some significant ways. Auerbach notes that the death of Thorton frees Buck to achieve his "apotheosis as immortal Ghost Dog, a kind of concluding emblem for London's career aspirations as a writer" (108). The film, on the other hand, reaches it climax with Ghost Dog's death: he allows Louie to kill him so that the latter may restore his "honor" and fulfill his own duty by avenging the death of his bosses. In the moments immediately preceding what is described as a *High Noon*–style confrontation, Ghost Dog offers the following analysis of his situation: "Samurai must always stay loyal to his boss no matter what happens. Me and him, we're from different ancient tribes, and now we're both almost extinct. Sometimes you gotta stay with the ancient ways, the old-school ways." What this film is thus centrally *about* is the passing of these "old-school ways." (Moreover, the samurai film tradition upon which Jarmusch draws here is also about a similar moment of monumental social and cultural transition.) Earlier Louie had complained that "nothing makes any sense any more"; and one of the Mafiosi shot by Ghost Dog confesses with his dying breath that Ghost Dog has restored a certain sense of pride in him, "sending us out in the old way, like real fuckin' gangsters." It is this sense of disorientation, of the destruction of a certain set of masculine cultures, that pervades this film. And in its concluding scene, it does appear as if these two "ancient tribes" will be continued, in a much diminished capacity, through young women, the daughter of the Vargos (who had witnessed Ghost Dog's murders) and Pauline, a young African American girl who has befriended Ghost Dog and who, in the final image of the film, is seen reading his copy of *The Way of the Samurai* (quotations from this quintessential professional's manual appear throughout the film).

Auerbach's description of the anxieties at play in London's text offer us an important clue as to the central ideological contents of this film and *Fight Club* as well:

> London's progressive disenchantment with work registers the growing fear felt by many turn-of-the-century American men that the market, increasingly abstract and rationalized, could no longer offer the grounds to define manhood, particularly in terms of those ideals of self-reliance, diligence, and mastery at the heart of nineteenth-century liberalism. Once the workplace diminishes in significance in the new century, then masculinity threatens to become primarily a performance or a pose for its own sake. (110–11)

Both films, I would suggest, finally give expression to current middle-class and masculine anxieties about status and identity in an emerging global political economy—anxieties that have been driven to new levels of intensity in the economic aftermath of September 2001. And yet, whereas *Ghost Dog* can offer us a brilliant critique of the destructive nature of these older cultures, it, very much like its contemporary *Fight Club*, fails to generate a vision of the politics that would lead us beyond this impasse. In the end, both films pass beyond the engagements of the critical dystopia and give way to the "resigned pessimism" of the naturalist ideologies from which the form arises in the first place.

IV

By way of the briefest of afterwords, I want to take this opportunity to raise a question about the continued role of the dystopia in our present moment. Moylan's work has the value of helping us grasp the significance of the critical dystopias of the 1980s and 1990s, emphasizing the ways they maintained at least the horizon of historical possibility in the seemingly bleak enclosures of that historical conjuncture. However, the best critical dystopias are, as I suggested earlier, very much about their own erasure, and the ultimate resignation of the two films that I explore above may tell us something about the price to be paid for being forced to occupy this critical position for too long (a similar warning about the consequences of an extended "patient and obstinate perseverance" in the face of tremendous political opposition was offered long ago by Antonio Gramsci). In contrast, we might hold up as exemplary the intellectual trajectory of Robinson in the period following the publication of his critical dystopia *The Gold Coast*: rather than repeat this gesture, he took it as the opening for the production, or Event, of his utopian texts, *Pacific Edge*, the *Mars* trilogy, and most recently, *The Years of Rice and Salt*. All of these are utopias of process rather than location, finding their deepest pleasures in the voyage rather than the destination. Do these works mark at least the beginning of real transformation of the historical situation in which the great critical dystopias necessarily flourished? Signs of such a shift do appear to be everywhere—in the events in Seattle, Quebec City, and Porto Allegre to name only a few prominent sites (and to which the machinations of post–September 11 appear more as a form of reaction than real reversal). Will such a revival of utopian speculation and collective political action continue? This is a question that of course can only be answered in time. However, in such a situation as our own, this observation by Jameson feels especially apt: "The Kairos is then Lenin in April: you cannot know whether a thing was possible until it is tried; only after the fact does it transpire that what finally happened had to happen that way and no other" ("Religion" 44).

Notes

1. Jameson's point of reference here is Goode; see also Thompson.
2. For a discussion and application of a dialectical theory of genre as a way of understanding the development of these forms in history, see McKeon.
3. For further discussion, see Wegner, "The Occluded Future: *Red Star* and *The Iron Heel* as 'Critical Utopias,'" in *Imaginary Communities* (99–146).
4. See Wegner, "A Map of Utopia's 'Possible Worlds': Zamyatin's *We* and Le Guin's *The Dispossessed*," in *Imaginary Communities* (147–82).
5. For Orwell's admiration of Gissing's work, see Shelden (359).
6. Mannheim maintains that the conservative mentality is first and foremost a form of counter-utopia, its primary antagonist being "the liberal idea which has been translated into rationalistic terms. Whereas in the latter, the normative, the 'should' is accentuated in experience, in conservatism the emphasis shifts to existing reality, the 'is'" (234–35). More important, he argues:

   > The time-sense of this mode of experience and thought is completely opposed to that of liberalism. Whereas for liberalism the future was everything and the past nothing, the conservative mode of experiencing time found the best corroboration of its sense of the determinateness in discovering the significance of the past, in the discovery of time as the creator of value. . . . Consequently not only is attention turned to the past and the attempt made to rescue it from oblivion, but the presentness and immediacy of the whole past becomes an actual experience. (235)

   Such an outlook can still be described as "utopian" because, as with his other three mentalities, it too "is incongruous with the state of reality within which it occurs": the conservative mentality maintains this ideal of the full self-presence of the past in the present precisely in a moment when the possibility of such an unbroken continuity begins to disappear—that is, in a moment of dramatic historical upheaval (192). Also see Wegner,

"Modernity, Nostalgia, and the Ends of Nations in Orwell's *Nineteen Eighty-Four*," in *Imaginary Communities* (183–228).

7. The relationship of the superhero form to dystopian fiction is an area ripe for investigation. For some recent "critical" expressions of the genre that interrogate this relationship, one might look at Alan Moore and Dave Gibbon's graphic novel *The Watchmen*; Frank Miller's *The Dark Knight Returns*, as well as its current sequel, *The Dark Knight Strikes Again*, a text that is also interesting for making the movement into dystopia proper; and the two Josh Wedon television series, *Buffy the Vampire Slayer* and *Angel*.

8. For Jameson's discussion of cyberpunk as "dirty realism," see *Seeds* (150–59).

9. For useful introductions to the Regulationist School of political economy and their theorizations of Fordism and Post-Fordism, especially in the U.S. context, see Aglietta, Boyer, and Harvey.

10. Barthes too emphasizes the alienation experienced by the critic of myth in ways that resonate with this discussion: "This harmony justifies the mythologist but does not fulfill him: his status still remains basically one of being excluded. Justified by the political dimension, the mythologist is still at a distance from it. His speech is a metalanguage, it 'acts' nothing; at the most it unveils—or does it? To whom? His task always remains ambiguous, hampered by its ethical origins" (156).

11. I examine this aspect of *Independence Day* in more detail in "A Nightmare."

12. For a useful analysis of the central characters' hybridity and the relationship of this to Jarmusch's archival revisionist project, see Nieland.

Works Cited

Aglietta, Michel. *A Theory of Capitalist Regulation: The US Experience.* Trans. David Fernbach. New York: Verso, 1979.

Auerbach, Jonathan. *Male Call: Becoming Jack London.* Durham: Duke UP, 1996.

Barthes, Roland. *Mythologies.* Trans. Annette Lavers. New York: Hill, 1972.

Bellamy, Edward. *Looking Backward, 2000–1887.* New York: New American Library, 1960.

Bloch, Ernst. *The Principle of Hope.* Trans. Neville Plaice, Stephen Plaice, and Paul Knight. Oxford: Blackwell, 1986.

Boyer, Robert. *The Regulation School: A Critical Introduction.* Trans. Craig Charney. New York: Columbia UP, 1990.

Dead Man. Dir. Jim Jarmusch. 1996.

de Certeau, Michel. *The Practice of Everyday Life.* Trans. Steven Rendall. Berkeley: U of California P, 1984.

Fight Club. Dir. David Fincher. 1999.

Freud, Sigmund. "The Uncanny." *The Standard Edition of the Complete Psychological Works of Sigmund Freud.* Vol. 17. Trans. and ed. James Strachey. London: Hogarth, 1964. 219–56.

Ghost Dog. Dir. Jim Jarmusch. 1999.

Giroux, Henry A. "Brutalized Bodies and Emasculated Politics: *Fight Club*, Consumerism, and Masculine Violence." *Third Text* 53 (Winter 2000–01): 31–41.

Goode, John. "Gissing, Morris, and English Socialism." *Victorian Studies* 12 (1968): 201–26.

Harvey, David. *The Condition of Postmodernity: An Enquiry into the Origins of Cultural Change.* Oxford: Blackwell, 1989.

Jameson, Fredric. *The Political Unconscious: Narrative as a Socially Symbolic Act.* Ithaca: Cornell UP, 1981.

———. *Postmodernism, or, The Cultural Logic of Late Capitalism.* Durham: Duke UP, 1990.

———. "Religion and Ideology: A Political Reading of *Paradise Lost.*" *Literature, Politics and Theory: Papers from the Essex Conference 1976–84.* Ed. Francis Barker et al. London: Methuen, 1986. 35–56.

———. *The Seeds of Time.* New York: Columbia UP, 1994.

London, Jack. *The Call of the Wild, White Fang, and Other Stories.* New York: Oxford. 1998.

———. *The Iron Heel.* New York: Macmillan, 1908.

Mannheim, Karl. *Ideology and Utopia: An Introduction to the Sociology of Knowledge.* Trans. Louis Wirth and Edward Shils. New York: Harcourt, 1936.

McKeon, Michael. *The Origins of the English Novel, 1600–1740.* Baltimore: Johns Hopkins UP, 1987.

Meet John Doe. Dir. Frank Capra. 1941.

Morris, Meaghan. *Too Soon Too Late: History in Popular Culture.* Bloomington: Indiana UP, 1998.

Moylan, Tom. *Scraps of the Untainted Sky: Science Fiction, Utopia, Dystopia.* Boulder: Westview, 2001.

Nieland, Justus. "Graphic Violence: Native Americans and the Western Archive in *Dead Man.*" *CR: The New Centennial Review* 1. 2 (2001): 171–200.

Orwell, George. *The Collected Essays, Journalism and Letters of George Orwell.* Ed. Sonia Orwell and Ian Angus. New York: Harcourt, 1968.

———. *Nineteen Eighty-Four.* New York: Harcourt, 1949.

Palahniuk, Chuck. *Fight Club.* New York: Holt, 1996.

Sargent, Lyman Tower. "The Three Faces of Utopianism Revisited." *Utopian Studies* 5.1 (1994): 1–37.

Shelden, Michael. *Orwell: The Authorized Biography.* New York: Harper, 1991.

Thompson, E. P. *William Morris: Romantic to Revolutionary.* Rev. ed. New York: Pantheon, 1977.

Wegner, Phillip E. *Imaginary Communities: Utopia, The Nation, and the Spatial Histories of Modernity.* Berkeley: U of California P, 2002.

———. "'A Nightmare on the Brain of the Living': Messianic Historicity, Alienations, and *Independence Day.*" *Rethinking Marxism* 12.1 (2000): 65–86.

Williams, Raymond. *George Orwell.* New York: Columbia UP, 1971.

Zamyatin, Yevgeny. *We.* 1924. Trans. Clarence Brown. New York: Penguin, 1993.

Žižek, Slavoj. "Georg Lukács as the Philosopher of Leninism." Postface. *A Defense of History and Class Consciousness: Tailism and the Dialectic.* By Georg Lukács. Trans. Esther Leslie. New York: Verso, 2002. 151–82.

CHAPTER 10

Theses on Dystopia 2001

DARKO SUVIN

Usà puyew usu wapiw. (Backward going forward looking.)
—Swampy Cree tribe phrase and image taken from a porcupine backing
into a rock crevice

I. Premise

1. All of us on planet Earth live in highly endangered times. Perhaps the richer among us, up to 15 percent globally but disproportionately concentrated in the trilateral United States–western Europe–Japan and its appendages, have been cushioned from realizing it by the power of money and the self-serving ideology it erects. But even those complain loudly of the "criminality" and general "moral decay" of the desperately vicious invading their increasingly fortress-like neighborhoods. We live morally in an almost complete dystopia—dystopia because anti-utopia—and materially (economically) on the razor's edge of collapse, distributive and collective.

2. Utopianism is an orientation toward a horizon of radically better forms of relationships among people. It establishes orientations: vectors of desire and need toward radically better horizons. This was being discussed at length in the 1960s and 1970s. But in the endangered today (Benjamin's *Jetztzeit*) this is, while still supremely necessary, not enough. Utopian reflections, in and out of fiction, have now to undertake openings that lead toward agency: action.

3. We therefore have to talk first about epistemology (imagination, semiotics, semantics) and then about ontology (application of imagination to

really existing power relationships, politics). "Reality is not at all the same as the empirical being—reality is not a being, it is a becoming . . . the moment in which the new is born. Reality is admittedly the criterion of accurate thinking. But it does not just exist, it becomes—not without participation of the thinking" (Lukács).

II. Epistemology

Introductory: The discourse around utopia/nism is not far from the Tower of Babel. Its ideological cause (capitalist maligning of non-capitalist alternatives) is difficult to affect. But it behooves us to try and affect the secondary semantic muddiness. A tool kit needed to talk intelligibly has to be proposed, subsuming my own earlier attempts and selected illuminations from criticism in English, German, Italian, French, and so on.

4. *Utopia* will be defined as the construction of a particular community where sociopolitical institutions, norms, and relationships between people are organized according to a *radically different principle* than in the author's community; this construction is based on estrangement arising out of an alternative historical hypothesis; it is created by social classes interested in otherness and change.

Gloss 4: This definition backgrounds the tradition arising out of Thomas More's island and title, in which the relationships between people are organized according to a radically more perfect principle than in the author's community. I believe we have to abandon the meaning and horizon of utopianism as automatically entailing radically better relationships. More perfect relationships have to be proved (or disproved) for each particular case or type of texts. Confusing *radical otherness* and *radically greater perfection* leads to muddle: incommunicability or wilful obscurantism.

5. In case the imaginatively constructed community is not based principally on sociopolitical but on other radically different principles, say biological or geological, we are dealing with science fiction (sf). The realization that sociopolitics cannot change without all other aspects of life also changing has led to sf's becoming the privileged locus of utopian fiction in the twentieth century.

Gloss 5: This means that utopian fiction is, today and retrospectively, both an independent aunt and a dependent daughter of sf. The lines of consanguinity begin to intertwine in H. G. Wells's sociobiological sf, where biology is mainly a metaphor for social class.

6. Utopia may be divided into the polar opposites of *Eutopia*, defined as in Thesis 4 but having sociopolitical institutions, norms, and relationships among people organized according to a *radically more perfect* principle than in the author's community; and the symmetrically opposed *Dystopia* (cacotopia), organized according to a *radically less perfect* principle. The radical difference in perfection is in both cases judged from the point of view and within the value system of a discontented social class or congerie of classes, as refracted through the writer.

Gloss 6: As in all other entities in these theses, we are dealing with ideal types. Example of proximity to eutopia: More's *Utopia*; to dystopia: Yevgeny Zamyatin's *We*.

7. Dystopia in its turn divides into anti-utopia and what I shall call "simple" dystopia. *Anti-Utopia* finally turns out to be a dystopia, but one explicitly designed to refute a currently proposed eutopia. It is a pretended eutopia—a community whose hegemonic principles pretend to its being more perfectly organized than any thinkable alternative, while our representative "camera eye" and value-monger finds out it is significantly *less* perfect than an alternative, a polemic nightmare. *"Simple" Dystopia* (so-called to avoid inventing yet another prefix to *topia*) is a straightforward dystopia, that is, one which is not also an anti-utopia.

Gloss 7a: The intertext of anti-utopia has historically been anti-socialism, as socialism was the strongest "currently proposed" eutopia ca. 1915–1975. The intertext of "simple" dystopia has been and remains more or less radical anti-capitalism. Zamyatin, individualist but avant-garde critic of mass society, straddles both.

Gloss 7b: Examples of proximity to anti-utopia: all the poorer followers of Zamyatin, from Ayn Rand and George Orwell on; of proximity to "simple" dystopia: Frederik Pohl and C. M. Kornbluth's *Space Merchants* (and in general the U.S. "new maps of hell" of the 1950s–1960s) or the movies *Soylent Green* and *Blade Runner*.

8. More clearly than for other genres of writing, all the delimitations above function only if understood within the *historical space-time* of a text's inception. In that too, utopia is akin to satire and pamphlet (Frye's "anatomy") rather than to the standard individualist novel. It is obvious that for a post-industrial reader the statics of Plato's *Politeia* (*Commonwealth*) or Tommaso Campanella's *Civitas Solis* (*City of the Sun*) translate the historically intended eutopian horizon into a dystopian one.

Gloss 8a: A reader of Plato in, say, the twentieth century is reading against a different horizon of experiences and values, which colors all, so that the shadow of the SS falls on the Guardians' politics and erotics; we might call this the "Pierre Ménard" syndrome or law.

Gloss 8b: This is not a defect but a strength of utopian horizons and artefacts: born in history, inciding on history, they laicize eternity and demand to be judged in and by history.

9. Given this history it is mandatory to insert satire into the utopian tradition, at the latest since Cyrano's *États et Empires de la Lune* (*States and Empires of the Moon*). It took the second major step in that tradition: to import into utopia's other spatial (later: temporal) locus a radically worse sociopolitical organization, and to do this by exfoliating the perceptive and evaluative strategy of estrangement into an array of deeply critical microdevices. Historically and psychologically, dystopia is unthinkable without, and as a rule mingled with, satire.

Gloss 9: Untranscended example: Jonathan Swift's *Gulliver's Travels*; but the twentieth-century sf texts from Stanislaw Lem to Robert Sheckley, Philip K. Dick, and Iain M. Banks run a close second.

10. To use Swiftian terms: in utopia a Thing Which Is Not is posited as being (in eutopia as being supremely valuable), while in satire a Thing Which Is is posited as being despicable; one condemns what is by indirection and the other by direction. If utopia is to be seen as a formal inversion of salient sociopolitical aspects of the writer's world which has as its purpose the recognition that the reader truly lives in an axiologically inverted world, then satire wittily foregrounds the inherent absurdity, and thus counteracts utopia's necessary but often solemn doctrinal categorization. It adds the Ass to the Savior's crib and entry into Jerusalem.

11. We have here, as already in Thesis 2, come up against the necessity of another set of analytic tools. From Plato's term *topos ouranios* (heavenly place) on, it is clear that utopia's location, while a very important signifier, is only seemingly spatial: it abounds in maps but it is not photographable. In the best cases it is less significant than the orientation toward a place somewhere in front of the orienter; and furthermore, even the place to be reached is not fixed and completed: it moves on. It is thus situated in an imaginary space that is a measure of and measured as value (quality) rather than distance (quantity). The necessary elements for utopian movement—of which stasis is a zero-form—are an agent that moves and an imaginary space (or time—but all the metaphors for time are spatial) in which it moves. I shall return to the agential aspects, which open up the properly political problematics of who is the bearer of utopia/nism. The pertinent aspects of space are: a) the place of the agent who is moving, the

Locus; b) the *Horizon* toward which that agent is moving; and c) the *Orientation*, the vector that conjoins locus and horizon.

Gloss 11: It is characteristic of horizon that it moves with the location of the moving agent, as demonstrated by Giordano Bruno. But it is, obversely, characteristic of orientation that it can through all the changes of locus remain a constant vector of desire and cognition.

12. A combinatorics of locus/horizon gives the following possibilities:

1) H > L: open-ended or dynamic utopia;
2) L = H or L > H: closed or static utopia;
3) L (H = 0): heterotopia;
4) H (L = 0): abstract or non-narrative utopianism.

There seems to be no obstacle to applying these terms (as well as a further set of agential terms) as analytic tools to the whole range of utopian studies—fictions, projects, and colonies.

13. Finally: what is not usefully discussed as utopia but as some other beast? Among other things, any construction, I would say, that does not significantly deal with a radically changed community but with dreams of individual felicity within the social status quo (Don Juan) or outside of society (Robinson Crusoe). No doubt, these are multiply connected with utopianism, by contraries or eversion, but englobing all dreams of betterment under the illicit metaphor of utopia—as in the most meritorious Ernst Bloch—leads to a loss of all explicative clarity. While supremely important today, Utopia is not the same as Being, or even as Supreme Good.

Gloss 13: Much of the otherwise highly interesting sf, from Dick to cyberpunk, backgrounds, fragments, or indeed represses all kinds of utopianism so strongly that, although inescapably written between the eutopian and dystopian horizons, it would need too complicated analogical mediations to be usefully discussed here.

III. Politics and Dystopia

Introductory: If in Parts I and II a scholar can be formal and impersonal, calling attention to rules of method (suggesting what delimitations may be required), this is scarcely the case for Parts III and IV. Even where I don't expressly introduce the first-person singular, it is implied, so that the following theses are at best stimuli for what may be further debated.

14. If history is a creatively constitutive factor of utopian writings and horizons, then we also have to recognize the epistemic shift beginning in

the 1930s and crystallizing in the 1970s: capitalism co-opts all it can from utopia (not the name it abhors) and invents its own, new, dynamic locus. It pretends this is a finally realized eutopia (end of qualitative history); but since it is in fact for 85 percent of humanity clearly and for 13–14 percent subterraneously a dystopia, it demands to be called Anti-Utopia. We live in an ever faster circulation of a whirligig of fads that do not better human relationships but allow heightened oppression and exploitation, especially of women, children, and the poor, in "a remarkably dynamic society that goes nowhere" (see Noble). The economists and sociologists I trust call it Post-Fordism and global commodity market—unregulated for higher profit of capital, very regulated for higher exploitation of workers.

15. The unprecedented Post-Fordist mobilization and colonization of all non-capitalized spaces, from the genome to people's desires, was faced with the insufficient efficacy of orthodox religions (including scientism and liberalism). After "belief became polluted, like the air or the water" (see de Certeau), culture began supplying authoritative horizons for agency and meaning. It does so either as information or as aesthetics: information-intensive production in working time (for example biotechnology, with its output of information inscribed in and read off living matter) and "aesthetic" consumption in leisure time, the last refuge of desire. The new orthodoxy of belief proceeds thus "camouflaged as facts, data and events" (see de Certeau) or as "culture industry" images.

16. Early on within Post-Fordism, Raymond Williams sniffed the winds of change and drew attention to a new dominant in pragmatic as well as cultural history in which radical change (communist revolutions) has failed, largely because capitalism has managed to co-opt change. This went beyond the superficial yearly fashions, consubstantial to consumerist capitalism (see Benjamin), to a truly different mode of doing business, soon to be known as globalization and post-modernism. Change is now permanently on the agenda but "primarily under the direction and in the terms [and on terms] of the dominant social order itself" (see Williams). This led to the battle cry "death to systems," meaning in practice not what the working classes earlier meant when opposing the System but an end to all-englobing alternative projects. Those taking up the cry with François Lyotard, Gianni Vattimo, and co. did not mean that they themselves should not form a system of institutional and other power ties and that their writings should not become the dominant academic form of criticism known as deconstruction, but that all talk of wholeness and totality be henceforth terrorized into extinction. The dogmas to be found in Soviet-type pseudo-socialism were fiercely ripped apart; the dogmas of "free market" (meaning

demolition of public control over huge capitalist conglomerates), which I'd argue are at least as pernicious and murderous, were not questioned. This transfers into utopianism, Williams noted, taking up terms by Miguel Abensour, as heuristics vs. systematics, and he went on to discuss even-handedly their strengths and weaknesses.

Gloss 16a: I can here identify three exemplary Post-Fordist constructions, all "aesthetic." One is dystopian and anti-utopian, Disneyland (Theses 18–20); two are refurbishings of old stances and genres, *Fallible Utopia* and *Fallible Dystopia* (Theses 21–24). This already points to the fact that mainstream bourgeois ideology (say in TV and newspapers) has kept resolutely systematic, albeit in updated guises such as Disneyfication. Obversely, what may perhaps be called the "New" (not New) Left has in and after the 1960s found new ways to proceed in heuristic guise.

Gloss 16b: Of course, the overarching dystopian construct is the "informational" one of Post-Fordism and global capitalism itself, the killer whale inside which we have to live, but obeying my Thesis 13, I shall not discuss it directly here.

17. However, heuristic means "serving to find out" and it is not incompatible with systematic, which originally meant both pertaining to "the whole scheme of created things, the universe" and to "a set of principles, etc., a scheme, method" (OED): you can very well find out a universal scheme. This became rigid in the nineteenth century, when Frederick Engels ironized that "the 'system' of all philosophers springs from an imperishable desire of the human mind—the desire to overcome all contradiction." Rather, the heuristic should be contrasted to what philosophers call the "ostensive" mode: concentrating on the right formulation of a question vs. handing down received wisdom. The heuristic method induces the questioner to collaborate in finding the answer, which is indispensable in times of fast change, in learner or world: it foments a dis-covering rather than giving doctrinal (dogmatic) answers. But any teacher—or other practitioner, say practical theologian (see Bastian)—would know that you cannot reach anybody without using both methods: only on the basis of existing understanding can new knowledge be gained. When vanguard knowledge began to proceed heuristically—as of 1905, when Albert Einstein did not call his paper on relativity a theory but considerations from a "heuristic viewpoint," or indeed as of Karl Marx, who called his considerations not a theory but "a critique"—it was taking off from improperly absolutized systematicity.

Gloss 17: This can be clearly seen in the static eutopias that infested the positivist age (Louis Sébastien Mercier, Cabet, Edward Bellamy), which swallowed horizon in locus. They were fiercely combated by the Right (anti-utopias such as Emile Souvestre's) and the Left (metamorphic eutopias such as Restif de la Bretonne's or William Morris's).

18. *Disneyfication as Dystopia.* An exemplary (bad) case of a dystopian misuse of eutopian images are the edulcorated fables and fairy tales of Disneyland. I shall use it as a privileged *pars pro toto* of the capitalist and especially U.S. admass brainwash. Its spatial rupture with everyday life masks its intensification of commodity dominance. Its central spring is what I shall (adapting Louis Marin) call *reproductive empathy*. As Benjamin remarked, "the commercial glance into the heart of things demolishes the space for the free play of viewing" by abolishing any critical distance. This empathy functions (perverting Sigmund Freud's dreamwork) by *transfer ideologizing* and *substitution commodifying*.

Gloss 18a: Transfer ideologizing is the continually reinforced empathizing immersion, the "thick," topologically and figurally concrete, and seamless false consciousness that injects the hegemonic bourgeois version of U.S. normality into people's neurons by "naturalizing" and neutralizing three imaginative fields: *historical time* as the space of alternative choices; the *foreign/ers*; and the *natural world*. Historical time is turned into the myth of technological progress, while the foreign and natural become the primitive, the savage, and the monstrous.

Gloss 18b: In substitution commodifying, the Golden Calf is capillarized in the psychic bloodstream as *commodity*. The pervasive upshot of Disneyland is: "*life is a permanent exchange and perpetual consuming*" (see Marin, emphasis original); it commodifies desire, and in particular the desire for happiness as signification or meaningfulness. The dynamic and sanitized empathizing into the pursuit of commodity is allegorized as anthropomorphic animals who stand for various affects that make up this pursuit. The affects and stances are strictly confined to the petty-bourgeois "positive" range where, roughly, Mickey Mouse introduces good cheer, the Lion King courage and persistence, and so on.

19. Psychologically, the Disneyfication strategy is one of *infantilization* of adults. Its images function as an infantile "security blanket," producing constantly repeated demand to match the constantly recycled offer. The infantilization entails a double rejection. First, it rejects any intervention into the real world that would make the pursuit of happiness collectively attainable: it is a debilitating daydream that appeals to the same mechanism as empathizing performances and publicity. Second and obversely, it rejects any reality constriction of one's desire, however shallow or destructive. Wedded to consumer dynamics of an ever expanding market, Disneyland remains deeply inimical to knowledge, which crucially includes an understanding of limits

for any endeavor—and in particular of the final personal limit of death. Snow White must always be magically resuscitated, to circulate again.

Gloss 19: "Main Street, USA," the central thoroughfare of Disneyland, was constructed as an exact replica of the main street of Walt Disney's boyhood small town, except that it was, "down to every brick and shingle and gas lamp," five-eights normal size and created a sense of depth, both shortening and stretching the perception, by having each exterior level built larger than the one above it: "the intended effect was to recall the main street of every adult's distanced youth . . . with the remembered perspective of a child's eye" (see Eliot). Disney passed most days inside his apartment above Main Street, "where he would stand by the window with tears streaming down his face as people walked along the boulevard of his dreams" (see Eliot).

20. In sum: Disneyland's trap for desire, this fake Other, is a violence exercised upon the imaginary by its banalized images. Disneyfication is a shaping of *affective investment into commodifying which reduces the mind to infantilism* as an illusory escape from death: a mythology. It can serve as a metonymy of what Fredric Jameson has discussed as the post-modern "consumption of the very process of consumption," say in TV.[1] It preempts any alternative imagination, any fertile possibility of a radical otherness or indeed simply of shuttling in and out of a story.

21. *Fallible Eu-Dys-Topia.* From Tom Moylan's pioneering delimitation and the wealth of his analyses of fictional and critical texts in *Demand*, I draw the following scheme for what I prefer to call the *Fallible Eutopia*, a new sub-genre of the U.S. 1960s–70s: 1) the society of textual action is eutopian, in open or subtle contradiction to the human relations and power structures in the writer's reality; 2) this new Possible World is revealed as beset by dangers—centering on inner contradictions, but often including also outer, hegemonic counter-revolutionary violence—that threaten to reinstate class stratification, violence, and injustice; 3) our hero/ine, often a multifocal collective, fights against this threat with some chance of success. This form supplements the usual utopian critique of the writer's (dystopian) reality with a second front against the involution and downfall of the eutopian society.

Gloss 21a: Examples: Robert Nichols's wonderful tetralogy *Daily Lives in Nghsi-Altai*; Sally M. Gearhardt's *Wanderground*; Suzy M. Charnas's *Motherlines* dilogy (now tetralogy); the culmination of the first wave of this form, Le Guin's *The Dispossessed*, explicating in its two-loci, braided chapter structure and the book's subtitle ("An Ambiguous Utopia") the two fronts; and Kim Stanley Robinson's work culminating so far in the *Mars* trilogy, the masterpiece of its second, dialectically post-feminist wave.

Gloss 21b: The evident basis of such works in the counter-hegemonic U.S. and European movements of the times, from anarchist ascendancies through the centrally situated feminist ones to other counter-cultural ones (gay, ecological, "rainbow"), is clear in this "plague on both your houses" thrust typical of the anti-Stalinist New Left. It is confirmed by the abrupt cessation of its first wave with the advent of Reagan and its reappearance when the shock of Post-Fordism had been digested.

22. From Moylan's pioneering delimitation and the wealth of his analyses of fictional and critical texts in *Scraps*, I draw the following scheme for what I prefer to call the *Fallible Dystopia*, a new sub-genre arising out of both the shock of Post-Fordism and its imaginative mastering: 1) the society of textual action is dystopian, in open extrapolation or subtle analogy to human relations and power structures in the writer's reality; 2) this new Possible World is revealed as resistible and changeable, by our hero/ine, often with great difficulty. In the best cases, such as Robinson and Marge Piercy, it begins to visit the "periphery" of capitalism, usually the Arabic world. Obversely, the escape to a eutopian enclave as illusion of bliss, finally to the stars, inherited from earlier dystopian sf (for example, Pohl and Kornbluth's *The Space Merchants*), is an individualist temptation persisting in sf from John Brunner (if not A. E. Van Vogt) to Octavia Butler.

Gloss 22: Representative works are to my mind Pamela Sargent's *The Shore of Women*, an exceptionally explicit self-criticism of separatist feminism, Robinson's *Gold Coast*, Piercy's *He, She and It*, Butler's *Parable of the Sower*. The great ancestor is Jack London's *Iron Heel*, while Aldous Huxley's *Island* already prefigured the fall from fallible eutopia into fallible dystopia. Pat Cadigan's *Synners* melds the fallible dystopia and cyberpunk. A ludic variant at its margin is the "Culture" series by Banks beginning with *Consider Phlebas*. The reader should draw her own conclusion from the preponderance of female names, within an incipient regrouping of opposition to unbridled speculative capitalism.

23. The epistemic and political impulse of those two genres seems very similar, and their differences stem mainly from the different structure of cognitive feeling in their historical moments. This can be well seen in Robinson's switch from the mainly dystopian *Gold Coast* to the mainly eutopian *Pacific Edge*. Rooted in a Gramscian "pessimism of the intellect, optimism of the will," interweaving glimpses of far-off horizons with the closure inside the belly of the beast, these are hybrid and often polyphonic writings. In the pragmatic absence and indeed breakdown of collective agencies, such as centralized parties, the writings focus on the *choices* by one or more focal single agents, themselves endangered and fallible, who

undergo a heuristic awakening to be followed by the reader—not least toward new collective agencies from the bottom up. Sometimes the choice is formalized as different time horizons flowing out of some crucial choice/s (Joanna Russ, Le Guin, Piercy). Fallible eutopia had to devise more innovative textual strategies to counteract the dogmatic systematicity of its tradition and make room for the presence of the old hegemony inside and outside the eutopias. It is therefore as a rule heuristic and open, fit for epic action and articulation of change as process and not blueprint. Fallible dystopia, with a shorter tradition, has no such rigid format to break, either formally or ideologically (nobody ever set out to realize a dystopia): it can simply follow the riverbed of societal history. Since dystopia can incorporate rather than—as eutopia—counteract the ancestral proceedings, its strategies seem more similar to dystopian sf from Wells and Karel Capek through the "new maps of hell" of Pohl, William Tenn, or Sheckley to Dick and Thomas M. Disch.

Gloss 23: A polar opposition between the fallible eutopia and the fallible dystopia is thus possible only in terms of ideal types that allow for a spectrum of intermediate possibilities. A balance of eutopian and dystopian horizons makes of Russ's *Female Man* and Piercy's *Dance the Eagle to Sleep*, which deal partly or wholly with a flawed eutopian struggle within a fierce repression, ancestors of both these genres. Samuel R. Delany's *Triton* rejects both horizons in favor of the micropolitics of his anti-hero, and seems to me not to belong in either subgenre.

24. In sum, the strategies of what we may call a refurbished utopianism for sadder and possibly wiser times add to the panoply of deeply critical devices for creating inverted worlds whose salient aspects show up the author's pragmatic world as one of upside-down, death-dealing values and rules. This enriched horizon clarifies and activates liberating desire by means of textually embodied—not only ideological—alternative images and actions. To the illusory mythology of Disneyfication (as example of hegemonic strategies for "commodity aesthetics"), a Lotosland for the weary, they oppose epic struggle. To addictive consumption they oppose cognitive and practical creation. Through narrative choices, they affirm the possibility of a radical otherness, indeed its absolute necessity for the survival of human values and lives.

IV. *Ausklang*: Who Are We? Where Are We Going To? (free after Gauguin)

25. At the end of Piercy's *He, She and It*, an anti-capitalist alliance is in the making between the high-technology intellectuals and politicized urban

gangs. While it is not useful to blur the ontological differences between fact and fiction, both partake of, incide on, and are shaped by the same human imagination. It seems to me mandatory to end these much too long theses (testimony to the confusing times that we live through and that live through us) by a brief attempt to identify who might be talking to whom, in this endangered moment under the stars. My answer is (maybe alas): various stripes or fractions of intellectuals. What can, and therefore must, intellectuals do today within, under, and against dystopia? If I may define this type as one who responds, who is responsive and responsible, a possible answer is: not too much, but perhaps, with much effort and much luck, this might prove just enough.

Gloss 25: The above Bakhtinian dialogical definition excludes of course the great majority of those whom sociologists call "the professionals," people who work mainly with images and/or concepts and, among other functions, "produce, distribute and preserve distinct forms of consciousness" (see Mills): the engineers of material and human resources, the ad writers and "design" professionals, the new bishops and cardinals of the media clerisy, most lawyers, as well as the teeming swarms of supervisors (we teachers are increasingly adjunct police officers keeping the kids off the streets). The funds for this whole congerie of "cadre" classes "have been drawn from the global surplus" (see Wallerstein): none of us has clean hands. I myself seem to be paid through loans to the Québec government by German banks, or ultimately by the exploitation of people like my ex-compatriots in eastern Europe.

26. This our intermediate class-congerie in the world has since 1945 in the capitalist core countries been materially better off than our historical counterparts: but the price has been very high. Within the new collectivism, we are "a dominated fraction of the dominant class" (see Bourdieu), a living contradiction: while essential to the *encadrement* and policing of workers, we are ourselves workers—a position memorably encapsulated by Bertolt Brecht's "Song of the Tame Eighth Elephant" helping to subdue his recalcitrant natural brethren in *The Good Person of Setzuan*. Excogitating ever new ways to sell our expertise as "services" in producing and enforcing marketing images of happiness, we decisively contribute to the decline of people's self-determination and non-professionalized expertise. We are essential to the production of new knowledge and ideology, but we are totally kept out of establishing the framework into which, and mostly kept from directing the uses to which, the production and the producers are put. Our professionalization secured for some of us sufficient income to turn high wage into minuscule capital. We cannot function without a good deal of self-government in our classes or artefacts, but we

do not control the strategic decisions about universities or dissemination of artefacts.

27. And what of the swiftly descending future? To my mind, but not only mine, the hope for an eventual bridging of the poverty gap both worldwide and inside single countries is now over. It is very improbable the Keynesian class compromise can be dismantled without burying under its fallout capitalism as a whole. Will this happen explosively, for example in a quite possible Third World War, or by a slow crumbling away that generates massive breakdowns of civil and civilized relations, on the model of the present "cold civil war" smoldering in the United States and indeed globally, which are (as Disch's forgotten masterpiece *334* rightly saw) comparable only to daily life in the late Roman Empire? And what kind of successor formation might come about? Worst fears and maddest hopes are allowable. The age of individualism and free market is over, the present is already highly collectivized, and demographics as well as insecurity will make the future even more so: the alternative lies between the models of the oligarchic (that is, centrally fascist) war-camp and an open plebeian-democratic commune.

28. In this realistically grim perspective, facing a dangerous series of cascading bifurcations, I believe that our liberatory corporate or class interests as intellectuals are twofold and interlocking. *First,* they consist in securing a high degree of self-management, to begin with in the workplace. But capitalism without a human face is obviously engaged in large-scale "structural declassing" of intellectual work, of our "cultural capital" (see Bourdieu, and Guillory). There is nothing more humiliating, short of physical injury and hunger, than the experience of being pushed to the periphery of social values—measured by the only yardstick capitalism knows, our financial condition—which all of us have undergone in the last quarter century. Our younger colleagues are by now predominantly denied Keynesian employment, condemned to part-time piecework without security. Capitalism has adjoined to the permanent reserve army of industrial labor that of intellectual labor. Thus our interests also consist, *second,* in working for such strategic alliances with other fractions and classes as would allow us to fight against the current of militarized browbeating. This may be most visible in "Confucian capitalism" from Japan to Malaya, for example in the concentration-camp fate of the locked-in young women of its factories, but it is well represented in all our "democratic" sweatshops and fortress neighborhoods as well as fortress nation-blocs, prominently in the United States (see Harvey). It can only be counteracted by ceaseless insistence on meaningful democratic participation in the control not only of production but also of distribution of our own work, and in the control

of our neighborhoods. Here the boundary between our dissident interests within the intellectual field of production and the overall liberation of labor as their only guarantee becomes permeable.

29. The modernist oases for exiles (the Left Bank, Bloomsbury, lower Manhattan, major U.S. campuses) are gone the way of a Tahiti polluted by nuclear fallout and venereal pandemic: some affluent or starving writers à la Pynchon or Joyce may still be possible, but not as a statistically significant option for us. Adapting Marina Tsvetaeva's great line "All poets are Jews" (*Vse poèty zhidy*), we can say that fortunately all intellectuals are partly exiles from the Disneyland and/or starvation dystopia, but we are an "inner emigration" for whom resistance was always possible and is now growing mandatory. The first step toward resistance to Disneyfied brainwashing is "the invention of the desire called utopia in the first place, along with new rules for the fantasizing or daydreaming of such a thing—a set of narrative protocols with no precedent in our previous literary institutions" (see Jameson). This is a collective production of meanings, the efficacy of which is measured by how many consumers it is able to turn, to begin with, into critical and not empathetic thinkers, and finally into producers.

30. All variants of dystopian-cum-eutopian fiction sketched above pivot not only on individual self-determination but centrally on collective self-management enabling and guaranteeing personal freedom. Whoever is not interested in this horizon will not be interested in them. And vice versa.

Note

1. My pervasive debt to Raymond Williams's and Fredric Jameson's work is not well indicated by the one reference for each. Much work of Lyman Tower Sargent and other colleagues from the Society for Utopian Studies and elsewhere is also implied.

Works Cited

Bastian, Hans-Dieter. *Verfremdung und Verkündigung*. München: Kaiser, 1965.

Benjamin, Walter. *Gesammelte Schriften*. Frankfurt am Main: Suhrkamp, 1980–87.

Bloch, Ernst. *Das Prinzip Hoffnung*. Frankfurt am Main: Suhrkamp, 1959.

Bourdieu, Pierre. *In Other Words*. Trans. M. Anderson. Stanford: Stanford UP, 1990.

de Certeau, Michel. "The Jabbering of Social Life." *In Signs*. Ed. M. Blonsky. Baltimore: Johns Hopkins UP, 1991. 146–54.

Eliot, Marc. *Walt Disney*. New York: Carol, 1993.

Guillory, John. "Literary Critics as Intellectuals." *Rethinking Class*. Ed. W. C. Dimock and M. T. Gilmore. New York: Columbia UP, 1994. 107–49.

Harvey, David. *Justice, Nature and the Geography of Difference*. Oxford: Blackwell, 1996.

Jameson, Fredric. *The Seeds of Time*. New York: Columbia UP, 1994.

Lukács, Georg. *Geschichte und Klassenbewusstsein*. Berlin: Luchterhand, 1968.

Marin, Louis. *Utopiques: jeux d'espaces*. Paris: Minuit, 1973.

Mills, C. Wright. *White Collar*. New York: Oxford UP, 1953.

Moylan, Tom. *Demand the Impossible: Science Fiction and the Utopian Imagination*. New York: Methuen, 1986.

———. *Scraps of the Untainted Sky: Science Fiction, Utopia, Dystopia*. Boulder: Westview, 2000.

Noble, David F. *America by Design*. New York: Knopf, 1977.

Suvin, Darko. "Horizon (Utopian)." Entry for "Lexicon: 20th Century A.D." *Public* 19: 72–75.

———. "Locus, Horizon, and Orientation: The Concept of Possible Worlds as a Key to Utopian Studies." *Not Yet: Reconsidering Ernst Bloch*. Ed. Jamie Owen Daniel and Tom Moylan. London: Verso, 1997. 122–37.

———. *Metamorphoses of Science Fiction: On the Poetics and History of a Literary Genre*. New Haven: Yale UP, 1979.

———. "Novum Is as Novum Does." *Foundation* 69 (Spring 1997): 26–43.

———. *Positions and Presuppositions in Science Fiction*. London: Macmillan; Kent State UP, 1988.

———. "Reflections on What Remains of Zamyatin's *We* after the Change of Leviathans: Must Collectivism Be Against People?" *3000, The Next New Millennium: Science Fiction Studies/Cultural Studies*. Ed. Marleen Barr. Middletown: Wesleyan UP (forthcoming 2003).

———. "System." Entry for "Lexicon: 20th Century A.D." *Public* 20: 81–84.

———. "Two Cheers for Essentialism & Totality." *Rethinking Marxism* 10.1 (1998): 66–82.

———. "Utopianism from Orientation to Agency: What Are We Intellectuals under Post-Fordism to Do?" *Utopian Studies* 9.2 (1998): 162–90.

Wallerstein, Immanuel. *Historical Capitalism* [, with] *Capitalist Civilization*. London: Verso, 1996.

Williams, Raymond. *Problems in Materialism and Culture*. London: Verso, 1980.

CHAPTER 11

Concrete Dystopia: Slavery and Its Others

MARIA VARSAM

Was not the whole world a vast prison and women born slaves?
—Mary Wollstonecraft, *Mary; and, The Wrongs of Woman*

Work or the Crematory—the choice is in your hands.
—Elie Wiesel, *Night*

I. Introduction

Is it possible to speak of slavery, a historical fact, in relation to dystopian fiction? At first glance there is an obvious discrepancy between the time-space parameters of each. On the one hand, slavery has been documented in history as an institution that has constituted an integral part of most societies' economic and cultural makeup. In fact, Orlando Patterson argues in *Slavery and Social Death* that there has never been a society that has not practiced slavery to some degree or another (vii). On the other hand, dystopian fiction belongs to the realm of the "fantastic," describing events that typically have not taken place, indeed may never take place. Yet, utopian narratives, oral or written, have also been a part of every society's artistic production, at least, as Lyman Tower Sargent argues, in the form of "social dreaming" of a better future, a *eutopia*.[1] Across space and time, then, the reality of slavery and the dream of a better future provide the co-ordinates for a cultural common denominator.

At the same time, slavery has not only been described in history books. As a result of the African-American slave experience, the eighteenth and nineteenth centuries have seen the production of a plethora of autobiographical texts that provide a unique insight into the institution of slavery. These texts in turn have inspired the creation of the twentieth-century neo-slave narrative and provided, according to the editors' introduction to *The Slave's Narrative*, the determining influence for what is now an African-American literary tradition (Davis and Gates xxxiii).[2] Most important for this essay, certain neo-slave narratives, while retaining many of the conventions of the early slave narratives, develop issues and themes common to those of the twentieth-century dystopian novel.

Though many different themes are developed in classic and neo-slave narratives and in dystopian narratives, one common thread unites them: a conspicuous preoccupation with obtaining freedom. In female-authored texts, in particular, this preoccupation centers on issues of reproductive freedom, sexuality, and the control over one's body. The focus of this essay will be on women's sexual and reproductive choices in three such texts: Harriet Jacobs's nineteenth-century slave narrative *Incidents in the Life of a Slave Girl* (1861), Margaret Atwood's dystopia *The Handmaid's Tale* (1985), and Octavia Butler's neo-slave narrative and critical dystopia *Kindred* (1979). My purpose is to bring together fact and fiction, reality and its representation, in order to elaborate on a frequently utilized motif in dystopian fiction—that of slavery—and its relationship to a discourse on freedom. This in turn will illuminate facets of slavery (both literal and literary) that remain unexamined in studies of dystopias because of the prevailing scholarly emphasis on slavery as a historical phenomenon.[3] My comparison will focus on the first-person narrator of these texts since it is with this point of view that the reader is asked to identify and empathize. I will draw common parameters between the fictional account of the institution of slavery—its constitutive elements, its function, and effects—and dystopian fiction, a particularly twentieth-century phenomenon (though one with ancient antecedents). As a result, I will expand the terms of slavery and dystopia to include a plethora of cultural manifestations that will reveal the outlines of a "dystopian continuum," one that a) spans the time-space axis, b) links fact and fiction in a non-representational mode, and c) expands the generic category of dystopian fiction while reframing the historical novel of the Afro-American slave experience in terms of a utopian impulse, a process of hope and resistance to oppression. Far from simplifying and/or belittling the experience of slavery, my reading will emphasize the importance of slavery as a living memory and constitute a warning of the danger of history repeating itself.

II. Dystopian Fiction and Representation

To begin with, how do we—the readers—know when a text "counts" as a dystopia? Because of the range of visions, one writer's eutopia is another

writer's dystopia, an issue that remains problematic in the history of interpretation of texts ranging from Plato's *The Republic* to modern-day works.
Sargent defines dystopian fiction as texts showing "a non-existent society
described in considerable detail and normally located in time and space
that the author intended a contemporaneous reader to view as considerably worse than the society in which the reader lived" ("Three Faces" 9). He
suggests examining the author's intentions for the limited purpose of determining whether the work can be classified more easily. Though he admits that this is not always possible, he insists that it remains necessary
(13). The author's intention may be easily discerned by a researcher, but
not by a reader who has no ready access to the sources that will enable
her/him to determine whether or not a text is a dystopia. What is needed is
a text-based definition that the reader takes an active part in generating,
since it is the reader's understanding of the narrator's message that will establish the distinction between what constitutes a "good" or "bad" future
world.

It follows that it would be more useful if this determination, rather
than being based on authorial intention, were to focus on the identification the reader is invited to make with the protagonist/narrator. Since it
is the protagonist who experiences his/her society as dystopian (to a
greater degree, at least, than the others), one criterion then should take
this positioning into account. It is also the protagonist who attempts to
answer the question "which world is this, and what place do I occupy
within it?" This is a useful distinction to make for the genre since it is the
perception of the protagonist that the reader is asked to accept as a valid
representation of the dystopian experience. It is usually the protagonist's
desires and hopes for a better present or future that distinguish him/her
from the rest of the population and additionally bring him/her into conflict with the dystopian establishment. Unlike eutopian fiction, in which
there seems to be an agreement of principles among all the citizens, the
multiplicity of voices in dystopian fiction renders it necessary for the
reader to accept the narrator's point of view as the most reliable; there
would otherwise be no exposure of the dystopia in question.[4] The narrator's perception is an important sign in the genre for signaling and documenting the discrepancy between the world as he/she experiences it and
the world he/she desires. The reader is then drawn into the dystopian
world via a series of formal devices utilized for the purpose of identification with the narrator's point of view. Without a successful process of
identification, the reader will not be convinced of the narrator's critique
of the present, and the utopian impulse implicit in the dystopian narrative will have failed in its purpose to warn of future, potentially catastrophic, developments. For the purpose of ensuring that identification
is successfully developed, formal strategies must be employed that function

independently of the author's actual intentions, which are inaccessible to the reader.

The main stylistic strategy employed to express this discrepancy is that of "defamiliarization."[5] This term, coined by the Russian formalist Victor Shklovsky, denotes a technique necessary (for him, to all literature) to the purpose of "renewing perception": "art exists that one may recover the sensation of life. It exists to make one feel things, to make the stone stony. The *purpose of art* is to impart the sensation of things *as they are perceived and not as they are known.* The technique of art is to make objects *unfamiliar*, to make forms difficult, to increase the difficulty and length of *perception*" (18, emphasis added). In this passage, the stress on "perception" in relation to "the purpose of art" points to two key concerns of the utopian genre. In the process of "making things unfamiliar," of defamiliarizing objects of reality, dystopian fiction invites the reader to observe the dystopian world as the narrator observes it, not merely to sympathize but also to judge. Via *this* perception of reality, the reader must empathize with the narrator/protagonist in order to condemn, as the narrator/protagonist does, those aspects of society that constitute the narrator's oppression. In fact, defamiliarization is the key strategy all utopian literature employs to some degree for the explicit purpose of social critique via renewed perception. Applied to dystopian fiction, defamiliarization makes us see the world anew, not as it is but as it *could* be; it shows the world in sharp focus in order to bring out conditions that exist already but which, as a result of our dulled perception, we can no longer see. In this sense, dystopian fiction acts as our new eyes onto the world, creating clues that we can become aware of if only we "tuned into" the right frequency. Reality becomes a site of interpretation, and the reader is asked to partake in this interpretation in order to elicit the exact parameters of the warning conveyed in any given dystopian text. Through the devices that "make strange" our perception of the world, dystopian texts continually demand readerly attention to our relationship to the real world in order to ask whether we are making, as Sargent points out, the "correct choices" ("Three Faces" 24).

In *Metamorphoses of Science Fiction*, Darko Suvin amends Shklovsky's term in the case of sf utopia to be a formal property called "cognitive estrangement" in order to delineate a "creative approach toward a dynamic transformation rather than toward a static mirroring of the author's environment" (9). His emphasis on interpretation rather than reflection points to the critical work of an author in his/her purpose to present the reader with a perception of reality that critiques accepted views of the world. In sf and utopian writing, then, the real world is made to appear "strange" in order to challenge the reader's complacency toward accepted views of history and awaken, through the "truth" of fiction, a new perception of the connections between history and the present world. The device of defamil-iarization, then, may serve in dystopian fiction as a formal strategy that cre-ates a bridge between certain elements of reality and fiction, the historical and the synchronic, on the one hand, the ahistorical and the diachronic, on the other. This makes it possible to draw parallels between disparate histor-ical events far removed from one another in space and time and to make connections between similar events placed in disparate contexts. Through the comparisons across time—future, present, and past—and across space, the author encourages the reader to critique the historical process and to as-sess what similarities and differences can be drawn. However, when one translates Shklovsky's term, it remains a device that is used for, as Suvin states, "a reflection *on* reality as well as *of* reality" (9).[6]

Furthermore, it is clear that with such an approach to the interpretation of reality, a mimetic theory of art in relation to dystopian fiction is insuffi-cient. Dystopias cannot be expected to adhere to a Platonic concept of *mimesis* since the world they are depicting does not exist in the present time of writing.[7] The mimetic approach to art also relies on a stable, recog-nizable reality as well as an interpretation of that reality that assumes a di-rect correspondence between the two. Instead, what is a more useful—and appropriate—hermeneutic is what Andrew Bowie emphasizes in the po-tential of literature to "disclose" the world by making connections where previously none were visible and to "reveal the world in ways that would not be possible without the existence of art itself" (18).[8] In this respect, utopian fiction is the quintessential art form for a hermeneutics of "disclo-sure" because of its self-conscious effort to select elements of the present material world in order to transform them in a narrative that illuminates their latent potential for evolving into a better or worse future. Utopian fic-tion performs an "education" of perception whereby certain truths are dis-closed via defamiliarization since at the level of plot, language, and character the reader is made to "see" the world in radically different ways. In short, the reading of utopian fiction accomplishes what P. B. Shelley claimed for the effect of reading poetry in his "A Defence of Poetry": "It creates anew the universe, after it has been annihilated in our minds by the recurrence of impressions blunted by reiteration" (505–06).

III. Concrete Utopia and Concrete Dystopia

How then does the term "concrete dystopia" relate to the above issues? In order to delineate what constitutes concrete dystopia it is first necessary to look to another, related term, Ernst Bloch's "concrete utopia." For Bloch, this term points to a perception of reality in process: "real historical possi-bilities and tendencies in the Not-Yet."[9] Though it refers to the present, it is anticipatory because it brings together past, present, and future by realizing the latent utopian forces in society in its focus on change in the future (*On Karl Marx* 72). In *The Principle of Hope*, Bloch elaborates on the implications of concrete utopia: "Reality without real possibility is not complete, the world without future-laden properties does not deserve a glance, . . . concrete utopia stands on the horizon of every reality, real possibility surrounds the open dialectical tendencies and latencies to the very last" (223). Bloch's utopian hermeneutic forms a bridge between art and reality that is otherwise absent from classical literary criticism, for what Bloch brings to critical discourse is a disruption of "the acceptance of given realities as the only realities" (McManus 2). Reality for Bloch is not a fixed, unchanging object of human inquiry, but rather, as Ruth Levitas points out, it "includes what is becoming and might become" and as such is "in a state of process" which incorporates future possibilities (70).[10] Utopia, then, is not merely escapist fantasy but a positive force in the present that enables the expression of the hope that, ultimately, happiness and fulfillment (including the absence of violence, fear, and alienation) will be tenable by all. Looking to the negative, therefore, if dystopian texts extrapolate from real events, then manifestations of concrete dystopia form the material basis through which literature, as a carrier of utopian hope, may convey its intention to critique and warn. Moreover, on a conceptual level, it expresses connotations both parallel and opposite to those of concrete dystopia.

What concrete utopia shares with concrete dystopia is an emphasis on the real, material conditions of society that manifest themselves as a result of humanity's desire for a better world. For both, reality is not fixed but fluid, pregnant with both positive and negative potential for the future. It implies that present and past conditions are dystopian in their function and effects because of the ever present need for change and improvement. If concrete utopia brings together the present and future by pulling "the present forward," as Tom Moylan writes in *Demand the Impossible*, then concrete dystopia brings together the past and present, creating thus a continuum in time whereby historical reality is dystopian, possibly punctuated by utopian ruptures in the form of literature, art, and other cultural manifestations (22). For Bloch, Utopia can be detected in every art form, from literature and music to architecture and painting, and is central to ethics, religion, and philosophy (683). It follows, then, that any forces that attempt or have attempted to crush the expression of hope by means of physical or psychological violence or to displace desire by means of a physical and/or propaganda machine form the basis from which fear becomes institutionalized in order to establish a new "reality" defined by hierarchy and stasis, censorship, and lack of freedom. Such forces include, but are not limited to, all forms of slavery, genocide, and political dictatorship. Their manifestation is not the prerogative of any one time or society but a potential reality in any time and space in which alienation has been imposed and hope replaced with despair and desire with fear.

In opposition to concrete utopia, concrete dystopia designates those moments, events, institutions, and systems that embody and realize organized forces of violence and oppression. Where concrete utopia envisions freedom from violence, inequality, and domination, concrete dystopia expresses coercion (physical and psychological), fear, despair, and alienation. Whereas concrete utopia is a manifestation of desire and hope for a better world and an "unalienated order" that upsets the status quo, concrete dystopia delineates the crushing of hope and the displacement of desire for the purpose of upholding that status quo (Bloch, *Principle* 624). So although utopian literature, both eutopian and dystopian, is an expression of utopian hope because of its revolutionary potential, only dystopian literature expresses the warning that what once happened, or took place to a limited degree, may happen again. Concrete dystopias are those events that form the *material* basis for the content of dystopian fiction which have *inspired* the writer to warn of the potential for history to repeat itself. To summarize, the terms "concrete utopia" and "concrete dystopia" share a common *space* in their referral to conditions that manifest themselves in the real world but stand in opposition in terms of *time*, the former being forward looking, the latter backward looking. Both however, retain a common space-time in the possibility of realization in the present.

The relationship of dystopian fiction to the reality it refers to and is inspired by is a key issue in the delineation of concrete dystopia. It is in this fiction that the reader may see what elements of reality the writer deems significant enough to extrapolate from in order to warn the reader of future, potentially catastrophic developments. For example, in writing *Nineteen Eighty-Four*, George Orwell expresses this fear: "I believe . . . that totalitarianism, if not fought against, could triumph anywhere" (*Collected* 502); and in *The Handmaid's Tale*, the religious fundamentalism of the Republic of Gilead is for Atwood not wholly imaginary: "There's nothing in it that we as a species haven't done, aren't doing now or don't have the technological capacity to do" (qtd. in Howells 129). In both novels, the experience of the "present" dystopian reality gives rise to reflection on the processes of history and the relationship between past, present, and future. In Atwood's text, this reflection leads, as Raffaella Baccolini has argued, not to a nostalgic desire for a better future along similar parameters with the past, but to a critique of the past and its continuing legacy in the present ("Journeying" 346). Equally, Octavia Butler has stated that for her slavery is not an event of the past but a reality in the present both in the American

South and in her native California: "And, frankly, there isn't anything in there that can't happen if we keep going as we have been. . . . It's already happening. I'm talking about people who can't even leave. If they try they're beaten or killed" (qtd. in Miller 352). Butler's and Atwood's novels, then, effect not only what Fredric Jameson calls an apprehension of "the present as history" (246), but also the past as present and the present as future. As a result, the experience of oppression and its effect on the present is reformulated in order to understand not merely a historical event but also a living present. In short, the relationship that dystopian fiction has to reality is a dialectical one in which historical events provoke artistic expression that in turn may provoke historical change.

IV. Dystopian Fiction, Slavery, and Slave Narratives

What events, then, have constituted concrete dystopias for writers of dystopian fiction? There have been many historical events that have provided *inspiration* but the most prominent of these has been the rise of fascism in Europe in the twentieth century.[11] Classic dystopias such as Orwell's *Nineteen Eighty-Four* and Katharine Burdekin's *Swastika Night* present authoritarian worlds and their physical and psychological effects on men and women respectively.[12] At the same time, these worlds are often represented as quasi slave societies that provide not only the content but often a stylistic framework within which to develop the themes of oppression, freedom, and liberation. In *Swastika Night*, for example, the women are illiterate, denigrated, and powerless in their position of reproductive slave labor. In Angela Carter's *The Passion of New Eve*, there is a micro slave society in which the female (though previously male) protagonist/narrator is captured by its tyrant, Zero, becomes a member of his harem, and is repeatedly raped and forbidden to speak. Slavery is also depicted more broadly, as in Butler's *Parable of the Sower*, to designate relations of economic dependence with the use of the term "debt slavery." On the level of content, then, the concerns of dystopian fiction often coincide with those of slave narratives in their discourse on freedom, inequality, and the nature of domination. On the formal level, dystopias such as *Handmaid* "borrow" from the classic slave narrative, and in Butler's critical dystopia *Kindred* slavery forms the main raison d'être for the novel's narrative.[13] Since slavery is depicted as a form of "totalitarian" oppression in future worlds, these dystopian fictions problematize its status as a system of oppression and exploitation located exclusively in the past.

Yet, defining slavery is not an altogether uncomplicated issue. For Patterson, to define slavery as a relation of domination—a relation defined by inequality, violence, and lack of freedom rather than a relation defined by property—makes a crucial difference. The former definition is for Patterson more fitting than the second because it can be accurately applied to the institution of slavery irrespective of its particular existence in time and place. Just as significant is the fact that it is one drawn from the point of view of the slaves themselves and the effects on *their* condition rather than an expression of their masters' point of view (*Slavery* 20–27, 334).[14] It is the relative power between the parties concerned that differentiates the master-slave relationship from any other because the slave master's power over the slave's life is total. Furthermore, unlike people exploited in other types of labor relations "only slaves entered into the relationship as a substitute for death" (Patterson, *Slavery* 26). The constant threat of violence, then, and the ultimate powerlessness of the slave—barring the power to choose suicide—is a definition both narrow and flexible enough to accommodate past and, I will argue, to present manifestations of slavery. Finally, this definition is supported by the evidence in the narratives of the slaves themselves. Slavery is shown to be primarily a relation of domination, while the issue of property, though important, is secondary.

In its classic form, the slave narrative achieves its effects on the reader as a form of autobiography with well-defined formal conventions as well as thematic ones. But as the essays in John Sekora and Darwin T. Turner's *The Art of the Slave Narrative* illustrate, it also utilizes conventions distinct from other autobiographical narratives that overlap with those of dystopian narratives.[15] From a formal point of view, the most obvious similarity between the slave narrative and the dystopia is the focus on the subjective point of view of the narrator with whom the reader must identify and sympathize. As with all autobiographies, first-person narration is a necessary means of expressing the immediacy of experience as well as its authenticity. But in the case of the slave narrative the emphasis on first-person point of view serves an additional purpose, that of critique and education. It is with these two functions that the slave narrative shares a common purpose with dystopian fiction.

But how do these functions manifest themselves in both slave narratives and dystopias vis-à-vis the institution of slavery? There are two important common points of reference here. Slave narratives were written "to persuade the reader of [slavery's] evils" and were thus used as one of the vehicles the abolitionist movement enlisted to convince its audience of the need to end the institution of slavery (Taylor xvii).[16] These narratives share a commitment to social critique that the dystopian text, as with all utopian fiction, practices implicitly if not explicitly. In *Incidents*, for example, Jacobs states from the beginning: "But I do earnestly desire to arouse the women of the North to a realizing sense of the condition of two millions of women of the south, still in bondage, suffering what I suffered, and most of them far worse. I want to add my testimony to that of abler pens to convince the people of the Free States what Slavery really is" (6). Since social critique is not a requirement of historical/autobiographical novels as such, nor of sf in general, in this instance two completely different genres meet at the point of extra-textual function, that is, in the author's desire to educate the reader and warn of certain evils inherent in particular institutions. And what does the dystopian novel contribute to a further understanding of slavery despite its conventional placement in a future time and place?

The answer lies in the second common function of the dystopia and the classic slave narrative in documenting the conditions of slavery, thus performing the education of perception that is also characteristic of utopian fiction in general (Taylor xvii). Thematically, African American slave narratives describe the violence inflicted on slaves and the ritual debasement they are subjected to throughout their lives, acts officially justified as a form of punishment ideologically supported by Christian rhetoric in favor of the institution of slavery. But slave narratives describe these events not merely to shock but also to reveal both the double standards and hypocrisy practiced by the slave masters as well as their cruelty.[17] The violence of slavery is crucially extended to the forced separation of families, with children sold away from their mothers, and to the surreptitious rape of slave women by their masters. The constant threat to slave women of being forced to bear children by their masters and the subsequent threat of being separated from their offspring through their sale is the dominant fear expressed in *Incidents*. As Jacobs poignantly laments: "Slavery is terrible for men; but it is far more terrible for women. Superadded to the burden common to all, *they* have wrongs, and sufferings, and mortifications peculiarly their own" (119). The educational force of slave narratives by women thus extends beyond the documentation of injustices to expose the gendered nature of oppression produced by the institution of slavery.[18]

Likewise, in dystopian texts, public as well as privately enforced violence and its threat ensure the obedience of the lesser powerful. If slavery is primarily a relation of domination, then from the point of view of their protagonists, these dystopias represent forms of domination at their most extreme: from the case of *Swastika Night*, in which women have no voice of their own, to the more open situation in which the context allows for a successful escape to freedom, as in *Parable of the Sower*. And as any reader of dystopias knows, to rebel against the status quo, to refuse one's slave status, results in certain death if escape or change is not accomplished. Atwood's descriptions of public hangings at "the wall" (chapters 6 and 44), "salvagings" or gender-segregated public executions (chapter 42), and "particicutions" or group-organized murder of "criminals" (chapter 43) exist alongside the monthly enforced "mating" of the Handmaids with the Commanders. As sexual/reproductive slaves, the Handmaids immediately hand over their children to the commanders' families and are denied any rights over them. Additionally, any preexisting children are forcibly separated from their own mothers and "reassigned" to childless households of the elite, never to be seen again by their parents. Even though the Handmaids' fear centers on the possibility of not being able to reproduce, they are already broken women on a psychic level because they are powerless to prevent the parting from their children or the "duties" required of them as Handmaids. Equally, as in slave narratives, religious rhetoric and its emphasis on sacrifice is often utilized to indoctrinate as well as to justify the new state of affairs, especially for new "recruits" who have little choice in their "assignments" (230–31).

In *Handmaid*, the only "choice" the narrator retains is to become a sexual slave or die. Though Offred claims, "nothing is going on here that I haven't signed up for," her options are extremely limited: she may provide children for the Commanders' families, become (unofficially) a prostitute, a "Jezebel," or work as an "unwoman" in a toxic waste site where death is inevitable (105).

It is striking evidence of Atwood's use of slave narrative conventions that the one unacknowledged group of women whose "services" buttress the Republic of Gilead share the same biblical name as that attributed to female slaves of the American South. The "Jezebel" was a carnal image of women slaves, one that Deborah Gray White argues was useful as a counter-image of the asexual and religious mother figure, the mammy (46).[19] The roles that women were assigned in slavery thus adhere to strict sexual functions that benefited the masters without regard for the women's own desires. Within these limited parameters, each woman may or may not practice a kind of precarious "freedom" within which to negotiate for her desires, but without the threat of violence ever receding from view.

In their common purpose to "warn," these texts perform at the level of narrative the function of what J. C. Austin calls, in *How to Do Things with Words*, an illocutionary speech act, an utterance that achieves a "certain force" by virtue of its saying something (121). At the same time, Austin asserts that "unless a certain effect is achieved, the illocutionary act will not have been happily, successfully performed" (116). For this to occur in the reading of dystopias, the reader will have to have understood the warning issued and, as a result, benefitted from the intended "education" of perception. Such an understanding leaves no room for ambiguity in the message conveyed and, in the case of slavery, the target of its critique. As in dystopias that extrapolate from real events, the narrative must be clear, for the reader, about the institutions it critiques and the context it refers to. This analogy then is fruitful for a comparison of two genres as distinct as nineteenth-century autobiography and twentieth-century sf because it brings out the texts' common concerns to warn of sexual and reproductive slavery without eliding the different contexts from which they emerged. In their intention to warn, dystopias and slave narratives alike express a utopian impulse that combines critique of the present with hope for a better future.

Although the value attached to each of these instances of forced reproduction are radically different (in Jacobs's text the woman is disgraced and ashamed, and in Atwood's text she is "officially" honored and celebrated), taken from the point of view of the women their experiences are more similar than different. In both, women's powerlessness and fear are a constant reminder of their lack of sexual and reproductive freedom. It is this theme that links the function of "educating" to that of "warning" in both slave narratives and dystopias. Despite the differences in time, women's vulnerability toward sexual slavery expresses itself in both genres as a danger inherent in the condition of womanhood in patriarchal institutions that must be fought and guarded against for themselves as well as for their daughters.

The forced separation of women from their children as well as other family members corresponds to what Patterson has termed "natal alienation"—"the loss of ties of birth in both ascending and descending generations" (*Slavery* 7). This does not mean, however, that there were no social ties, but rather that they were neither legally nor morally binding. As Jacobs expresses: "Always I was in dread that by some accident, or some contrivance, slavery would succeed in snatching my children from me" and "my mistress, like many others, seemed to think that slaves had no right to any family ties of their own" (227, 59). This regime placed slave women in the unique position of involuntary complicity since they were unlikely to attempt to escape without their children and any attempt to do so with them was more likely to fail. More often than not, as shown in these texts, women complied with their fate and tried to "make the best of it," without, however, this "ethic of compromise" completely eradicating the desire for freedom.[20] As a result of this constant threat of separation, women chose, unsurprisingly, to avoid attempts at escape in return for the possibility of retaining familial relationships, however precarious they were.

It is not so much the degree or quality of this "freedom" which is significant but the decision to reproduce at all that brings female-authored dystopias and slave narratives into a common framework. What links the discourse of freedom in both genres—and differentiates them from male-authored texts—is centered on the preoccupation with their reproductive rights, the freedom to choose motherhood, and their right to refuse it. According to Sarah Lefanu, "[w]omen's dystopias foreground the . . . denial of women's sexual autonomy. They show women trapped by their sex, by their femaleness, and reduced from subjecthood to function" (71). In fact, as Nan Bowman Albinksi writes, the central concerns in women's utopian writing from the 1920s to the 1990s are sexual freedom and, particularly for dystopias, reproductive freedom—the freedom to bear children or to avoid a compulsion to do so (79). In all the above novels, the narrators' fears of separation and the violence of punishment are ample deterrents from attempts at escape, and their acquiescence is manifest in their "choice" of slavery. But unlike them, not all characters share in their desire for freedom. How is it, then, that in dystopias, as well as in slavery, forced reproduction does not always take place against a woman's will but often willingly on her part?

To achieve such compliance, the forces of power enlist a range of practices that attempt to sublimate desire and eradicate hope via the violent practice of what Louis Althusser calls "Repressive State Apparatuses"—the army, the police, the courts, and the prisons. But fear of violence is not always sufficient, as desire for freedom is impossible to eradicate. To this purpose, then, are put further "Ideological State Apparatuses"—religious, educational, legal, political, and cultural institutions (145). If women are made to believe that everything in their society is as it should be and unchangeable, then there will be no desire for change or revolt. In dystopias as much as in slave narratives, this "belief" that change is futile leads many to accept the given reality and their place within it—though unsurprisingly, in both it is the narrator who resists such complacency and refuses the displacement of desire and the loss of hope.

By achieving the suppression of desire, dystopian worlds effect what is most characteristic of the genre's characters and/or narrator: that of both inter-subjective and intra-subjective alienation. Whereas eutopias utilize the technique of defamiliarization for a change of consciousness in the reader—a way of seeing the world as if for the first time and recognizing its forms—dystopias effect a double defamiliarization: between reader and narrator and within the narrator's psychic world. The first kind is positive and performs a transforming effect on the reader. The second is more appropriately called alienation. It is always accompanied by the narrator's cognition that the "official" language of the world he/she inhabits does not express experience; rather, it becomes an instrument of psychological manipulation and further alienation. For women, this alienation takes place most evidently in relation to their bodies, their sexuality, and their reproductive freedom.

Luce Irigaray's theory of women's alienating labor is useful for revealing how women's bodies become a commodity with an exchange value in both slavery and the dystopian context. Following from Marx, Irigaray argues that women's alienation from the "product" of their labor (their children), from themselves, and from other women is inextricably tied up with the sacrifice of their sexual and reproductive freedom and as such serves to maintain the patriarchal social order (172, 185). In Gilead as on slave plantations, women's bodies become the site of production of exploited relations as well as their reproduction (of the means of exploitation). A woman's body in effect becomes a commodity with an exchange value as the woman is not the owner of this commodity but instead the laborer who must provide the goods to those who will benefit directly from her services. Accordingly, in Gilead the newborn are immediately handed over to the commander's wives and, after a period of breastfeeding, separated forever from their real mothers. Yet women still "desire" to provide their masters with children: "What we prayed for was emptiness, so we would be worthy to be filled: with grace, with love, with self-denial, semen and babies" (240). If the state's ideological apparatuses "promote class oppression and guarantee the conditions of exploitation and its reproduction," then the enforced motherhood of Gilead constitutes the Handmaids as the most exploited class and thus the most alienated (Althusser 184).

Equally, on the plantations of the slave narratives, children may be sold away from their mothers at any age and as far away as necessary. Yet because of this over-emphasis on reproduction, female desire takes second place to maternity, since it is the latter that will determine a woman's "value" and the "quality" of her life: "Whatever slavery might do to me, it could not shackle my children. If I fell a sacrifice, my little ones were saved" (Jacobs 166). Because of this double exploitation (as slave and woman) in Jacob's story, the narrator chooses to become the mistress of another white man rather than her master, for the purpose of avoiding his absolute power over the children. Indeed, until she escapes to freedom, she can never be certain of her children belonging to her alone, and this justifies her continual efforts to outsmart her master: "For, according to Southern laws, a slave, *being* property, can *hold* no property. . . . Still, in looking back, calmly, on the events of my life, I feel that a slave woman ought not to be judged by the same standard as others" (13, 86, emphasis original). Jacobs makes the point repeatedly that it is not her plight alone that her children and her own body do not belong to her, but a reality for all slave women. Indeed, it constitutes a woman *as* slave.

Just as Jacobs in her narrative is preoccupied with her lack of freedom and continually struggles to obtain it, so the protagonist of *Handmaid* comes to understand freedom in a new light, one that she had never considered in her "free" life, before her enslavement in the Republic of Gilead.

This conceptual dependency of freedom on the experience of slavery is one that Patterson argues is a result of a historical process based on the particular socioeconomic and ideological forces that have shaped the history of the western world. As a result of the slave's need for a life of dignity and disalienation, "[t]he idea of freedom is born, not in the consciousness of the master, but in the reality of the slave's condition. Freedom can mean nothing positive to the master, only control is meaningful. . . . Before slavery, people could not have conceived of the thing we call freedom" (*Freedom* 98, 340). Though freedom here is defined negatively (i.e., by the lack of constraints on action), it is also defined, significantly from the point of view of the slave. It is the experience of slavery and, in these texts, sexual slavery that provides the discourse on freedom with its particular force and links two disparate genres in their common conceptual concerns.

In the narrator's dream of escape the first step is taken on the road of freedom from slavery. The only possible escape, however, apart from death, is to step outside the boundaries of the particular dystopian world in order to experience a life in a different geographical space. Accordingly, Jacobs finally escapes to the North and is reunited with her children; whereas the closest free state outside Gilead is Canada. As Heidi S. Macpherson points out: "Escape, with all its various meanings, is an important part of the dystopic tradition and any slave world is necessarily dystopic" (182). For Atwood's protagonist, what makes her condition dystopian is her status as sexual/reproductive slave; and for Jacobs, slavery is dystopian because without freedom she cannot be the "master" of her own body, her life, and her children's lives. For both women, slavery and the lack of freedom it entails is not a condition which is time bound but rather space bound: whether in the past or the future, to be denied the power over one's own reproductive choices alienates a woman from her children, her body, and her sense of womanhood. In short, what female-authored slave narratives and dystopias highlight is a theme often neglected or understated in their male-authored counterparts: that of the gendered nature of oppression and its repercussions on women's subjectivity, agency, and relationship to their children.

V. Dystopia and Neo-Slave Narratives

In *The Oxford Companion to African American Literature* under the entry for "Neo-Slave Narrative," Ashraf H. A. Rushdy maintains that despite variations within the genre, what unifies these works is that "they represent slavery as a historical phenomenon that has lasting cultural meaning and enduring social consequences" (533). Slavery in these texts is not seen solely as a historical event but as a living present, influencing the consciousness of every individual within the community, often in a destructive manner. In the category *Kindred* belongs to, "the palimpsest narrative," slavery is depicted as having an ongoing effect in the present for current relations between the descendants of masters and their slaves (Rushdy 535).

In this narrative, set in the California of the 1970s, Dana realizes that "the comfort and security" she has experienced all her life is dependent on her ignorance of the effect of slavery on the present (9). The judgments this ignorance leads to are challenged when she is forced to relive, literally, the experience of slavery firsthand in order to understand its ongoing legacy. Dana discovers she is being transported from 1976 Los Angeles to an early-nineteenth-century Maryland plantation every time her white ancestor Rufus (her great-grandmother's father as well as son of the plantation owner) finds himself in life-threatening danger. In her efforts to save him, and herself, she discovers firsthand the constraints that determined the choices slave women were forced to make in order to survive, and, as a result, she reaches an understanding of her own responsibility in the legacy of this past and a new understanding of her identity in the present. As a neo-slave narrative then, and a critical dystopia, *Kindred* is making a case for an interdependent relationship between history and present and its effect on women's sense of selfhood. As with the original slave narratives, the personal and political are linked in Dana's loss of sexual and reproductive freedom and her realization that she is in greater danger of a physical/sexual assault as a slave than as a free woman in contemporary Los Angeles.

But where do neo-slave narrative conventions stand in relation to the utopian literary tradition? Like the narrator in *Handmaid*, Dana comes to a realization of slavery as a system of domination where one group exists in almost total powerlessness sustained under the constant threat of violence (92, 142, 183). The ensuing result of psychic alienation is due to constant compromise which inevitably distorts all relations (97, 145, 178). As a system characterized by inequality, violence, and the domination of one community by another, slavery cultivates self-alienation, and a "slow process of dulling" (183). As such, *Kindred* names slavery as another example of concrete dystopia that constrains women's control over their bodies, either in their sexual expression or reproductive choices. As in Atwood's text, slave women's choices are limited to forced reproduction with their master—as Alice, one of Dana's ancestors, must accept—or failing that, separation from the mates of their choice. It is within the common themes of bondage and the desire for freedom from oppression that these two genres share the most narrative similarities.

Dana becomes an unwilling accomplice in Alice's oppression and forced mating with Rufus when she realizes that this is the only way to ensure her own eventual birth. Despite her efforts to console Alice and to educate Rufus when he misleads Alice, as a method of intimidation, into believing that he has sold her children away, Alice hangs herself (178). Since Alice had already been separated from the man of her choice, her only meaningful point of reference was her children; and her "choice" of death constitutes a tragic non-choice. As a result of this suicide, rather than making absolute judgments on the past and her ancestors' choices—as in the case of the household's "mammy"—Dana realizes that individual agency must be judged in the context within which it must function (145). She thus becomes more understanding of the choices slave women have had to make with regard to their children and the consequences they have had to suffer as a result. The influence of the original slave narratives is clear here, because of the emphasis on survival, as the message conveyed is one often repeated in both: that a corrupt system can only foster corrupt relations. As a neo-slave narrative, then, *Kindred* brings together the concerns of the dystopia and the classic slave narrative with its emphasis on sexual violence and enforced reproduction.

Most important, *Kindred* exemplifies the flexibility of slavery as a system of domination to manifest itself in many forms, irrespective of time or place. When Dana is forced to destroy a history book, her thoughts lead her to compare this act to Nazi book burning not only because of the physical violence but also because "[r]epressive societies always seemed to understand the danger of 'wrong ideas'" (141). She also realizes the importance of the effect of psychic as well as physical violence on agency when she draws parallels between the oppression of slavery and that of twentieth-century racism in South Africa: "South African whites had always struck me as people who would have been happier living in the nineteenth century, or the eighteenth. In fact, they were living in the past as far as their race relations went. They lived in ease and comfort supported by huge numbers of blacks whom they kept in poverty and held in contempt" (196). As a form of racial oppression, then, slavery lives on in the present, perpetuated by a minority "white supremacist government" (196). Having experienced the effect of institutionalized slavery, Dana discovers that she is safer not because of her temporal distance from oppression but because of a *spatial* distance while others, at the same moment in time, are less fortunate. It is this persistence of slavery, albeit in a different form, to which Butler, through the convention of time travel, draws attention in her fiction, in order to warn the reader against any complacency in the present.

By comparing aspects of slavery with Nazi Germany and the South African regime, Dana realizes the omnipresence of oppression and the nature of her own freedom. As a consequence of her time travel she comes to an understanding of the means, the consequences, and the physical and psychic effects of a system of domination and violent hierarchy as unlimited by time or space but merely different in terms of degree of severity. They are part of the history and the present time of humanity and as such, run the real danger of recurring in the future.

Within these parameters, it is possible to conceive of the real world as existing in a "dystopian continuum" in which not only do extreme forms of oppression and alienation co-exist with lesser forms, but also one's place on the continuum is subject to unpredictable change. It is thus possible to include phenomena from the past as concrete dystopias, since the connections *Kindred* makes betray how easily one can move from one point in the continuum to another across the time-space axis. A dystopian continuum brings together the history of the world on a space-time axis where both diachronically and synchronically extreme forms of alienation take over to form concrete dystopias. Not only slavery but also genocide, dictatorship, and any configuration that uses institutionalized fear evoked by physical and/or psychological violence to establish a "new reality" characterized by hierarchy and stasis, censorship, and terror for those who resist can be defined as concrete dystopias.[21]

My purpose here has not been to provide a detailed comparison of all the thematic and structural similarities among Atwood's, Jacob's, and Butler's novels but to draw attention to those features that reveal how all three express a dystopian worldview and trace its effects on women's consciousness and agency. In neo-slave narratives, the formal innovations shed new light on the thematic concerns of the classic slave narratives while adding an extra dimension to traditional dystopian novels that emphasize resistance and hope for a better future. The first-person narrative voice that emphasizes personal experience illuminates the plight inherent to enslaved motherhood at which history books on slavery could at best only hint at (Beaulieu 129). At the end of *Kindred*, Dana, despite having lost an arm and her old sense of security, is reborn through her understanding of the past with a sense of hope and "political renewal" (Donawerth 62); if some of her ancestors survived the horrors of slavery, then she too can struggle for a better world. For Baccolini, this privileging of personal narrative over official history constitutes a revolutionary strategy that reveals how "our present—and our future—depend on our past" ("Gender and Genre" 30).

VI. Conclusion

These novelists are not alone in their expositions of slavery as a continuing form of sexual oppression and exploitation. For Kevin Bales, author of *Disposable People: New Slavery in the New Economy*, the economic conditions created by global capital support the "new slavery" while at the same time masking it from view. From the trafficking of children for sexual purposes to the kidnapping of young girls for prostitution, the "new slavery" may not be a legally condoned institution, but it continues to exist in many forms in both developed and developing countries. For Bales, the new slavery, like the old slavery, is based on exploitation, violence, and injustice (262); but unlike the old slavery it focuses on "big profits and cheap lives" (4), and its selection criteria are based on the "weakness, gullibility and deprivation" (11) of its victims. Recent television documentaries (Woods and Blewett) and groups such as Anti-Slavery International are examples of a growing effort to inform the public and bring an end to modern slavery.

As with other examples of concrete dystopia, slavery's effect on its victims is to constitute them as powerless as possible in a system that functions by physical and psychological intimidation. For women it means an ever present danger to their reproductive choices and physical integrity. But although the potential for the emergence of a concrete dystopia appears to be a latent reality, the narrators' endeavors at resistance reveal what Moylan calls "traces, scraps, and sometimes horizons of utopian possibility" (*Scraps* 276). Despite, then, or because of, Italo Calvino's conclusion at the end of *Invisible Cities* that all is "inferno," the capability and responsibility lie within everyone not only to counteract oppression, violence, and alienation but also to do so by making connections, forming ties, and fostering hope in their promise (165). In this context, it is necessary to reassert the relevance of Bloch's concrete utopia as those moments that rupture the dystopian continuum to reveal glimpses of what the world may still become.

Notes

1. Sargent argues that "the traditional notion that utopianism is the peculiar invention of Christian culture is simply wrong" ("Utopian Traditions" 8). He then differentiates between utopias brought about by human effort and those brought about without human effort, and says, "Every culture that has ever been studied has had utopias brought about without human effort" ("Utopian Traditions" 8).
2. For the historical development and literary influences of the African-American novel, see Rushdy.
3. One notable example is Rhodes. See also Baccolini, "Gender and Genre" (13–24). I will return to Baccolini's work when I discuss *Kindred*. For a comprehensive listing of slave narratives, see Andrews.
4. An exception is the case of the "flawed utopia," where the "good" society appears to suffer from a fatal flaw that compromises its status as eutopia; see Sargent, in this volume.
5. Another strategy is the juxtaposition between memory of the past and desire for a better future; see Baccolini, "Journeying" (343–57).
6. Suvin prefers to translate *ostranenie* into "estrangement" rather than "defamiliarization" (6, n.2). For Suvin, it is "cognition" that performs this critical stance toward reality (10).
7. I am indebted to Nick Varsamopoulos for this point. In *The Republic*, Plato's main worry is over the possible pernicious effects of representation. In any case, fiction for Plato distorts reality and conveys "untruths" (363–64).

8. Compare the argument in *Basic Works of Aristotle*, esp. 1483–85, where Aristotle allows for a broader definition of representation to include things "as they have been, or ought to be" (1483).

9. See also Cavalcanti on the relevance of Bloch's utopianism in the context of the feminist utopia/dystopia.

10. Levitas makes this point in the context of arguing against the, ultimately untenable, distinction between abstract and concrete utopia (65–79).

11. On the relationship between dystopian fiction and modern history, see Booker. For a useful review, see Fitting.

12. For a comparative analysis of gender relations in these two novels, see Patai.

13. For a positive reaction to Atwood's use of slave narrative conventions see Macpherson (179–91). For a negative response, see Lauret (176–83). Lauret's accusation of Atwood's "disingenuousness" is misguided in my opinion as there cannot be a patent on generic conventions. For genre "blurring" as oppositional, see Baccolini, "Gender and Genre." Among borrowed elements from slave narratives, the practice of renaming and other rituals of indoctrination, especially for new "slaves," are standard in dystopia. In *Handmaid*, for example, Offred is so named after the master of the household. On rituals of indoctrination, see Patterson, *Slavery*, ch. 2.

14. In *Slavery*, Patterson argues for a third crucial difference between slaves and non-slaves who are nonetheless salable against their will: alienation from all ties of natality (26). For his argument against slavery as property, see ch. 1. For other definitions of slavery, see Garnsey, who focuses on the notion of property (1); D. B. Davis, who compares various societies' definitions (47–49); Finley, for his distinctions (67–68); and Bales, for definitions by international conventions (275–78).

15. For discussions on other aspects of the generic conventions as well as innovations of the slave narrative, see Cobb, Hedin, Jugurtha, and Niemtzow.

16. Taylor lists five distinct functions of the slave narrative: to "impart religious inspiration; to affirm the narrator's personhood; to redefine what it means to be black; to earn money; and . . . to delight or fascinate the reader" (xvii).

17. For a comprehensive list of slave narrative conventions, see Olney (152–53).

18. This is not to say that male-authored texts ignore the condition of women, merely that the focus of their text is more "male neutral" and less preoccupied with choices concerning sexuality and reproduction. See Douglass. For "solutions" to the "problem" of motherhood in utopias, see Lees.

19. White further argues for the ideological importance of the Jezebel/Mammy figures: "The black woman's position at the nexus of America's sex and race mythology has made it most difficult for her to escape the mythology" (27–29).

20. For the particular constraints on women slaves in North America and an attempt to separate myth from reality, see White. For more on the "ethic of compromise," see Baccolini, "Gender and Genre."

21. For contemporary comparative discussions of slavery and the Holocaust, see Lawrence. For an older (and controversial) view, see Elkins; and for a critique, see Du Press (150–77). On the Holocaust, see Bettelheim; concerning literary representations of the Holocaust, see Vice.

Works Cited

"Abolish: The Anti-Slavery Portal." Available at: http://www.iabolish.com/act/camp/stop/index.htm

Albinksi, Nan Bowman. *Women's Utopias in British and American Fiction.* New York: Routledge, 1988.

Althusser, Louis. "Ideology and Ideological State Apparatuses." *Lenin and Philosophy and Other Essays.* Trans. Ben Brewster. New York: Monthly Review, 1971. 127–88.

Andrews, William L., ed. *Documenting the American South* (DAS). The University of North Carolina at Chapel Hill, Academic Affairs Library. 1 Apr. 2002. Available at: http://docsouth.unc.edu/neh/neh/html

Aristotle. *Basic Works of Aristotle.* Trans. Ingram Bywater. New York: Random, 1941.

Atwood, Margaret. *The Handmaid's Tale.* London: Virago, 1985.

Austin, J. C. *How to Do Things with Words.* Ed. J. O. Urmson and Marina Sbisà. Oxford: Oxford UP, 1962.

Baccolini, Raffaella. "Gender and Genre in the Feminist Critical Dystopias of Katharine Burdekin, Margaret Atwood, and Octavia Butler." Barr 13–34.

———. "Journeying through the Dystopian Genre: Memory and Imagination in Burdekin, Orwell, Atwood, and Piercy." *Viaggi in utopia*. Ed. Raffaella Baccolini, Vita Fortunati, and Nadia Minerva. Ravenna: Longo, 1996. 343–57.

Bales, Kevin. *Disposable People: New Slavery in the New Economy*. Berkeley: U of California P, 1999.

Barr, Marleen S., ed. *Future Females, The Next Generation: New Voices and Velocities in Feminist Science Fiction*. Lanham: Rowman, 2000.

Beaulieu, Elizabeth Ann. *Black Women Writers and the American Neo-Slave Narrative: Femininity Unfettered*. Westport: Greenwood, 1999.

Bettelheim, Bruno. *Surviving and Other Essays*. New York: Vintage, 1980.

Bloch, Ernst. *On Karl Marx*. Trans. John Maxwell. New York: Syracuse UP, 1990.

———. *The Principle of Hope*. Trans. Neville Plaice, Stephen Plaice, and Paul Knight. Oxford: Blackwell, 1986.

Booker, M. Keith. *The Dystopian Impulse in Modern Literature: Fiction as Social Criticism*. Westport: Greenwood, 1994.

Bowie, Andrew. *From Romanticism to Critical Theory: The Philosophy of German Literary Theory*. London: Routledge, 1997.

Burdekin, Katharine. *Swastika Night*. 1937. Old Westbury: Feminist, 1985.

Butler, Octavia E. *Kindred*. London: Women's, 1979.

———. *Parable of the Sower*. London: Women's, 1995.

Calvino, Italo. *Invisible Cities*. Trans. William Weaver. London: Vintage, 1997.

Carter, Angela. *The Passion of New Eve*. London: Virago, 1977.

Cavalcanti, Ildney. "Articulating the Elsewhere: Utopia in Contemporary Feminist Dystopias." Diss. U of Strathclyde, 1999.

Cobb, Martha. "The Slave Narrative and the Black Literary Tradition." Sekora and Turner 36–44.

Davis, Charles, and Henry Louis Gates, Jr., eds. *The Slave's Narrative*. New York: Oxford UP, 1985.

Davis, David Brion. *The Problem of Slavery in Western Culture*. New York: Oxford UP, 1966.

Donawerth, Jane. "The Feminist Dystopia of the 1990s: Record of Failure, Midwife of Hope." Barr 49–66.

Douglass, Frederick. *Narrative of the Life of Frederick Douglass, An American Slave*. 1845. New York: Penguin, 1986.

Du Press, Terence. *The Survivor: An Anatomy of Life and Death in the Death Camps*. Oxford: Oxford UP, 1976.

Elkins, Stanley M. *Slavery: A Problem in American Institutional and Intellectual Life*. New York: Grosset, 1959.

Finley, M. I. *Ancient Slavery and Modern Ideology*. London: Chatto, 1980.

Fitting, Peter. "Impulse or Genre or Neither?" *Science-Fiction Studies* 22.2 (1995): 272–81.

Garnsey, Peter. *Ideas of Slavery from Aristotle to Augustine*. Cambridge: Cambridge UP, 1996.

Gates, Henry Louis, Jr., and Charles Davis. "Introduction: The Language of Slavery." Davis and Gates vi–xxxiv.

Hedin, Raymond. "Strategies of Form in the American Slave Narrative." Sekora and Turner 25–35.

Howells, Coral Ann. *Margaret Atwood*. London: Macmillan, 1996.

Irigaray, Luce. *This Sex Which is Not One*. Trans. Catherine Porter with Caroline Burke. New York: Cornell UP, 1985.

Jacobs, Harriet [Linda Brent]. *Incidents in the Life of a Slave Girl*. 1861. New York: Oxford UP, 1988.

Jameson, Fredric. "Progress Versus Utopia; or Can We Imagine the Future?" *Art After Modernism: Rethinking Representation*. Ed. Brian Wallis. New York: New Museum of Contemporary Art, 1984. 239–52.

Jugurtha, Lillie Butler. "Point of View in the African-American Slave Narratives: A Study of Narratives by Douglass and Pennington." Sekora and Turner 110–19.

Lauret, Maria. *Liberating Literature: Feminist Fiction in America*. London: Routledge, 1994.

Lawrence, Thomas Mordekhai. *Vessels of Evil: American Slavery and the Holocaust*. Philadelphia: Temple UP, 1993.

Lees, Susan H. "Motherhood in Feminist Utopias." *Women in Search of Utopia: Mavericks and Mythmakers*. Ed. Ruby Rohrlich and Elaine Hoffman Baruch. New York: Schocken, 1984. 219–32.

Lefanu, Sarah. *In the Chinks of the World Machine: Feminism and Science Fiction*. London: Women's, 1988.

Levitas, Ruth. "Educated Hope: Ernst Bloch on Abstract and Concrete Utopia." *Not Yet: Reconsidering Ernst Bloch*. Ed. Jamie Owen Daniel and Tom Moylan. London: Verso, 1997.

Macpherson, Heidi Slettedahl. *Women's Movement: Escape as Transgression in North American Feminist Fiction*. Amsterdam: Rodopi, 2000.

McManus, Susan. "Bloch's Utopian Imagination." Utopian Studies Society Conference. University of Nottingham, June 2000.

Miller, Jim. "Post-Apocalyptic Hoping: Octavia Butler's Dystopian/Utopian Vision." *Science-Fiction Studies* 25.2 (1998): 336–60.

Moylan, Tom. *Demand the Impossible: Science Fiction and the Utopian Imagination*. New York: Methuen, 1986.

———. *Scraps of the Untainted Sky: Science Fiction, Utopia, Dystopia*. Boulder: Westview, 2000.

Niemtzow, Annette. "The Problematic Self in Autobiography: The Example of the Slave Narrative." Sekora and Turner 96–109.

Olney, James. "'I Was Born': Slave Narratives, Their Status as Autobiography and as Literature." Davis and Gates 148–75.

Orwell, George. *The Collected Essays, Journalism and Letters of George Orwell*. Ed. Sonia Orwell and Ian Angus. London: Secker, 1968.

———. *Nineteen Eighty-Four*. 1949. London: Seker, 1984.

Patai, Daphne. "Orwell's Despair, Burdekin's Hope: Gender and Power in Dystopia." *Women's Studies International Forum* 7.2 (1984): 85–95.

Patterson, Orlando. *Freedom: Freedom in the Making of Western Culture*. Vol. 1. London: Tauris, 1991.

———. *Slavery and Social Death: A Comparative Study*. Cambridge: Cambridge UP, 1982.

Plato. *The Republic*. Trans. Desmond Lee. London: Penguin, 1987.

Rhodes, Jewell Parker. "Toni Morrison's *Beloved*: Ironies of a 'Sweet Home Utopia' in a Dystopian Slave Society." *Utopian Studies* 1.1 (1990): 72–92.

Rushdy, Ashraf H. A. "Neo-Slave Narratives." *The Oxford Companion to African American Literature*. Ed. William L. Andrews, Frances Smith Foster, and Trudier Harris. New York: Oxford UP, 1997. 533–35.

Sargent, Lyman Tower. "The Three Faces of Utopianism Revisited." *Utopian Studies* 5.1 (1994): 1–37.

———. "Utopian Traditions: Themes and Variations." *Utopia: The Search for the Ideal Society in the Western World*. Ed. Roland Schaer, Gregory Claeys, and Lyman Tower Sargent. New York: New York Public Library/Oxford UP, 2000. 8–17.

Sekora, John, and Darwin T. Turner, eds. *The Art of the Slave Narrative: Original Essays in Criticism and Theory*. Macomb: Western Illinois UP, 1982.

Shelley, Percy Bysshe. "A Defence of Poetry." *Shelley's Poetry and Prose: Authoritative Texts Criticism*. Ed. Donald H. Reiman and Sharon B. Powers. New York: Norton, 1977. 480–508.

Shklovsky, Victor. "Art as Technique." *Modern Literary Theory: A Reader*. Ed. Phillip Rice and Patricia Waugh. London: Arnold, 1996. 17–21.

Suvin, Darko. *Metamorphoses of Science Fiction: On the Poetics and History of a Literary Genre*. New Haven: Yale UP, 1979.

Taylor, Yuval. *I Was Born a Slave: An Anthology of Classic Slave Narratives Vol. 1, 1772–1849*. Edinburgh: Payback, 1999.

Vice, Sue. *Holocaust Fiction: From William Styron to Binjamin Wilkomirski*. New York: Routledge, 2000.

White, Deborah Gray. *Ain't I a Woman? Female Slaves in the Plantation South*. New York: Norton, 1985.

Wiesel, Elie. 1958. *Night*. Trans. Stella Rodway. London: Penguin, 1960.

Wollstonecraft, Mary. *Mary; and, The Wrongs of Woman*. Ed. Gary Kelly. Oxford: UP, 1980.

Woods, Brian, and Kate Blewett. *Slavery: A Global Investigation*. Channel 4. 28 Sept. 2000.

CHAPTER **12**

The Problem of the "Flawed Utopia": A Note on the Costs of Eutopia

LYMAN TOWER SARGENT

I. Introduction

The emergence of the category of a "critical dystopia" following on the development of the category of the "critical utopia" made me aware of a label I have used with increasing frequency in my bibliography *British and American Utopian Literature, 1516–1985*, particularly in the unpublished post-1985 supplement.[1] That label is the *flawed utopia* and refers to works that present what appears to be a good society until the reader learns of some flaw that raises questions about the basis for its claim to be a good society. The flawed utopia tends to invade territory already occupied by the dystopia, the anti-utopia, and the critical utopia and dystopia. The flawed utopia is a subtype that can exist within any of these subgenres. Thus, I make no pretence of having discovered a new subgenre.[2]

I have always argued that utopias are not descriptions of perfect places.[3] And J. C. Davis has argued in his *Utopia and the Ideal Society* that the utopia reflects "the collective problem: the reconciliation of limited satisfactions and unlimited desires within a social context" (36). While I have disagreements with Davis, here he catches the problem nicely. This might lead one to conclude that even such classic eutopias as Thomas More's *Utopia* and Edward Bellamy's *Looking Backward* are necessarily "flawed."

But this conclusion misses the point that while neither "perfect" people nor a "perfect" society designed for imperfect people is the norm in utopian literature, the norm is certainly not a society presented as good but deeply flawed. Rather, it is a good or significantly better society that provides a generally satisfactory and fulfilling life for most of its inhabitants. The range of mechanisms for achieving that goal is immense, but the label "flawed utopia" is inappropriate for all of them.

That label fits two categories of works. The first is more numerous and shows the ultimately dystopian nature of apparent perfection. Within this subset, a common trope is to demonstrate that the reason/perfection of computers/machines is anti-human. The other category, which is the focus of this essay, poses the fundamental dilemma of what cost we are willing to pay or require others to pay to achieve a good life. If someone must suffer to achieve that good life, is the cost worth paying?

There is a strong tradition in the literature on utopias, one that is at the root of much anti-utopianism, which insists that the cost is inevitably too high.[4] The anti-utopian argument is that there is a fatal flaw in the makeup of the human being, a failure of nerve perhaps, or too much nerve. According to this argument, utopians behave as follows: First, they develop a plan, a blueprint for the future. Second, they attempt to put the plan into operation and find it does not work because other people are unwilling to accept it, it is too rational for human nature, or it is out of touch with current realities. Third, knowing they are right, the utopians do not reject the plan, but reject reality. They attempt to adapt people to the plan rather than the plan to people. Fourth, such action inevitably leads to violence, to the movement from an attempt to encourage people to adapt the plan to forcing them to change to fit the plan. Fifth, in the end, the plan or utopia fails, and a new one is tried. Utopia is thus the ultimate tragedy of human existence, constantly holding out the hope of a good life and repeatedly failing to achieve it. Against this, I have argued that while the anti-utopian position identifies a serious problem (people who are willing to impose their utopia on others), this is not a problem with utopianism per se.[5] But the flawed utopia is not generally about these authoritarian figures; it is about the rest of us.

In this essay, I reflect on the issues raised by the "flawed utopia" and suggest that those issues are both common and important in utopianism. I also argue that understanding them gives us a more nuanced understanding of the significance of utopianism as a way of looking at contemporary social problems.

II. The Costs of Eutopia Are Too High

Ursula K. Le Guin's "The Ones Who Walk Away from Omelas" typifies the flawed utopia that asks questions of us, since the existence of the story's utopian society depends on the sacrifice of one child. Those who leave Omelas say no; those who stay apparently say yes.[6] The subtitle of "The Ones Who Walk Away from Omelas" is "(Variations on a Theme by William James)" and in the note to the story in her *The Wind's Twelve Quarters* (1975), Le Guin quotes two passages from James's "The Moral Philosopher and the Moral Life":

> Or if the hypothesis were offered us of a world in which Messrs. Fourier's and Bellamy's and Morris's utopias should all be outdone, and millions kept permanently happy on the one simple condition that a certain lost soul on the far-off edge of things should lead a life of lonely torture [Le Guin changes this word to "torment"],[7] what except a specifical and independent sort of emotion can it be which would make us immediately feel, even though an impulse arose within us to clutch at the happiness so offered, how hideous a thing it would be its enjoyment when deliberately accepted as the fruit of such a bargain? (144, qtd. in Le Guin 224)

Although this statement plays only a peripheral role in the essay, James is arguing that we must calculate the costs and benefits of our actions to produce the greater good. Thus, it is fair to conclude that James might argue that the child's suffering in Le Guin's story is justified by the creation of eutopia for everyone else. In this case, since it is impossible to meet all human needs and desires, some of them must be ignored. How better to calculate what can be ignored than by weighing the happiness of the multitude against the suffering of one?

Le Guin also indicates that she had forgotten about a similar theme in *The Brothers Karamazov*.[8] She labels the issue as concerning the problem of the "scapegoat," and clearly the problem of the scapegoat was a central issue in the twentieth century in the form, "Who is to blame?" For German National Socialists, Jews were the primary reason that Germany was not as great as it deserved to be. In the United States, blame has been placed variously on Jews, African Americans, immigrants, bankers, the United Nations, and communists, among others, by various groups at various times to explain/excuse one problem or another. Each of these examples is currently used as a scapegoat by some group in the United States.[9]

But Le Guin puts a different twist on this familiar theme and, in doing so, turns it into a much more interesting issue in which the word "scapegoat" seems misplaced. Rather than blaming someone for current problems or failures, she and James ask the crucial question, Would and should we be willing to punish someone or allow someone to suffer if to do so we would produce a good life for everyone else?

Dostoevsky has Ivan Karamazov assert that neither truth nor harmony (read eutopia) is worth the suffering of a child. He says, "I absolutely renounce all higher harmony. It is not worth one little tear of even that one tormented child," and he goes on, "if the suffering of children goes to make up the sum of suffering needed to buy truth, then I assert beforehand that the whole truth is not worth such a price" (245).

Le Guin, James, and Dostoevsky are raising questions about our behavior because in modernity people suffer so that others can live in the material eutopia of the world's developed countries. The sufferers include virtually everyone in the Third World but, of course, more specifically those who, from economic necessity, must work in sweatshop or worse conditions to produce the goods we purchase. They also include all those who must breathe polluted air and drink polluted water so that the prices we pay do not have to be raised to cover a clean environment in producing countries, or even consuming countries. And they include the children who are sold into prostitution to satisfy the sexual tourist. And in many developed countries, like the United States, racial and ethnic minorities suffer from unwillingness to provide the resources needed to improve their condition because doing so might reduce the standard of living of the rest of us.

Most people today seem to be happy to stay in Omelas. When asked if they would be willing to lower their standard of living so that people in the Third World could raise theirs, most Americans say "No." In fact, many take the position that the Third World should restrict its development so as not to further negatively affect the environment in the developed world. Thus, the choice is made that others should pay the costs of material eutopia. One could argue that by rejecting the Kyoto Agreement, the Bush administration made this official U.S. policy.

Of course, most people do not believe that children should be sold into prostitution for use by sexual tourists and support laws to punish the tourist in the hope that as a result the practice will go away. It will not, but solving the problem of Third World poverty that leads to child prostitution (which also exists in the developed world for similar reasons) is seen as too complex, too difficult, or even impossible.

But we must remember that there are eutopians who address all the problems outlined above and conclude that those who now benefit should pay the costs of eutopia rather than the suffering child. Perhaps these are the people who walk away from Omelas so as not to benefit from the suffering of the child. And perhaps there are a revolutionary few who choose to stay in Omelas to convince the others living there that all their lives will actually be better if the suffering of the child is eliminated. To me this is the force of the second passage from James that Le Guin quotes: "All the higher, more penetrating ideals are revolutionary. They present themselves far less in the guise of effects of past experience than in that of probable causes of future experience, factors to which the environment and the lessons it has so far taught us must learn to bend" (144, qtd. in Le Guin 224). It is possible to change; it is possible to behave in new and better ways. It is even possible that Ivan Karamazov is right.

Yet, there are still others who require us to think carefully about the calculation of cost. In *Walden Two*, B. F. Skinner sees a benefit where I and other readers see a cost.[10] Skinner clearly saw *Walden Two* as a eutopia, but many readers have seen it as a dystopia because the inhabitants of the community are manipulated by its leaders without their knowledge, let alone consent. Skinner contends that in order to achieve happiness we must give up the fiction that we are free.[11] Only then, and with the correct application of behavioral engineering, will it be possible to lead a good life.

Another example poses a greater problem for me personally because I find the eutopia immensely appealing. In *Island* by Aldous Huxley, children who are identified as having certain physical/psychological characteristics that might produce "Little Hitlers" and "Little Stalins" are given training designed to offset these characteristics and channel their energies and talents into socially useful rather than socially destructive directions. To me this raises the possibility of someone giving in to the temptations of power and using these techniques to manipulate people for personal rather than social benefit. Of course, the process is supposed to make this impossible.

Huxley was well aware of the potential problem and Pala, the eutopia in *Island*, is full of devices designed to allow people to cope with or eliminate the temptation. Because we are all flawed, eutopia must be designed to allow us to correct those flaws, but that process itself produces a flawed utopia.

III. Utopia and/as Tragedy

In one of the fundamental elements of Greek tragedy, each individual is born into a specific role (*moira* or allotted portion) in a well-structured society. But through hubris or pride, individuals break through the boundaries containing them. These are the heroes and heroines, larger-than life figures who are unwilling to be limited to the normal, the acceptable, who challenge the given, the "way things are." Because of who they are and what they do, they are fated to meet their nemesis and are punished for their effrontery, their challenge to the established order. Utopians and the utopias they create, on paper and in practice, are like these heroes and heroines. They challenge the normal and proclaim that people do not have to live lives of "quiet desperation." They say that life can be richly fulfilling, if only enough people insist that poverty, disease, and degradation are not the portion allotted to human beings.

Utopians say that challenging the gods or the power structures is essential. In Genesis 2:9, Eve sets the human race free from the animal-like existence that God had prepared for her and Adam by recognizing that "the knowledge of good and evil" is essential to being human. Eve is the first rebel and the first creator of a flawed utopia. God clearly overreacts and harshly punishes Adam, Eve, and the serpent for the heinous crime of disobedience, thus setting the stage for all the eutopias to come. God condemns women to pain in childbirth and subservience to their husbands and men to labor and death (Genesis 3:16–19). Clearly, many utopias are concerned with overcoming the curse of the Fall and hark back to the Garden of Eden. Others insist that eutopia can be created within the boundaries set by God's punishment or contend that some aspect of the punishment, such as subservience to men, can be overcome.

We must *commit* eutopia knowing that it is *not* perfect and that, like the ideal *polis* in Plato's *Republic*, it contains within it the seeds of its own destruction. We must commit eutopia again and again because each time we do we have the opportunity, as Oscar Wilde put it, of landing there and then setting off after another. Wilde concludes that "progress is the realization of utopias" (27), and while we believe in progress much less than in Wilde's day, not believing in the possibility of betterment, however flawed, condemns us to live in someone else's vision of a better life, perhaps one forced on us. As a result, denying eutopia ensures that we live in dystopia.

Notes

1. On critical dystopia, see Baccolini, Moylan, *Scraps*; on critical utopia, see Moylan, *Demand*.
2. For my definitions of the standard types of utopia, see Sargent, "Three Faces" 9. See also Sargent, "Eutopias and Dystopias."
3. See, for example, Sargent, "A Note on the Other Side" and "Three Faces."
4. See, for example, Popper.
5. See Sargent "Authority and Utopia" and "Three Faces."
6. On "Omelas," see the essays in the special issue of *Utopian Studies* 2.1–2 (1991).
7. In a letter to the author of 30 January 2001 Le Guin wrote that the change was unintentional and that she did not know if it came from a corrupt text, her typing error, or a typesetting error.
8. On Le Guin and Dostoevsky, see Knapp and Tschachler.
9. See Sargent, *Extremism in America*.
10. See, for example, Stillman.
11. On fictions of this sort, see Bentham.

Works Cited

Baccolini, Raffaella. "Gender and Genre in the Feminist Critical Dystopias of Katharine Burdekin, Margaret Atwood, and Octavia Butler." *Future Females, the Next Generation: New Voices and Velocities in Feminist Science Fiction Criticism*. Ed. Marleen S. Barr. Lanham: Rowman, 2000. 13–34.

Bentham, Jeremy. "The Theory of Fictions." *Bentham's Theory of Fictions*. Ed. C. K. Ogden. Paterson: Littlefield, 1959.

Davis, J. C. *Utopia and the Ideal Society: A Study of English Utopian Writing, 1516–1700.* Cambridge: Cambridge UP, 1981.
Dostoevsky, Fyodor. *The Brothers Karamazov.* Trans. Richard Pevear and Larissa Volokhonsky. New York: Vintage, 1990.
Huxley, Aldous. *Island.* New York: Harper, 1962.
James, William. "The Moral Philosopher and the Moral Life." *The Works of William James.* Vol. 6. Ed. Frederick Burkhardt, Fredson Bowers, and Ignas K. Skrupskelis. Cambridge: Harvard UP, 1979. 141–62.
Knapp, Shoshona. " 'The Morality of Creation.' Dostoevsky and William James in Le Guin's 'Omelas.' " *Journal of Narrative Technique* 15.1 (1985): 75–81.
Le Guin, Ursula K. "The Ones Who Walk Away from Omelas (Variations on a Theme by William James)." *The Wind's Twelve Quarters.* New York: Harper, 1975.
Moylan, Tom. *Demand the Impossible: Science Fiction and the Utopian Imagination.* London: Methuen, 1986.
———. *Scraps of the Untainted Sky: Science Fiction, Utopia, Dystopia.* Boulder: Westview, 2000.
Popper, Karl. *The Open Society and Its Enemies.* 4th ed. rev. Princeton: Princeton UP, 1962.
Sargent, Lyman Tower. "Authority and Utopia: Utopianism in Political Thought." *Polity* 14.4 (1982): 565–84.
———. *British and American Utopian Literature, 1516–1985: An Annotated, Chronological Bibliography.* New York: Garland, 1988.
———. "Eutopias and Dystopias in Science Fiction: 1950–75." *America as Utopia.* Ed. Kenneth M. Roemer. New York: Burt Franklin, 1981. 347–66.
———. "A Note on the Other Side of Human Nature in the Utopian Novel." *Political Theory* 3.1 (1975): 88–97.
———. "The Three Faces of Utopianism Revisited." *Utopian Studies* 5.1 (1994): 1–37.
———, ed. *Extremism in America: A Reader.* New York: New York UP, 1995.
Skinner, B. F. *Walden Two.* New York: Macmillan, 1948.
Stillman, Peter. "The Limits to Behaviorism: A Critique of B. F. Skinner's Social and Political Thought." *American Political Science Review,* 69.1 (1975): 202–13.
Tschachler, Heinz. "Forgetting Dostoevsky; or, The Political Unconscious of Ursula K. Le Guin." *Utopian Studies* 2.1–2 (1991): 63–76.
Wilde, Oscar. *The Soul of Man under Socialism.* 1891. Boston: Luce, 1910.

Critical Dystopia and Possibilities

RAFFAELLA BACCOLINI AND TOM MOYLAN

Preface

What follows is a continuation of what has become our ongoing dialogue about history and Utopia—about form, critique, and transformation. We choose to work in dialogue form in order to make space for our distinct cultural and geographical positions and voices. Also woven into our text and extending the discussion are the words and ideas of the contributors to this volume. In these comments, the events of 11 September 2001 and beyond provide an immediate point of departure, but we make no claim to encompass that complex event in what is more pointedly a discussion about the persistence of Utopia.

TM: On 11 September 2001, I saw dystopia come off the page and screen once again. When the passenger planes were flown into the World Trade Towers and the Pentagon, the "concrete dystopian" (Varsam) reality which most people already suffer daily was condensed into a single morning. For the terrible destruction in New York and Washington, D.C., was not an isolated event. While it was a pointed act of fundamentalist terror, its perpetration did not arise from some ahistorical hell. Rather, it grew out of a very real, worldwide situation for which the economic logic of capital and the arrogance of the U.S. superpower are deeply to blame.

In this world situation, as the essays in our volume each argue in their own way, the utopian impulse that would say *no* to "widening inequalities, persistent armed conflict, ecological destruction and the tightening grip of 'globalization,' or more properly, global capitalism" and *yes* to "a real transformation of the global social and economic system" (Levitas) in the interest of everyone and not a privileged few has, since the conservative backlash of the 1980s and the onset of neoliberal hegemony in the 1990s, already been silenced and attacked on one hand and co-opted on the other. And so, in the aftermath of that day in September—in the imploded space between the "phantom Twin Towers," as Rosalind Petchesky put it, of "terrorist networks and global capitalism"—the anti-utopian denial of possibility and enforcement of the new order did not suddenly begin. Rather, it continued along its established path, now opportunistically drawing on people's genuine grief and fear to lock in an ideological common sense that valorizes the centrality of the market along with an unquestioning, patriotic loyalty (3). For me, those phantom towers now stand as signposts for a locus of power that refuses any vestige of a radical utopian horizon.

Yet, as the horrendous material and ideological dust clears, we again see manifestations of critique, and perhaps movement toward transformation, "as people persist in trying to find better ways of living": "People are protesting, including protesting about the erosion of civil liberties under the guise of 'security.' . . . People are prepared to say 'not in my name.' So that perhaps . . . there is hope—the hope which Bloch, again, construed 'not . . . only as emotion . . . but *more essentially as a directing act of a cognitive kind*" (Levitas, quoting Bloch, her emphasis). As that dust clears, and new, and stronger, expressions of utopian thought and action emerge, perhaps we can better grasp the analytical and anticipatory value of the critical dystopias that offered their warnings, and possibilities, as early as the 1980s.

RB: Your comment about dystopia coming off the pages and screen once again is certainly true for me too. For a moment, I had the impression I was watching a film, but unfortunately it was no film that we were watching on 11 September. The political climate of these past years, with the shift to the Right almost everywhere, makes me feel as if I were living in a dystopia. Therefore, I think that today, when Utopia is entering one of the most antiutopian of times and communication seems to have broken down if not become impossible, lucidity is most needed. In light of this, I would like to address Darko Suvin's comment that "the discourse around utopia/nism is not far from the Tower of Babel" and that we need a tool kit "to talk intelligibly." I'm reminded, once more by the events of this last year, that communication has become a real challenge these days. But I'd like to think of critical dystopias as a common ground from which to resume communication, and to offer a quotation from George Steiner's *After Babel* as another possible image of hope:

> *After Babel* argues that it is the constructive powers of language to conceptual- ize the world which have been crucial to man's [read humanity's] survival in the face of ineluctable biological constraints, this is to say in the face of death [read Anti-Utopia]. It is the miraculous [read Utopia]—I do not retract the term—capacity of grammars to generate counter-factuals, "if"-propositions and, above all, future tenses, which have empowered our species to hope, to reach far beyond the extinction of the individual. We endure, we endure cre- atively due to our imperative ability to say "No" to reality, to build fictions of alterity, of dreamt or willed or awaited 'otherness' for our consciousness to inhabit. . . . [T]he affair at Babel was both a disaster and—this being the ety- mology of the word "disaster"—a rain of stars upon man [read humanity]. (xiii–xiv, xviii)

Perhaps we can be helped by this image: as a critical or open dystopia, with its disasters and representations of worse realities, retains the potential for change, so we can discover in our current dark times a scattering of hope and desire that will arise to aid us in the transformation of society. A need for clarity, a sort of Raymond Carver "what we talk about when we talk about utopia," and a desire for (or "a dream of) a common language" (Adrienne Rich) with which to speak inform this project, in order to attempt to under- stand what we are living and to resume a possibly transformative dialogue. Indeed, I agree that "the exploration of alternatives is a transformative pro- cess in itself" (Sargisson), and in this I find one of the strengths of the thought experiments that we deal with in our volume. In this respect, it may be true that some offer primarily personal responses to—almost personal refuges against—dystopia, and that "the personal is not political enough" (Levitas). But I think that, today, we nonetheless cannot afford to lose the personal. I would add, in defense of an ambiguous, if not an altogether happy, ending, that this is precisely one of the reasons why critical dystopias are important: to show us that the opening of hope toward Utopia (not as at- tained and finished, but rather as reachable and in process) is a way to make Utopia part "of the process which must be entered into now, rather than postponed always beyond the horizon" (Levitas).

This is not to say that I don't agree with what you and others say about the co-optation of Utopia. Too often, in these times, Utopia has been con- flated with materialist satisfaction, and thus has been commodified, deval- ued, abused, and tarnished. It is important to recognize this because "people suffer today so that others can live in the material eutopia of the world's developed countries" (Sargent). I have recently seen, in an Italian magazine, an advertisement for a series of jewels called "utopia." The ad, as often is the case, plays on contrast at the level of both image and text: a young woman in "hippie" clothes wears the sophisticated jewels. The text says that while some utopias fade, *this* "utopia" is here to stay. It all seems part of the Disneyfication strategy that is going on around us, where Disneyland is another way to sell us "utopia" as a materialist dream, that which "commodifies desire, and in particular the desire for happiness as signification or meaningfulness" (Suvin). After all, consumerism has come to represent the contemporary modality of happiness. But if it is particularly evident today, such a modality was already present some thirty years ago, as the critique of the affluent American society in a counter-epic like Samuel R. Delany's *Dhalgren* makes clear (Donawerth). In a way, the Disneyfication strategy is not that different from the dream sold to Italians by the present government: the pursuit of individual happiness, which is none other than material success, is embodied by the proliferation of posters of today's prime minister's face (altered so that he appears younger, less bald, and leaner) during the electoral campaign. "Vote for me and my dream will be true for you too"—this is the message behind the campaign. This strategy reduces Utopia to the Land of Cockaigne, by suggesting that Utopia is something that will magically happen rather than come about by hard work, if only we leave it up to him. Such manipulation of reality makes me feel like a citizen of a dystopian novel, but what I really am is a citizen of Anti-Utopia.

TM: You get right to the heart of the matter. As Suvin puts it: "Utopian reflections, in and out of fiction, have now to undertake openings that lead toward agency: action." In these times (since 1980, right now?), how can the world be made otherwise? In the face of the commodification of everything and the growing suppression of dissent, how can a critical perspective develop? How can we work together (you and I, but also all of us) not only to develop a critical language and perspective but also to join in developing transformative actions (since I agree here with Raymond Williams's distinction) that are actually oppositional and not only alternative? As someone who cut his political teeth in the civil rights, anti-war, and socialist-feminist movements of the United States in the 1960s, I agree with you about the importance of the *personal* as the point from which not only revisioning but also radical choice proceeds. However, I also take Ruth Levitas's point about the personal not being political enough. Whether the utopian moment of the 1960s movements failed, or was, temporarily, beaten, the subsequent "fragmentation of those utopian projects into local issues and identity politics" (Fitting), however necessary in their own right, resulted in a pullback into a micro-politics (what gets expressed and explored as enclaves in critical dystopias such as Octavia Butler's) that in the long run is not sufficient to take on the macro-system of global capital and its military mercenaries in the United States. What has happened—as seen in the anti-capitalist protests, but also in the globalizing labor, human rights, indigenous, and ecological movements—is precisely such a shift to a more totalizing level of analysis and a larger scale of alliance politics. While we now might well be seeing a stronger form of these tendencies than existed in the 1990s, it is to the credit of the critical dystopias that, rather than hiding out in a resigned pessimism, they tracked the possibilities of just such alliances—and did so in ways that held on to the deep and dialectical relationship between personal choice and systemic change (see Cadigan, Butler, Robinson, Piercy, Le Guin, and films such as *The Matrix* and *Pleasantville*). It may well be time for new forms of utopian thought and imagination, but while that time has been coming, the work of the dystopian turn did its job in generating a collective and forward-looking structure of feeling in a social context that worked against such a future-oriented optimism in every possible way.

And, yes, the anti-utopian "market utopia" prevents the possibility of an emancipatory memory (of which you write) and a radically new form of everyday life (see, for one example, Jacobs on Butler's consideration of a transformed humanity living out a new posthuman collectivity), by taking up "utopia" and selling it back to us as an already-achieved dream. The use of "utopia" in a recent Irish ad goes a step further than your example in that it is the name given to a new type of bank loan: now, not only can you immediately live utopia but you can have the "perfect" overdraft to afford that living!

Regarding Disneyland, I'd also think of how New York City itself has become a theme park: beginning in the years of Rudolph Giuliani's regime of gentrification and zero tolerance, but now, after 11 September, entering a new phase, as Ground Zero is bounded by scaffolding erected to accommodate tourists. Perhaps, in the immediate aftermath of the 11th, a critical dystopian openness existed in the wake of the bombing, as possibilities for new ways of knowing the world (and the place of the United States in it) hovered in the political unconscious of the newly victimized population. But very soon (especially as government and media spin took over) the potential for utopian vision growing out of an atmosphere of genuine grief and honest re-assessment hardened into an ideological amber of patriotism and vengeance, frozen in the spirit of the past, as in the evocations of Pearl Harbor, and closed to the opportunity for a new clarity regarding the place of America (and its own "dream") in the world.

On yet a darker note, this moment of capitalist intensity has so claimed and exploited Utopia, at the "end of history," that some of the biggest corporations (e.g., Enron, Worldcom) fell prey to their own non-realistic, "utopian" over-reaching. With the collapse of such mega-enterprises, we see capital exposed in its lies and thievery on a grand scale. The rush to wealth in the 1990s has consequently produced its own terrible event. Here, however, it is not a crashing plane but a crashing market that is eviscerating savings, pensions, and the tax base, and eliminating jobs—consequently impoverishing millions of people. This dystopian event, on top of the U.S. military response to 11 September that has resulted in killing hundreds of Afghan civilians in its anti-terrorist campaign, offers evidence of an anti-utopian reality produced not only through fundamentalist rage but even more by the ruling economic and political power.

RB: Since you refer to your personal experience in the 1960s, I will try to add another personal reason for my interest in dystopia. I have noted that Phil Wegner thinks that the best critical dystopias are "very much about their own erasure," "self-consuming text[s]" doomed to disappear, while Peter Fitting wonders whether "our attention to the critical dystopia is misplaced." Suvin, on the other hand, chooses the term "fallible" to refer to the open and critical dystopia of the 1980s and 1990s. I don't want to sound at all prescriptive, and for this reason I see our volume and these provisionary conclusions only as points of departure for an ongoing dialogue. However, I do think that it is important to engage with the critical dystopias of these last decades, as this is what the times have produced. After all, Bertolt Brecht was writing in 1939, "Yes, there will also be singing/ About the dark times."

But I also think that dystopia as a genre speaks to me more than other forms because of "when and where I was born." Personally, 1968 does not belong to my memory. Rather, it is 1970s Italy with its "leaden years" (*anni di piombo*) of terrorism that forms my background—the years between 1976 and 1980 when almost 100 people were killed and many more wounded in terrorist attacks by the Brigate Rosse and similar groups (Ginsborg 511–521). During that time, many more lost their lives through bombings perpetrated by extreme-right terrorists together with state apparatuses, which had their beginning with what has been called the *strage di stato* in Milan's Piazza Fontana, on 12 December 1969. So the 1960s with their utopias have less to say to me than do dystopias, which is another way of saying that I have little room for nostalgia of a better time.

I need stories that speak to me, and I am reminded of a similar statement by Marge Piercy that can help us recognize the value of the critical dystopias:

> When I was a child, I first noticed that neither history as I was taught it nor the stories I was told seemed to lead to me. I began to fix them. I have been at it ever since. To me it is an important task to situate ourselves in the time line so

that we may be active in history. We require a past that leads to us. After any revolution, history is rewritten, not just out of partisan zeal, but because the past has changed. Similarly, what we imagine we are working toward does a lot to define what we will consider double action aimed at producing the future we want and preventing the future we fear. (1–2)

Therefore, I don't think that our attention is misplaced if it means that things will change, if these works point us toward change. We need to pass through the critical dystopia to move toward a horizon of hope. That's why I think that to call these works "fallible" is to reduce their potential, impact, and criticism. It writes off the intentional critique of our society that they enact and portrays them as false at worst, ineffectual because erroneous at best. These, on the other hand, are works that through the portrayal of dystopian worlds can lead to an "education of desire that focuses anger, a view of the present as defamiliarized and historical, and a radical hope for better ways of living" (Donawerth). Next to the education of desire, these works also enact an "education of perception" through the affinities to the "concrete dystopias" they represent (Varsam).

TM: It's tricky, but important, to sort out the nostalgic from the continuing useful when looking back at a period of intense political activity like the 1960s. Certainly, society was in motion, and the whole world was watching. Societal affluence (albeit barely trickling down to many) and (in a contradictory manner not always acknowledged) the security of U.S. hegemony (expressed positively, at least as some of us initially took it, in Kennedy's "ask . . . what you can do for your country") gave to those of us who were to become activists a confidence that we could stand up to the power structure and change it. In this way, the systemic wealth and power that we opposed gave us a sense of utopian possibility that we turned against that very system. Or, to put it in the spirit of the critical utopias of the 1970s, one (conservative) utopian moment, that of postwar American hegemony, led through its contradictions to another utopian trajectory that overtly opposed it (here, Ursula K. Le Guin's *The Dispossessed* becomes the most prescient of the utopian revivals). One way of understanding the 1960s movements is therefore to see them in terms of a concrete utopian politics of *choice* that worked at both the personal and systemic levels. Certainly, at the level of the personal, choice was central to the claiming of a fuller, more authentic (to use the existentialist language of the time) life: whether that involved deciding to set aside a career in favor of activism, putting one's safety on the line in some form of nonviolent civil disobedience, (for men) refusing military service, or (for all) retaining the right to choose one's options regarding reproductive and sexual behavior. But this politics of choice also played out at the macro-level, as the movement challenged basic policy decisions regarding the distribution of wealth and the delivery of civil rights as well as the waging of war. If this was not a struggle driven by the totalizing perspective of Utopia, nothing was. Having said that, while I think a politics of utopian choice is still apt, I agree with you that the conditions we are now in—leaner, harder, meaner as they are—call for a concrete politics suited to the dystopian moment and not one that is abstractly rehashed from another time.

RB: Lest we fall into a simplistic discussion of nostalgia, I want to add that I agree that a primitivist nostalgia is a trap in which the classical dystopian narrative often falls (Wegner). At the same time, a nostalgia for another world that is possible—one that is often found in feminist novels and not one of the real past because our present originates from that very past—is not necessarily a drawback. In an interview, Le Guin laments that any alternative to capitalism these days is written off as nostalgia (Gevers on line). Similarly, I think that too often dystopia is written off as the absence of hope and therefore antithetical to Utopia. If this *may* be true for classical dystopias where hope is maintained outside the pages of the story, it is not so for critical dystopias where hope remains within the pages for protagonists and readers alike. To paraphrase Isabel Allende, writing (or the critical dystopia) "is an act of hope . . . to illuminate the dark corners. Only that, nothing more—a tiny beam of light to show some hidden aspect of reality, to help decipher and understand it and thus to initiate, if possible, a change in the conscience of some readers" (qtd. in Cavalcanti). In this, I think, lies the didactic and ethical value of utopian writing, as the reading of critical dystopias becomes "not only a public affair, but also, one hopes, a shared political stance, and a utopian statement in itself" (Cavalcanti).

TM: You bring our discussion right to the question of the politics of form, and this is a matter that all our contributors address. In particular, Jane Donawerth and Wegner look at dystopia's roots in other, more "conservative" modes such as satire and naturalism. While Donawerth sees the critical dystopia, especially, shifting the textual valence of dystopia's relationship to satire by way of a more progressive appropriation that offers not only an interrogation of a "decayed" social order but also a hopeful exploration of other horizons, Wegner is less sanguine about dystopia's capability to outgrow its "genetic" roots in nineteenth-century naturalism's anti-utopian evocation of despair. So too, David Seed reminds us of the intertextual links between critical dystopias and cyberpunk, even though, as he argues, a writer such as Cadigan moved beyond the early nihilism of that strain of sf.

However, as several contributors argue (e.g., Sargent, Fitting, Suvin, as well as Donawerth, Wegner, and Seed), dystopia cannot be conflated with the orientation or mechanisms of anti-utopian writing (whether in its overtly anti-utopian mode or its related forms of satire, naturalism, heterotopia, or cyberpunk). "Illuminating the dark corners" in a critical fashion is central to the work of the classical dystopia, even if its complementary evocation of eutopia is present only in its denial rather than its achievement. Ildney Cavalcanti explains how this illumination occurs by way of the rhetorical devices of *catachresis*—wherein "unusual, far-fetched metaphors" allow for a perceptual break with the surface realities of everyday life (see Varsam's "education of perception")—and what Fredric Jameson terms *world-reduction*, which delivers "an attenuation in which the sheer teeming multiplicity of what exists, of what we call reality, is deliberately thinned and weeded out, through an operation of radical abstraction and simplification" (qtd. in Cavalcanti). However, rather than a fantastic move out of reality, in utopian writing these devices enable what Suvin terms a "cognitive art"—that is, an art form that gives us an analytical and critical "reflection *on* reality as well as *of* reality" (qtd. in Varsam). While in the critical dystopias—which, as a later and more self-reflexive development, are as concerned about challenging and sublating the limits of dystopia as critical utopias were of the classical eutopia—the formal strategy makes possible the exploration of the "mediatory link between the dystopia and absent present utopian future" (Wegner).

One of the lessons of both the classical and critical dystopia, therefore, is that the world is capable of going from bad to worse, not only in a punctal moment but more often in a complex series of steps arising from the existing social order and the choices people make within it (as you write). Another lesson is that whatever bad times are upon us have been produced by systemic conditions and human choices that preceded the present moment—but also that such conditions can be changed only by remembering that process and then organizing against it. One of the dangers of the official and popular responses to an event like 11 September is therefore the erasure of memory of such root causes—an erasure intensified by the ideological work of the political apparatus. It lies, however, within the remit of dystopian narrative to challenge that closure and thus to reopen society, and history. As a form of what you, in another essay, call "moral" and what others call "didactic" art, utopian writing in general (and dystopia when it opts for a critical, militant, open stance) can therefore be of use (if we as readers are interested) in teaching us that choices have consequences, in helping us to see why and how things are as they are, and, perhaps, in showing how we can act to change the conditions around us: not simply to do no harm but utterly to transform reality in favor of all (see Baccolini).

Quite to the point, Le Guin, in *The Telling*, traces how fundamentalist rule and action can grow out of hegemonic conditions that are already unjust and violent. And, in what must have been a painful task, Piercy, in *He, She and It*, gives us her prophetic account of the nuclear destruction of the

Middle East, by a "zealot to be sure," but one who was driven by the deep injustice and suffering caused by state policies in the region and in the centers of world power. As well, writers such as Butler, Pat Cadigan, Suzy McKee Charnas, and Kim Stanley Robinson give us critical maps of how a social system can opt for profit and power for those who are privileged in race, class, and gender and thereby destroy the lives of the entire population, not in a single explosion but in a process of daily exploitation and violence that destroys slowly, like water eroding the rock below it.

RB: In your discussion of form, you touch upon subjects like choice, responsibility, and memory which are very important to me, and I can only agree with what you say. You are right in saying that an event like 11 September becomes a contested terrain for memory and its erasure. When an event of that magnitude occurs, one of the dangers is the tendency to co-opt it and, as you say, to erase the "memory of such root causes." What we are left with, today, is a dispute about what to do with Ground Zero. The meeting of some 5,000 ordinary people, which took place in July 2002 in New York to discuss what should be done, speaks to those forms of oppositional alliance now needed to counter economic and political exploitation (of which you, Fitting, and Jacobs, among others, write). I think it is an important moment, despite my pessimism about the outcome. I have the feeling, in fact, that nothing good will come out of this reconstruction project, and an indication of this is to be found in the fact that the city has decided to start with the construction of a series of buildings first and to postpone that of a memorial. Economic profit takes precedence over memory.

But the erasure of memory plays also at another level and can be linked, I think, to the lessons that you find in dystopia. In your essay, you say that the primary lesson of the dystopian imaginary is that it is the "totalizing machinery of the hegemonic system that brings exploitation, terror, and misery to society." I think that it is also the constant erosion and erasure of hard-fought pieces of the civil society that contribute to the totalizing climate of Anti-Utopia. It is also in the apparently insignificant (compared to dramatic events like 11 September) gestures that Anti-Utopia is maintained and strengthened. For example, in Bologna where I live, the conservative local government is slowly destroying, "like water eroding the rock below it," many of the hard-won battles by, for example, trying to eliminate the adjective "fascist" from the plaque at the Bologna Railway Station commemorating the 85 people killed by a bomb on 2 August 1980, or by restarting the station clock, which stopped at 10:25 on that day and has remained that way. Again, memory is attacked when, in the name of reconciliation, in a small town near Ferrara, a member of the former fascist party is invited to speak at the 25 April celebration (Liberation Day in 1945). Or when, after the recent killing of the socialist lawyer and professor Marco Biagi by the new Brigate Rosse, the premier, Silvio Berlusconi, used words from a speech by Benito Mussolini to say that the government would not be intimidated by people's demonstrations in the squares. On a more general level, this pattern can be seen in the politics of place-naming: conservative local governments are slowly eliminating street names attributed to Resistance leaders and introducing a "rehabilitative practice" of naming streets after fascists. Because I value memory and I live in a country that has little historical memory, I want to share with you something Giuliano Giuliani, the father of Carlo Giuliani who was killed during the G8 protest in Genoa, has written, trying to straighten out what happened on 20 July 2001. Quoting Claudio Magris, he says that "memory is neither revenge nor resentment but the keeper of truth and liberty" ("la memoria non è né vendetta né rancore, ma custode di libertà e verità" 86). For this, I think that an emancipatory notion of memory is important to our discussion of Utopia.

TM: Your mention of the practice of renaming makes me think of Brian Friel's play *Translations*, which is based on the British ordinance survey renaming of Irish-language place-names in the nineteenth century. It also makes me think of the practice of geographical erasure and occupation implicit in the Israeli settlement campaign.

I think this connection of memory, truth, and agency, so well put by Magris, is what makes dystopia so compelling for so many readers. As you say about yourself, and as I have seen over and over in my own reading responses and those of my students (having now taught dystopias to students of many subject positions and ages in Milwaukee, Washington, Liverpool, Galway, and Limerick), there is an attraction in these dark narratives that eutopian texts (which Jameson notes in *The Seeds of Time* are a "non-narrative" meditation on the nature of society without a privileged subject position) lack, at least in this historical period. That is, "in a world drained of agency" (Jacobs), dystopian narratives with their account of what happens to a specific character offer a readerly pleasure that lies in the process of following the protagonist as she or he finally comes to see the society for what it is and then acts against it. At a visceral level, the success or failure almost doesn't matter, for it is the dignity, acuity, and agency of the character that stimulates and inspires. Again, what the critical dystopia adds to this formal strategy, and thus to the readerly experience, is the additional matter of the actual, and at least temporarily successful, oppositional movement along with the critical analysis of causes that Fitting and others write of.

RB: Your comment about students' preference for dystopian narrative is something that I have also noticed. Perhaps, as we have said in other conversations, this might be a generational thing, but again I would still argue that, in general, critical dystopias speak to us more today than utopias do also because of the historical time in which we live. At the risk of sounding naïve or romantic, I want to say that I try to make the "connection of memory, truth, and agency" a primary concern of what I write and teach. And to go back to the issue of choice, I too do not want to "pass off responsibility for who we are onto external structures" (Levitas). For this, I think that your judgment of Butler's micro-politics may be too hard, because if it is important to recognize that an "entirely independent and self-determining subject was never more than a fantasy" of the West (Jacobs), it is equally important to stress the necessity for accountability, responsibility, and agency. I like what Adrienne Rich says, that "historical responsibility has, after all, to do with action," and it all starts with who we choose to be and how we "come to be where we are and not elsewhere" (145).

Haidi Giuliani's invitation to join her in Genoa a year later to remember her son and to resume the interrupted dialogue is, in a way, an instance of what Rich says. It is a powerful message that combines memory and agency without denying accountability:

> To Genoa, to resume a broken conversation, an argument that was torn by the violence of those who wanted to silence a voice of justice; to Genoa, to reaffirm an alliance, a pact among different people who recognize and respect each other and decide to be on the same side—the side of honest people. A year later, to give solidarity to those who were wounded and offended in their bodies and souls. To say that we will not accept it and that we will continue on the road that we never left. Together, despite our differences: indeed stronger and richer because of those differences that distinguish us but do not divide us. Because the stakes are too high: because it's not about a little more money in our paycheck, a crumb of illusory well-being, or our own little garden. At stake is the world's equilibrium, with the people who live in it, the animals, the plants, the waters and the lands, the air we breathe, the art, and the culture made over millions of years by billions of human beings who, with patience and hard work, with joy and with pain, have created it. We cannot afford to leave everything in the petty hands of a few arrogant bullies, nor to leave it to the bleakness of indifferent people or the obtuseness of greedy fools. We must recognize our fellow travelers even when they speak a language that is different from ours; we have to walk together without being shocked if somebody stumbles, if there are those who are slow, or if others run: what is important is that the horizon is clear. To Genoa, for all this. And to walk by Piazza Alimonda to bring our greetings to Carlo. (on line, my translation)[1]

TM: Your references to Genoa, a year ago and now, and your citations of Haidi and Giuliano Giuliani give me a way into saying that even as the punctal events of 11 September stand as a stark moment of concrete dystopia, the ongoing anti-globalization or anti-capitalist movement continues as a concrete utopian space and process, one that is no doubt flawed and fallible in all its "differences that distinguish us but do not divide us" (H. Giuliani) but is nevertheless strong and persistent in its call to disrupt "the structural closure of the present" (Levitas). In this growing movement, in Genoa as elsewhere, women and men of all ages, races, religions, and regions, and workers and citizens in all sectors of global society—groups previously isolated in the politics of their own situatedness or issues—have joined together in a "new alignment of those who are opposed to the status quo and disgusted with conventional electoral politics but are also unwilling to abandon the political arena" (Fitting), the very sort of alignment portrayed in the more militant of the critical dystopias. We do, therefore, seem to be entering a new phase of oppositional thought, imagination, and practice. As opposed to the now dated postmodern "weak thought" proposed by the likes of Gianni Vattimo or François Lyotard, new forms of utopian *strong thought* are appearing—interestingly, in political theory. Works by Subcomandante Marcos, Roberto Unger, Arundhati Roy, David Harvey, Daniel Singer, Michael Hardt and Antonio Negri, and others are once again proposing radical alternatives to global capitalism, neoliberal ideology, and U.S. power. While some (such as Hardt and Negri) write at a level of abstraction that certainly recognizes the eutopian goals of the "multitude" but then steps away from exploring what concretely needs to be done to achieve those goals, others have been effectively forged in the crucible of direct relationships with successful oppositional movements (e.g., Marcos and Unger) and still others have worked in the realm of theory but nevertheless have examined ways to move forward both within and against/beyond existing state structures (e.g., Roy, Harvey, Singer). In a more localized version of this utopian strategy, addressing our own sectoral position (and no doubt that of many of our readers), Suvin urges those of us in the "intermediate class-congerie" of people who, as C. Wright Mills put it, "produce, distribute and preserve distinct forms of consciousness" to pursue two "interlocking" goals: that of "securing a high degree of self-management" in our own workplaces, and then joining in building alliances "with other fractions and classes" in winning such "self-management" on a global, systemic scale (qtd. in Suvin). Overall, then, it is time to build on and work from the dystopian era of the 1980s and 1990s, a time to take what Jameson in *Seeds* called the "absent next step," a time to, yet again, "commit utopia" (Sargent).

Along with such theory is the practice. Here, however, it cannot just be a matter of the anti-capitalist protest movement, for that movement is but an initial, critical step in the transformation of the world society. As Leo Panitch put it, speaking at a Canadian conference called "Protest, Freedom and Order in Canada": "There can be no effective change unless and until well-organized new political forces emerge in each country that have the capacity, not just to protest vociferously, but to effect (although the anarchists may not like this way of putting it) a democratic reconstitution of state power, turn it against today's state-constituted global American empire, and initiate cooperative international strategies among states that will allow for inward-oriented development" (29–30). Here, then, an emergent eutopian strategy works by way of the braided threads of "seeking a seat at the table of power" while continuing to carry on mass protests (Genoa and beyond) and grass-roots organizing (as seen in Brazil, Mexico, Ireland, Italy, and elsewhere).

RB: On the issue of change, Utopia, and, I would add, language: even if it is true that capitalism has co-opted Utopia, we need to reclaim it, and to speak of the critical dystopia might just be one way to do so. Since language plays such an important role in dystopian novels, I agree with Cheris Kramarae that "those who have the power to name the world are in a position to influence reality," and I think that we cannot underestimate the transformative and potentially subversive power of language (165). This is another reason why the term "critical" works better than "fallible" in describing the dystopian works of this period. In this context, I am also reminded of the strategy of *reappropriation* of language and memory, one that the so called minorities or ex-centric subjects (ethnic groups, women, gays and lesbians, etc.) have successfully employed in the past. I'm not so naïve as to think that it is enough to name things differently to eradicate racism or promote Utopia in society, but I think that reclaiming meaning is an important step in the transformative process, one that allows us to question shared assumptions and to envision and enact alternatives (see, for example, what Sargisson says about this process in intentional communities).

TM: Yes, however much capitalism has co-opted change, it has not acquired (by hostile means or otherwise) *critique* (nor would it really "want" to), at least not critique in its fullest sense, in which the negative supersession of what is leads to at least the empty space of a provisionally positive, systemic transformation. Yet, it's good to bear in mind Levitas's warning in *The Concept of Utopia* that critique is but one step toward transformation and does not necessarily include that next step (and at its worst can detract from that step by settling for a resigned cynicism or accommodation). However, at its most engaged, it does continue to offer, in these times, the *possibility* of an active break with the present. So, some expressions of negation, as in the first round of cyberpunk, reject the current system but tend to look no further; while others, like the critical dystopias and the continuing critical utopias of the likes of Robinson, discover within the existing conditions hopeful possibilities and new sources of agency, reminding us at the same time that none of this is easy or guaranteed.

Your invocation of *reappropriation* for me echoes as well with Ernst Bloch's notion of a recoverable heritage, but actually it's an activity far more transformative (at least at the level of consciousness) than Bloch was suggesting. Because appropriation of traditions, tales, and genres plays a key role in the ongoing reformulation of utopian expression (just as at the end of the nineteenth century the new dystopian form grew out of borrowings from forms such as satire and naturalism), we need to stay open to new forms as they emerge. Perhaps, as you suggest in your work on the critical dystopia, the concept of *hybridity* can provide a means of reading such texts in ways that recognize their subversive, critical, utopian qualities. In addition, Cavalcanti's argument for "utopian writing" and Jameson's concept of "cognitive mapping" also contribute to our ability to recognize new utopian forms. In this context, I think of Subcomandante Marcos's writing as a good example of a new utopian hybrid—which in this case blends manifesto, poetry, and folk tale, both western and indigenous.

RB: In light of what you say, it seems to me that we agree that forms do change, but they change by way of the historical context and not simply by way of our intentions or desires. Therefore, despite what has been repeated over and over again (that the world will not be the same after 11 September; that reality has overcome imagination, etc.), I like to think that there will still be imaginative texts (be they recognizably dystopias or utopias or, as you suggest with your example of Marcos, new forms that will require new critical formulations) about which we will become passionate and with which we'll engage—in short, texts that will move us, surprise us, and make us think and hope.

Finally, to come back to what you said at the beginning about 11 September—such a huge thing and of such major proportions that it is difficult to talk about. As Petchesky says, these are hard times and yet we must begin to think through them, "even while we know our understanding at this time can only be very tentative and may well be invalidated a year or even a month or a week from now by events we can't foresee or information now hidden from us" (1). One of the things that worries me is that the event has been co-opted in such a way that it is difficult to say something "different" without being accused of being insensitive. It feels like one cannot try to understand and be critical without being accused of complicity. I am reminded here of Barbara Lee, the only woman in the U.S. Congress who voted against military intervention, and she has been attacked for it. One cannot dissent without being automatically accused of affinities with "the other side." But I am also afraid, at times, that the search for an adequate language with which to talk about this event may lead to a silencing altogether or to just *one* appropriate—read normative—use of language (which is another form of silencing). For example, as Mike Davis notes, " 'Irony' . . . is now an illegal alien in the land of liberty" (42). Similarly, in a recent interview, Art Spiegelman, while condemning how the Bush administration has appropriated and exploited 11 September, said that his new work, "In the Shadow of No Towers," has only circulated in the United States on the pages of a minor periodical, *Forward*, and that the editor of the *New York Review of Books* found it more suited for a European public (Farkas 125, 127).

I want to close (or open?) with a quote from the poet Mahmoud Darwish, which to me well captures the respect and the perspective needed at this time:

> We know that the American wound is deep and we know that this tragic moment is a time for solidarity and the sharing of pain. But we also know that the horizons of the intellect can traverse landscapes of devastation. Terrorism has no location or boundaries, it does not reside in a geography of its own; its homeland is disillusionment and despair. The best weapon to eradicate terrorism from the soul lies in the solidarity of the international world, in respecting the rights of all peoples of this globe to live in harmony and by reducing the ever increasing gap between north and south. And the most effective way to defend freedom is through fully realizing the meaning of justice. (qtd. in Petchesky 6)

Premilcuore, Liverpool, Limerick, Bologna
November 2002

Note

1. The untranslated text:
   A Genova per riprendere un discorso interrotto, un ragionamento strappato dalla violenza di chi avrebbe voluto ridurre al silenzio una voce di giustizia; per confermare un'alleanza, un patto tra diversi che si riconoscono, si rispettano e decidono di stare dalla stessa parte, quella degli onesti. Un anno dopo, per testimoniare solidarietà a chi è stato ferito, umiliato, offeso nel corpo e nell'anima. Per dichiarare che non ci stiamo, no, e continueremo la strada che non abbiamo mai interrotto. Insieme, nonostante le differenze: resi più forti e più ricchi, anzi proprio da quelle differenze, che ci distinguono ma non ci dividono. Perché la posta in gioco è troppo grande: perché in gioco non c'è qualche soldo in più nella busta paga, qualche briciola di illusorio benessere, l'orticello di casa nostra. In gioco c'è l'equilibrio del mondo, con i popoli che lo abitano, i suoi animali, le piante, le acque e le terre, l'aria che respiriamo, l'arte e la cultura di milioni di anni, di miliardi di esseri che l'hanno pazientemente, faticosamente creata, con gioia e con dolore. Non possiamo abbandonare tutto nelle mani meschine di pochi prepotenti arroganti, al grigiore degli indifferenti, all'ottusità degli avidi stolti. Dobbiamo saper riconoscere i compagni di strada anche quando parlano un linguaggio diverso dal nostro;

dobbiamo camminare fianco a fianco senza scandalizzarci se qualcuno zoppica un po', se c'è chi è più lento, se altri corrono: l'importante è che l'orizzonte sia chiaro. A Genova, per tutto questo. E per passare da piazza Alimonda, a portare un saluto a Carlo.

Works Cited

Baccolini, Raffaella. " A place without pity': Images of the Body in Cynthia Ozick's *The Shawl.*" *The Controversial Women's Body: Images and Representations in Literature and Art.* Ed. Vita Fortunati, Annamaria Lamarra, and Eleonora Federici. Bologna: Bononia UP, 2003. 165–85.

Davis, Mike. "The Flames of New York." *New Left Review* 12 (2001): 34–50.

Farkas, Alessandra. "L'11 settembre? Non chiamatelo Olocausto." *Sette* 45 (7 Nov. 2002): 124–27.

Gevers, Nick. "Driven by a Different Chauffeur: An Interview with Ursula K. Le Guin." *SF Site.* Available at: http://www.sfsite.com/03a/ul123.htm

Ginsborg, Paul. *Storia d'Italia dal dopoguerra a oggi.* Torino: Einaudi, 1989.

Giuliani, Giuliano. "Dalla lettera di Giuliano Giuliani al direttore de *L'Unità.*" *Genova. Il libro bianco.* A cura del Gruppo Comunicazione del Milano Social Forum. Milano: Nuova Iniziativa Editoriale, 2002.

Giuliani, Haidi. "Genova perché." E-mail message circulated by the Bologna Social Forum (info@contropiani2000.org), 18 July 2002.

Hardt, Michael, and Antonio Negri. *Empire.* Cambridge: Harvard UP, 2000.

Harvey, David. *Spaces of Hope.* Berkeley: U of California P, 2000.

Jameson, Fredric. "Cognitive Mapping." *Marxism and the Interpretation of Culture.* Ed. Cary Nelson and Lawrence Grossberg. Urbana: U of Illinois P, 1988. 347–60.

———. *The Seeds of Time.* New York: Columbia UP, 1994.

Kramarae, Cheris. *Women and Men Speaking: Frameworks for Analysis.* Rowley, MA: Newbury House, 1981.

Levitas, Ruth. *The Concept of Utopia.* Syracuse: Syracuse UP, 1990.

Panitch, Leo. "Violence as a Tool of Order and Change: The War on Terrorism and the Antiglobalization Movement." *Monthly Review* 54.2 (2002): 12–32.

Petchesky, Rosalind P. "Phantom Towers." *The Women's Review of Books* 19.2 (2001): 1–6.

Piercy, Marge. "Telling Stories about Stories." *Utopian Studies* 5 (1994): 1–3.

Rich, Adrienne. "Resisting Amnesia: History and Personal Life." *Blood, Bread, and Poetry. Selected Prose 1979–1985.* London: Virago, 1987. 136–55.

Roy, Arundhati. *The Cost of Living.* New York: Modern Library, 1999.

Singer, Daniel. *Whose Millennium? Theirs or Ours?* New York: Monthly Review 1999.

Steiner, George. *After Babel. Aspects of Language and Translation.* New York: Oxford UP, 1992.

Subcomandante Marcos. *Our Word Is Our Weapon: Selected Writings.* Ed. Juana Ponce de Leon. New York: Seven Stories, 2001.

Unger, Roberto. *False Necessity: Anti-necessitarian Social Theory in the Service of Radical Democracy.* London: Verso, 2002.

Notes on Contributors

Raffaella Baccolini, Associate Professor of English at the University of Bologna at Forlì, is the author of *Tradition, Identity, Desire: Revisionist Strategies in H.D.'s Late Poetry*, and articles in English and Italian on women's writing, dystopia, sf, poetry, and modernism. She has co-edited several volumes, including *Viaggi in utopia* (with V. Fortunati and N. Minerva) and *Critiche femministe e teorie letterarie* (with M.G. Fabi, V. Fortunati, and R. Monticelli), and is currently working on history and memory in fiction and film. She is associate editor of *Utopian Studies*.

Ildney Cavalcanti is Assistant Professor of English at the Universidade Federal de Alagoas. She has published interviews, reviews, and articles on literary utopianism, especially in feminist fiction, in English and Portuguese. She is currently coordinating a research group called "Literatura e Utopia."

Jane Donawerth, Professor of English and Women's Studies at the University of Maryland, is the author of *Frankenstein's Daughters: Women Writing Science Fiction*, co-editor (with C. Kolmerten) of *Utopian and Science Fiction by Women*, and the author of four other books. She is currently completing, with Julie Strongson, a translation of the rhetorical writings of Madeleine de Scudéry.

Peter Fitting is Professor of French and Director of Cinema Studies at the University of Toronto. He has had a longtime interest in sf and utopia and is the author of numerous essays on this subject. He is a past president of

251

the Society for Utopian Studies (North America). He is currently completing an edition of his collected essays.

Naomi Jacobs is Professor of English at the University of Maine. She is the author of *The Character of Truth: Historical Figures in Contemporary Fiction*, as well as articles on nineteenth-century literature, women's literature, and utopian writers including Ursula K. Le Guin, William Morris, and Austin Tappan Wright. She is a past president of the Society for Utopian Studies (North America). She is currently working on two projects: one on utopianism in the feminist poetry movement, and another on the monstrous in Fourier.

Ruth Levitas, Professor of Sociology at the University of Bristol, is the author of *The Concept of Utopia* and *The Inclusive Society? Social Exclusion and New Labour*, and editor of *The Ideology of the New Right*. She has published numerous articles on aspects of utopianism and political thought and is a past president of the Utopian Studies Society (Europe). Pulling together concepts of space, time, and Utopia, she is currently working on a book on William Morris, *News from Nowhere*, and Hammersmith.

Tom Moylan is Glucksman Professor of Contemporary Writing in the Department of Languages and Cultural Studies at the University of Limerick. He is the author of *Demand the Impossible: Science Fiction and the Utopian Imagination*; *Scraps of the Untainted Sky: Science Fiction, Utopia, Dystopia*; and essays on sf, utopia, and cultural studies. He co-edited (with Jamie Owen Daniel) *Not Yet: Reconsidering Ernst Bloch* and (with P. Fitting) a special issue of *Utopian Studies* called "Fredric Jameson and Utopia." He is currently working on a study of Irish utopianism.

Lyman Tower Sargent, Professor of Political Science at the University of Missouri-St. Louis, is the author of numerous articles and books, including *British and American Utopian Literature, 1516–1985: An Annotated, Chronological Bibliography* and *Contemporary Political Ideologies*; editor of *Extremism in America* and *Political Thought in the United States*; and co-editor (with G. Claeys) of *The Utopia Reader*. Co-adviser for the Bibliothèque Nationale and the New York Public Library exhibit "Utopie: La quête de la société idéale en Occident/Utopia: The Quest for the Ideal Society in the West," he is co-editor of the exhibit catalogs (with R. Schaer and G. Claeys). He is a past president of the Society for Utopian Studies (North America) and founder and editor of *Utopian Studies*.

Lucy Sargisson is Senior Lecturer in Politics at the University of Nottingham. She is the author of *Contemporary Feminist Utopianism* and *Transforming Bodies and the Politics of Transgression*. She is a political theorist who has worked on utopias and utopianism and she is currently researching the connections between intentional communities and utopianism. She is the president of the Utopian Studies Society (Europe).

David Seed is Professor of American Literature at Liverpool University. He has published books on Pynchon, Heller, Joyce, and American Cold War sf, and is editor of *Anticipations: Essays on Early Science Fiction and its Precursors*. He is senior editor of the Liverpool University Press Science Fiction Texts and Studies Series. He is completing a study of representations of brainwashing in fiction and film.

Darko Suvin is Professor Emeritus at McGill University. He has written ten books, including *Metamorphoses of Science Fiction, Victorian Science Fiction in the UK, Positions and Presuppositions in Science Fiction*, and two books of poetry, as well as many articles. He was a founding editor of *Science-Fiction Studies*. His latest publication on sf is "Science Fiction Parables of Mutation and Cloning as/and Cognition" in *Biotechnological and Medical Themes in Science Fiction* (ed. D. Pastourmatzi).

Maria Varsam is completing her Ph.D. in American and Canadian Studies at the University of Nottingham. She is writing a dissertation on utopian ethics that focuses largely on the ethics of dystopian narratives. She has presented papers at utopian studies conferences on neo-slave narratives, post-colonial utopias, dystopian film, and feminist ethics.

Phillip E. Wegner is Associate Professor of English at the University of Florida, where he teaches modern literatures, cultural studies, and critical theory. He is the author of *Imaginary Communities: Utopia, the Nation, and the Spatial Histories of Modernity* and numerous essays on cinema, sf, critical theory. He is currently working on a book on globalization and questions of political agency in sf, chapters of which have appeared in *Rethinking Marxism, The Comparatist*, and *World Bank Literature*.

Index

Lightning Source UK Ltd.
Milton Keynes UK
UKOW050308281112

202815UK00016B/782/P